'Ramsey' by Les Edwards

Ramsey Campbell. Photograph by Peter Coleborn

Phantasmagoria Presents

Phantasmagoria

Presents

a RAMSEY CAMPBELL SPECIAL

RAMSEY CAMPBELL

CONTENTS

Editor: Trevor Kennedy

Editorial Consultant: Stephen Jones

***Phantasmagoria* Editorial Team**: Adrian Baldwin, John Gilbert,
Marc Damian Lawler, G.C.H. Reilly, Helen Scott and Allison Weir

Cover and logo design: Adrian Baldwin, www.adrianbaldwin.info

Front cover artwork: 'Ramsey Campbell' by Pete Von Sholly

Interior artwork: Randy Broecker (including all spot illustrations), Dave Carson,
Les Edwards, Eddie Jones, Stephen Jones, Allen Koszowski, Jim Pitts,
Pete Von Sholly and Joe X. Young

Contributors: Peter Atkins, Abdul-Qaadir Taariq Bakari-Muhammad,
Clive Barker, Eddy C. Bertin, David Brilliance, Randy Broecker, Jenny Campbell,
Ramsey Campbell, Jonathan Carroll, Mike Chinn, Adrian Cole, Con Connolly,
Peter Crowther, Dean M. Drinkel, Frank Duffy, Jeremy Dyson, Harlan Ellison,
Jo Fletcher, Barry Forshaw, Christopher Fowler, Neil Gaiman, Stephen Gallagher,
Richard Gavin, Ed Gorman, Muriel Gray, Carl R. Jennings, Stephen Jones,
S.T. Joshi, Pat Kearney, Stephen King, Joel Lane, John Langan, Joe R. Lansdale,
Thomas Ligotti, Alison Littlewood, Alessandro Manzetti, Patrick Marcel,
RC Matheson, David Mathew, Louise McVeigh, Paul Meloy, China Mieville,
Mark Morris, Lisa Morton, Adam Nevill, Kim Newman, Thana Niveau,
Jonathan Oliver, Reggie Oliver, Barnaby Page, Alan David Price,
John Llewellyn Probert, David R. Purcell, Tony Richards, David A. Riley,
Nicholas Royale, Mark Samuels, David J. Schow, Carol Smith,
Michael Marshall Smith, Jessica Stevens, Simon Strantzas, Peter Straub,
David A. Sutton, Steve Rasnic Tem, Lisa Tuttle, Conrad Williams and Joe X. Young

With thanks to: Gerry Adair, Peter Coleborn, Valerie Edwards, Maria Tissot and
Flame Tree Publishing, Jo Fletcher, Mandy Slater, Phil and Sarah Stokes
and Tamsin Traves and PS Publishing

To **Dr. David Mathew** for planting the idea of this publication in our heads

And, of course, to **Ramsey Campbell** and **Stephen Jones**

INTRODUCTION: RAMSEY @ 75

Stephen Jones

*Ramsey Campbell and Stephen Jones. London, February 15th, 2018.
Photograph by Mandy Slater*

MY INITIAL MEETING with Ramsey Campbell took place at the very first science fiction convention I ever attended – Novacon 4 – in 1974. Of course, I had already known who he was for some years before that.

Ramsey was already a legend to me because he had sold his first book, the short story collection *The Inhabitant of the Lake and Less Welcome Tenants*, while still only in his early teens. More importantly, he has sold it to August Derleth at the legendary Arkham House imprint. How cool was that?

So when, having barely entered the grotty bar of Birmingham's Imperial Centre Hotel, I was invited to join Ramsey and other luminaries of the British Fantasy Society at their table, I was already aware of his work through various anthology and magazine appearances, and his lively film review columns in the fanzines of the time. I guess, looking back, Ramsey was the first genuine author I ever met.

I don't think I was prepared for how friendly and approachable he and the others were to a neophyte fan such as myself. But pretty soon I found myself editing the Society's journal, *Dark Horizons*, and Ramsey proved to be as staunch a supporter as anyone could wish. He was there when David Sutton and I started *Fantasy Tales* and, when I became a full-time editor in the late 1980s, Ramsey was the one constant I knew I could call upon when I needed a story, an introduction, or simply some sound advice. In fact, Ramsey has contributed to more of my books than any other writer, for which I shall always remain eternally grateful.

There was no doubt in my mind when I was approached by Nick Robinson to edit an annual *Best New Horror* anthology series that I wanted Ramsey to be my co-editor. Nobody knows more about the genre than he does, and I respect his taste and judgement above all others. Of course, that doesn't prevent us disagreeing on occasions, and I don't think we will ever concur on the merits – or lack thereof – of *The Blair Witch Project*, or the need to adapt English spelling and punctuation for American editions! He also has a wickedly dry sense of humour, as anyone who has ever read one of his 'Ramsey Campbell, Probably' columns will attest to.

That Ramsey eventually had to withdraw after five volumes from *Best New Horror* because of a combination of slush-pile burnout and a need to concentrate on his own work remains a great disappointment to me. Yet I was secure in the knowledge that he was always there whenever I ever need some guidance.

Of course, since our inaugural encounter all those decades ago, we have remained firm friends. Whether it is having adventures with the late and lamented Dennis Etchison in Baja, California, sharing yet another panel about horror publishing in some drab convention hotel, or enjoying a raucous meal with friends in an out-of-way the restaurant he has learned about, Ramsey is always fun to hang out with. His wife, Jenny, has been like a second mother to me (though I'm not sure I would have gone to a sleazy Mexican strip show with my actual mother), and I have watched their children Matt and Tammy grow up into sensible and well-adjusted adults – and who would ever have thought it with a father like Ramsey?

We have also been guests in each other's homes, although it was only afterwards that he revealed that the room I had been staying in at his house was reputedly haunted. In fact, I can remember a convention breakfast some years ago where he managed to completely freak me out before the waitress had even taken our orders with a description of a night he had spent in that same room. That's the mark of a consummate storyteller.

Ramsey Campbell is not only the most important horror writer we have, he is also one of the most important *writers* we have – period. I have always said that given a choice between having J.K. Rowling's millions or Ramsey Campbell's body of work to my credit, I would always chose the latter. He has had a remarkable career so far, and he's only getting better as time goes on.

And time *is* moving on. Ramsey celebrated his seventy-fifth birthday this year. How the hell did that happen? Has it really been more than five decades since we first met each other in that Birmingham hotel bar? Apparently it has.

However, I doubt that he'll be slowing down much soon. Most likely we can put that down to his devotion to the field of horror fiction, those regular bottles of wine and whatever's in that pipe of his.

He's been voted "the horror writers' horror writer", and that's an accolade that nobody can argue with. He is truly a giant of the field, and his dedication to his craft and refusal to suffer fools gladly puts him head-and-shoulders above the rest of us working in the same genre.

So I salute you, my friend, on this auspicious occasion. You richly deserve all the tributes and plaudits that follow in this very special edition of *Phantasmagoria* magazine. As always, I look forward to our next adventure, and our next project working together. Until then, all I ask is that you please don't make me sleep in that haunted room again . . .!

Ramsey and friends. From left to right: Sean Hogan, Stephen Jones, Jenny Campbell, Barry Forshaw, Ramsey Campbell, Kim Newman and Paul McAuley. London, February 15th, 2018. Photograph by Mandy Slater

Artwork by Allen Koszowski

RAMSEY CAMPBELL: SELECTED BIBLIOGRAPHY

Compiled by Stephen Jones

Novels

The Doll Who Ate His Mother (1976)
The Bride of Frankenstein (1977) [as by Carl Dreadstone]
Dracula's Daughter (1977) [as by Carl Dreadstone/E.K. Leyton]
The Wolfman (1977) [as by Carl Dreadstone/E.K. Leyton]
The Face That Must Die (1979)
To Wake the Dead (aka *The Parasite*, 1980)
The Nameless (1981)
Incarnate (1983)
The Claw (aka *Night of the Claw*, 1983) [as by Jay Ramsay]
Obsession (1985)
The Hungry Moon (1986)
The Influence (1988)
Ancient Images (1989)
Midnight Sun (1990)
The Count of Eleven (1991)
The Long Lost (1993)
The One Safe Place (1995)
The House on Nazareth Hill (aka *Nazareth Hill*, 1996)
The Last Voice They Hear (1998)
Silent Children (1999)
Pact of the Fathers (2001)
The Overnight (2004)
Secret Stories (aka *Secret Story*, 2005)
The Grin of the Dark (2007)
Thieving Fear (2008)
Creatures of the Pool (2009)
The Seven Days of Cain (2010)
Solomon Kane: Official Movie Novelisation (2010)
Ghosts Know (2011)
The Kind Folk (2012)
Think Yourself Lucky (2014)
Thirteen Days by Sunset Beach (2015)
The Searching Dead (2016)
Born to the Dark (2017)
The Way of the Worm (2018)
The Wise Friend (2020)
Somebody's Voice (2021)

Collections

The Inhabitant of the Lake and Less Welcome Tenants (1964) [as by J. Ramsey Campbell]
Demons by Daylight (1973)
The Height of the Scream (1976)
Solomon Kane: Skulls in the Stars (with Robert E. Howard, 1978)
Solomon Kane: The Hills of the Dead (with Robert E. Howard, 1979)
L'homme du souterrain (1979) [as by J. Ramsey Campbell]
Dark Companions (1982)
Cold Print (1985)
Dark Feasts: The World of Ramsey Campbell (1987)
Scared Stiff: Tales of Sex and Death (aka *Scared Stiff: Seven Tales of Seduction and Terror*, 1987)
Waking Nightmares (1991)
Alone with the Horrors (aka *Alone with the Horrors: The Great Short Fiction of Ramsey Campbell 1961–1991*, 1993)
Strange Things and Stranger Places (1993)
Far Away & Never (1996)
Ghosts and Grisly Things (1998)
Scared Stiff: Tales of Sex and Death (2002)
Told by the Dead (2003)
Hungriger Mond und Das Kettenbriefmassaker (2004)
Derrière le masque . . . (2006)
Inconsequential Tales (2008)
Just Behind You (2009)
The Inhabitant of the Lake & Other Unwelcome Tenants (restored and expanded edition, 2011)
Holes for Faces (2013)
Visions from Brichester (2015)
By the Light of My Skull (2018)
Masters of the Weird Tale (two volumes, 2019)
The Companion & Other Phantasmagorical Stories (2019)
The Retrospective & Other Phantasmagorical Stories (2020)
Needing Ghosts and Other Novellas (2021)

Edited

Superhorror (aka *The Far Reaches of Fear*, 1976)
New Tales of the Cthulhu Mythos (1980)
New Terrors 1 (aka *New Terrors*, 1980)
New Terrors 2 (aka *New Terrors II*, 1980)
The Gruesome Book (1983)
Omnibus of New Terrors (1985)
Fine Frights: Stories That Scared Me (1988)
Best New Horror (with Stephen Jones, 1990)
Best New Horror Volume Two (with Stephen Jones, 1991)

Uncanny Banquet (1992)
Best New Horror Volume Three (with Stephen Jones, 1992)
Horror Writers of America Present Deathport (1993)
The Giant Book of Best New Horror (with Stephen Jones, 1993)
Best New Horror Volume Four (with Stephen Jones, 1993)
Best New Horror Volume Five (with Stephen Jones, 1994)
The Giant Book of Terror (with Stephen Jones, 1994)
Meddling with Ghosts: Stories in the Tradition of M.R. James (2000)
Gathering the Bones (with Jack Dann and Dennis Etchison, 2003)
The Folio Book of Horror Stories (2018)

Chapbooks

Through the Walls (1978)
Watch the Birdie (1984)
Slow (1986)
Medusa (1987)
Needing Ghosts (1990)
Two Obscure Tales (1993)
Point of View (2000)
The Decorations (2005)
The Long Way (2008)
The Render of the Veils (2010)
Holding the Light (2011)
Cut Corners: Volume 1 (with Ray Garton and Bentley Little, 2012)
The Last Revelation of Gla'aki (2013)
The Pretence (2013)
The Booking (2016)
The Enigma of the Flat Policeman (2019)

Poetry

Ramsey Campbell's Limericks of the Alarming and Phantasmal (2016)

Non-Fiction

Ramsey Campbell, Probably: Essays on Horror and Sundry Fantasies (2002)
Ramsey Campbell, Probably: Revised and Expanded (2020)

On a school trip, Dominic begins to suspect his teacher has reasons to be there as secret as they're strange. Meanwhile a neighbour joins a church that puts you in touch with your dead relatives, who prove much harder to get rid of. As Dominic investigates, he can't suspect how much more terrible the link between these mysteries will become.

Book 1 in the Three Births of Daoloth trilogy.

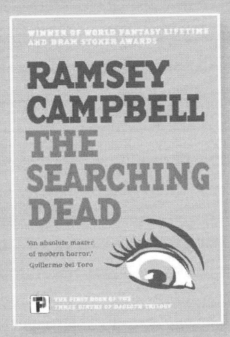

Order online and in your local bookstore.
Available in hardcover, paperback, and ebook.

Search online for
Flame Tree Ramsey Campbell
flametreepublishing.com

An Independent Publisher

FOR RAMSEY

A note from Trevor Kennedy and Allison Weir

Trevor Kennedy meets Ramsey Campbell at the Dublin WorldCon in 2019

RAMSEY CAMPBELL IS a gentleman. And a hell of a writer to boot. Just take a look at his highly impressive bibliography on the previous pages and the list of names included in this brand new *Phantasmagoria Special* and you'll get something of an idea of the sheer scope of respect and love Ramsey deservedly commands as both a man and an author.

I first encountered the work of Ramsey Campbell as a young boy in my school years of the 1980s through my regular correspondence with the fantasy artist Dave Carson and John Gilbert's *FEAR* magazine (readers of my previous editorial notes in our *Special Edition* series will notice a pattern developing here – basically, blame Dave and John on everything!). It was through Ramsey's collaborations with the above (Dave's *Haunters of the Dark* portfolio publication, stories and a piece about film censorship for *FEAR*, for example) that immediately embedded his name in my psyche from a very early age. Whilst back then I had not read much of Ramsey's fiction (the main bulk of it being in more recent years – and there is a *lot* to get through!), his was a name that always stayed with me in the intervening decades, one I knew even then was of a very well admired and revered horror author. I was, of course, correct, but to somewhat prove what you already know about Ramsey's professionalism and kindness, please allow me to regale you with an anecdote that I believe only Ramsey and I know about . . . until now . . .

Back in those halcyon days of 2016(!), pre-*Phantasmagoria*, I was putting together my first anthology, what would become the first volume in the *Gruesome Grotesques* series. To say I was inexperienced and naive (as both a writer and editor) is something of an understatement. I was also very enthusiastic and excitable – too much so! You see, one Friday evening whilst working on the antho, I had a brainstorm and impulsively – and quite 'cheekily' – privately messaged Ramsey on social media, asking him if I could print one of his stories in this upcoming book of mine. I mean, what a coup that would have been! The problem was I didn't have a specific story of Ramsey's in mind, which I should have, and whenever he asked me which tale of his I was thinking of I was completely taken aback and *hugely* embarrassed (I believe I literally went red and held my hands in my head). I hadn't thought my diabolical plan through properly and had made a fool out of myself in front of one of the greatest writers of our time. I suppose I could have just grabbed one of my old copies of *FEAR* or Stephen Jones' *Best New Horror* and located one, but that would have been rather disingenuous of me, plus I just *knew* at this point Ramsey had also figured out I was – for want of a better phrase – 'brass-necking it'.

I had been caught out, I felt like a fraud, the ground could have swallowed me up whole at that particular moment in time, and I would have deserved it too! However, Ramsey – to my great relief – was a complete gent about it all, not making a fuss and telling me not to fret (the actual phrase he used). I believe his kindness on that evening saved me from dying of some sort of self-induced cringe attack.

Over the resulting years, I've gotten a little more professional and less impulsive (I hope so anyway!), thanks to the support and friendship of guys like Ramsey, the aforementioned Steve Jones and John Gilbert, David Sutton, and many others, a list which is now a very long one indeed. Following my previous debacle, I've now interviewed Ramsey three times for *Phantasmagoria* (four if you count publishing John Gilbert's brand new interview with him in this *Special*) and reprinted several of his stories, all of this down to the amazing generosity of the great man himself.

It is now, naturally, a massive honour to be presenting this edition dedicated to the life and work of Ramsey Campbell, in this the year of his 75th birthday, a publication which is, I believe, something rather extraordinary, featuring an A-list conglomerate of writers, artists, friends and family of Ramsey's over the past half a century and more, not to mention three stories, two competitions, limericks and an interview to boot!

So, here's to a class act with such professionalism and grace! Here's to one of the best and most prolific writers of modern times! Here's to many more years of profoundly unsettling horror stories and enlightening, entertaining non-fiction! Here's to Ramsey Campbell!

—**Trevor Kennedy**

2019 SEEMS JUST A dot in the distance, but it was a fantastic year for many in the writing world. Let's rewind back to the 77th World Science Fiction Convention: WorldCon 2019, Dublin Convention Centre.

I remember ascending the escalators to the Green Room, a magnificent sunny view awaiting us over the River Liffey with the Samuel Beckett Bridge visible in the background. A cracking day awaited us, I was assured of that!

Trevor and I shared so much enjoyment over a mega busy schedule, but I did not realise how much I would look forward to meeting the legendary Ramsey Campbell until later that afternoon.

Yes, the same Ramsey Campbell who has impressed with his horror fiction writing tenure spanning over fifty years. Crossing genres of the dark fantasy and thriller kind, and much more, as well as being one of Britain's most respected horror writers of his generation – Ramsey really does set the bar high in everything he has done and is still doing!

When I did strike up a conversation with him over one of his many works, *Told by the Dead*, I quickly realised what a quirky chap this Liverpudlian was, and a gentleman to boot!

As we are still in a despicable Covid-19 deadlock, it will give me chance to finally complete my tiny reading wish-list, for I don't read too quickly but when I do, I pick my reads wisely and I know I have to tick off Ramsey's 2020 release with *The Wise Friend*.

Trevor will agree with me when I say this – Ramsey is one of the most down to earth writers I have ever had the pleasure of meeting, one that advises well across the horror writing spectrum and most importantly, one that has time for his audience and devoted fans.

—Allison Weir

Allison Weir meets Ramsey Campbell at the Dublin WorldCon in 2019

'Rising Generation' by Stephen Jones

RISING GENERATION

Ramsey Campbell

Back in 1974, I had been a member of the British Fantasy Society for less than two years. I had already started contributing to the Society's B.F.S. Bulletin *— reviews, news items and spot-illustrations — when the editor of a new monthly newsstand magazine,* World of Horror, *contacted me and asked if they could reprint one of my pieces of art from the* Bulletin.*

They used it to illustrate a story entitled 'The Clown That Cried Blood' by "Georgianna Lee" (actually associate editor Lee Kennedy) in issue No.2 (October 1974), but it was reproduced too small and too dark. However, it did lead to other things . . .

The editor, "Gent Shaw" (Jim Shier), contacted me again and asked if I would be willing to contribute an original full-page story illustration to the magazine. Not only that, but they would actually pay *me for it this time!*

Obviously, I jumped at the chance, and you can see the result opposite. It appeared in World of Horror *No.4 (January 1975) — the one with Mr. Spock on the cover — and was my first professionally paid job in the genre. But, even better, it illustrated Ramsey Campbell's story 'Rising Generation'.*

Soon afterwards, Jim Shier and I moved on to Legend Horror Classics, *and I never worked for* World of Horror *again. The story subsequently appeared in America in* Night Cry *magazine (Fall, 1987) and in Ramsey's 1993 collection* Strange Things and Stranger Places. *In a nice piece of synchronicity, I also ended up reprinting it in my 1993 anthology,* The Mammoth Book of Zombies.

It's rarely been reprinted since, and this special edition of Phantasmagoria *marks the first time that Ramsey's story and my illustration for it have been reunited in forty-six years . . .*

—Stephen Jones

AS THEY APPROACHED the cave beneath the castle some of the children began to play at zombies, hobbling stiffly, arms outstretched. Heather Fry frowned. If they knew the stories about the place, despite her efforts to make sure they didn't, she hoped they wouldn't frighten the others. She hadn't wanted to come at all; it had been Miss Sharp's idea, and she'd been teaching decades longer than Heather, so of course she had her way. The children were still plodding inexorably towards their victims. Then Joanne said "You're only being like those men in that film last night." Heather smiled with relief. "Keep together and wait for me," she called.

She glanced up at the castle, set atop the hill like a crown, snapped and bent and discoloured by time. Overhead sailed a pale blue sky, only a wake of thin foamy clouds on the horizon betraying any movement. Against the sky, just below the castle, Heather saw three figures toiling upward. Odd, she thought, the school had been told the castle was forbidden to visitors because of the danger of falling stone, which was why they'd had to make do with the cave. Still, she was glad she hadn't had to coax her class all the way up there. The three were moving slowly and clumsily, no doubt exhausted by their climb, and even from where Heather stood their faces looked exceptionally pale.

She had to knock several times on the door of the guide's hut before he emerged. Looking in beyond him, Heather wondered what had taken his time. Not tidying the hut, certainly, because the desk looked blitzed, scattered and overflowing with forms and even an upset ink-bottle, fortunately stoppered. She looked at the guide and her opinion sank further. Clearly he didn't believe in shaving or cutting his nails, and he was pale enough to have been born in a cave, she thought. He didn't even bother to tum to her; he stared at the children lined up at the cave entrance, though by his lack of expression he might as well have been blind. "I'd rather you didn't say anything about the legend," she said.

His stare swivelled to her and held for so long she felt it making a fool of her. "You know what I mean," she said, determined to show him she did too. "The stories about the castle. About how the baron was supposed to keep zombies in the cave to work for him, until someone killed him and walled them up. I know it's only a story, but not for the children, please."

When he finished staring at her he walked towards the cave, his hands dangling on his long arms and almost brushing his knees. At least he won't interrupt, she thought. I wonder how much he's paid, and for what? There was even a propped-up boot poking out from beneath the desk.

As she reached the near end of the line of children he was trudging into the cave. Daylight slipped from his back and he merged with the enormous darkness, then the walls closed about him as his flashlight awakened them. Heather switched on her own flashlight. "Stay with your partner," she called, paragraphing with her fingers. "Stay in the light. And don't lag."

The children, fourteen pairs of them, were hurrying after the guide's light. The cave was wide at the entrance but swiftly narrowed as it curved, and when Heather glanced back a minute later, lips of darkness had closed behind them. As the guide's flashlight wavered, the corrugations of the walls rippled like the soft gulping flesh of a throat. The children were glancing about uneasily like young wild animals, worried by the dark sly shifting they glimpsed at the edge of their vision. Heather steadied her beam about them, and the thousands of tons of stone above their heads closed down.

Not that it was easy to steady the beam. In the cave the guide had picked up speed considerably, and she and the children had to hurry so as not to be left behind. Maybe he feels at home, she thought angrily. "Will you slow down, please," she called, and heard Debbie at the front of the line say "Miss Fry says you've got to slow down."

The guide's light caught a wide flat slab of roof that looked as if it were sagging. Scattered earth crunched softly beneath Heather's feet. About now, she was sure, they would be heading up and out the other side of the hill. Joanne, who hadn't let Debbie convince her as a zombie, and Debbie squeezed back to Heather along the contracting passage. "I don't like that man," Joanne said. "He's dirty."

"What do you mean?" Heather said, sounding too worried. But Joanne said "He's got earth in his ears."

"Will you hold our hands if we're frightened?" Debbie said.

"Now I can't hold everyone's hand, can I?" Earth slid from beneath Heather's feet. Odd, she thought: must come from the guide's ears and beneath his nails, and began to giggle, shaking her head when they asked why. He was still forcing them to hurry, but she was beginning to be glad that at least they wouldn't have to depend on him much longer. "If you think of questions don't ask them yet," she called. "Wait until we're outside."

"I wish we didn't have to come underground," Joanne said.

Then you should have said before, Heather thought. "You'll be able to look for things in the field later," she said. And at least you haven't had Miss Sharp herding you as well as her own class. If they hadn't come on ahead they would have had to suffer her running their picnic.

"But why do we have to come down when it's nice? Sharon didn't have to."

"It'll be nice this afternoon. Sharon can't go into places that are closed in, just as you don't like high places. So you see, you're lucky today."

"I don't feel lucky," Joanne said.

The ridges of the walls were still swaying gently, like the leaves of a submarine plant, and now one reached out and tugged at Heather's sleeve. She flinched away then saw that it was a splintered plank, several of which were propped against the wall, looking as if they'd once been fastened together. Ahead the cave forked, and the children were following the shrinking rim of light into the left-hand passage, which was so low that they had to stoop. "Go on, you're all right," she told Debbie, who was hesitating. Stupid man, she raged.

It was tighter than she'd thought. She had to hold one arm straight out in front of her so that the light urged the children on, leaving herself surrounded by darkness that coldly pressed her shoulders down when she tried to see ahead. If this passage had been fenced off, as she suspected, she was sorry it had been reopened. The children's ridged shadows rippled like caterpillars. Suddenly Debbie halted. "There's someone else in here," she said.

"Well?" Joanne said. "It's not your cave."

Now all the children had gone quiet, and Heather could hear it too: the footsteps of several people tramping forward from deeper within the cave. Each step was followed by a scattering sound like brief dry rain. "Men working in the caves," she called, waiting for someone to ask what the dry sound was so that she could say they were carrying earth. Don't ask why, she thought. Something to do with the castle, perhaps with the men she'd seen on the hill. But the footsteps had stopped.

When she straightened up at last the darkness clenched on her head; she had to steady herself against the wall. Her vertigo gradually steadied, and she peered ahead. The children had caught up with the guide, who was silhouetted against a gaping tunnel of bright pale stone. As she started towards him he pulled something from his pocket and hurled it beyond her.

Debbie made to retrieve it. "It's all right," Heather said, and ushered the pair of them with her light towards the other children. Then, cursing his rudeness, she turned the beam on what she assumed he'd thrown her to catch. She peered closer, but it was exactly what it seemed: a packed lump of earth. Right, she thought, if I can lose you your job, you're out of work now.

She advanced on him. He was standing in the mouth of a side tunnel, staring back at her and pointing his flashlight deeper into the main passage. The children were hurrying past him into the hard tube of light. She was nearly upon him when he plodded out of the side tunnel, and she saw that the children were heading for a jagged opening at the limit of the beam, surrounded by exploded stone sprinkled with earth. She'd opened her mouth to call them back when his hand gripped her face and crushed her lips, forcing her back into the side tunnel.

His cold hand smelled thickly of earth. His arm was so long that her nails flailed inches short of his face. "Where's Miss Fry?" Debbie called, and he pointed ahead with his flashlight. Then he pushed Heather further into the cave, though she hacked at his shins. All at once she remembered that the boot beneath the desk had been propped on its toe: there might have been a leg beyond it.

Then the children screamed; one chorus of panic, then silence. Heather's teeth closed in the flesh of his hand, but he continued to shove her back into the cave. She saw her flashlight gazing up at the roof of the main passage, retreating. His own flashlight drooped in his hand, and its light drew the walls to leap and struggle, imitating her.

Now he was forcing her towards the cave floor. She glimpsed a mound of earth into which he began to press her head, as if for baptism. She fought upwards, teeth grinding in his flesh, and saw figures groping past her upturned flashlight. They were the children.

She let herself go limp at once, and managed to twist out of the way as he fell. But he kept hold of her until she succeeded in bringing her foot forward and grinding his face beneath her heel like a great pale insect. He still made no vocal sound. Then she fled staggering to her flashlight, grabbed it and ran. The stone wrinkles of the low roof seemed more hindering, as if now she were battling a current. Before she was free of the roof she heard him crawling in the darkness at her heels like a worm.

When the children appeared at the end of her swaying tunnel of light she gave a wordless cry of relief. She could feel nothing but relief that they were covered with dirt: they'd been playing. They still were, just short of the border of daylight, and they'd even persuaded Joanne to be a zombie. "Quickly," Heather gasped. "Run to Miss Sharp's class." But they continued playing, turning stiffly towards her, arms groping. Then, as she saw the earth trickling from their mouths and noses, she knew they weren't playing at all.

RAMSEY CAMPBELL INTERVIEW: MASTER STORYTELLER, LITERARY GIANT

John Gilbert chats to Ramsey Campbell

Ramsey Campbell. Photograph by Peter Coleborn

In an exclusive interview with the man at the centre of this very special issue of Phantasmagoria, ***Ramsey Campbell*** *discusses with **John Gilbert** aspects of his career past, present and future.*

ASK A CONTEMPORARY Horror writer to name their influences and it is likely they will mention Liverpool native Ramsey Campbell in the conversation. He may not have the sales figures of Stephen King but his novels and short stories continue to haunt and inspire readers and writers. He is a living legend whose name is mentioned in the same breath as M.R. James, Arthur Machen and H.P. Lovecraft.

His fiction has a timeless quality that resonates with the nightmares of a worldwide audience that continues to grow.

I first interviewed Ramsey thirty years ago when I was a newbie editor and he already had a good few decades of fiction under his belt. I began that interview with a question about his own influences, so it is only natural this time around that I ask whether Covid has had an impact on his writing output or content: "For quite a while I would have said neither. I'm certainly no less productive, and I don't think there has been any falling off in quality, to judge by reactions I've had. There's been a fair amount of discussion among writers about how to respond to the pandemic – quite a lot take the view that we can't ignore it in our fiction. I'm inclined to think the opposite. After all, where is Spanish flu to be found in Hemingway or Scott Fitzgerald or Virginia Woolf or D. H. Lawrence or Evelyn Waugh or Aldous Huxley or Faulkner, to name just a few crucial writers who brought out novels in the succeeding decade? (We can be forgiven for not looking for it in *The Velveteen Rabbit* or *Winnie the Pooh* or even *Just William*.) It seems more prevalent in recent historical fiction that deals with the period. Art is often longer than the present, after all, and wider in its scope.

"Incidentally, I was unsure how folk would take to anything new of mine, or indeed new horror generally, while the virus was so much at large. I was heartened by the way *The Wise Friend* seemed to go down, even though it was released early in the first lockdown. I hope this means the uncanny offers something valuable to folk even in the midst of our present grim situation. I'd call it more than simple escapism – certainly the works I admire in the field mean more than that to me.

"Inspiration – if you'd asked me during that lockdown I would have said it had given me none and no sense that it was remotely likely. I may say I've recently read two fine tales involving the pandemic in John Taff's forthcoming Tor anthology *Dark Stars*, but even they wouldn't have sent me in that direction by themselves. However, ideas for the novel I was mulling (*The Lonely Lands*, to be written this year) began to intersect with it, and I believe the pandemic may be crucial to it. Often enough stories of mine take shape from the collision or mating of separate ideas."

FOREWORD

Born John Ramsey Campbell on January 4, 1946, he began reading and writing at a very early age, inspired and encouraged by the works of an eclectic mix of authors. "I believe I was trying to pay back some of the pleasure the field had given me. I was monstrously precocious, reading Edith Wharton ('Afterward') when I was six, and Lovecraft ("The Colour out of Space") a year later. I began to write seriously, though badly, as I turned eleven. I wonder if I was unconsciously aware of my limitations, because the stuff I wrote then wasn't based on these writers, nor on other masters – M.R. James, Poe, Le Fanu and others – whose work I'd read. Instead my attempts were patched together from the likes of the contents of *Phantom* and the lesser fiction in the digest issues of *Weird Tales* (then remaindered for sixpence a copy, and I grabbed every one I could find), and they were as ungainly as any version of Frankenstein's creature. Horror of horrors, the longest and most ambitious tale – nearly five thousand words of it – was an imperfectly digested version of *The Devil*

Rides Out. The entire book of tales was written with pen and ink in an exercise book (the way I still write first drafts) and illustrated in ink and crayon, hardly evidence of professionalism. Just the same, at the behest of my mother I submitted that copy to publishers, and even had an encouraging letter from Tom Boardman Jr, encouraging me to carry on. Any sense that I was any kind of real writer didn't linger long, and so when I wrote my first Lovecraft pastiches I sent them to August Derleth purely to see whether he thought they were any good, with no thought of publication. I wasn't to know how lucky my timing was, sending him Lovecraftian fiction at the point when he felt he'd run out of the energy to write any more along those lines himself, which he'd done increasingly in order to keep Lovecraft's name alive. It was only when he said that, given sufficient editing and with extra tales, Arkham House might publish a book of mine that I started to feel like the kind of writer I read."

INSPIRATION

Ramsey was educated by the Catholic brothers at St Edwards School in Liverpool but, although he credits several of the teachers for inspiring him academically he was very much a self starter as a writer. "I always read years above my age and picked up correct usages in the process. I actually had to unlearn a few of the stricter grammatical rules the grammar school taught – for instance, never writing a sentence without a verb – in order to loosen my style a bit once I saw publication. I should praise some teachers, though. Brother Kelly at St Edward's in Liverpool encouraged me to read my tales, even the gruesome ones, to the class in my first year. In my last, Ray Thomas was a splendid teacher who conveyed enormous enthusiasm for English literature and made it speak to this fifteen/sixteen-year-old. And by some magic Brother Butler rendered geometry enjoyable for me in that final year, whereas previous years (or being taught by dullards) hadn't.

"On the other hand, too many of the staff at each of the three Liverpool schools I attended – Christ the King and then Ryebank Primary, and eventually St Edward's – should never, for a variety of reasons, have been let anywhere near children. I'm sure various incidents back then lent me my recurring theme of the vulnerability of the young. Stories such as 'The Interloper' and *The Hungry Moon* draw upon some of those experiences without exaggerating them. In the interests of fairness I should acknowledge that the school in *The Searching Dead* is quite like my old grammar in its more benign aspects.

"Family life – I've written at length about that in *Ramsey Campbell, Probably*, and I'd recommend anybody interested to look there. Just to sketch it, my mother was a paranoid schizophrenic, undiagnosed as far as I know until almost the end of her life, which meant that from a very early age – say three years old – I had to distinguish what she insisted was true from what was real. I suspect that's why so much of my fiction is preoccupied with shifts of perception and why many of my stories convey mental instability or more extreme states. As for my father, my parents were estranged well before I started school, but he continued to live in the same very small house (40 Nook Rise in Liverpool) and became a presence I never saw face to face, only heard in the night or on the other side of doors, a situation that persisted for about twenty years. My mother emphasised his monstrousness and claimed he might try to murder us. Even his voice, which I overheard during their occasional confrontations, seemed somehow inhuman. I think we may assume that my early decades helped to shape me as a writer.

"My mother encouraged me to finish stories and submit them. Making my way – well, I didn't try that until eleven years after my first publication. Emboldened by T. E. D. Klein's essay on *Demons by Daylight* – my second book, in which he found everything I'd hoped to communicate – I decided to go fulltime. If Jenny hadn't supported us both from her teaching, I would certainly not have succeeded. I didn't start to make a living as a writer for another five years. Jenny supported me in many other ways as well, which are among the reasons why I say she's the best part of me and of my life."

Ramsey Campbell and his wife Jenny. Photograph by Peter Coleborn

LOCATION, LOCATION

Liverpool, its landscape and its people, regularly appear in and have had a profound effect on Ramsey's work and career. This great city is a centre for the creative arts spawning many who have gone on work in the worlds of film, visual arts and books. It also seems to be something of a hub for the Horror genre. "We are all creatures of the pool. To some extent we knew each other, of course. Clive Barker cites the talk I gave at his school as a spur to his early work, and Clive knew Pete Atkins and Doug Bradley and Nick Vince, all of whom I later got to know.

"Locations are frequently the source rather than simply the setting of my stories. The very first that I still regard as more mine than just an amalgam of influences is

'The Cellars', which arose from an actual location of the kind, very much as described. It was my first overtly Liverpudlian tale (whereas 'The Stone on the Island', for instance, relocated my Liverpool workplace to Brichester), and I think this was a liberating development. Many other stories owe their soul to Merseyside – *Creatures of the Pool*, of course, and the trilogy, for another instance – but stories have also been brought to life by other places: Greek islands in *Thirteen Days by Sunset Beach*, the Peak District in *The Hungry Moon*, the Lakes in 'Above the World', Wales in *The Influence* . . ."

Yet, Liverpool is a literary territory to which he has returned during his writing career and is obviously important to him so I asked if he had ever thought of relocating from his home in Wallasey where he lives with wife Jenny and, if so, where would that be to: "I've never really considered it. We're pretty ideally located where we are, not least in terms of nearby countryside, and I can't imagine moving. Purely as a fantasy, one place that tempts me is New Orleans, one of our favourite places to eat in the world."

Stephen Jones, Peter Atkins and Ramsey Campbell. Tropicon XI, West Palm Beach, Florida, January 1993. Photograph by Gerry Adair

RELOCATION

One of the initial sparks that eventually brought Ramsey to the attention of Horror readers was his lengthy correspondence with the American Arkham House publisher August Derleth who played a large role in the career of H.P. Lovecraft. It was a long distance literary relationship that would provide Ramsey with encouragement and inspiration. "My old friend and correspondent Pat Kearney (to be found elsewhere in this magazine) suggested I should contact August. Here's how I did, complete with Americanisms I then used:

16 / 8 / 61
Dear August Derleth:
Being a great fan of HPL myself, I have recently been attempting a number of pastiches of the Lovecraft Mythos. There is obviously nobody better than yourself to criticize such work, and I therefore wonder if you could spare the time to discuss mss. of mine, if I sent them along to you. Several fans have praised my work (one of them is running a novelet of mine in his fanzine) but I think you, as the greatest authority on HPL, should have the final word. Please let me know if you want them handwritten or typed (if at all!)
While I am writing, I hope you will not object if I ask for information on a few matters. Firstly, I have noticed that in HPL's Commonplace Book in The Shuttered Room and Others, there are many plot-ideas still unused: presumably you hold copyright. Would you have any objection to my using them in tales of my own? . . .

Hoping for a long future correspondence,
　Cordially,
　　John Campbell

And his response, in part:

19 August 1961
Dear Mr. Campbell,
All thanks for your letter of the 16th. I should say at the outset that we had better see your pastiches of Lovecraft Mythos stories because a) the Lovecraft material is copyrighted and so protected and b) the approval of Arkham House is necessary before any copyrighted material can be released for publication. This is a necessary provision, of course, because if we did not enforce it scores of cheap imitations would flood the market, reflecting unfavorably on Lovecraft and his work. I do much prefer typed MSS., though your writing seems quite readable.
Re the plot ideas in the COMMONPLACE BOOK. I should be extremely wary of using any of them—one cannot copyright an idea, of course—largely because we cannot be certain when those jottings are original with HPL and when they have simply been put down to note a theme he had read in use somewhere. Should you use one of the latter, you would soon find yourself in trouble with someone who had used it and had it under copyright . . .

So began my career."
Derleth suggested that some of his early short stories which he had located in America should be relocated to England.
"Indeed he did:

6 October 1961
Dear Mr. Campbell,

I have received your stories, but I have had time to read only one or two of them. I don't want to comment on them in extended fashion until I've read all, but I do think them competent. However, there is one alteration I think you should definitely make; and I know that as the joint copyright-holder, Mr. Wandrei would insist on it, and that is to remove your stories from the Lovecraft milieu. I mean, keep the Gods, the Books, etc., but establish your own place. This would give the stories vastly more authenticity as an addition to the Mythos rather than pastiche pieces, and it might then be possible for us to consider their book publication in a limited edition over here.

What I suggest you do is establish a setting in a coastal area of England and create your own British milieu. This would not appreciably change your stories, but it would give them a much needed new setting and would not, in the reader's mind, invite a direct comparison with Lovecraft, for in such a comparison they would not show up as well as if you had your own setting and place-names for the tales . . .

"Ironically, I knew just about as little of the Severn Valley as I did of Massachusetts, and nothing at all from experience. My version of it wasn't much more authentic than my American attempt, but presumably it seemed so to Derleth. I do regret not fixing on the Chester area as a solution – I could easily have travelled there and got more sense of place."

ENGAGING THE IMAGINATION

In this time of Covid when all our lives and preconceptions have been thrown into disarray, it is perhaps not surprising that the tropes of Horror fiction continue to prove popular even with authors and audiences who would not normally associate with the genre. In Ramsey's work, horror can seep into everyday lives and the main aim of a writer is to ". . . engage the imagination – the writer's in the first place, of course, and then with luck the reader's – and enrich it too. To make us – again, both writer and reader – to look again at things we've taken for granted. Mind you, all that should be true of good art generally. As for a purpose that's specific to horror, I'd say that ranges all the way from disturbing the reader to conveying a sense of the uncanny or exploring the darker (indeed, darkest) regions of human psychology to (as in Barker and Cronenberg) compelling us to confront and examine things we might ordinarily look away from. For me, though, aspiration to awe is the highest horror reaches, as in 'The White People' and 'The Willows' and 'The Colour out of Space', just three of quite a small number."

Whilst novels such as *Ancient Images*, *Midnight Sun* and *The Doll Who Ate His Mother* have all proved immensely popular to a readership that continues to grow, it is Ramsey's multi-award-winning short fiction that often provides his introduction to new fans. Whilst the market for short stories has shrunk over the past decade, the form continues to prove popular and Ramsey is one of a select band of authors whose short stories are eagerly sought out by readers. But why is the short form especially popular with Horror fans? "Perhaps because it compresses the experience and intensifies it, whether we're talking about supernatural dread or psychological insight. That said, I think the expansiveness of novels has merits of its own."

Ramsey Campbell and James Herbert. FantasyCon 2012, Brighton, England. Photograph by Mandy Slater

LITERARY CHILDREN

So, does he have any favourites amongst his own literary children? Are there any particular stories or novels that he would suggest for newcomers to his work? And are there works by other writers that he would suggest to recent converts to the genre? "I've talked about favourites of my own stuff elsewhere in the magazine. For newcomers to me, I do think the trilogy represents me pretty well, and the two *Phantasmagorical Stories* collections are a good overview of my first sixty years as a short story writer, though my more Lovecraftian tales are to be found in two other PS Publishing collections.

"Other folk – two fine introductions to a breadth of work, *The Dark Descent* (edited David Hartwell) and the more global anthology *The Weird* (edited by Ann and Jeff VanderMeer). And let's not forget Steve Jones's essential annual anthology *The Mammoth Book of Year's Best Horror*. All these books will give the reader new to horror any number of fine writers to follow up. Films – Jacques Tourneur's *Night of the Demon* (my favourite horror film), almost any features by David Lynch (the only director whose work frequently terrifies me almost to the limit), *The Innocents*, Robert Wise's *The Haunting*, Hitchcock's *Psycho* . . ."

A growing number of 'literary' authors and thriller writers are now writing what are without doubt Horror stories and yet seem keen to distance themselves from the genre and feel it necessary to deny any link to the genre. Though Horror has always been seen by some critics and creatives as the runt of literary endeavour, Ramsey feels the it is the right of every author to categorise their work (or not) as they see fit – even when readers may have a different view.

"I do think writers have the right to define their own work. I hope everyone who needs to know it knows that I say I write horror, but I admit my definition of the genre is a lot more capacious than some – it has been, I suppose, ever since I read Herman Melville's 'Bartleby the Scrivener' in *Best Horror Stories* when I was eleven and felt instinctively that it fitted somehow. The definition includes many ghost stories, and I'm reminded that M.R. James declared horror to be necessary to the form. I certainly think there's a considerable area of overlap between the ghost story and supernatural horror, and it's a pity that some of the writers who work in that area won't admit it, even dismissing it as beneath them. Robert Aickman and I used to disagree genially about it, not least since his ghostly anthologies for Fontana include a number of horror tales. He seemed happy enough for me to use stories of his in some of my horror anthologies, and I was too happy about having them to twit him about it."

WRITING SPACE

Ramsey shows no sign of retiring or in slowing his literary output. "I'm here at my desk by seven each morning or earlier, having started work as soon as I got up an hour before, composing prose in my head and these days dictating it to the phone notebook. That's if I'm working on a first draft, which I do every day, Christmas and my birthday included, until it's finished. It's always handwritten. I reread when it's completed, and then edit with gleeful severity on the computer. If I go away, the first draft goes with me to be written. For me there's nothing worse than staying somewhere with no space for me to write.

"Real events can certainly germinate in my head. Look no further than my latest novel *Somebody's Voice*. A couple of years back I was listening to a phone-in on the local BBC, where the presenter interviewed a survivor of child abuse who had just brought out a ghostwritten memoir of her experience. A listener commented that the victim was very brave, which she certainly was, and the presenter remarked that she was also a very good writer. Since the book was ghostwritten, this bothered me, and almost immediately suggested the theme of a ghostwriter whose sense of self and memory is shaken by writing such a book, particularly since not all the material he works with may be reliable. In a few days I'd come up with many of the crucial developments in the book.

"One more example – some years ago (in those mythical days when we could travel abroad for a holiday) we were on a jeep tour of Zante and passed through a young folks' resort early in the day, when it was utterly deserted except for a few taverna staff sweeping their floors. The driver remarked that the guests in the resort never came out in daylight, and maybe a minute later I'd got my notebook out. By the end of the day I'd scribbled down most of the ideas that grew into my Greek novel *Thirteen Days by Sunset Beach*.

"Somewhere in limbo is a novel called *The Black Pilgrimage*. I've twice tried to develop it, but the process took me so far away from the basic idea that I left it behind and followed the new route (in *The Kind Folk* and *The Wise Friend*). Perhaps there's still enough of the original concept left unused that I may give it another shot in due course.

"Real people – there are bits of them in various characters of mine, but few portraits from life. I remember two friends of ours both felt I'd based Jack Orchard in *The Count of Eleven* on them, but I hadn't really had either of them consciously in mind. Elsewhere, I was amused when one of the few characters I'd portrayed from life was criticised as a caricature. In fact I'd toned down some of their actual behaviour because I thought the reader would never believe in it."

Ramsey Campbell, Shaun Hutson and Iain Banks. Photograph by Peter Coleborn

BY ANY OTHER NAME

Whilst remaining prolifically true to the Horror genre, Ramsey has also written a number of books pseudonymously, including Jay Ramsey and Carl Dreadstone: "Jay was born for just one book, because Macmillan in New York had at least two of mine in the pipeline and I was giving them a break. They understandably didn't want me to bring out a new novel elsewhere to compete with theirs, and so I adopted that pseudonym, which I thought wouldn't fool anyone who knew my history. *Claw / Night of the Claw / The Claw* (as it was variously known) was planned as the first novel by a new horror writer, to be enthusiastically promoted by the publisher. In the event the book came out as a library hardcover with no promotion whatsoever (copies of which are now excruciatingly pricey). Perhaps I should have expected no better, since the editor concerned was unique in those days for not taking me out to lunch to discuss the project, instead giving me a plastic cup of coffee in her office and requiring me to tell her the story I had yet to write (a potentially disastrous approach, and one I would refuse to countenance now). The Americans treated the novel far better, and it did pretty well.

"As for Dreadstone, Piers Dudgeon at Star Books – my first British editor – had struck a deal with Universal to create novels from six of their classic monster movies. Initially he suggested I should write all six, but two werewolf books were one too many for me, and since I can't swim, I didn't think I was the man to do the Gill-man justice. I bagged *The Bride of Frankenstein, The Wolfman* and *Dracula's Daughter* (which I thought would be my only vampire novel, and was until recently). Piers asked me to think up a house name, and I suggested Carl Thunstone but checked with our friend Manly Wade Wellman, who felt the surname might cause folk to assume he was the author (since it was the name of a character of his, which was where I'd pinched it from). Dreadstone was our compromise, although just to confuse everyone some editions renamed the writer E. K. Leyton.

"I'm occasionally confused with Errol Undercliffe, perhaps because so little of his work is readily available these days. I also fused bits of two British filmmakers, Lance Comfort and Montgomery Tully, into a pseudonym for a single tale – Stuart Schiff wanted to use two of my stories in an issue of *Whispers* but preferred not to have the same byline in the contents listing twice.

HONOURED

It is only natural that due to the quality of his work and its resonance with readers, critics and the publishing industry, Ramsey has has been honoured with national and international awards for his fiction. "I appreciate them all! I'm honoured and flattered. I suppose the lifetime awards are especially meaningful. I do have a particular fondness for the honorary fellowship Liverpool John Moores University gave me for 'outstanding services to literature'. At the ceremony I said I'd like to accept for my field as well as on my own behalf . . .

"If the folk who like my tales feel I've haunted their imaginations and perhaps occasionally made them see the world through new eyes, that would make me happy. More generally, I hope I'm a stage, however minor, in the continuity and development of our field."

FUTURE TRENDS

And so to the future of the genre and his own work and there are definite trends he can see in genre fiction. "Two developments I can identify are the growth of the horror novel – there were few good ones when I started reading in the field, but there are many more to be reckoned with now – and the increasing diversity of authors. I believe the genre is as vital as ever, and that's how it will survive. Perhaps eventually it will need once more to rise from its own grave, but then it always does. As long as people value intensity of experience (which certainly includes terror) in the arts, it will have an audience.

"As for my own future, I don't plan to slow down any time soon. Right now I'm rewriting the first draft of a new supernatural novel, *Fellstones*. Another novel, *The Lonely Lands*, awaits writing. PS Publishing will bring out a third volume of my collected shorter tales, *Needing Ghosts and Other Novellas*, including a new one, *The Village Killings*. They also have my second non-fiction collection – *Ramsey Campbell, Certainly* – in the works, and their Electric Dreamhouse imprint is preparing a collection of my columns from *Video Watchdog*. Another work I have in progress for that imprint is *Six Stooges and Counting*, a personal wander through the Stooges' films. I won't be retiring just yet, folks, or – if I have anything to do with it – at all."

Karl Edward Wagner and Ramsey Campbell. FantasyCon VI, Birmingham, England, October 1980. Photograph by Jo Fletcher

COMPETITION!

WIN a signed and slipcased copy of PS's forthcoming **RAMSEY CAMPBELL CERTAINLY** edited by S.T. Joshi

As it's a celebration of the horror master himself, let's have some fun . . . PS would like a limerick that includes Ramsey's full name and the number 75 to celebrate his 75th birthday.

Email info@pspublishing.co.uk

RAMSEY CAMPBELL: THE EARLY YEARS

*In a trilogy of articles by **Pat Kearney**, **Eddy C. Bertin** and **S. T. Joshi** we take a look back at the earlier aspects and influences of **Ramsey Campbell**'s career.*

*Front cover of Goudy magazine issue 2 from 1961,
which featured some of Ramsey's earliest work. Artwork by Eddie Jones*

THE INHABITANT OF LIVERPOOL

Pat Kearney

*Artwork by Eddie Jones for (J.) Ramsey Campbell's story
'The Tower from Yuggoth' which appeared in* Goudy *magazine,
number two, in 1961*

THE INVITATION FROM *Phantasmagoria* to contribute to a *Festschrift* issue for Ramsey came at an unfortunate moment. My wife and I, wearying of the all too frequent evacuations from the wildfires in northern California, decided to relocate to the relative safety of Bakersfield, her home town. The approach from Trevor Kennedy, the magazine's editor, arrived less than a month after the move. With a house full of unpacked boxes and much else still to be done, the prospect of sitting down to write something appropriate was daunting. Nevertheless, I felt it was something I should do in order to mark my appreciation for an excellent author who is some small way I helped unleash onto the world. I'll leave criticism of his work to those who do that sort of thing, and confine myself to a few personal anecdotes . . .

I no longer recall how, in the early 1960s, John Ramsey Campbell, as he was then known, and I first got to know each other. I was barely out of my teens and living in London, Ramsey a couple of years younger and 220 miles away in Liverpool, and both of us were relative newcomers in science fiction fandom. It seems probable that somebody who knew of our shared interest in the work of H.P. Lovecraft put us in touch with each other, but however it happened we were soon corresponding regularly and at length.[1]

The news that Ramsey had been writing stories heavily influenced by the Lovecraft 'mythos' struck an immediate cord. At the time I was publishing a fanzine at irregular intervals and was experiencing difficulties in finding original material. The whole thing was amateurish even for something that was supposed to be amateurish. I even went through several different titles for the 'zine – *The Elizabeth Street Bugle*, from the street where I lived at the time, *In Focus, Enfocado* and *Goudy*. But they did had some positive qualities. So far as I know I am the only fan to have published something by Henry Miller, an author who was still heavily banned in both England and the United States. I was also one of the early users of electronic stencils, and able to illustrate the issues with some excellent art by some of the best fan artists like Eddie Jones, Arthur Thompson and Harry Douthwaite. Something original in the vein of one of my favourite authors would fit in very well with my publishing empire, and so I cautiously asked Ramsey if he'd let me see some samples of his work, hoping that he'd trust a relative stranger with original manuscripts.

When a package arrived a few days later, I was surprised to find in it two – I think – school exercise books filled cover-to-cover with amazingly neat, almost calligraphic handwriting. Having seen the chaotic state of manuscripts by James Joyce and other authors displayed in the public galleries of the British Museum I had to assume that those by Ramsey laying before me were the finished products of several drafts, each improvements over their predecessors, but if memory serves this wasn't the case at all. The stories themselves were excellent, and had I not known otherwise would have believed them to have been hitherto undiscovered works by Lovecraft. I immediately wrote to Ramsey asking whether he'd agree to let me publish one them in the second issue of *Goudy*. Happily he agreed, and 'The Tower from Yuggoth' appeared in late 1961. It was Ramsey's first appearance in print.

Soon afterwards, Ramsey wrote asking me if I had any thoughts as to how he might have his tales published in more professional – and more profitable – venue. In my reply, I proposed that he might submit his work directly to August Derleth in Wisconsin whose Arkham House imprint had been set up in 1939 specifically in order to preserve in hardcover form the work of Lovecraft which had appeared originally in *Weird Tales* and other pulp magazines.[2] Ramsey took up my suggestion, and in 1964 Arkham House published *The Inhabitant of the Lake and Less Welcome Tenants*, a collection of ten short stories, in edition of 2009 copies. To the best of my

---

[1] Ramsey kindly nudged my memory on this. It was Peter Mabey who introduced us. At the time Peter ran the postal library of the British Science Fiction Association, and noted that both Ramsey and I were both working our way through their file of *Weird Tales* simultaneously.

[2] Again I have Ramsey to thank for clarifying a cloudy memory of mine. In fact, what happened was I wrote to a fan in Indiana named Betty Kujawa mentioning his Lovecraft stories, and she suggested that he submit them to August Derleth. I merely passed on her recommendation. However, I made the mistake of giving Betty's postal address to Ramsey without her advance permission, and she did not take kindly to a letter out of the blue from someone she didn't know. Betty was a woman of strong opinions, and I was treated to a figurative spanking for the intrusion.

knowledge it was Ramsey's only book to which he attached his full name, 'John' being subsequently dropped.

Encouraged by the positive reception of his work by Arkham House, I suggested to Ramsey that we might collaborate on something Lovecraftian. He agreed, and a manuscript of lengthening size was soon moving back and forth between Liverpool and London. When it was completed, I mailed it off to Sauk City and waited in keen anticipation of a positive reply. Instead, I received an extremely hostile letter from Derleth. I forget exactly what he wrote, but I do recall in general terms that he dismissed the tale as being unworthy of even being characterized as a parody of Lovecraft, let alone a pastiche. It is to Ramsey's credit that, knowing as he must how appalling the story was, he still put his name to it, jeopardizing his relationship with his publisher; it is to Derleth's credit in turn that he knew perfectly well who owned the responsibility for a story so awful even its title is now forgotten.

Artwork by Eddie Jones for (J.) Ramsey Campbell's story
'The Tower from Yuggoth' which appeared in Goudy *magazine,*
number two, in 1961

Ramsey and I quickly discovered interests in common other than Lovecraft. We shared a passion for cinema, and at one science fiction convention we shared the stage with some others for a discussion following a screening of Murnau's 1922 film *Nosferatu, eine Symphonie des Grauens*, an adaptation of Bram Stoker's novel *Dracula*. More memorable for me was an occasion when for some reason long forgotten Ramsey was in London, and we spent literally a whole night wandering the Thames embankment and its environs talking about our beloved films until, as I noticed, the sun rose over the Endell Street clap hospital shortly after we parted company.

Another shared interest was erotic literature, and specifically the output of the

Olympia Press in Paris, a subject which for me developed into something of a passion, resulting in three two catalogues and a full-blown bibliography of their publications over a span of almost forty years. This would lead to a brace of interesting incidents.

```
                    GOUDY - Number two.


Contents:-

      Rumble!                          By Pat Kearney.
                                       Illustrated By Eddie Jones.

      Super Fan (Fiction)              Ken Cheslin & Dave Hale
                                       Illustrated By Pearson

      Dialectical Materialism          Kathleen Norbury
                                       Illustrated By Kearney

      Walt Willis Fund                 Arthur Thomson

      Are Monster Films Coming Or Cohen?   Alan Dodd
                                       Illustrated By Eddie Jones

      The Tower From Yuggoth (fiction)   John Ramsey Campbell
                                       Illustrated by Eddie Jones
      Last Minutes                     Pat Kearney

      Like - Mail - er....             You lot out there

Front cover By Eddie Jones
Back cover By Arthur Thomson.

      Art Editor - Eddie Jones
      Duplicator - in Chief - Bruce Burn, assisted by Alan Dodd and Messrs.
      Gestetner.
      Duplicator used on this issue, is the property of Skyways Coach/Air Ltd,
      (£8:15s, Return London/Paris......Bloody reasonable, but watch how you
      go - my father's in charge of the trips, and there has been talk of
      white slavery.......).
Extracts from Evan Hunter's "A MATTER OF CONVICTION" reprinted by permission
of CORGI BOOKS LTD.
      All correspondence, parcels, bombs, etc, should be sent to the nit
      who published this ....er.... this.. er... who lives at:-
      33, Elizabeth Street, London, S.W.1. Oh, yes my name is Pat Kearney.
```

Contents page of Goudy *magazine, number two, 1961*

The first occurred when Ramsey's mother read one of my interminably long letters to her son in which I had written enthusiastically about the Olympia Press English translation of Sade's *Les 120 Journées de Sodome*; my father holding a high position in a small airline company, I was fortunate in that I could travel freely between London and Paris to obtain the latest titles emanating from the dingy offices of the Olympia Press on rue Saint-Séverin. Ramsey had not yet got a copy of his own, and was anxious to hear my opinion, but it appeared that his mother didn't share his enthusiasm for the 'divine marquis' and fired off a letter of her own to me in which she expressed her sadness at my literary interests, and wondered what my 'poor mother' would think of them. Something she wrote made me suspect she believed I was a Roman Catholic – my Irish-sounding name I suppose – and in my reply I quickly disabused her of the notion, and also assured her that my mother didn't give a fig for the books I read, which wasn't strictly speaking true. When I was later to get my book *A History of Erotic Literature* published by Macmillan, my mother pressed me earnestly not to dedicate the book to her and my step-father, a request I was pleased to circumvent by having "By special request this book is not dedicated to my parents" printed on p. [5].

Whether Ramsey's mother was mollified by my reply I am unable to say, but since my correspondence with Ramsey continued unabated I have to imagine she was and when we finally met, in the circumstances comprising the second incident, the matter was not spoken of.

A year or two later, Ramsey, accompanied by his mother, took a trip to Paris. Knowing full well that he'd be buying some Olympia Press titles for his own collection, I asked him whether he'd do me a solid and pick up a volume of either bawdy ballads or obscene limericks – I now forget which – that had been cobbled together by 'Count Palmiro Vicarion' [Christopher Logue] and published by the Olympia Press. He agreed, and we arranged to meet on his return from Paris at platform 2 at Victoria Station, which is the London terminus of the boat train connection between the two cities. Since what followed has been described elsewhere, I imagine an encore presentation won't be out of place. The cross-Channel trip had not been kind to Ramsey. Having had an identical experience myself when returning from a school holiday to the Black Forest in Germany, I felt deeply for him, who looked pale and whose coat was garlanded with the remains of his last meal. There was a touch of envy too since his sense of composure was greater than mine had been. During my own little episode, I'd vomited almost continuously from midway across the Channel until after I'd returned home to Bromley in Kent and was miserable as sin. Yet here was Ramsey, clearly the worse for wear, but ready with a smile, albeit a weak one, and triumphantly holding aloft the volume I'd asked him to get for me. He'd evidently purchased it from one of the *bouquinistes* that lined the banks of the Seine since it was still neatly protected in their favoured heavy glassine protective wrappers with the price marked in black crayon. Clearly a true bibliophile, an excellent author and a good friend.

40

creeping horror... twisted tales...

creeping crawlers

A bumper anthology of creeping, crawling, slithering horror, Science Fiction and Fantasy by 19 of today's top authors. Edited by award winner, Allen Ashley.

Including stories by Adrian Cole, Storm Constantine, Andrew Darlington, John Grant, Andrew Hook, Mark Howard Jones and others. (£11.99)

Worse Things Than Spiders

Samantha Lee can tell a great story... These are dark stories indeed, told with just the right dollop of horror to thoroughly unnerve the reader.

Samantha Lee is the author of several SF, fantasy and horror novels, including Demon, Demon II, Amy, The Belltower and The Bogle. (£8.99)

Get them at Amazon.co.uk / Amazon.com
From the publisher at: https://www.shadowpublishing.net/shop
Text 07484 607539

Shadow Publishing

THE UNEASY WORLDS OF RAMSEY CAMPBELL

Eddy C. Bertin

Front cover of Shadow #16, March 1972. *Cover artwork by Alan Hunter*

Originally published in Shadow: Fantasy Literature Review, *#16, March 1972. (The text has been subject to minor revisions since first publication).*

This is a survey of his critical work and his fiction, published and unpublished, with some notes. I want to thank J. Ramsey Campbell[1] specially for all the information about his stories as well as personal notes, which, he gave me so willingly, and for the manuscripts he sent me for lecture and dissection in this article, more than two years ago. All the quotations are reprinted here with Ramsey Campbell's grateful permission and are copyrighted by him. (ECB).

---

[1] In the early part of his career the author's by-line was J. Ramsey Campbell.

IF EVER THERE was a fan critic who managed to accumulate quite a crowd of pen-enemies in a rather short time, it surely was Ramsey Campbell. Campbell is a fanatic film goer (RC: "I like people, though!") possessing, an explicit knowledge about 'le septieme art' and a remarkably sharp eye for details formulating the artistic value of a film. Add to this a witty but poisoned pen and a healthy disdain of the so-called 'cults' around single films, actors or studios, and it is easy to foresee the results of some of his better-known pieces.

'King Kong: Classic or Catastrophe'[2] raised howls and cries from the Kong-cult, who felt almost personally attacked when Campbell very logically dismembered the film piece by piece, commenting on its story, treatment, acting and artistic and entertainment value. Even Michel Parry in his rebuttal, had to fall back on its age and simple entertainment value, in order to put up a defence for poor old Kong.

In his long, detailed piece on the then current horror films between 1958-67, 'The Horror of Horror'[3] Campbell viciously dissects, with a critic's scalpel, all the famous or infamous modern horror classics which magazines and fans have been raving about for years, (including Hammer's first *Dracula*), searching for the real reasons which contributed to their success, and often comparing them with certain scenes out of mainstream films. Neglecting bitter counter attacks, Campbell continued his one-man crusade against the "accepted classics" and often in favour of lesser (and supposedly "inferior") productions in 'Imagination· and its substitutes on the British Screen'[4], where he puts the axe into Terence Fisher, Daniel Haller and other directors, explaining in elaborate detail (something which many film critics don't seem to think necessary) his reasons for liking or disliking some particular director's work.

He searches for the fantasy values in some mainstream films and in the so-called "third rate" SF films in 'But is it SF?', ending his article with the ironic but very economical comment, "But is it SF, you ask? Who cares?" Having finished the vivisection of films, film makers and others, there's someone left: the actors, and they do get their share of the knife (not always cutting however) in 'Performances in Context'[5], where he frankly states his own personal opinions on the performances of such celebrities as Christopher Lee, Peter Cushing, Dahlia Lavi, Barbara Steele and others. One must admit that Campbell has a sharp eye for women also.

Campbell's pieces have often been called "mere checklists", but how else do you write a four-page article in which you want to decapitate some twenty film directors? When reading through the collected mass of his criticism, one often has the impression that Campbell in fact tries to see too much; he searches for hidden clues, of symbolism and eroticism where they are not apparent, and therefore often neglects the simple, straightforward entertainment value of a film. On the other hand, wherever he does find something, he forces one's nose down onto the proofs

---

[2] *Alien Worlds*, 1965.

[3] *Twylight* #1, 1967.

[4] *Twylight* #2, 1968.

[5] *Supernatural* #1, 1969.

of his statement — mainly negative — and there's no way to infuriate a fanatic horror film fan more than to show and explain to him why the film he liked so much, is in fact very poor.

In the literary field Campbell tried the same with his denial of Lovecraft in 'Lovecraft in Retrospect'[6], where — while analysing Lovecraft's story building very briefly and superficially — he discards him completely with the words, "Whatever impression he left on the genre as a whole has faded, except as preserved by a few faithful admirers, the last romantics . . ." The upsurge of interest in Lovecraft's work in the USA (where all his work is now available in paperback; in boxed sets, and even posters coming along), England and Europe (with new editions in Germany, France and Holland to name but a few), has surely disproven that last statement. Book publishers are hardly likely to be the last romantics! Campbell can't be accused of being unfair however, no matter how hard his put-down on Lovecraft was. He goes as far as dismembering one of his own, early Lovecraft pastiches 'The Face in the Desert' in his essay, 'Reflections on Juvenilia'[7], in which he shows — using himself as an example — the dangers of dutiful pastiche writing in the development of the future career of a beginning author. He advises the development of completely original models for the pastiche author, not the blind imitation of someone else's ideas or style, both as deadly.

RC: "Let people you've observed wander in and let them bring a milieu with them. If the idea of the story collapses, then find yourself a new idea. If you have no new ideas, then forget it. Don't write because it would be nice to see your name in print; write because you have to."

Practical and very sound advice to beginning writers, with which I wholeheartedly agree. At the same time, it also gives a clue to the underlying fundamentals of many of Campbell's own stories, which very often reflect his own milieu, or contain fragments of his own experiences.

Ramsey Campbell was "born of man and woman 4th January 1946" in Liverpool and received a primary education first at a local Roman Catholic school, where for some reason he contracted psychosomatic asthma, and then at a strange little private school under a railway bridge, where he liked to scare his classmates by gloatingly re-telling the more gruesome episodes of Margaret St Clair's 'The Gardener'. At the age of seven, he was sneaking adult fantasy books out of the library, and in 1956 discovered *Astounding* on the stands. He soon turned to darker visions with *Weird Tales* which he used to buy whenever remainder copies turned up at the bookstalls. At the age of five, a local newspaper had already published a children's poem of Campbell's in their 'All Your Own Work' section (RC: "But happily I don't recall any more of that!"). Without any special interest he wrote a few stories, recalling among them the title 'Black Fingers from Space', but no examples of this earliest period remain. During the first two years at the Roman Catholic college, his English master often used to excuse him from homework so that he could write tales which he later used to read to the class. He sent off "an unpleasant piece of juvenile morbidity

---

[6] *Shadow* #7, 1969.

[7] *Weird Fantasy* #1, 1970.

called 'Lover's Meeting' to *The Magazine of Fantasy and SF*, which they quickly (and understandably) returned . . ." He picked up a copy of the paperback *Cry Horror* at the age of fourteen, and was hooked on Lovecraft immediately, so far even, that in a very short time he turned out no less than five Lovecraft pastiches.

Why precisely Lovecraft as a model for these pastiches? RC: "He'd affected my perception to such an extent that I actually began to see ruined houses, underground passages, and ancient books and the like, much as he did. This was probably already inherent in me: I'm not sure that it didn't relate to a confusion, of adolescent morbidity and awakening sexuality."

Lovecraft didn't start Campbell writing, there had never been a time-lag between his pastiches and the earlier weird juvenilia, though nothing remains of these early examples. Though Campbell has now shook off all Lovecraft's influences completely, denying his earlier inspiration, they were still the start of real publication. But why in fact did Campbell begin writing at all?

RC: "Probably because I had to: at the age of five or seven you don't think in terms of publication. One good answer might be: enjoyment of the use and capabilities of words. Why horror? Well, I was the archetypical introverted only child, given to solitary fantasy: it was probably inevitable that I'd read fantasy stories and then, of course, try writing them myself."

On the advice of Betty Kujawa, Campbell sent those original five pastiches to August Derleth, who returned them immediately, with, however a kind letter and some suggestions for revision. The correspondence continued, and two stories finally saw print in small publications: 'The Tower from Yuggoth' in *Goudy*, 1963, a story which was later rewritten as 'The Mine on Yuggoth' for his first book collection, and 'The Face in the Desert' in *Mirage* in 1965. This is the story he dissected himself in *Weird Fantasy* in 1970. In 'Face' a traveller goes in search of what Abdul Alhazred found in the desert before he left for the Nameless City. The traveller discovers enormous statue-like cylinders, bearing on top of them the sculpted heads of indescribable monstrosities. He begins to read the alien inscriptions on the pillars, astounded at his ability to read them at all, then looks up as he is standing before a headless pedestal. And: "For even as I chanted that horrific ritual, a likeness had been forming to surmount the pedestal. As I stared upwards, I glimpsed a loathsome and foetal replica materialising at the centre of the translucent bulb – a ghastly but recognisable likeness of my own face!" The whole Lovecraft pandemonium is there, complete with shunned places, hidden secrets too loathsome to speak about, and as Campbell has amply demonstrated himself, is very far from faultless, but remembering that it is one of his first tries at professionalism, it doesn't come out so very badly at all.

Campbell's first book collection *The Inhabitant of The Lake and Less Welcome Tenants* was published by Arkham House in 1964, and from the ten stories included, only four were re-writes based on his early pastiches: 'The Room in the Tower', containing a monstrous growing entity; 'The Horror from the Bridge', where the Old Ones once again walk the Earth for a short time, when someone removes the Elder Sign keeping them prisoner; 'The Insects from Shaggai', in which the narrator in typical Lovecraft style visits other worlds and dimensions through a vampiric entity in his mind, and 'The Mine on Yuggoth', an unconvincing story about a mountain staircase opening a gateway to the weird planet Yuggoth and its inhabitants. All the stories are set in the Severn Valley at Brichester, a detailed British counterpart of Lovecraft's Arkham-Dunwich-Innsmouth setting. So are the other tales in the collection, but here the influence of Lovecraft is already less apparent. 'The Render of the Veils' deals with things seen as they really are, not as we see them with our limited 'veiled' eyes, while 'The Moon Lens' brings a more gruesome variation on Shub Niggurath. A dead witch tries to raise her disintegrating body from the grave, and then take over the mind of her house's new tenant in 'The Return of the Witch'. The opposite is 'The Plain of Sound' which is almost straight science fiction, putting forward the notion of another plane of existence where the sounds from our dimension materialise in deadly form. 'The Will of Stanley Brooke' is a poor little variant on the old theme of the doppelganger. Still one of my favourite Lovecraftian stories (Lovecraftian not Lovecraft-pastiche) remains the title story, 'The Inhabitant of the Lake' a powerful weird novelette. In this, an extraterrestrial being, Gla'aki, has fallen to Earth with its whole city in the middle of an enormous meteorite and sunk below a lake.

> *"You've got to look into the lake at a special angle, otherwise you can't see anything. Down on the bottom, among the weeds – stagnant water, everything dead, except . . . There's a city down there, all black spiraling steeples and walls at obtuse angles with the streets. Dead things lying on the streets – they died with the journey through space – they're horrible, hard, shiny, all red and covered with bunches of trumpet-shaped things . . . And right at the centre of the city is a transparent trapdoor. Gla'aki's under there, pulsing and staring up – I saw the eye-stalks move toward me –"* (p.135).

The story is told in first person, who has come to the Severn Valley to help his friend Cartwright, an artist, interested in the macabre, and who through his dreams has contacted the horrible world of Gla'aki. His first meeting with Gla'aki in person is frightening enough:

> *". . . I could look down into the lake. The ferns and water were unusually mobile tonight, but I didn't realise what was making them move until an eye rose above the surface and stared moistly at me. Two others followed it and, worst of all, none of them was IN A FACE!"* (p.115).

But seeing the whole of the being is even worse:

> *"The centre of each picture was, it was obvious, the being known as Gla'aki. From an oval body protruded countless, thin, pointed spines of multicoloured metal; at the more rounded end of the oval a circular, thick-lipped mouth formed the centre of a spongy face, from which rose three yellow eyes on thin stalks. Around the underside of the body were many white pyramids, presumably used for locomotion . . ."* (p,132).

46

Gla'aki is served by a cult of zombie-like walking corpses, victims it killed and revived into a semblance of life. 'Inhabitant' is an excellent blend of weird SF and gruesome horror and though the general development of the story follows the way of most Lovecraft tales, the ideas exposed are fully original.

The final rewrite under Lovecraft's influence was 'The Church in the High Street' (which didn't fit in the above collection as it had already been published by Arkham House in 1962). In this story the memory of the horrible life-forms glimpsed through a portal into another dimension drives the narrator to suicide. The final published version was heavily cut and re-written by August Derleth. (I won't go into any more details on this Lovecraft period of Campbell, as I have dealt with these before in my article 'The Followers of Cthulhu' in *Shadow* 9[8].

Two other stories from the period just after *The Inhabitant of the Lake* had been put together, are 'The Childish Fear', a minor but enjoyable horror tale in a very modern setting, and dealing with nightmarish things of the dark, visiting among other places a cinema where nothing but horror films are played; and 'An Offering to the Dead', a vampire tale, awaiting publication at this time.

By this time, Campbell was schooled at St Edwards Roman Catholic college where he first became agnostic and then a confirmed atheist: "I do not believe in God or in life after death. If it exists, then it is in a form so unrecognizable that it doesn't concern me anyway."

Campbell "left the oppressions of school in 1962 for the oppressions of Civil Service", and "finally reacted against the conservatism of the latter in 1966" when he started working as a librarian in Liverpool. Two years later he announced that he had stopped fan-writing altogether though occasionally a piece of his still sees the light. On the whole, he appreciates what every man in his right mind likes: smoking (his former hang-up on Turkish brands turns up in 'The Cellars'), drinking (anything which is good to the taste, he is even a member of a wine and food appreciation society), and girls, "though I had various troubles along the way." Some of these psychological and sentimental influences can be found back in such stories as 'Concussion', 'The Cellars', 'Napier Court' and 'The Stocking'. He seems to have solved his problems, as on January first, 1971 he changed his address (though still-living in Liverpool) and married Jenny Chandler. Now we know who 'Jenny, the White Witch' was to whom so many of his articles have been dedicated.

Among his favorite authors he cites Mervyn Peake, J.R.R. Tolkien, Errol Undercliffe, Alfred Bester, Cordwainer Smith, Roger Zelazny, Fritz Leiber and M.R. James. Quite a mixed crowd, but Campbell's choice of literature is far from restricted to fantasy and science fiction; among the mainstream authors he prefers the work of F. Scott Fitzgerald, Vladimir Nabokov, Kenneth Patchen, Graham Greene and Jorge Louis Borges. As to preferred works, there is a long list with many classics of fantasy, but he has reserved a special niche for the controversial mainstream novels *Last Exit to Brooklyn*, *L'Histoire d'O* ("the only really pornographic. novel I know about") and *Why we are in Vietnam*. Another of his favorite things is – as seems to be the case with many authors of the macabre – music, which may be apparent from many of his stories. As well as the obvious classics such as Beethoven, and Mozart, he is particularly fond of Mahler, Sibelius,

---

[8] Jan-Feb 1970, reprinted in *Nyctalops* 5, Dec 1971.

Debussy, Stravinsky, Britten and Shostakovich, and of the more contemporary Henze, Penderecki and some of Stockhausen and Beiro.

Campbell still feels a certain affection for his early published work because "at least it's dead serious, not all camp", but he doesn't consider it much more than "a sustained homage to the pre-war *Weird Tales* period." He continues, "However you'll notice a definite stylistic break with Lovecraft in 'The Stone on the Island'. I'd become tired of his predictable effects, standardised and occasionally absurd characterisations, and heavy and unsubtle style." The effects in this story are indeed far from predictable, dealing with weird face-like creatures who take horrible revenge upon an intruder on the island, where they guard an ancient stone.

RC: "But it wasn't until I wrote 'The Cellars', which is largely autobiographical, the cellars do exist – and my first real story, that I began to see what I wanted to write." Not without reason 'The Cellars' has been called a love story, and it marks indeed a certain change in subject matter as well as in treatment in Campbell's fiction.

A quote from one of his articles is very well suited, here, At the end of his piece 'Note of Doubt'[9] Campbell writes ". . . let's not draw back from avant-garde music or soft drugs or what you will in blind horror. We must perceive the horror in the everyday and personally confront, not recoil, from the unknown."

Until this point, Campbell's stories had been clear-cut. They took some weird subject, mostly influenced by his counter-creation of Lovecraft's myth patterns; his narrators almost always either ran and escaped from the unknown and horrible fate, or else became its easy prey. His stories had a linear development from beginning to end, the horror was suggested, then imposed on the reader and it won or lost the battle. Even 'The Stone on the Island' had been straightforward, but 'The Cellars' was something very different indeed. July, a young woman, is dated by a man whom she finds rather boring. With him she visits hidden catacombs, 'the cellars' below Liverpool, among crumbling walls covered with mold. The man later strangely disappears from the office where they both work, yet July receives a valentine card written in a magnified and unsteady hand and discovers a patch of mold on the envelope. A face watches her through a window, and after it has disappeared, she notices traces of mold on the glass where the face was pressed. Later she silently watches a horribly deformed creature stumble into the water, but already interest and memory of the girl passing away.

Not only much more care is given to originality in the art of writing and the use of new comparisons ("Several minutes later he left her reluctantly, detaching himself from her presence as from fly-paper"), but also the setting changes from the near-Gothic Severn Valley into a modern city, and interest in real human relationships develops. The horror is never fully mentioned, never explained in fact, but everything is suggested with hints between the lines. The real horror of the story lies not so much in the change of the young man into a lumbering mass of mold, but rather in the cold, indifferent psychological reaction of the girl to the change and to his remaining feelings.

RC: "From this point onwards, you can trace recurrent themes: those of unresolved sexuality and of the fragility of relationships." The former, especially,

---

[9] *Stardock* #3, 1970.

come strongly through in the final Cthulhu tale (though only because it happens to include a new weird deity and a horrible forbidden book, continuing those he created in *The Inhabitant of the Lake*.

'Cold Print'. The anti-hero, in his ques for pornographic and erotic books, ends up in the possession of an ancient volume on forbidden gods. In turn he has to accept the position of high priest and obtain suitable food for the deity, Y'golonac, an undead thing which feeds on the living, and takes their form upon itself. It comes when its name is spoken or read, which happens to the unfortunate Strutt. In vain he tries to escape from the unmentionable thing before him. "This was happening because somewhere, someone had WANTED this to happen to him. It wasn't playing fair, he hadn't done anything to deserve this – but before he could scream out his protest his breath was cut off, as the hands descended on his face and the wet red mouths opened in their palms."

Campbell motivates his own preference for the horror story as follows: "The horror story, with its sense of the instability of 'reality' and its innumerable sexual undercurrents, seems to me to be a more than relevant means of expression. This is, of course, retrospective justification, but I'm probably not the first writer to have started writing in a field without conscious justification and only later to have selected those aspects of the form he finds relevant to what he wants to say." 'Cold Print' is full of hints of hidden horror, morbidity and sexuality, and they are all blended together in the gruesome final lines with their striking sexual symbolism; in which the narrator is really absorbed by the final vagina-symbol, the hungry wet red mouths.

"The most important line," Campbell says, "is: 'somewhere, someone had wanted this to happen to him' . . . namely, the reader! If we recoil from his (the narrator, Strutt) sexual-pornographic tendencies, why not from our quest of horror?" Which brings us to a sharp insight not only into the horror story itself, but also of those who read them – "Nous sommes tous des assassins" would be well suited in a way – because we can only feel antipathy for Strutt and his search for a meaning in his empty life through pornography, we expect the horrible ending which is brought to his life, we anticipate it and rejoice in it. We are horrified, yes, but we feel no pity for Strutt. Yet which of the two is more inhuman: Strutt's pathetic quest for arousing literature to fill his dreary days, or our sadistic-indifferent anticipation of his gruesome death?

These themes appear in most of Campbell's stories from then onwards, and so do many autobiographical – though masked – details. Many are the stories which have been inspired by some small and otherwise unimportant incident in reality. Some particularly bizarre personal ads in a newspaper formed the basis for 'Reply Guaranteed' in which a girl, as a joke, answers one of those weird advertisements asking for someone for company, though the girl certainly didn't expect her visitor to be something which should be dead but wasn't quite in a way. The accumulation of psychical stress through small, unimportant details until its breaking point of madness makes the climax of 'The Stocking', another analysis of human relationships, and as in some of the other stories, this one also ends just BEFORE the final horror, which the reader knows is bound to happen now. Campbell says about this: "I *want* my characters to escape . . ." and in a way, he leaves this possibility open to the reader. If the reader really wants it, he can change what comes after the story ends . . . but probably he won't.

We often meet someone in the street or on a bus, already turn and open our mouth to speak to him or her . . . and then notice that it isn't the person we thought it was at all but a complete stranger. Such an everyday incident started 'The Scar', a nightmarish tale on the doppelganger theme, about things which not only take on our external form but also our place in society. An obsessed conscience formed the fundamentals for the short prose-poem 'The Drowned Car'. A woman's possessive desire for a younger man's sexual attentions starts 'Cyril', a weird, voodoo-like doll which the young man brings with him to the woman's apartment, a doll which in some way seems partly alive and bizarrely related to the man's own body.

Not all of Campbell's recent work is "horror" however, or at any rate not "horror" as we think of the term. Campbell himself doesn't like the sound of the word horror so very much, he calls 'The Stocking' a comedy of menace and 'Concussion', a science-fantasy. Campbell says that he prefers to use John Burke's inspired phrase "tales of unease", a term which describes Campbell stories in general perfectly. In the following stories Campbell shows a full mastery of the craft of literary writing, but on the other hand unfortunately the story lines are much less clear, often very confusing: more and more the reader has to follow what he himself THINKS is happening, relying on – often too vague – hints and suggestions. The "horror" is almost never shown now, nor even immediately suggested. The whole impact of this new group of stories relies on a general atmosphere of lurking menace, mounting psychological stresses, and the uneasy feeling that any second now something is bound to happen. Unfortunately, in many cases it never DOES happen, and the reader feels cheated.

Take 'The Sunshine Club' which literally seen is an excellent piece of writing, but seen as a horror story is a confusing mess. It deals with a psycho-analytical explanation of vampirism, by which means a psychiatrist rids his patients of their fears of garlic, crosses, fire etc. The liking for blood, however, stays. Two quotes are in order here, examples of the mixture of weird fact with symbolism:

"I closed his file on my desk and glanced at him to detect impatience or a plea, but his eyes had filled with the sunset as with blood. He was intent on the cat outside the window, waiting huddled on the balcony. There was the spider's cocoon of eggs like a soft white marble in the corner, belling with minute hectic birth . . ."

And later on in the story: "I stood above the lights of the city clustering towards the dark horizon, and the tiny struggling red spiders streamed out from the window on threads, only to drift back and settle softly, like microscopic drops of blood, on my face . . ."

In 'Napier Court', Alma, a young, intelligent and sick woman is a recluse in the house of Napier, an old family house where a man committed suicide, who refused the wealth of the world, and who is supposed to haunt the house. Alma breaks with her boyfriend whom she considers uneducated, and, alone with her French books and her flute, she waits in an atmosphere of mounting tension where delirium and hallucinations begin to mingle with reality. 'Napier Court' is remarkable for its fluent stream of semi-poetical prose and fresh images, the central theme is very carefully treated, never giving away too much, and the story ends on a screaming note of unexpected terror.

Martin, the hero of another story, is on his way to London, with nothing to lose there except his last ten pounds. He doesn't care anymore about his life, and this brings in the powers of evil, when he ends up in the middle of a weird poker game with three grotesque companions with lightning eyes and who are surrounded by flies. Playing by their own rules, Martin has to play 'The Last Hand' if he wants to survive. But does he really want to?

On Christmas Eve, 1969, BBC Radio Merseyside broadcast another very subtle story 'The Christmas Present' with music commissioned by Don Henshilwood. The narrator and his friend receive a wrapped present from a strange character, a Christmas gift, which they are, however, only allowed to open at midnight exactly. Campbell carefully builds up the suspense and curiosity about the "present", slowly creating a haunting suggestion of immense powers of materialising evil, as reality slowly changes into the realms of darkness and the supernatural. Again however, the ending is too subtle, too open for many different interpretations. Is it a ghost story? A symbolisation of our primeval superstitions, still inherent in us, today's people? Is it only a joke on the narrators, and on the reader/listener? We can guess what it's all about, but somehow this way of ending leaves us unsatisfied.

'The Void' deals with the ghost of a man whose hand has been transplanted to another man, and his eye to a woman. The schizophrenic changing points of view however, make this story completely non-understandable and Campbell himself, having observed that it doesn't work out as it should, will probably rewrite it.

Schizophrenia in another, even more nightmarish way, crops up in 'The Telephones', in which a long-haired hitchhiker is pursued by telephone calls through all the public boxes along his route, made by an anonymous homosexual who says he's coming for him. As it turns out, it is his own repressed fear of homosexuality which haunts him, though the frightening climax, real or imagined – but in both extremes absolutely horrible – leaves, open no less than three possible interpretations to the reader.

My own personal favorite among Campbell's work is the short story, 'The Previous Tenant', one of the finest ghost stories I've ever read . . . and I have read many! A very sensitive young painter and his very ordinary wife move into the furnished flat of a young girl who committed suicide. This is not openly stated – mark the subtle and yet very clear way which Campbell takes to bring this knowledge over to the reader with one sentence: "How could she have become a scream above the city, a broken figurine beneath the window?" The shy presence of the dead girl is all over the flat, felt and absorbed by the painter, who finally is almost able to see her, but the insensitiveness and routine-housewife mentality of his wife is slowly driving away the presence by imposing her own dull routine on the flat. The woman doesn't know about the ghostly, fading presence of the dead girl . . . or maybe unconsciously she does know? The story is excellently written, full of hidden sexual and psychological symbolism. The cold, buried hatred of the sensitive artist against everyday reality, personified by his dull wife never comes into the open until the last striking sentences. His wife is busy with dinner, and she succeeds finally in discarding the last lingering essence of the dead girl, leaving her husband full of fury at his loss.

"His hands closed on the carving knife, 'This'll do,' he said."

Campbell's second book, *Demons By Daylight* was announced by Arkham House for 1971, but now with Derleth's regretted death, it probably will be postponed for this year or thereabouts. It is a strange collection of stories, only half of which are real horror stories, though they all have undercurrents of the strange and the macabre.

'Potential' opens the book. This shocking story was inspired by an abortive freak-out in Southport, and – which touching on the generation gap, drugs, pop, pot, flower-power etc – deals with an elderly accountant, who is searching for something to make him special, something to bring some colour into his dreary life. He mixes with the in-groups and at a flower-power party meets someone who invites him to an experiment. In a room above a lonely inn at Severnford, he and his friends experiment with the mind, trying to find something to release its potential, with total neglect of human rules and laws. A nude girl is bound on a rack, and Charles, the accountant, receives a set of knives in his hands. The choice is his now, he has the absolute power of the life of the girl, and of the way she is going to die. The climax is far from anything the reader might suppose. 'The End of a Summer's Day' deals with a young married couple who visit a cave of absolute darkness with a mixed bunch of tourists. We all know that feeling of helplessness when being alone with a group of people one can't understand and when something goes wrong. It is a striking tale of mounting fear, as well as a sharp picture of complete alienation, human disinterest and cruelty. 'At First Sight' projects a frustrated young girl's fears of and attraction to sex as a menace, symbolised and materialised in a strange man upstairs in her own room. 'Errol Undercliffe: A Tribute' (or 'The Franklyn Paragraphs') is something entirely different. RC wrote me: "Errol "Undercliffe is the most important Brichester-born writer, as far as I know." Not being able to check this, and never having heard of Undercliffe, I don't know in how far RC is writing the truth and in how far he is playing a joke on me, so I will consider the whole thing as fiction.[10] In the story, RC himself is in correspondence with Undercliffe, a horror author, who is on the trail of a book by R. Franklin titled "We all Pass from View". This book states that the number of spirits is limited so that when a body dies and is not cremated, the spirit has to linger in the dead body. Undercliffe mysteriously disappears, after having found the grave of R. Franklin, whose mind is still ghostily alive. Undercliffe writes: "No longer could I trust the surface of the world. It was as though it had been instantaneously revealed to me that there were countless forces awake in everything, invisible things lurking in daylight, shifting, planning . . ."

This is in fact the essence of *Demons by Daylight*! Nothing is what it seems, unease, terror and menace are everywhere surrounding us, hiding their real face in the ordinariness of daylight. This story also contains two interesting quotations, which Campbell relates through the mouth of his own alter-ego as a horror author:

"Even the supernatural story-writer who believes what he writes (and I'm not saying I don't) isn't prepared for an actual confrontation. Quite the reverse, for every time he fabricates the supernatural in a story (unless based on experience) he clinches his skepticism, he knows such things can't be, because he wrote them. Thus for him a confrontation would be doubly upsetting."

And a bit further on: "There was this idiot at the party, wanting to know what I did, 'Horror stories', I said. Should have seen him blanch. 'Why do you write those things?' he asked as if he'd caught me picking my nose? 'For the money,' I said."

---

[10] Errol Undercliffe is of course Ramsey Campbell.

Typical for many of the modern stories is the inclusion of allusions to details only known to in-people, names and places which only carry meaning to those who know about the fields of horror and SF literature, and fandom. Some examples which turn up in some way or other: Michel Parry, the first issue of *Alien Worlds*, *Castle of Frankenstein* magazine, August Derleth, the deity Daoloth, Cthulhu, Robert Blake (from 'The Haunter of the Dark'), 'The Yellow Wallpaper', film producer Harry Nadler. Even Dennis Wheatley's warnings about the enormous dangers on the misuse of magic and witchcraft turns up.

After 'The Franklyn Paragraphs' RC offers as a final tribute to Errol Undercliffe 'The Interloper' by Errol Undercliffe. In this ghoulish little shocker, very reminiscent of 'The Cellars' two young boys searching for a practically unknown dance The Catacomb, stumble upon real catacombs hidden under the city, inhabited by slimy, semi-human beings who prey on the force of the living.

'The Second Staircase' again, is set in very contemporary times, with talks about Ravi Shankar, Richard Davis, George Harrison and – Ramsey Campbell included. It is another story of projected menace, which might or might not be a ghost story.

'Concussion' is one of Campbell's own favorite stories, what he calls "a romantic science-fantasy", and though very slow moving, it is a beautiful and touching story. Kirk Morris, an old man, tries to regain his past and love affair with Ann, a girl he once met on a coach. Past, present and reflections on the future into the past, intermingle in a bizarre mosaic: after a short summer idyll, Morris tries to find the girl, but in her native town the address she gave him doesn't exist, the street isn't even built yet! He goes in search of her relative, an aunt, who she told him is an old woman with a birthmark disfiguring her face, but he finds her as a young unmarried girl . . . carrying the birthmark. Has he loved a projection of Ann from the future in his own real or imagined past? The reader will have to puzzle out the solution for himself, reading between that which "really" happens. Because how do you define reality, and objectiveness?

In 'The Enchanted Fruit' the narrator, while strolling through the woods, discovers a strange, unknown fruit on a tree, and he eats it. Afterwards anything he eats tastes as the fruit at first, but then as decaying fruit, worse and worse, so that finally he can't keep anything down. The story, which begins modernistic soon dashes off into what seems like a kind of fairy-tale at first, but then changes into a psychological nightmare. RC: "'The Enchanted Fruit' is a meditation on the meaning of pain . . . a story about the inevitability of suffering." When human science and belief in a god fail the narrator, "the love of a woman can conquer in such a situation . . ." (RC). But does it? Again the reader himself has to provide his own answer to the riddle, but frankly I haven't been convinced by the treatment of this story. The symbolism lies too thick on it and in a short space it requires three changes of mood, which is asking a bit too much of the reader.

'Made in Goatswood' (RC): "decides after a good deal of thought not to be a horror story after all . . .", though I am not so sure about that. Oedipodian possessive love, religious fanaticism, modern paganism, the power of suggestion, ancient evils . . . they all turn up in this subtle, terror tale, in which a young atheist presents three evil garden gnomes to his very Catholic fiancé. Again the reader has to decide for himself whether the weird happenings are due to the suggestive power of the gnomes, or if they are really possessed by alien and dangerous powers. This attitude of leaving the reader several possibilities to conclude what has happened has its strong points, but also when it happens too often, it can be quite frustrating.

A good example is Campbell's most recently published story (at this time of writing), 'Broadcast', in which two schoolboys and their favorite teacher visit a broadcasting station, where they lose him in a very strange way. The atmosphere of tension and terror mounts to what should be a shattering climax, but I'm still wondering what happened in fact.

Late in 1969 Campbell started working on a series of connected stories in novel form, titled *Shifts*, the project has been abandoned since then. At the moment he is working on a collection of tales set (where else?) in Liverpool, which should include 'The Cellars', 'The Christmas Present', 'The Last Hand', 'Beside the Seaside', 'The Dark Show' and 'The Wounds' among others.

He has been working as a film critic for BBC Radio Merseyside for almost three years now and has also taken to reading his stories in public to a live jazz improvisation. The first tale treated in this way so far was 'In the Shadows', and it proved quite effective. Recently Radio Merseyside did his 'Writer's Curse', and one of his latest contracts was with the Norwegian Broadcasting Corporation (Norsk Rikskringkasting) in Oslo who are looking for horror stories for dramatization in a series of late-night broadcasts.

Ramsey Campbell has high hopes for his next collection: "A great many people are going to dislike *Demons by Daylight*, but I hope a good many more will find parts of it they like," he wrote late in 1969, when the assembling of the collection was nearly complete (only two stories were replaced since then). Since that time, many of his "new" stories have appeared through various sources and have openly marked his change of style and subject matter for the early period of straight horror and weird SF into another dimension of terror: the worlds of unease, where reality is never what it seems, and where the most ordinary, everyday incident can be the start of some hideous happening, the opening doorway for a Demon by Daylight.

EDDY C. BERTIN (1944–2018)

MY FIRST CONTACT with Eddy was when he began to submit essays to my small press magazine, *Shadow: Fantasy Literature Review*. His first article appeared in the second issue in 1968, 'Charles Birkin: Master of Cruelty and Horror'. It soon became apparent that Eddy was one of those horror aficionados who could turn his hand to anything—book reviews, articles and fiction. In the following seven years he contributed more than eighty essays, biographies, bibliographies and reviews to the magazine, often providing biographies of the lesser-known European writers, such as Maurice Limat and Jean Ray. He contributed many items on H.P. Lovecraft's work, amongst reams of other useful and interesting material. I owe Eddy a great debt of gratitude—*Shadow* was improved immeasurably by his input.

And it was through *Shadow* that I discovered Eddy's fiction, publishing 'A Taste of Rain and Darkness' in my short-lived fiction magazine *Weird Window* in 1970. His first professional sale was to Herbert van Thal's *The Ninth Pan Book of Horror Stories*, 'The Whispering Horror', which appeared in 1968. In the same year 'The City, Dying' appeared in John Carnell's *New Writings in SF* volume 13.

A great many genre stories followed, written in Dutch, Flemish and German as well as English. His significant body of work includes many short stories, poetry and novels, including translations into various languages. He authored many novels in the horror genre as well as pulp novels and serials, thrillers, murder mystery and historical romances, some under various pseudonyms. But his greatest contribution was in horror fiction with a distinctly European flavour, and fiction based in H.P. Lovecraft's Cthulhu Mythos. His only collection of short stories in English is *The Whispering Horror* (Shadow Publishing 2013).

—David A. Sutton

Front cover of The Whispering Horror *by Eddy C. Bertin (Shadow Publishing)*

FROM 'THE FRANKLYN PARAGRAPHS' TO DAOLOTH: RAMSEY CAMPBELL AND LOVECRAFT OVER FIFTY YEARS

S. T. Joshi

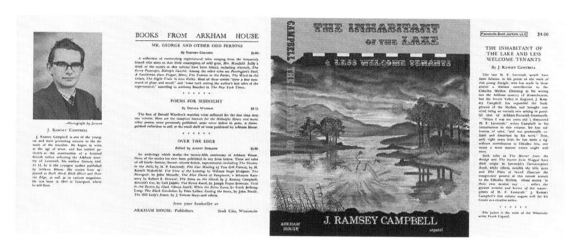

Dust jacket for Ramsey Campbell's (as J. Ramsey Campbell)
The Inhabitant of the Lake and Less Welcome Tenants

IT HAS LONG been known that Ramsey Campbell's first published volume, *The Inhabitant of the Lake and Less Welcome Tenants* (1964), consisted of pastiches of H.P. Lovecraft's Cthulhu Mythos. Some of these stories, we learn, were initially written when he was as young as eighteen. These works are somewhat crude and derivative, but even they reveal an incipient innovativeness that would lead Campbell to approach Lovecraft in increasingly distinctive ways over the next several decades.

One of the most remarkable of Campbell's post-*Inhabitant* tales is 'The Franklyn Paragraphs', written in 1967 and first published in the landmark collection *Demons by Daylight* (1973). This story is a masterful adaptation (and perhaps partial parody) of Lovecraft's "documentary style", in which letters, newspaper articles, telegrams, and the like are directly cited to augment a tale's verisimilitude. Campbell is himself a character, narrating the story in the first person and claiming to have established a correspondence with the horror writer Errol Undercliffe, who disappeared from his flat in Lower Brichester in 1967. Several real individuals—from August Derleth to Campbell's agent Kirby McCauley to J. Vernon Shea, a correspondent of and commentator on Lovecraft—are all cited by name in the tale; to complete the confusion, Robert Blake (a character in Lovecraft's 'The Haunter of the Dark') is also mentioned.

Undercliffe has stumbled upon a very obscure volume, Roland Franklyn's *We*

Pass from View (1964); and Campbell provides both the British National Bibliography catalogue entry for the work as well as a dismissive review of it from the *Times Literary Supplement*. On the surface, it appears to be the usual mélange of grandiosity and ominous prophecy that makes so many occultist works comical instead of frightening; but Undercliffe seems impressed with it and even joins a band of initiates once led by Franklyn, who has died. He seems to do so primarily as a lark, remarking flippantly, "I'd give a lot for a genuine supernatural occurrence." He gets his wish sooner than he expects. While looking at a blank page of *We Pass from View,* he sees lines of print suddenly appearing:

> FEEL THEM COMING SLOWLY BURROWING WANT ME TO SUFFER CANT MOVE GET ME OUT SAVE ME SOMEWHERE IN BRICHESTER HELP ME

It turns out that Franklyn was killed violently by his wife, a circumstance that has caused his soul to be trapped in his body and to be ravaged by nameless "burrowers of the core".

This synopsis cannot begin to convey the richness of texture and subtlety of execution that make 'The Franklyn Paragraphs' a masterwork of cumulative horror. The relationship between writing and reality—a theme that dominates Campbell's work from beginning to end—receives one of its most potent expressions here. It might be thought that a horror writer would welcome the actual experience of the supernatural, but in fact the reverse is the case; as Franklyn's wife scornfully tells Undercliffe, "God! You'd never write about it, you'd never write about anything again"—and this makes us realise why Undercliffe's last letter to the narrator trails off in a fragment. The ultimate message of 'The Franklyn Paragraphs' is exactly that of Lovecraft's best work—"No longer could I trust the surface of the world"—but it is expressed in a mood and idiom that are entirely Campbell's own.

The recent collection *Visions from Brichester* (2015) prints the early version of this story, written in 1965. It is much less Lovecraftian than its revised version and also commits the gaffe of placing its supernatural dénouement at the beginning of the story. The basic motif of both stories is again that of the "forbidden book", already well used by Lovecraft himself and his disciples; by the time Campbell got around to using it, something new had to be done. He did so—but bunglingly in this first version. Here a character named Harvey Shea (presumably derived from J. Vernon Shea, a correspondent of Lovecraft cited by name in the revised version) who comes upon a strange book by Roland Franklyn, *Magic, Legend and the Infinite Self* (a far less evocative title than the revised version's *We Pass from View*). But whereas in the later version the climax—the fact that the book begins writing words of its own accord in front of the narrator's eyes, as the spirit of Franklyn seeks to escape from the tomb in which his vindictive wife buried him—is placed well along in the story for maximum impact, in the early version it is matter-of-factly introduced toward the beginning. What is more, Campbell in the later version has incorporated his own persona into the narrative, presenting a series of letters from Roland Franklyn to himself and thereby radically enhancing (and in some senses subtly parodying) the "documentary style" so frequently used by Lovecraft to create verisimilitude.

Campbell went on to write many other Lovecraftian tales over the coming decades, but I wish to focus on some works that allowed Campbell to expand the scope of his (and Lovecraft's) conceptions to novel length. Consider a novel published in 2002, *The Darkest Part of the Woods*. Here Campbell returns to Brichester, but this Brichester, far from being the implausibly archaic nexus of Lovecraftian horror that it was in the *Inhabitant of the Lake* stories, is a town fully enmeshed in the modern world, with its computers, cellphones, and televisions. And yet, Lovecraft is perhaps not far from Campbell's vision in this richly complex, meticulously crafted, and chillingly terrifying work.

We learn that Heather Price, struggling to support herself and her adult son, Sam, as a librarian, is the daughter of Lennox Price, a man confined in the Arbour, a nearby mental hospital. Lennox, the author of a scholarly work, *The Mechanics of Delusion,* has himself become unhealthily fascinated with the dense woods that surround Brichester, and on occasion he leads other inmates in conducting anomalous rituals in a clearing deep in the heart of the woods. He refuses to explain what he is searching for aside from uttering the curious name "Selcouth".

The name Selcouth is finally elucidated (initially by an Internet site) as one Nathaniel Selcouth, a sixteenth-century magician who built a dwelling in the Brichester woods and sought to "create a messenger or servant that would mediate between him and the limits of the universe, both physical and spiritual". It is here that the Lovecraft influence manifests itself, and even more so when Sylvia discovers Selcouth's journal in an underground cavity deep in the woods. The echoes of *The Case of Charles Dexter Ward,* with Ward's discovery of the journal of the seventeenth-century American wizard Joseph Curwen, are evident, and Campbell makes no secret of it: Curwen, it appears, "is known to have visited England in search of Selcouth's journals but failed to locate them". What follows are some of the most terrifying passages in all Campbell's work, as successive characters brave the depths of the woods either to carry out or to thwart the sinister plans of the ancient mage.

In 2017–18, Campbell published a trilogy of novels collectively titled *The Three Births of Daoloth*. The reference, of course, is to the entity Campbell cited in several of his early Lovecraftian tales, beginning with 'The Room in the Castle'. Conveniently for Campbell, this entity is generally mentioned in only the vaguest of terms in his early stories. The one clear elucidation of Daoloth's nature and purpose is found in 'The Render of the Veils', where a character states:

> "Daoloth is a god—an alien god. He was worshopped in Atlantis, where he was the god of the astrologers. I presume it was there that his mode of worship on Earth was set up: he must never be seen, for the eye tries to follow the convolutions of his shape, and that causes insanity. That's why there must be no light when he is invoked—when we call on him later tonight, we'll have to switch out all the lights."

It is, however, not at all clear that, in his trilogy, Campbell is portraying Daoloth in accordance with this passage. Accordingly, the trilogy becomes less an homage to Lovecraft as a grand summation of Campbell's nearly sixty years of life and writing.

The first novel in the trilogy, *The Searching Dead* (2017), opens in 1952 and is told in the first person by Dominic Sheldrake, whose exact age is never specified but who appears to be in his early teenage years, living with his parents in Liverpool. Postwar rationing is still in effect, and parts of the city still remain devastated from German bombing. Our attention is arrested when a neighbour, Mrs Norris, tells Dominic's parents that the new church she has joined allows members to see the dead in the flesh; she, in fact, has spoken to her recently deceased husband. Dominic's father, Desmond, a strict Catholic, scoffs at this assertion as routine (and potentially blasphemous) spiritualism; but Dominic learns from Mrs Norris that it is his own teacher at the Catholic school he is attending, Christian Noble, who is the head of this new church, which calls itself the Trinity Church of the Spirit. This superficially Christian-sounding name clearly masks a much darker secret.

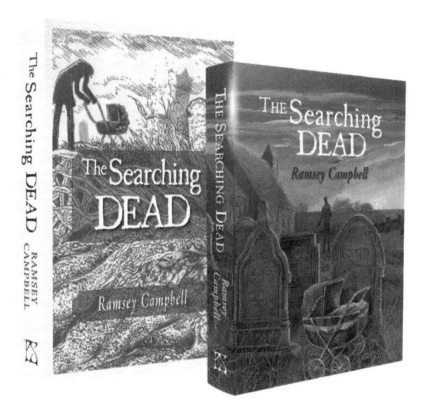

PS Publishing editions of The Searching Dead

Dominic, who since childhood has teamed up with two friends, Jim Bailey and Roberta (Bobby) Parkin, in various adventures under the nickname of the Tremendous Three, believes something sinister is going on, and that Noble is behind it. Dominic had seen Noble in a nearby cemetery, pushing a pram; he now sees that Noble has a baby daughter, Tina, but Tina's mother, Bernadette, seems quite hostile to her husband. Noble now proposes to take some of the students on a field trip to World War I battlefields in France; his father, Jack Noble, tells the students hideous stories of life as a soldier in that war. The students go to France, where they come upon a field whose trees are all leaning away from it; could this be the "hungry place" that Jack Noble had mentioned? One night, Christian Noble sneaks out of the dormitory; Dominic and Jim follow him and see him perform some kind of ritual.

Later, when Dominic's and Jim's parents learn of the dubious church Noble has founded, they bluntly confront him: "Mr Noble, are you a Christian?" After various evasive answers, he finally admits, "Of course I believe . . . In the three persons." Of course, he fails to specify which persons these are. By the beginning of the next school term, the students learn that Noble is no longer at the Catholic school. Soon thereafter, Jack Noble shows up at the school, revealing fear of his own son and making the astonishing statement: "The world would be better off without him." Jack hides a notebook of some sort in the gymnasium of the school, but Dominic has seen him do so and takes the notebook. It is manifestly a diary written by Christian Noble and addressed to his daughter, Tina, and it is full of cryptic and darkly terrifying hints of his plans for the future. He tells of his experiments in raising the dead ("Then I felt my mind catch hold of something more solid than the vision, and the plot of earth began to stir, quivering the flowers that leaned against the headstone") and refers to Bernadette as follows: "Previously, I had found no use for her kind, but the time for your birth was approaching, and so I sought a suitable candidate without knowing why I did." He goes on to write: "My visit to the field in France whence I originated has revealed to me how many secrets we have yet to learn. He who lies beneath the field has gained strength from them, though centuries of searching for them has left him monstrously transformed." There is a later reference to "Daoloth, which is the name of that which rends the veils", an explicit nod to his early story. But Dominic is forced by school authorities to give back the notebook to Christian Noble.

But is Noble merely interested in resurrecting the dead? Something far more baleful seems to be at work, as a terrifying incident in a movie theatre suggests. When Dominic goes to the men's room, he feels a hand grab his neck. Initially he sees nothing in the mirror, but then he observes a "naked whitish hulking shape . . . pressing its hands or the approximation of hands against the glass". Dominic manages to flee, and when he brings Jim into the room, nothing is visible—but then they notice that there are fingerprints on the mirror, and that, incredibly, "They were inside the mirror". In a later discussion by the Tremendous Three with Jack Noble, he confirms that his son's church is "just a front for what he's planning". He also demands that the three take him to their parents, but they flee, and as he pursues them he perishes when he is hit by a tram and cut to pieces.

Dominic tries desperately to persuade his friends to take action against Noble and his church, but they are stymied by their parents' opposition to any such action. In a tense conversation with Christian and Tina Noble, the precocious Tina at last specifies who the members of the church's "Trinity" are: "The past and the present and the future.. Even this apparent blasphemy does little to change his parents' minds; but then a newspaper reporter, Eric Wharton, who himself has infiltrated the church's membership, writes a column betraying hostility to the church. Dominic subsequently finds that the windows of the church have been broken and the interior of the church vandalised—apparently by shocked townspeople. In exploring the basement of the church, Dominic finds hundreds of potted plants on tables—are these the flowers planted on graves that Christian Noble believes have some occult power to raise the dead? Some of the flowers look exceptionally odd, like no flowers known to earthly botanists. Dominic systematically destroys all the plants, especially those that seem vaguely animate: "a bunch of swollen leaves groped to close around my wrist."

The Lovecraft influence is covert but telling in certain segments of the novel. The general scenario of a man begetting strange offspring with a human mother echoes both 'The Dunwich Horror' and *The Case of Charles Dexter Ward*. In the former story, the huge, goatish Wilbur Whateley is ultimately revealed to be one of the twin sons of the hideous cosmic entity Yog-Sothoth and a hapless female member of the Whateley clan. In the latter tale, the preternaturally aged Joseph Curwen wishes to secure an advantageous marriage both to repair his standing in the community—he is regarded by his fellow citizens in Providence, Rhode Island, as a sorcerer and worse—and to secure an heir who will ultimately effect his resurrection. Curwen himself seems to be engaging in the revival of the dead, just as Christian Noble is; but, like Noble, Curwen has much bigger fish to fry. The notebook that Christian Noble has written is a clear nod to 'The Dunwich Horror', where extracts of Wilbur Whateley's diary are presented to the reader.

Howard Phillips Lovecraft

61

As *Born to the Dark* (2017) opens, we have leapt thirty years, to the height of Thatcherite England in 1985. Bobby has become an investigative reporter, now partnered with a woman named Carole; Jim has become a policeman; and Dominic (now calling himself Dom) is married to a woman named Lesley, with a five-year-old child, Toby. He teaches film at the university. Our concern through much of the novel focuses on little Toby, who has apparently been subject to seizures from infancy. In desperation, Lesley enrols him in a facility called Safe To Sleep, which practises some kind of specialised sleep treatment. Initially, Toby seems to improve, but disturbing hints quickly emerge. Lesley tells Dom that Toby has "been scaring some of the children at school", stating that they may see "a giant face that lives in the dark" when they sleep. Toby himself describes some of his dreams about that face with unnerving naïveté: "It's like it's waiting for you to go to sleep so it can have your dreams to make a bit more of itself."

Dom, who has been sceptical of Safe To Sleep from the start, wonders if Toby has managed to read the extracts of Christian Noble's diary—which contain all manner of cryptically cosmic passages—that Dom had copied in an exercise book. Dom also realises that the name of one of the proprietors of the facility, a pediatrician named Chris Bloan, is a partial anagram for Chris Noble: could this be Christian Noble's daughter, whom he had referred to as Tina (i.e., Christina)? She herself has a son named Christopher (or Toph), an infant who seems incredibly precocious in numerous ways.

Dom's worst fears are confirmed when he sneaks onto the grounds of Safe To Sleep and sees the redoubtable Christian Noble himself come into the room where the children are sleeping. Noble, his daughter Tina, and her son Toph seem to be chanting the name Daoloth over and over again. It is at this point that Dom experiences a clutching moment of terror when he attempts to flee the grounds:

> A wind that I couldn't sense was enlivening the foliage, which responded with a whisper unnecessarily reminiscent of the kind of hush you might address to a child who was unable to sleep. As the dangling carkins writhed they might almost have been striking to imitate the insects I saw everywhere I looked, squirming out of the trees but remaining embedded as if rather than nesting in the timber they might be extensions of the material. I was desperate not to touch them, especially those that reared up towards me, revealing how transparently gelatinous they were, as I tried to sidle past the trees. When a bloated tendril found my cheek it felt like a cold dead tongue, somehow animated.

It gets worse. When, later, Dom goes to the hospital where Tina Noble works, he sees her making strange hand gestures over the newborn babies—and he comes to the staggering realisation that she and her father have actually *induced* the seizures into Toby and other children so that her family can later gain control of them through their facility.

But horror and tragedy follow upon this revelation. When Dom frantically attempts to explain the situation to Lesley, she (perhaps rightly) believes that Dom is simply paranoid, a result of his boyhood encounter with Noble. She orders Dom from the house and immediately initiates divorce proceedings. (Lesley's sudden turning on her husband does not seem entirely plausible. They had been married for at least six or seven years, but her extreme reaction—even if it was motivated by a desire to protect her son from what she believed to be Dom's harmful behaviour toward him—is not wholly credible.) Dom comes to a dispiriting conclusion: "It looked as if I needed to protect Toby on my own, which left me feeling worse than isolated."

Things get worse for Dom before they get better. After confronting both Tina and Christian (both of whom appear to know who he is and what he has done in the past), Dom crashes his car near the facility after a hand-like object touches his face. He wakes up in the hospital with a serious head injury; his father, Desmond, is in the same place, suffering from the effects of an infection following a fall. And while Desmond is sympathetic to Dom's concerns about Toby and vows to take care of the matter, there is little Desmond can do; indeed, he dies shortly thereafter. At the funeral, Dom is disturbed when Toby makes the bland claim: "I don't think grandad's really gone." This may be nothing more than a conventional belief that Desmond is in heaven; but does it have a more sinister signification?

Dom may not be quite as isolated as he thinks. Perhaps the Tremendous Three can take up the matter. Bobby becomes interested in investigating Safe To Sleep, and she wants Dom to fax her the extracts from Noble's diary; but Dom is dismayed (a word, incidentally, that Campbell tends to overuse) to find the diary missing. Can Toby, under Noble's instructions, have taken it? Bobby nonetheless carries on her investigation; but when she meets Dom later at a pub, he is startled to find that she has become a convert to Noble's ideas. "Tina Noble's doing everything she can for the children," she says, adding even more ominously: "I've joined in." She actually advises Dom to try a sleep session at the facility; Dom agrees—but he has other plans in mind.

During the session, Dom manages to wake up and clumsily take Toby away in his car. Noble, incredibly, is fully aware of what Dom has done, but doesn't seem to care. In a brief confrontation he declares, "It matters much less than you imagine." Toby expresses a desire for his parents to be reunited, and Lesley drops her plans for the divorce. At a later stage Dom persuades Jim to conduct some private investigation of Safe To Sleep; but when they arrive there, they find the place almost entirely vacant. That, however, certainly does not seem to be the end of the matter; for in a dream Dom appears to hear Toph's voice saying: "You're ours when we want."

Born to the Dark is so powerful and skilful a novel that it is difficult to enumerate its virtues. But the one element where the novel may come up short is its purportedly Lovecraftian substratum. The references to Daoloth are too slight and tangential to be fully comprehensible. What we are led to infer, insofar as we can make any sense of the supernatural manifestations involved, is the notion of astral projection—which is certainly not a Lovecraftian conception. (Campbell refers several times to Rose Tierney, the protagonist of his earlier novel *The Parasite* [1980], where astral projection is suggested.) The raising of the dead might, as with *The Searching Dead,* be a nod to *The Case of Charles Dexter Ward,* but it is so common a motif in weird fiction that no specifically Lovecraftian implication need be assumed.

With *The Way of the Worm* (2018), Campbell's cosmic trilogy comes to a triumphant conclusion. We now reach the present day, where Dominic in his seventies and calling himself by his full name, is facing multiple trials and tribulations—not the least of them the death of his beloved wife, Lesley. Toby is now married to a woman named Claudine; and the moment we learn this we are alarmed, for Claudine was one of the children in a facility called Safe To Sleep organised by the baleful Christian Noble along with his daughter and grandson. We have seen that much of *The Searching Dead* and *Born to the Dark* was devoted to increasingly frenzied efforts by Dominic—as well as his compatriots Jim Bailey and Bobby Parkin—in exposing the nefariousness of the Nobles. Even though the latter novel ended with the apparent destruction of the Safe To Sleep facility, we are hardly reassured that the danger represented by the Nobles is in any way over.

And, indeed, it is not. Both Dominic and the reader are distressed to find that the Nobles are now the leaders of a church or cult called the Church of the Eternal Three—suspiciously similar to the Trinity Church of the Spirit whose building was destroyed in *The Searching Dead*. Christian Noble must now be incredibly old, but he and his daughter and grandson are still thriving. What's more, Toby and Claudine are now members of the church, as are many other former patients of Safe To Sleep; still more disturbingly, Dominic's son and his wife are even inculcating their five-year-old daughter, Macy, into the church.

But is it possible that the church is really benign? Toby does his best to persuade his father of that, and some of the keenest moments of tension in *The Way of the Worm* focus on intense discussions between Toby (who is clearly sincere in his belief that the church has benefited his family) and Dominic, who knows all too well that the Nobles are anything but benevolent. Campbell may well be underscoring the dangers of religious brainwashing here: he himself has long struggled with the Catholicism he was forced to absorb as a child, and there is a clear implication of his disapproval of any sort of indoctrination of the young before they are mentally and emotionally ready to decide matters for themselves. The fact that the names of both of the churches established by the Nobles have unquestionably Catholic resonances underscores this point.

What the members of the Church of the Eternal Three seem to be engaging in is a series of deep meditation sessions—and what could be the harm in that? When Dominic grudgingly agrees to participate in such a session—which, to his alarm, takes place in the very building, Starview Towers, where Toby and his family live—he appears to dredge up memories of when he was a newborn baby. That is bad enough, but it is at this point that Dominic learns that the church is led by one Christopher Le Bon—which he easily recognises as an anagram for Noble. Later, Dominic attends a sermon by the entire Noble family, where Christopher delivers an ominous sermon about the imminent return of chaos to the world.

The novel gains dynamism when Dominic uses his phone to record a private conversation among the Nobles in which Christian essentially admits the appalling fact that he himself begat Christopher through an incestuous union with his own daughter. Dominic passes on the tape to Bobby, who writes a blog about it. A furore erupts, and the Nobles are arrested. In a subsequent trial, Christopher is found guilty of incest—but, to the astonishment and dismay of Dominic and others, his ten-year sentence is suspended, and the Nobles calmly walk out of the courtroom. This whole episode is narrated with such compelling intensity—including gripping cross-examinations of both Bobby and Dominic by the Nobles' attorney—that the reader comes to believe that Campbell could easily have excelled at courtroom dramas if he had not (thankfully for readers of weird fiction) chosen to work in another genre.

Dominic realises he must take more decisive action to thwart the Nobles. But before he can do so, others do the work for him. A gang of citizens, outraged at the outcome of the trial, set the Nobles' house ablaze. The Nobles, apparently naked, burn to death: "I thought I saw their bodies start not just to melt but to merge into a single monstrous shape." But the entire course of the trilogy has led us to discount the possibility that the Nobles could be so easily dispensed with.

There is much more to *The Way of the Worm* than the menace of the Nobles and the familial tension between Dominic and his son. Subsequent events, directly or indirectly engineered by the hideous entity that the Nobles have now become, cause Dominic to be bereft of nearly all his friends and family; and yet, even this is not the worst fate that befalls him. In a climax that melds otherworldly, cosmic horror with the distinctively intimate tragedy in which Dominic finds himself enmeshed, Campbell unifies his own worldview with Lovecraft's—and at the same time shows that richly detailed and loving characterisations of the human protagonists not only are not a barrier to the expression of cosmic insignificance, but can actually enhance it by rendering more poignant the fates of the hapless human beings who fall into the clutches of those forces (i.e., the Nobles) who symbolise cosmic dread.

There is little doubt that Ramsey Campbell's trilogy—for the three novels must be regarded as a tightly knit unity—will take its place among the stellar accomplishments in the realm of weird fiction. I struggle to find any trio of novels in our field that could match its achievement—an achievement that extends not merely to its deft portrayal of numerous characters over six decades and the impeccable elegance and mellifluousness of its prose, but above all to the grimly terrifying nature of its weird manifestations. It is too early to say that this trilogy is the summit of Campbell's achievement, for he (unlike his protagonist, Dominic Sheldrake) remains a vigorous septuagenarian, with much more work to come in the future; but readers, critics, and literary historians will have little hesitation in regarding it as a landmark that few of his rivals could hope to match.

RAMSEY CAMPBELL
a Portfolio

by Les Edwards

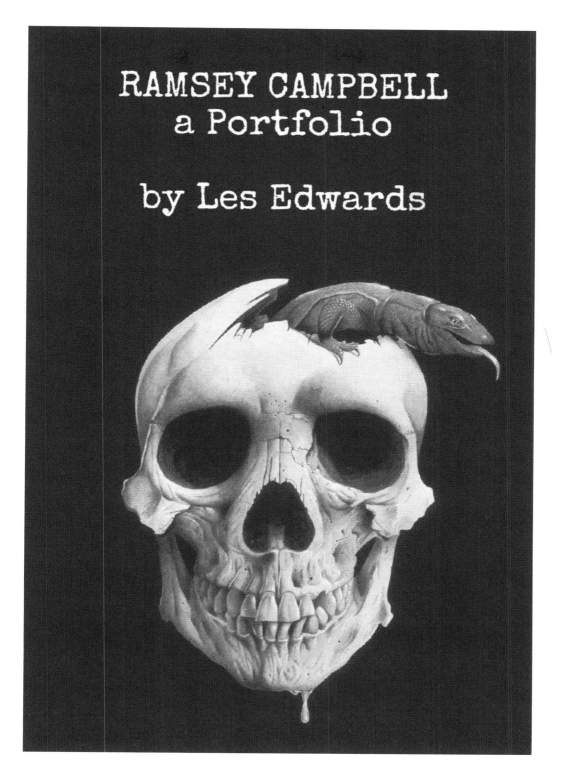

'Demons By Daylight'

'The Nameless'

'Born to the Dark'

'Ghosts and Grisly Things'

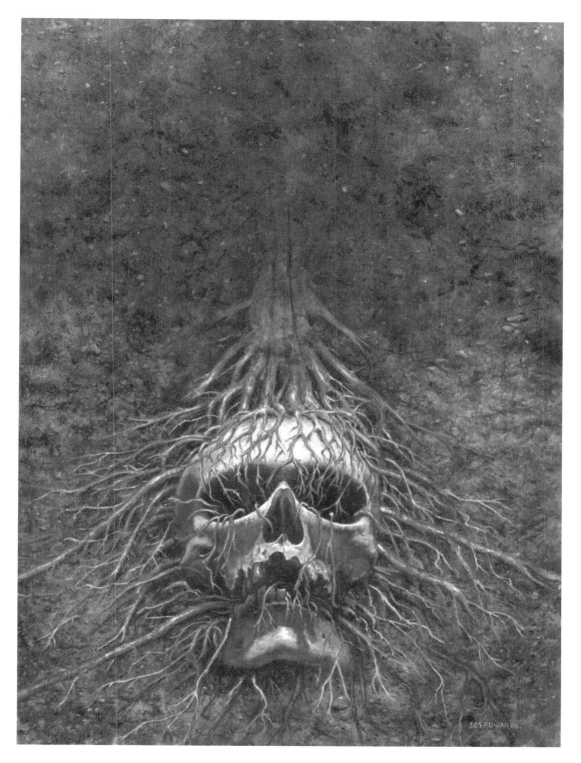

'The Searching Dead'

'The Way of the Worm'

'The Way of the Worm' wrap

'The Searching Dead' wrap

'Born to the Dark' slip

'Darkest Part of the Woods'

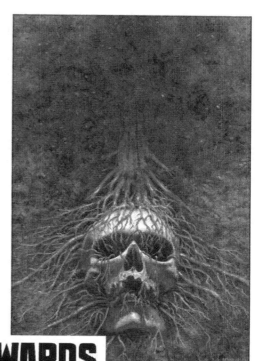

LES EDWARDS
www.lesedwards.com

MY FAVOURITE RAMSEY CAMPBELL STORY . . .

Phantasmagoria asked 35 of Ramsey Campbell's friends, colleagues and even his wife(!) to choose their favourite story by him . . .

Artwork by Allen Koszowski

Introduction

MY FAVOURITE RAMSEY Campbell story . . . is Ramsey Campbell.

When I was a schoolboy, and very uncertain of what I wanted to do with my life, my then art teacher the late Helen Clarke (who was in herself an extraordinary and influential power in my life) invited her friend Ramsey to Quarry Bank grammar school which is where I was a pupil.

It was to be a life-changing experience for me.

Here was this young man who was very clearly not accustomed to speaking to audiences, confronted by a class of schoolboys who didn't know who he was and probably weren't too interested in the idea of growing up to be writers. I was, looking back on it. I knew the process of writing was a complex one and very often it led to failure and disappointment. But Ramsey was the living proof that my deepest fears about the idea of being a writer were not true. Here he was talking to us with great passion about the genre of horror fiction.

Looking back, I probably invented a story for Ramsey Campbell's life which wasn't true. I probably thought of him as being far more deeply advanced into his career than he was. Later on, I discovered that he was still working in a library and though he'd had some things published nothing so far had really hit the mark. But that's not what I saw. That's not what I heard. I confronted for the first time A REAL WRITER. He spoke about the business of writing, particularly the business of writing horror fiction, with passion and authority and wit. As I say, I probably projected upon him the life that he was not yet living but my God, what a change he wrought in me!

Ramsey, you're seventy-five, though that's very hard to believe. I'm nearly sixty-nine and that's equally hard to believe. But six years between us when we first met was a chasm which you taught me to cross. If that is a part of your life, if *I* am part of your life, I could not be more proud. I love you, Ramsey – take care.

—**Clive Barker**

'The Inhabitant of the Lake' (*The Inhabitant of the Lake and Less Welcome Tenants*, 1964)

The story 'The Inhabitant of the Lake' is one of my favourite works by Ramsey Campbell, for a number of reasons. First of all, considering that it was written when Ramsey was eighteen, it sort of presages his later imagining and writing abilities, which over the years have reached the peaks we all know. Also, in this story, Gla'aki – the Great Old One created by Ramsey – appears for the first time, joining H.P. Lovecraft's Cthulhu Mythos and pantheon of Elder Gods. Not only that, but Gla'aki's arrival on Earth inside a meteor – forming the lake as a result of the impact – inspired my own novel, *Naraka: L'Apocalisse della Carne*, set in a dystopian world changed by the crash of a giant radioactive meteor on our planet. I could therefore only choose this story, since – just like what happens to the main character, Cartwright – I was deeply influenced by that lake, and what it hides.

—**Alessandro Manzetti**

'The Cellars' (*Travellers by Night*, 1967)

One thing I've always loved about 'The Cellars' when I first read it in *The Height of the Scream* is just how self-involved and oblivious its protagonist, Julie, is. Even when awkward Vic shows her something truly mysterious, she can't get beyond her own petty desires to care or even be curious. And when Vic's own curiosity leads him to do something he shouldn't, Julie hardly notices his absence or cares. The entirety of the horror happens in the background, flashing in and out while she lives her empty surface-level life. Vic's transformation is horrific without a doubt, but he ends up the lesser monster by the story's end. Ramsey's morbid and wicked sense of humour is on full display in this one.

—**Simon Strantzas**

'The Scar' (*Startling Mystery Stories*, Summer 1969)

Doubles and doubling permeate Ramsey Campbell's 'The Scar'. The story begins with a man's account of seeing his brother-in-law's doppelgänger. Subsequently, the narrative splits points of view between the brothers-in-law, as the setting divides between upper and lower Brichester, the former comfortably middle-class, the latter lower-class, still not fully recovered from the Blitz. During a visit to lower Brichester, the more affluent brother-in-law is attacked by a masked man who wounds his face hideously. Subsequently, he secretly revisits the site of the assault, returning changed, a different, less pleasant self. Or a double self, the one glimpsed by his brother-in-law, who follows in his footsteps, venturing from above ground to below ground (another doubling), discovering in the basement of a ruined building masked creatures capable of taking our faces. A story about trauma, the war, what waits to wear our skin, the meanings of 'The Scar' double and double again.

—**John Langan**

'Cold Print' (*Tales of the Cthulhu Mythos*, 1969)

'Cold Print' was the first horror story that struck me as being realistically set in a world I could recognise. PE teacher Sam Strutt's obsession is pornographic novels. Wandering around a snow-bound Brichester shortly before Christmas, Strutt is searching for enough new books to keep him going over the festivities. While feeling disgruntled at his lack of success in a local bookshop, he is approached by a tramp who tells him he knows where he can buy what he wants. Though distrustful, Strutt is desperate enough to follow the man into an insalubrious part of town. But from then on Strutt is drawn into something ominously more dangerous than his favoured tales of flagellation, hinted at by half-glimpsed newspaper headlines – BRUTAL MURDER IN RUINED CHURCH. If only he had taken time to read their stories! 'Cold Print' is filled with a claustrophobic atmosphere which Strutt, too blinded by his obsessions, fails to see until too late. The final line, when everything becomes clear, is a study in understatement – and as chilling as you can get.

—**David A. Riley**

'The End of a Summer's Day' (*Demons by Daylight*, 1973)

A coach party, including honeymoon couple Tony and Maria, visits subterranean caves. The same number exit as entered, but are they the same people? Put baldly, that is the story, but there is so much more. A case could be made that everything is internal to Maria. For her, sex is equated with darkness, she isn't ready to make love in daylight. She says the blind man who leaves with them isn't Tony, but would she know? Making love in the dark she feels "the hands exploring blindly, were no longer Tony." Like a fairy-tale princess she needs the deep sleep from which she can emerge as an adult woman, but instead finds herself lost in the forest. In the caves the rock formations show her faces like those of the puzzle picture forests of childhood. She re-enters the caves in search of Tony, and I always hope that they will emerge together into the light.

—**Jenny Campbell**

'The Franklyn Paragraphs' (*Demons by Daylight*, 1973)

On its surface, here we have Ramsey himself receiving increasingly disturbed letters from an obscure horror writer, Errol Undercliffe, concerning, in turn, a third individual, Roland Franklyn, the author of an occult tract entitled *We Pass from View*. Franklyn, in both double-crossing his own seedy witch-cult (as well as his creepy wife), has been buried alive – though even Poe did not conceive of such a horrid premature burial as this one. Undercliffe's investigation into Franklyn's demise proves to be the writing of his own epitaph and leads to the discovery of Franklyn's literally bookish self-interment. One cannot, then, hide from horror in horror: there is always some deeper, even more terrifying, "movement behind the scenes" – there are still "facets" yet to be discerned. Believe me, this is a bad trip of a tale; and with Ramsey dealing out the real dope, you won't be coming down after it.

—**Mark Samuels**

'Concussion' (*Demons by Daylight*, 1973)

'Concussion' achieves an equivalency with the great modernist writers: Sartre, Eliot, Greene, Camus, Joyce, Dostoyevsky, Lowry, to name a handful. It's a highly successful example of existential literature. A disorienting and nightmarish journey through a deeply confused, perhaps delusional man's consciousness. A paranoid, often bewildered mind that is engulfed by an obsessive urge to make sense of itself and reality. Actual awareness becomes the horror on a journey that travels backwards and forwards in time, through an unreliable memory. The tone passes into elation and lucidity and on to bafflement and despair. Repeatedly. Aural and visual hallucinations and false memories – or are they? – surge towards annihilation, not resolve. Oblivion might be the only blessing when the self's dread, its feelings and thoughts, become such a torment. A poetic, multi-sensory story that captures the oppression of madness, perhaps schizophrenia. A demonstration of what literary horror can do and should attempt.

—**Adam Nevill**

'The Enchanted Fruit' (*Demons by Daylight*, 1973)

Ramsey Campbell is the master of the slow burn, of inch by inch, step by step degradation, until you realise there is no escape – and there will *never* be an escape. This story perfectly encapsulates that. I love the way this tale of a man who discovers and eats an unknown fruit starts gently, described with such bucolic love you can almost touch the quivering leaves in the wood, hear the birds in the canopy above. By the time the strange fruit, the size of an apple but velvety, almost peach-like, drops into his hand, you are smelling that scented juice, tasting that luscious flesh – and then, in typical Campbell style, it *twists*, for now he can *only* taste the fruit, at first glorious, then the taste filling his mouth changes, no longer sublime, but worsening, bit by bit, almost as if it were rotting in his mouth, his roiling stomach . . . and now *everything* is tainted . . .

—**Jo Fletcher**

'The Man in the Underpass' (*The Year's Best Horror Stories: Series III*, 1975)

'The Man in the Underpass' was written in 1973. In it we see the new Ramsey Campbell at work: he has paid his dues as a beginner, he is exploring, away from his early Lovecraft pastiches, finding his own voice, honing his craft. And yet . . . RNA, DNA, HPL . . . Those three-letter systems are stealthy. They have a tendency to burrow deep and leave their mark. You can still feel the skeleton of a Lovecraftian design. Forgotten gods with unpronounceable names, dark places where bloody rituals are enacted. But those are only bones: they are now covered with powerful new sinews. The setting is all too real. Sex, disdained by HPL, is a major force here. What is Tonia doing? Has she met a god or turned dark longings into more than mere paint? Horror has given way to deep, deep unease . . .

—**Patrick Marcel**

'Call First' (*Night Chills*, 1975)

By any measure, Ramsey Campbell's 'Call First' is a remarkable benchmark in the author's staggering canon and one of Ramsey's most anthologised tales. The story's hapless breaking-and-entering protagonist is perhaps also his most sympathetic, though most of us would applaud the burglar's inevitable comeuppance. First appearing in Kirby McCauley's glittering *Night Chills* anthology before going on to secure for many readers joint pole position (alongside 'The Companion') in one of the author's own collections, *Dark Companions*, just seven years later, 'Call First' enmeshes the tale's three players: the would-be crook, the terrifying and protective devoted husband, and the all-too-familiar and inescapable Liverpool setting. One can almost smell the lonely terraced streets, the shimmering television sets and even the occasional faces at the windows . . . all of them, strangely complicit in the story's inevitable conclusion.

—**Peter Crowther**

'The Tugging' (*The Disciples of Cthulhu*, 1976)

H.P. Lovecraft famously wrote that ". . . the strongest kind of fear is fear of the unknown . . ." and I'd add an observation that fear is also the *anticipation* of pain. Few writers of horror fiction have understood and interpreted these views better than Ramsey, who demonstrates them succinctly and often powerfully in his tales of deep unease. I recall him speaking at an early Fantasycon about HPL pastiches and a common fault of writers being a tendency to imitate the worst aspects – the over-writing, the (ironically) indescribable horror, the lack of subtlety. In 'The Tugging' we have a Lovecraft pastiche that exemplifies the anticipation of fear, the gradually ascending terror, and the sense of bewildering cosmic horror. It is a perfect matching of scenes from our inner eye linked to an ultimate external vision of overwhelming nightmare.

—**Adrian Cole**

'The Companion' (*Frights*, 1976)

I came to 'The Companion' via Stephen King's rhapsodic praise in *Danse Macabre*. By the time I finished reading the story I'd decided I wanted to be a writer too, a thought that had never occurred to me before (I was eighteen at the time). There's just so much packed into its 4,500 words: the fresh take on contemporary urban gothic; the sophisticated psychology and skilful rendition of character; the flashes of dark humour; the exquisite eye for the eerie in the everyday. But it was the element of social critique that really got to me, a sensitivity to a frightening breakdown in public morality that was there in many of the other stories in *Dark Companions*, too. Knox's memory of turning to an adult for help when escaping from a childhood bully, only to find out the man is his nemesis' father, is in its way as frightening as the story's insidiously terrifying conclusion.

—Jeremy Dyson

'The Chimney' (*Whispers: An Illustrated Anthology of Fantasy and Horror*, 1977).

Although Ramsey started his career as a teenager, writing pastiches of H.P. Lovecraft, he soon developed his own style of urban horror based around his home city of Liverpool. Aptly described by the *Oxford Companion to English Literature* as "Britain's most respected living horror writer", he has produced a prolific number of novels and short stories, with most of his work falling into the category of "best in genre". Choosing a favourite was always going be difficult – there are just so many – so I will go for the World Fantasy Award-winning 'The Chimney', one of the creepiest Christmas horror stories I've ever read, given an extra poignant twist by the author's own – often disturbing – childhood experiences. I haven't yet done a Christmas reprint anthology yet but, if I did, 'The Chimney' would definitely be in it!

—Stephen Jones

'In the Bag' (*Cold Fear*, 1977)

When I come to a horror story, I hope for it to have a very clear direction, that it is rich in characterisation, thick with atmosphere, dotted with ambiguity and uncertainty, and carrying the *frisson*. I want the hairs on the back of my neck to get a workout. Ramsey's 'In the Bag' ticks all of these boxes. It's a story about a man trying to run away from his past while also, perhaps subconsciously, attempting to atone for what he did then by doing the right thing now. A current echo of his old crime suggests an imminent balancing of the books, and there are signs everywhere. A simple story effectively told, and utterly devastating.

—Conrad Williams

'Above the World' (*Whispers II*, 1979)

This story showcases Campbell's signature hallmarks: meaningful resemblances between objects (a stamp, or a patch of moss?), disturbing anthropomorphism, self-conscious questioning as the protagonist struggles with the facts, sinister descriptions. Knox descends to an empty reception area. No one at the front desk, no one sitting at the place settings. Absence haunts him: people heard but not seen, the rows of tents unoccupied, a favourite café closed. He claims cool, disinterested memories of a failed marriage. They'd come here on vacation. Later she and her new husband died here. Is it a coincidence he has the same room? Knox feigns the memories do not bother him, yet they pursue and consume. He is haunted by the past and his own emptiness. This story is a masterwork of tone and mood, with a controlled palette resulting in the eeriest of hauntings.

—**Steve Rasnic Tem**

'Mackintosh Willy' (*Shadows 2*, 1979)

I have long regarded 'Mackintosh Willy' as perhaps the single most frightening story that Ramsey Campbell has written. It tells of a derelict who terrorises a group of boys both in life and in death. He seems to live in a bus shelter, and the thoughtless boys plague him with the mercilessness of their kind. When he dies in the shelter, he is likened to an *old bag of washing, decayed and mouldy*. With heedless disrespect, one of the boys places bottle-caps on his eyes. Some time later a man is noted in the shelter, wearing some strange kind of spectacles. It is, in fact, Mackintosh Willy, who now seems *like a half-submerged heap of litter*. He hideously avenges the desecration of his corpse by killing the boy who placed the bottle-caps on his eyes. 'Mackintosh Willy' is a masterwork because of the insidious gradualness with which the tale unfolds and the cumulative horror it achieves.

—**S.T. Joshi**

'The Fit' (*New Terrors*, 1980)

I love everything about Ramsey Campbell's two-volume anthology project *New Terrors*, including the editor's own story, 'The Fit'. Adolescent Peter stays with his Aunt Naomi, a dressmaker, near Keswick in the Lake District, where the fells are "deceptively gentle monsters that slept at the edges of lakes blue as ice". To escape the confines of his aunt's house, where the dressmaker's dummies are becoming animated and the washing just won't stay still on the line, Peter wanders off and discovers a crack in the earth concealing a damp cottage, the home of Fanny Cave. As if that weren't enough to set alarm bells ringing, Peter has always thought his aunt, who insists her nephew calls her Naomi, seemed much younger than his mother and he was "vaguely aware that she often wore tight jeans". A one-off masterpiece of Freudian horror.

—**Nicholas Royle**

'Writer's Curse' (*Night Flights*, Winter 1980–81)

There was a time when both Ramsey Campbell and I were fresh-faced young men in Liverpool, and I could look forward to having the odd book of his dedicated to me (such as his exemplary collection of short stories, *Demons by Daylight*). We both recorded programmes for BBC Radio Merseyside, and I was able to do my utmost for several of his short stories (using my best BBC voice – neither of us sported a Scouse accent), including my particular favourite, a piece that Stephen Jones and David Sutton reprinted in *Fantasy Tales* #17 (Summer 1987) and that Ramsey himself included in *Inconsequential Tales*: 'Writer's Curse'. It's a brief, pithily atmospheric piece in which an experienced writer finds himself at the mercy of manifestations from a resentful beginner. Who couldn't feel unsettled by a paragraph such as this: *Even when the light lay inert on the bowling-green I could see the white egg of a face framed between two boards across a window . . . when the light framed the building again and as if on cue half a dozen pale featureless eggs clustered into the space between the boards. While I watched, unbelieving, more of the eggs crowded into the space. I thought distractedly of those myriad eggs one finds in dead trees. But I knew these were faces. Paralysed, I imagined the unseen bodies piling over one another in the dark . . .*

—**Barry Forshaw**

'The Brood' (*Dark Forces*, 1980)

The Gothic castle, the isolated house in the country and other remote locations have long been the standard background for a horror story, but Ramsey Campbell is known for having brought horror home to stay in ordinary, grimy, contemporary British cities, and using real places. 'The Brood', which combines elements of haunted house and alien intrusions as it gradually reveals the utter monstrousness lurking behind the façade of ordinary life, and is one of the best. Who hasn't wondered about the strangers they see every day, or what could be going on inside the house over the road? And who but Ramsey could come up with such horrible suggestions? He doesn't explain; he shows you the horror, and makes you feel it.

—**Lisa Tuttle**

'Again' (*Rod Serling's The Twilight Zone Magazine*, November 1981)

I can lose myself in a Ramsey Campbell story. I mean this literally. My world will not make sense. That the Ramsey Campbell I have known for almost forty years now is cheerful, affable, sensible, and profoundly sane, and in all ways a delight to know, does not lessen the effect of the fiction on me as a reader. 'Again' is, on the surface, simple: Bryant leaves Liverpool to walk the Wirral Way, and encounters an old woman locked out of a white bungalow who says to him, "Can you get in?". He enters the bungalow, sees what's in there, and leaves. Everything in the story is in the atmosphere, the word choice, the details. The story reminds me of Robert Aickman's fictions, but Aickman would never have taken the story to the dark place that Ramsey takes it, to the awful inevitable conclusion, to that final simple word. The story was elegantly and beautifully adapted into comics form by Michael Zulli, but I still prefer the word-pictures: with a handful of Ramsey's perfectly chosen words I find myself back in the white bungalow with Bryant, in his journey that (one fears) may never have an ending, and I am, as always, lost. Again. Again.

—**Neil Gaiman**

'Calling Card' (*65 Great Spine Chillers*, 1982)

I feel ashamed that it took me so long to discover Ramsey Campbell. I was in my early twenties when I was captivated by Stephen King's article on Ramsey in his book *Danse Macabre*. Soon afterwards I devoured the collection *Dark Companions*, relishing every word. Ramsey's use of imagery, particularly his skill in imbuing everyday objects and mundane situations with a sense of dread, I found electrifyingly inspirational. 'Calling Card', a gruesomely prolonged joke, which wouldn't have been out of place in an Amicus portmanteau movie, is a perfect example. Inanimate objects acquire a sinister aspect (*O O O, the washing machines said emptily*) and the senses are assailed by details from which we recoil – the pervasive odour of stagnant water, the glimpses and touches of slimy, snail-like flesh – as the tension builds towards a punchline that, although not unexpected, is nonetheless a gloriously repulsive treat.

—**Mark Morris**

'The Ferries' (*The 18th Fontana Book of Great Ghost Stories*, 1982)

Waking from sleep, a man witnesses his uncle being taken away on a sinister, mould-stained boat, triggering a growing realisation that some unspeakable horror is also coming for him. Although originally published in 1982, I initially encountered this story when reviewing *Dark Feasts: The World of Ramsey* Campbell, a collection published by Robinson in 1987. While it is not the most well known of Ramsey's short fiction, it resonates with me as it combines all the key signatures of his craft: unsettling visions, location as character, a creeping tide of paranoia and a sense of inherited doom highlight the influences of those other masters of horror, M.R. James and H.P. Lovecraft, on Ramsey's already stellar horror writing career. It is, however, Campell's unique, rich and evocative narrative voice that, for me, puts this tale at the top.

—**John Gilbert**

'The Depths' (*Dark Companions*, 1982)

Ramsey Campbell's 'The Depths' is a delirium of dread and madness. Suffering writer's block, as if an extinguished sun, a prominent author is assailed by predictive flashes of crimes; atrocities marauding like unwelcome plots. Stuck in his casket of entropy, craving a muse, he can't refuse the rogue horrors, however traumatic or lurid; origin irrelevant. But voicing the perversity of others, he discovers he's forever damned; a conduit for their purged sins. Things violently twist into bad outcomes; the story eluding imagined resolution, soaked in blood, vile need. As in fiction and life, blame is an irresistible rush . . . and murder always sells. In this sinister jewel box, Campbell sharpens pre-cognition and anguish to a vicious glisten, slowly, brilliantly sliding in the knife.

—**RC Matheson**

'The Show Goes On' (*Dark Companions*, 1982)

The cinema is still frequently cited as the escape hatch of bothered youth, but in Ramsey Campbell's case, the escape was fundamentally necessary, because his youth was substantially more dire – and threatening – than the average pre-teen discord. Just read Ramsey's own account of his childhood: haunted, conditioned by fears both real and convincingly imagined, a deadly spring-trap perpetually on the urge of snapping. Ramsey cited going to the movies as both a lifeline and a refuge, making my choice of 'The Show Goes On' a natural for inclusion in *Silver Scream* (1988), the first real anthology of "cinema horror". The story echoes the investigative, "probing" aspect of much of Ramsey's short fiction, also expressed at greater length and in the same idiom in *Ancient Images* (1989): characters search deeper and deeper into maze-like, seemingly mundane surroundings until they are hopelessly lost, without compass, and definitely in the shadow of peril. Ramsey always invites us along for the disturbance we know awaits. Can *you* remember where the exit is?

—David J. Schow

'The Voice of the Beach' (*Fantasy Tales* #10, Summer 1982)

Maybe it's a bit of a cop-out considering such a huge body of work, but of all Ramsey's stories which I myself (and also along with Stephen Jones) have published, it's his *tour-de-force* published in *Fantasy Tales* #10 that I have settled upon as a favourite. 'The Voice of the Beach' is recognisably affiliated to Lovecraft's Mythos. Ramsey described it, alongside a reprint of the story in 1988, as "my last Cthulhu Mythos story". Elements of the Mythos permeate this long, intense first-person narrative: the other-worldly impinging on our everyday reality; an uncaring, mechanistic universe; a peculiar book and its mad ravings; something so monstrous and alien it almost defies description; characters on the edge of madness. Unremitting in its intensity, imbued with a seething undercurrent of horror, 'The Voice of the Beach' is hauntingly good and I heartily recommend it.

—David A. Sutton

'The Sneering' (*Fantasy Tales* #14, Summer 1985)

Jack is an angry, stubborn, embittered old man (the story's title could describe him as much as the people from a nearby housing estate, of whom he has a very poor opinion). The life he knew is slowly eroding as the modern world encircles him. His wife, Emily, is also drifting away from him as dementia slowly erases her memories, over-writing them with childlike innocence and confusion. Early on in their marriage, Jack was found to be infertile; now, at the end of their life together, Emily is becoming as dependent as any child. He frets, is over-protective, making things worse. Near the story's beginning there is a terrible accident. Emily cannot remember it, while Jack finds himself haunted – literally and figuratively – by the tragedy. The ending is as poignant as it is inevitable.

—Mike Chinn

'Slow' (*Slow*, 1986)

A man is trapped in a cottage on a distant planet, menaced by a faceless alien creature. The thing can never hope to catch him, given its excruciatingly slow rate of motion. In an hour, it only moves a few centimetres. The constant hovering presence of the thing is frightening, but even as it eventually moves through the wall and into the cottage, the man scoffs, knowing he can easily outmanoeuvre it. Or can he? This story is as unnerving to me now as when I first read it. It's a masterpiece of relentless, inescapable dread, featuring a truly nightmarish creature.

—Thana Niveau

'Boiled Alive' (*Interzone* #18, Winter 1986)

"Boiled Alive," it repeated in an explanatory tone that sounded almost peevish, and rang off. No doubt the caller was on drugs and phoning at random, and Mee wanted to believe the phrase was just as meaningless. So begins the inexorable descent into paranoia and dread for another Ramsey Campbell protagonist, whom the author meticulously unravels for our disquieting pleasure. Highlighting a single tale from Ramsey's *oeuvre* is no mean feat, though for me 'Boiled Alive' shines as a masterful exploration of derangement. All the classic Campbellian touches are here: the drab workplace that thinly conceals menace, a reworking of horror's familiar imagery and themes (in this case, the eponymous "video nasty"), and an ingenious journey into the worldview of a character whose grip on reality is nowhere near as firm as they (and by extension we, the readers) want to believe.

—Richard Gavin

'Needing Ghosts' (1990)

Ramsey's often used Liverpool's history, geography and people as triggers for memorable excursions into the glorious wilds of his imagination and, amongst these surreal trips (or, as certain of our fellow Scousers might call them, Magical Mystery Tours), a particular favourite of mine is the novella *Needing Ghosts*. It takes place (perhaps) over a single day and is about a man trying to find his way home; in fact, to torture my Merseybeat analogy a little more, it could be described as *A Day in the Life* of Simon Mottershead as he takes a *Ferry Cross the Mersey*. As with much of Ramsey's best work, it is as rich in awe and melancholy as it is in anxiety and horror – its dream-like dislocations include a spectacular moment where the ferry appears ready to make anchor at Böcklin's *Isle of the Dead* – and leads us inexorably to one of Ramsey's most devastating conclusions: that this disorienting, disturbing nightmare in which we have been trapped is one from which it might, in fact, be better not to wake.

—Peter Atkins

'The Alternative' (*Darklands Two*, 1994)

Alan Highton is a professional, middle-class man with a good job, nice house and loving wife and family, but he has been having dreams of another life where he lives in a run-down flat, in a poverty-stricken, squalor-ridden council estate. Problems soon arise when Highton realises that what he is dreaming about also appears to exist in the waking world. As with many Campbell stories, 'The Alternative' is set in the real world, although a subtly differing version to the one in which we live, where you just know something is not quite right but can't put your finger on it. Aside from being a perplexing, fascinating mystery, it also addresses the theme of how our circumstances affect the path our lives will take. A superb strange tale, and the first story by the author which I had the honour of reprinting in one of my own publications!

—**Trevor Kennedy**

'Between the Floors' (*Destination Unknown*, 1997)

'Between the Floors' is classic Campbell. If Hannah Arendt's great theme was the banality of evil, Ramsey's is the evil of banality: the sinister in the apparently commonplace. We are in one of those ineffably drab hotels (where horror conventions are all too often held) and Jack, who is attending a cinema manager's conference, has been accidentally relegated to a remote annex with a very strange lift attendant. What begins in unease and frustration starts to slide inexorably into a nightmarish existential crisis. All the characteristic features of Campbell's work – a meticulously crafted atmosphere, a powerful sense of dread and entrapment, a quirky humour which, far from dissipating the horror, only heightens it – are present in this perfectly paced tale.

—**Reggie Oliver**

'The Entertainment' (*999: New Tales of Horror and Suspense*, 1999)

It's not easy to pick a favourite from Ramsey's stories, but 'The Entertainment' is certainly one of them. A drab stretch of English coastline in the rain, a strange and run-down hotel, and a hapless fellow taken for the evening's entertainment – this is incredibly atmospheric, not to mention claustrophobic. Full of vivid images and encapsulated in Ramsey's brilliant prose, the story's prickling sense of something not quite right is skilfully ramped up into full-blown dread. Ramsey was generous enough to allow me to play with his toys in my story 'The Entertainment Arrives', which is reprinted in this volume. I remain grateful, and not remotely messed up at all – no, sir . . .

—**Alison Littlewood**

'The Place of Revelation' (*13 Horrors: A Devil's Dozen Stories Celebrating 13 Years of the World Horror Convention*, 2003)

Young Colin's Uncle Lucien has a habit of sitting on his bed when he comes to visit and encouraging him to tell stories about the strange forest that he visits. Many of Ramsey Campbell's works exhibit the influence of Welsh writer Arthur Machen, perhaps most notably *Needing Ghosts* and *The Kind Folk*, but 'The Place of Revelation' is the story Campbell wrote specifically to "pay a debt to this giant of the field" (to use RC's own words). While the Machen influence is strong throughout, the sense of sheer cosmic terror the story builds to, and the feeling of utter gibbering insignificance it instils, is entirely Mr. Campbell's own doing. And how we love him for it.

—**John Llewellyn Probert**

'The Announcement' (*Dark Delicacies*, 2005)

'The Announcement' is not only a wonderfully vicious and lethal satire on the age-old battle in writing between art and business, it also has particular sentimental value for me because it appeared in *Dark Delicacies*, a book edited by my friends Del Howison and Jeff Gelb, and which also featured my story 'Black Mill Cove'. I was proud to have a story in a book that also featured Clive Barker, Ray Bradbury and Nancy Holder (among others), but being under the covers with Ramsey was a special delight for me.

—**Lisa Morton**

~~~~~

The Last Revelation of Gla'aki *cover spread artwork by Pete Von Sholly*

Phantasmagoria Magazine

Phantasmagoria
SPECIAL EDITION SERIES
#1

Britain's Prince of Chill
R. CHETWYND-HAYES

STORIES, ARTICLES, ARTWORK,
REVIEWS AND MUCH MORE!

R. CHETWYND-HAYES
CENTENARY COLLECTOR'S EDITION

Phantasmagoria
SPECIAL EDITION SERIES
#2

FEATURING
MIKE CHINN
ADRIAN COLE
DOUGLAS KLAUBA
LISA MORTON
KIM NEWMAN
JOHN LLEWELLYN PROBERT
ANGELA SLATTER
MICHAEL MARSHALL SMITH
and series creator STEPHEN JONES!

ALSO IN THIS ISSUE
H. P. LOVECRAFT'S
CLASSIC STORY
THE OUTSIDER
Plus Articles
Artwork Galleries
Lovecraftian Fiction
Reviews and More!

THE LOVECRAFT SQUAD
SPECIAL COLLECTOR'S EDITION

SPECIAL COLLECTOR'S EDITIONS

Phantasmagoria
SPECIAL EDITION SERIES
#3

FEATURING
M.R. JAMES
RAMSEY CAMPBELL
STEPHEN GALLAGHER
STEPHEN JONES
MARK MORRIS
ADAM L.G. NEVILL
KIM NEWMAN
AND MORE!

ALSO IN THIS ISSUE
ARTWORK FROM
RANDY BROECKER
DAVE CARSON
PETER COLEBORN
LES EDWARDS
STEPHEN JONES
ALLEN KOSZOWSKI
JAMES McBRYDE
JIM PITTS
and G.C.H. VERLEY

M. R. JAMES
SPECIAL COLLECTOR'S EDITION

OUT NOW on AMAZON

and FORBIDDEN PLANET
INTERNATIONAL (Belfast)

THE INHABITANT WITH VISIONS FROM DEMONS!

Randy Broecker

OKAY. I'M NOT picking a *single* Ramsey Campbell story for this issue of *Phantasmagoria* – no siree! Too hard! There are too many good ones, and too many already staked out. I'm kind of taking on a whole bunch of 'em. Only because I've more of a "personal" interest here; however I'm not going into specific story details, in case someone else has picked one of these little "gems" to rightly celebrate elsewhere in this issue.

I'll get to the point. A little over ten years ago, Peter Crowther – major-domo of PS Publishing – asked would I be interested in illustrating a new edition of *The Inhabitant of the Lake*, Ramsey's first book, originally published by Arkham House in 1964.

Would I??????

Does Gla'aki have three eye-stalks????

After reviving myself with a dose of "essential saltes", I of course told Pete that I'd love to, and thanked him for thinking of me. I had inherited a copy of that book from my late brother, which I'd had Ramsey sign at the 1979 Fifth World Fantasy Convention in Providence, Rhode Island.

Revisiting that collection after so many years was brilliant. Right from the start I was once again struck by the story-telling skill on display, and I couldn't help but think that had Ramsey started writing during the heyday of *Weird Tales*, I've no doubt he would have been part of that select group of H.P. Lovecraft and his acolytes. I also couldn't keep from thinking that all of this was written by a young British fan in his teens. It still amazes me.

Corresponding with, and submitting stories to August Derleth, and getting your first book published by Arkham House – what a *brilliant* start to what would become a long and celebrated career!

Those stories, both wonderful and disturbing, in the words of Claude Rains "seemed to light up my brain!" They were just what I needed at that point in time – inspiring me artistically, just as I'd like to think that Lovecraft had inspired Ramsey so many years earlier.

The title story is a particular favourite, along with 'The Moon-Lens' and 'The Return of the Witch' – although *all* are finely crafted tributes to Lovecraft. It was a real pleasure to illustrate them. Having read, via correspondence published between August Derleth and Ramsey, that at one time Lee Brown Coye would be providing the dust-jacket art for the book (in fact, it turned out to be Frank Utpatel's, not Coye's, art on the cover), I decided to use Utpatel's composition somewhat – but giving it more of a Coye spin. I also had Coye in mind for my approach to 'The Return of the Witch'.

In 2015 PS published a companion volume, *Visions from Brichester*, and I very happily picked up my illustration pens again. Containing the rest of his Lovecraftian short stories, the volume also included 'The Last Revelation of Gla'aki', a new novella wherein Ramsey was doing some revisiting of his own.

The following portfolio represents a selection of some of my artwork from both the PS Publishing editions of *The Inhabitant of the Lake* and *Visions from Brichester.*

Thanks to you and your words, Ramsey, they were a joy to work on, and I feel that they are some of my finest pieces.

Finally, there is a new illustration done specifically for this tribute edition of *Phantasmagoria* magazine. It's for the story 'Made in Goatswood', first published in *Demons By Daylight* (1973), the second of your Arkham House collections.

I'm delighted to say I'm *still* being inspired *and* disturbed by you!

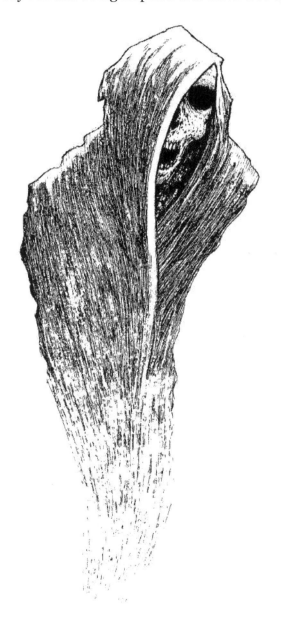

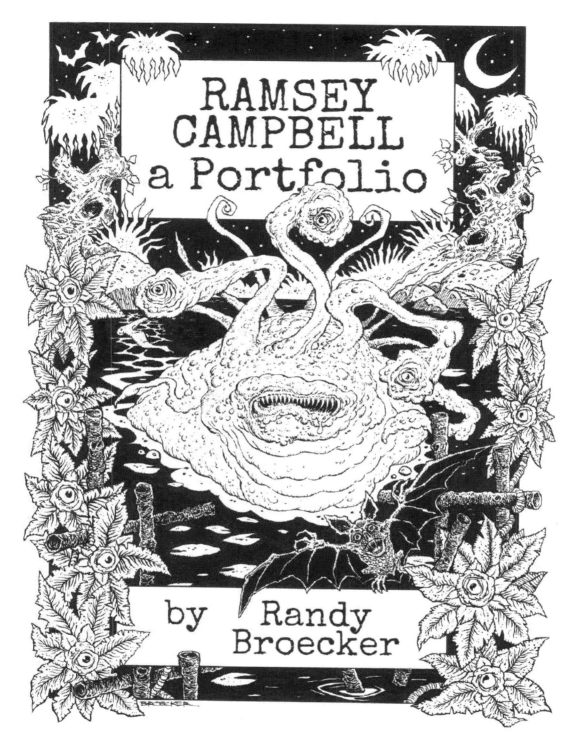

The Inhabitant of the Lake & Other Less Welcome Tenants *front cover artwork*

'The Room in the Castle'

'The Horror from the Bridge'

'The Return of the Witch'

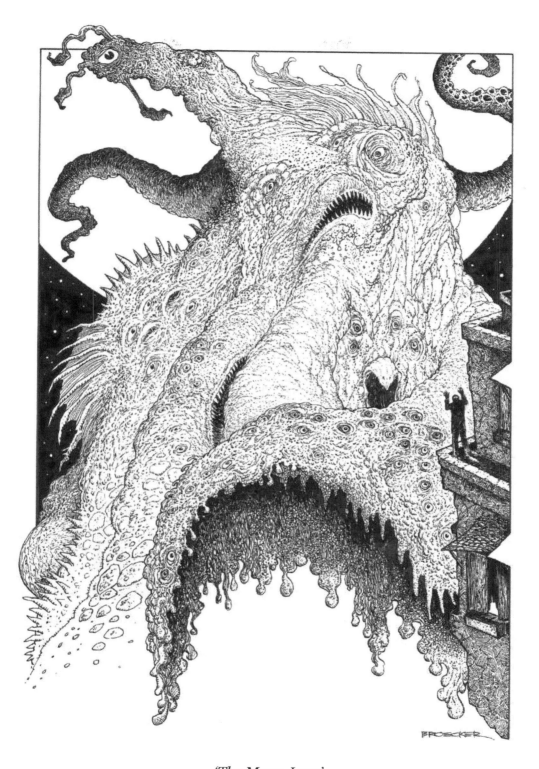

'The Moon-Lens'

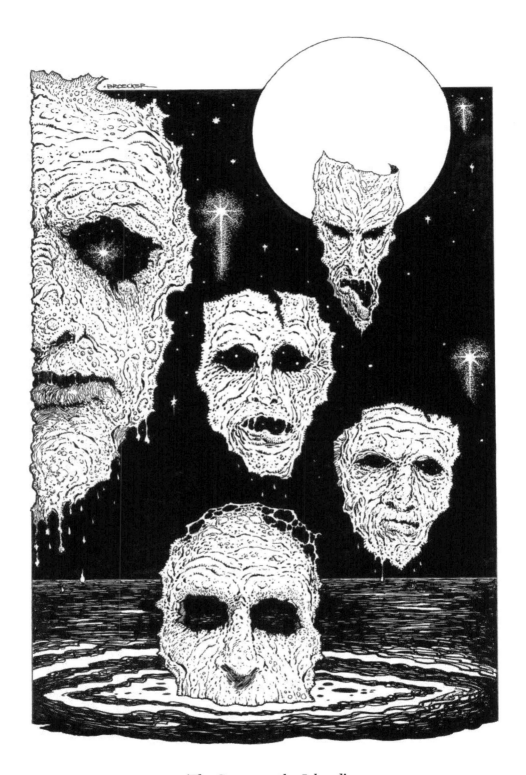

'The Stone on the Island'

'Before the Storm'

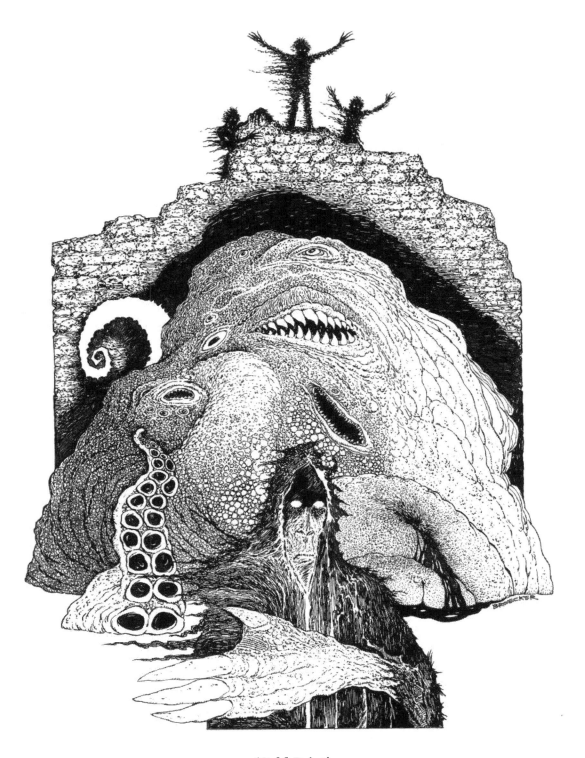

'Cold Print'

'The Other Names'

'The Last Revelation of Gla'aki'

'Made in Goatswood'

RAMSEY'S FAVOURITES

Introduced by Ramsey Campbell

Ramsey Campbell. Photograph by Peter Coleborn

The man at the centre of this very special issue of Phantasmagoria *introduces two favourite tales of his own, followed by reprints of them.*

OUR HOST, THE good Trevor Kennedy, asked me to select a favourite tale of mine. That proved to be a struggle when my old friend Dennis Etchison asked me decades back, and the swarm of new tales since then has made the choice harder still. For Dennis's anthology I chose "The Words That Count", partly on the basis that I thought it had been somewhat overlooked in terms of my total output. I'm no surer now than then whether readers don't spot what's going on in that story or find it too obvious to be worthy of remark. While I haven't chosen it this time round, interested readers can find its first complete appearance in *The Companion and Other Phantasmagorical Stories* (no connection with the present magazine) from PS Publishing. I'd previously managed to omit two of the words that counted, but that's fixed now. We must hope that the omission wasn't my subconscious way of protecting everyone from an insidious influence.

So which tale should I settle on for *Phantasmagoria*? In quite a few cases I like bits enough to wish the rest of the story were better, and that's no basis for selection, though some of those stories have been praised. *Needing Ghosts* has a special place in my heart and indeed head, since it seemed to render my unconscious directly eloquent, but it's a novella, and will be lending its name to a new PS collection of novellas (including my latest, previously unpublished) soon. "The Cellars" remains a favourite, since it was where I first seemed to read more like myself than like my literary inspirations, perhaps because it grew out of a location very much like the one I described, under Rumford Place in Liverpool (and incidentally incorporates a prose snapshot of the city in the sixties, the first of my portraits of Merseyside). I think my best pure horror story is "Again", but my instinct is to represent wider aspects of my stuff, and so I'll just mention that both those stories too can be found in the PS *Companion* volume. While most of my stories are founded on character, "A Street was Chosen" depicts none at all, instead listing their experiences in an experimental report given in the passive voice. I was struck by how responsive audiences have been when I read it aloud, demonstrating how minimalist horror can be and still have an effect, which is why it stays a favourite. Among recent tales I'm really quite fond of "The Rounds", perhaps because it seems to have attracted little favour.

I've selected none of these, however, despite cheating with a choice of two. "The Voice of the Beach" stands for my feeble leaps towards awe and the cosmic. It was my first Lovecraftian piece to do without overt mythos references, a bid to depict a vast manifestation by accumulating details of its effects. "Just Behind You" represents the uncanny as rooted in the psychological (though not to be explained away by it) and the domestic, a common situation in my work. I won't deny the influence of M.R. James – it would be idle for me to try – but as with Lovecraft, I've attempted to modernise the mode in my own way, however small, and give the characters more room to breathe, even if they aren't always doing so by the end of the tale. If folk don't like one of my choices, I hope perhaps they'll like the other.

THE VOICE OF THE BEACH

Ramsey Campbell

I

I MET NEAL at the station.

Of course I can describe it, I have only to go up the road and look, but there is no need. That isn't what I have to get out of me. It isn't me, it's out there, it can be described. I need all my energy for that, all my concentration, but perhaps it will help if I can remember before that, when everything looked manageable, expressible, familiar enough—when I could bear to look out of the window.

Neal was standing alone on the small platform, and now I see that I dare not go up the road after all, or out of the house. It doesn't matter, my memories are clear, they will help me hold on. Neal must have rebuffed the station-master, who was happy to chat to anyone. He was gazing at the bare tracks, sharpened by June light, as they cut their way through the forest—gazing at them as a suicide might gaze at a razor. He saw me and swept his hair back from his face, over his shoulders. Suffering had pared his face down, stretched the skin tighter and paler over the skull. I can remember exactly how he looked before

"I thought I'd missed the station," he said, though surely the station's name was visible enough, despite the flowers that scaled the board. If only he had! "I had to make so many changes. Never mind. Christ, it's good to see you. You look marvellous. I expect you can thank the sea for that." His eyes had brightened, and he sounded so full of life that it was spilling out of him in a tumble of words, but his handshake felt like cold bone.

I hurried him along the road that led home and to the He was beginning to screw up his eyes at the sunlight, and I thought I should get him inside; presumably headaches were among his symptoms. At first the road is gravel, fragments of which always succeed in working their way into your shoes. Where the trees fade out as though stifled by sand, a concrete path turns aside. Sand sifts over the gravel; you can hear the gritty conflict underfoot, and the musing of the sea. Beyond the path stands this crescent of bungalows. Surely all this is still true. But I remember now that the bungalows looked unreal against the burning blue sky and the dunes like embryo hills; they looked like a dream set down in the piercing light of June.

"You must be doing well to afford this." Neal sounded listless, envious only because he felt it was expected. If only he had stayed that way! But once inside the bungalow he seemed pleased by everything—the view, my books on show in the living-room bookcase, my typewriter displaying a token page that bore a token phrase, the Breughel prints that used to remind me of humanity. Abruptly, with a moody eagerness that I hardly remarked at the time, he said "Shall we have a look at the beach?"

There, I've written the word. I can describe the beach, I must describe it, it is all that's in my head. I have my notebook which I took with me that day. Neal led the way along the gravel path. Beyond the concrete turn-off to the bungalows the gravel was engulfed almost at once by sand, despite the thick ranks of low bushes that had been planted to keep back the sand. We squeezed between the bushes, which were determined to close their ranks across the gravel.

Once through, we felt the breeze whose waves passed through the marram grass that spiked the dunes. Neal's hair streamed back, pale as the grass. The trudged dunes were slowing him down, eager as he was. We slithered down to the beach, and the sound of the unfurling sea leapt closer, as though we'd awakened it from dreaming. The wind fluttered trapped in my ears, leafed through my notebook as I scribbled the image of wakening and thought with an appalling innocence: perhaps I can use that image. Now we were walled off from the rest of the world by the dunes, faceless mounds with unkempt green wigs, mounds almost as white as the sun.

Even then I felt that the beach was somehow separate from its surroundings: introverted, I remember thinking. I put it down to the shifting haze which hovered above the sea, the haze which I could never focus, whose distance I could never quite judge. From the self-contained stage of the beach the bungalows looked absurdly intrusive, anachronisms rejected by the geomorphological time of sand and sea. Even the skeletal car and the other debris, half engulfed by the beach near the coast road, looked less alien. These are my memories, the most stable things left to me, and I must go on. I found today that I cannot go back any further.

Neal was staring, eyes narrowed against the glare, along the waste of beach that stretched in the opposite direction from the coast road and curved out of sight. "Doesn't anyone come down here? There's no pollution, is there?"

"It depends on who you believe." Often the beach seemed to give me a headache, even when there was no glare—and then there was the way the beach looked at night. "Still, I think most folk go up the coast to the resorts. That's the only reason I can think of."

We were walking. Beside us the edge of the glittering sea moved in several directions simultaneously. Moist sand, sleek as satin, displayed shells which appeared to flash patterns, faster than my mind could grasp. Pinpoint mirrors of sand gleamed, rapid as Morse. My notes say this is how it seemed.

"Don't your neighbours ever come down?"

Neal's voice made me start. I had been engrossed in the designs of shell and sand. Momentarily I was unable to judge the width of the beach: a few paces, or miles? I grasped my sense of perspective, but a headache was starting, a dull impalpable grip that encircled my cranium. Now I know what all this meant, but I want to remember how I felt before I knew.

"Very seldom," I said. "Some of them think there's quicksand." One old lady, sitting in her garden to glare at the dunes like Canute versus sand, had told me that warning notices kept sinking. I'd never encountered quicksand, but I always brought my stick to help me trudge.

"So I'll have the beach to myself."

I took that to be a hint. At least he would leave me alone if I wanted to work. "The bungalow people are mostly retired," I said. "Those who aren't in wheelchairs go driving. I imagine they've had enough of sand, even if they aren't past walking on it." Once, further up the beach, I'd encountered nudists censoring themselves with towels or straw hats as they ventured down to the sea, but Neal could find out about them for himself. I wonder now if I ever saw them at all, or simply felt that I should.

Was he listening? His head was cocked, but not towards me. He'd slowed, and was staring at the ridges and furrows of the beach, at which the sea was lapping. All at once the ridges reminded me of convolutions of the brain, and I took out my notebook as the grip on my skull tightened. The beach as a subconscious, my notes say: the horizon as the imagination—sunlight set a ship ablaze on the edge of the world, an image that impressed me as vividly yet indefinably symbolic—the debris as memories, half-buried, half-comprehensible. But then what were the bungalows, perched above the dunes like boxes carved of dazzling bone?

I glanced up. A cloud had leaned towards me. No, it had been more as though the cloud were rushing at the beach from the horizon, dauntingly fast. Had it been a cloud? It had seemed more massive than a ship. The sky was empty now, and I told myself that it had been an effect of the haze—the magnified shadow of a gull, perhaps.

My start had enlivened Neal, who began to chatter like a television wakened by a kick. "It'll be good for me to be alone here, to get used to being alone. Mary and the children found themselves another home, you see. He earns more money than I'll ever see, if that's what they want. He's the head of the house type, if that's what they want. I couldn't be that now if I tried, not with the way my nerves are now." I can still hear everything he said, and I suppose that I knew what had been wrong with him. Now they are just words.

"That's why I'm talking so much," he said, and picked up a spiral shell, I thought to quiet himself.

"That's much too small. You'll never hear anything in that."

Minutes passed before he took it away from his ear and handed it to me. "No?" he said.

I put it to my ear and wasn't sure what I was hearing. No, I didn't throw the shell away, I didn't crush it underfoot; in any case, how could I have done that to the rest of the beach? I was straining to hear, straining to make out how the sound differed from the usual whisper of a shell. Was that it seemed to have a rhythm that I couldn't define, or that it sounded shrunken by distance rather than cramped by the shell? I felt expectant, entranced—precisely the feeling I'd tried so often to communicate in my fiction, I believe. Something stooped towards me from the horizon. I jerked, and dropped the shell.

There was nothing but the dazzle of sunlight that leapt at me from the waves. The haze above the sea had darkened, staining the light, and I told myself that was what I'd seen. But when Neal picked up another shell I felt uneasy. The grip on my skull was very tight now. As I regarded the vistas of empty sea and sky and beach my expectancy grew oppressive, too imminent, no longer enjoyable. "I think I'll head back now. Maybe you should as well," I said, rummaging for an uncontrived reason, "just in case there is quicksand."

"All right. It's in all of them," he said, displaying an even smaller shell to which he'd just listened. I remember thinking that his observation was so self-evident as to be meaningless.

As I turned toward the bungalows the glitter of the sea clung to my eyes. After-images crowded among the debris. They were moving; I strained to make out their shape. What did they resemble? Symbols—hieroglyphs? Limbs writhing rapidly, as if in a ritual dance? They made the debris appear to shift, to crumble. The herd of faceless dunes seemed to edge forward; an image leaned towards me out of the sky. I closed my eyes, to calm their antics, and wondered if I should take the warnings of pollution more seriously. We walked toward the confusion of footprints that climbed the dunes. Neal glanced about at the sparkling of sand. Never before had the beach so impressed me as a complex of patterns, and perhaps that means it was already too late. Spotlighted by the sun, it looked so artificial that I came close to doubting how it felt underfoot.

The bungalows looked unconvincing too. Still, when we'd slumped in our chairs for a while, letting the relative dimness soothe our eyes while our bodies guzzled every hint of coolness, I forgot about the beach. We shared two litres of wine and talked about my work, about his lack of any since graduating.

Later I prepared melon, salads, water ices. Neal watched, obviously embarrassed that he couldn't help. He seemed lost without Mary. One more reason not to marry, I thought, congratulating myself.

As we ate he kept staring out at the beach. A ship was caught in the amber sunset: a dream of escape. I felt the image less deeply than I'd experienced the metaphors of the beach; it was less oppressive. The band around my head had faded.

When it grew dark Neal pressed close to the pane. "What's that?" he demanded.

I switched out the light so that he could see. Beyond the dim humps of the dunes the beach was glowing, a dull pallor like moonlight stifled by fog. Do all beaches glow at night? "That's what makes people say there's pollution," I said.

"Not the light," he said impatiently. "The other things. What's moving?"

I squinted through the pane. For minutes I could see nothing but the muffled glow. At last, when my eyes were smarting, I began to see forms thin and stiff as scarecrows, jerking into various contorted poses. Gazing for so long was bound to produce something of the kind, and I took them to be after-images of the tangle, barely visible, of bushes.

"I think I'll go and see."

"I shouldn't go down there at night," I said, having realised that I'd never gone to the beach at night and that I felt a definite, though irrational, aversion to doing so.

Eventually he went to bed. Despite all his travelling, he'd needed to drink to make himself sleepy. I heard him open his bedroom window, which overlooked the beach. There is so much still to write, so much to struggle through, and what good can it do me now?

II

I had taken the bungalow, one of the few entries in my diary says, to give myself the chance to write without being distracted by city life—the cries of the telephone, the tolling of the doorbell, the omnipresent clamour—only to discover, once I'd left it behind, that city life was my theme. But I was a compulsive writer: if I failed to write for more than a few days I became depressed. Writing was the way I overcame the depression of not writing. Now writing seems to be my only way of hanging onto what remains of myself, of delaying the end.

The day after Neal arrived, I typed a few lines of a sample chapter. It wasn't a technique I enjoyed—tearing a chapter out of the context of a novel that didn't yet exist. In any case, I was distracted by the beach, compelled to scribble notes about it, trying to define the images it suggested. I hoped these notes might build into a story. I was picking at the notes in search of their story when Neal said "Maybe I can lose myself for a bit in the countryside."

"Mm," I said curtly, not looking up.

"Didn't you say there was a deserted village?"

By the time I directed him I would have lost the thread of my thoughts. The thread had been frayed and tangled, anyway. As long as I was compelled to think about the beach I might just as well be down there. I can still write as if I don't know the end, it helps me not to think of "I'll come with you," I said.

The weather was nervous. Archipelagos of cloud floated low on the hazy sky, above the sea; great Rorschach blots rose from behind the slate hills, like dissolved stone. As we squeezed through the bushes, a shadow came hunching over the dunes to meet us. When my foot touched the beach a moist shadowy chill seized me, as though the sand disguised a lurking marsh. Then sunlight spilled over the beach, which leapt into clarity.

I strode, though Neal appeared to want to dawdle. I wasn't anxious to linger; after all, I told myself, it might rain. Glinting mosaics of grains of sand changed restlessly around me, never quite achieving a pattern. Patches of sand, flat shapeless elongated ghosts, glided over the beach and faltered, waiting for another breeze. Neal kept peering at them as though to make out their shapes.

Half a mile along the beach the dunes began to sag, to level out. The slate hills were closing in. Were they the source of the insidious chill? Perhaps I was feeling the damp; a penumbra of moisture welled up around each of my footprints. The large wet shapes seemed quite unrelated to my prints, an effect which I found unnerving. When I glanced back, it looked as though something enormous was imitating my walk.

The humidity was almost suffocating. My head felt clamped by tension. Wind blundered booming in my ears, even when I could feel no breeze. Its jerky rhythm was distracting because indefinable. Grey cloud had flooded the sky; together with the hills and the thickening haze above the sea, it caged the beach. At the edge of my eye the convolutions of the beach seemed to writhe, to struggle to form patterns. The insistent sparkling nagged at my mind.

I'd begun to wonder whether I had been blaming imagined pollution for the effects of heat and humidity—I was debating whether to turn back before I grew dizzy or nauseous—when Neal said "Is that it?"

I peered ahead, trying to squint the dazzle of waves from my eyes. A quarter of a mile away the hills ousted the dunes completely. Beneath the spiky slate a few uprights of rock protruded from the beach like standing stones. They glowed sullenly as copper through the haze; they were encrusted with sand. Surely that wasn't the village.

"Yes, that's it," Neal said, and strode forward.

I followed him, because the village must be further on. The veil of haze drew back, the vertical rocks gleamed unobscured, and I halted bewildered. The rocks weren't encrusted at all; they were slate, grey as the table of rock on which they stood above the beach. Though the slate was jagged, some of its gaps were regular:

windows, doorways. Here and there walls still formed corners. How could the haze have distorted my view so spectacularly?

Neal was climbing rough steps carved out of the slate table. Without warning, as I stood confused by my misperception, I felt utterly alone. A bowl of dull haze trapped me on the bare sand. Slate, or something more massive and vague, loomed over me. The kaleidoscope of shells was about to shift; the beach was ready to squirm, to reveal its pattern, shake off its artificiality. The massive looming would reach down, and

My start felt like a convulsive awakening. The table was deserted except for the fragments of buildings. I could hear only the wind, baying as though its mouth was vast and uncontrollable. "Neal," I called. Dismayed by the smallness of my voice, I shouted "Neal."

I heard what sounded like scales of armour chafing together—slate, of course. The grey walls shone lifelessly, cavitied as skulls; gaping windows displayed an absence of faces, of rooms. Then Neal's head poked out of half a wall. "Yes, come on," he said. "It's strange."

As I climbed the steps, sand gritted underfoot like sugar. Low drifts of sand were piled against the walls; patches glinted on the small plateau. Could that sand have made the whole place look encrusted and half-buried? I told myself that it had been an effect of the heat.

Broken walls surrounded me. They glared like storm-clouds in lightning. They formed a maze whose centre was desertion. That image stirred another, too deep in my mind to be definable. The place was—not a maze, but a puzzle whose solution would clarify a pattern, a larger mystery. I realised that then; why couldn't I have fled?

I suppose I was held by the enigma of the village. I knew there were quarries in the hills above, but I'd never learned why the village had been abandoned. Perhaps its meagreness had killed it—I saw traces of less than a dozen buildings. It seemed further dwarfed by the beach; the sole visible trace of humanity, it dwindled beneath the gnawing of sand and the elements. I found it enervating, its lifelessness infectious. Should I stay with Neal, or risk leaving him there? Before I could decide, I heard him say amid a rattle of slate "This is interesting."

In what way? He was clambering about an exposed cellar, among shards of slate. Whatever the building had been, it had stood furthest from the sea. "I don't mean the cellar," Neal said. "I mean that."

Reluctantly I peered where he was pointing. In the cellar wall furthest from the beach, a rough alcove had been chipped out of the slate. It was perhaps a yard deep, but barely high enough to accommodate a huddled man. Neal was already crawling in. I heard slate crack beneath him; his feet protruded from the darkness. Of course they weren't about to jerk convulsively—but my nervousness made me back away when his muffled voice said "What's this?"

He backed out like a terrier with his prize. It was an old notebook, its pages stuck together in a moist wad. "Someone covered it up with slate," he said as though that should tempt my interest.

Before I could prevent him he was sitting at the edge of the beach and peeling the pages gingerly apart. Not that I was worried that he might be destroying a fragment of history—I simply wasn't sure that I wanted to read whatever had been hidden in the cellar. Why couldn't I have followed my instincts?

He disengaged the first page carefully, then frowned. "This begins in the middle of something. There must be another book."

Handing me the notebook, he stalked away to scrabble in the cellar. I sat on the edge of the slate table, and glanced at the page. It is before me now on my desk. The pages have crumbled since then—the yellowing paper looks more and more like sand—but the large writing is still legible, unsteady capitals in a hand that might once have been literate before it grew senile. No punctuation separates the words, though blotches sometimes do. Beneath the relentless light at the deserted village the faded ink looked unreal, scarcely present at all.

> FROM THE BEACH EVERYONE GONE NOW
> BUT ME ITS NOT SO BAD IN DAYTIME EXCEPT
> I CANT GO BUT AT NIGHT I CAN HEAR IT
> REACHING FOR (a blot of fungus had consumed a
> word here) AND THE VOICES ITS VOICE AND
> THE GLOWING AT LEAST IT HELPS ME SEE
> DOWN HERE WHEN IT COMES

I left it at that; my suddenly unsteady fingers might have torn the page. I wish to God they had. I was on edge with the struggle between humidity and the chill of slate and beach; I felt feverish. As I stared at the words they touched impressions, half-memories. If I looked up, would the beach have changed?

I heard Neal slithering on slate, turning over fragments. In my experience, stones were best not turned over. Eventually he returned. I was dully fascinated by the shimmering of the beach; my fingers pinched the notebook shut.

"I can't find anything," he said. "I'll have to come back." He took the notebook from me and began to read, muttering "What? Jesus!" Gently he separated the next page from the wad. "This gets stranger," he murmured. "What kind of guy was this? Imagine what it must have been like to live inside his head."

How did he know it had been a man? I stared at the pages, to prevent Neal from reading them aloud. At least it saved me from having to watch the antics of the beach, which moved like slow flames, but the introverted meandering of words made me nervous.

> IT CANT REACH DOWN HERE NOT YET BUT
> OUTSIDE IS CHANGING OUTSIDES PART OF
> THE PATTERN I READ THE PATTERN THATS
> WHY I CANT GO SAW THEM DANCING THE
> PATTERN IT WANTS ME TO DANCE ITS ALIVE
> BUT ITS ONLY THE IMAGE BEING PUT
> TOGETHER

Neal was wide-eyed, fascinated. Feverish disorientation gripped my skull; I felt too unwell to move. The heat-haze must be closing in: at the edge of my vision, everything was shifting.

> WHEN THE PATTERNS DONE IT CAN COME
> BACK AND GROW ITS HUNGRY TO BE EVERY-
> THING I KNOW HOW IT WORKS THE SAND
> MOVES AT NIGHT AND SUCKS YOU DOWN OR
> MAKES YOU GO WHERE IT WANTS TO MAKE (a
> blotch had eaten several words) WHEN THEY BUILT
> LEWIS THERE WERE OLD STONES THAT THEY
> MOVED MAYBE THE STONES KEPT IT SMALL
> NOW ITS THE BEACH AT LEAST

On the next page the letters are much larger, and wavery. Had the light begun to fail, or had the writer been retreating from the light—from the entrance to the cellar? I didn't know which alternative I disliked more.

> GOT TO WRITE HANDS SHAKY FROM CHIP-
> PING TUNNEL AND NO FOOD THEYRE
> SINGING NOW HELPING IT REACH
> CHANTING WITH NO MOUTHS THEY SING
> AND DANCE THE PATTERN FOR IT TO REACH
> THROUGH

Now there are very few words to the page. The letters are jagged, as though the writer's hand kept twitching violently.

> GLOW COMING ITS OUT THERE NOW ITS
> LOOKING IN AT ME IT CANT GET HOLD IF I
> KEEP WRITING THEY WANT ME TO DANCE SO
> ITLL GROW WANT ME TO BE

There it ends. "Ah, the influence of Joyce," I commented sourly. The remaining pages are blank except for fungus. I managed to stand up; my head felt like a balloon pumped full of gas. "I'd like to go back now. I think I've a touch of sunstroke."

A hundred yards away I glanced back at the remnants of the village—Lewis, I assumed it had been called. The stone remains wavered as though striving to achieve a new shape; the haze made them look coppery, fat with a crust of sand. I was desperate to get out of the heat.

Closer to the sea I felt slightly less oppressed—but the whispering of sand, the liquid murmur of the waves, the bumbling of the wind, all chanted together insistently. Everywhere on the beach were patterns, demanding to be read.

Neal clutched the notebook under his arm. "What do you make of it?" he said eagerly.

His indifference to my health annoyed me, and hence so did the question. "He was mad," I said. "Living here—is it any wonder? Maybe he moved there after the place was abandoned. The beach must glow there too. That must have finished him. You saw how he tried to dig himself a refuge. That's all there is to it."

"Do you think so? I wonder," Neal said, and picked up a shell. As he held the shell to his ear, his expression became so withdrawn and unreadable that I felt a pang of dismay. Was I seeing a symptom of his nervous trouble? He stood like a fragment of the village—as though the shell was holding him, rather than the reverse.

Eventually he mumbled "That's it, that's what he meant. Chanting with no mouths."

I took the shell only very reluctantly; my head was pounding. I pressed the shell to my ear, though I was deafened by the storm of my blood. If the shell was muttering, I couldn't bear the jaggedness of its rhythm. I seemed less to hear it than to feel it deep in my skull. "Nothing like it," I said, almost snarling, and thrust the shell at him.

Now that I'd had to strain to hear it, I couldn't rid myself of the muttering; it seemed to underlie the sounds of wind and sea. I trudged onwards, eyes half shut. Moisture sprang up around my feet, the glistening shapes around my prints looked larger and more definite. I had to cling to my sense of my own size and shape.

When we neared home I couldn't see the bungalows. There appeared to be only the beach, grown huge and blinding. At last Neal heard a car leaving the crescent, and led me up the path of collapsed footprints.

In the bungalow I lay willing the lights and patterns to fade from my closed eyes. Neal's presence didn't soothe me, even though he was only poring over the notebook. He'd brought a handful of shells indoors.

Occasionally he held one to his ear, muttering "It's still there, you know. It does sound like chanting." At least, I thought peevishly, I knew when something was a symptom of illness—but the trouble was that in my delirium I was tempted to agree with him. I felt I had almost heard what the sound was trying to be.

III

Next day Neal returned to the deserted village. He was gone for so long that even amid the clamour of my disordered senses, I grew anxious. I couldn't watch for him; whenever I tried, the white-hot beach began to judder, to quake, and set me shivering.

At last he returned, having failed to find another notebook. I hoped that would be the end of it, but his failure had simply frustrated him. His irritability chafed against mine. He managed to prepare a bedraggled salad, of which I ate little. As the tide of twilight rolled in from the horizon he sat by the window, gazing alternately at the beach and at the notebook.

Without warning he said "I'm going for a stroll. Can I borrow your stick?"

I guessed that he meant to go to the beach. Should he be trapped by darkness and sea, I was in no condition to go to his aid. "I'd rather you didn't," I said feebly.

"Don't worry, I won't lose it."

My lassitude suffocated my arguments. I lolled in my chair and through the open window heard him padding away, his footsteps muffled by sand. Soon there was only the vague slack rumble of the sea, blundering back and forth, and the faint hiss of sand in the bushes.

After half an hour I made myself stand up, though the ache in my head surged and surged, and gaze out at the whitish beach. The whole expanse appeared to flicker like hints of lightning. I strained my eyes. The beach looked crowded with debris, all of which danced to the flickering. I had to peer at every movement, but there was no sign of Neal.

I went out and stood between the bushes. The closer I approached the beach, the more crowded with obscure activity it seemed to be—but I suspected that much, if not all, of this could be blamed on my condition, for within five minutes my head felt so tight and unbalanced that I had to retreat indoors, away from the heat.

Though I'd meant to stay awake, I was dozing when Neal returned. I woke to find him gazing from the window. As I opened my eyes the beach lurched forward, shining. It didn't look crowded now, presumably because my eyes had had a rest. What could Neal see to preoccupy him so? "Enjoy your stroll?" I said sleepily.

He turned, and I felt a twinge of disquiet. His face looked stiff with doubt; his eyes were uneasy, a frown dug its ruts in his forehead. "It doesn't glow," he said.

Assuming I knew what he was talking about, I could only wonder how badly his nerves were affecting his perceptions. If anything, the beach looked brighter. "How do you mean?"

"The beach down by the village—it doesn't glow. Not any more."

"Oh, I see."

He looked offended, almost contemptuous, though I couldn't understand why he'd expected me to be less indifferent. He withdrew into a scrutiny of the notebook. He might have been trying to solve an urgent problem.

Perhaps if I hadn't been ill I would have been able to divert Neal from his obsession, but I could hardly venture outside without growing dizzy; I could only wait in the bungalow for my state to improve. Neither Neal nor I had had sunstroke before, but he seemed to know how to treat it. "Keep drinking water. Cover yourself if you start shivering." He didn't mind my staying in—he seemed almost too eager to go out alone. Did that matter? Next day he was bound only for the library.

My state was crippling my thoughts, yet even if I'd been healthy I couldn't have imagined how he would look when he returned: excited, conspiratorial, smug. "I've got a story for you," he said at once.

Most such offers proved to be prolonged and dull. "Oh yes?" I said warily.

He sat forward as though to infect me with suspense. "That village we went to—it isn't called Lewis. It's called Strand."

Was he pausing to give me a chance to gasp or applaud? "Oh yes," I said without enthusiasm.

"Lewis was another village, further up the coast. It's deserted too." That seemed to be his punch line. The antics of patterns within my eyelids had made me irritable. "It doesn't seem much of a story," I complained.

"Well, that's only the beginning." When his pause had forced me to open my eyes, he said "I read a book about your local unexplained mysteries."

"Why?"

"Look, if you don't want to hear—"

"Go on, go on, now you've started." Not to know might be even more nerve-racking.

"There wasn't much about Lewis," he said eventually, perhaps to give himself more time to improvise.

"Was there much at all?"

"Yes, certainly. It may not sound like much. Nobody knows why Lewis was abandoned, but then nobody knows that about Strand either." My impatience must have showed, for he added hastily "What I mean is, the people who left Strand wouldn't say why."

"Someone asked them?"

"The woman who wrote the book. She managed to track some of them down. They'd moved as far inland as they could, that was one thing she noticed. And they always had some kind of nervous disorder. Talking about Strand always made them more nervous, as though they felt that talking might make something happen, or something might hear."

"That's what the author said."

"Right."

"What was her name?"

Could he hear my suspicion? "Jesus *Christ*," he snarled, "I don't know. What does it matter?"

In fact it didn't, not to me. His story had made me feel worse. The noose had tightened round my skull, the twilit beach was swarming and vibrating. I closed my eyes. Shut up, I roared at him. Go away.

"There was one thing," he persisted. "One man said that kids kept going on the beach at night. Their parents tried all ways to stop them. Some of them questioned their kids, but it was as though the kids couldn't stop themselves. Why was that, do you think?" When I refused to answer he said irrelevantly "All this was in the 1930s."

I couldn't stand hearing children called kids. The recurring word had made me squirm: drips of slang, like water torture. And I'd never heard such a feeble punch line. His clumsiness as a storyteller enraged me; he couldn't even organise his material. I was sure he hadn't read any such book.

After a while I peered out from beneath my eyelids, hoping he'd decided that I was asleep. He was poring over the notebook again, and looked rapt. I only wished that people and reviewers would read my books as carefully. He kept rubbing his forehead, as though to enliven his brain.

I dozed. When I opened my eyes he was waiting for me. He shoved the notebook at me to demonstrate something. "Look, I'm sorry," I said without much effort to sound so. "I'm not in the mood."

He stalked into his room, emerging without the book but with my stick. "I'm going for a walk," he announced sulkily, like a spouse after a quarrel.

I dozed gratefully, for I felt more delirious; my head felt packed with grains of sand that gritted together. In fact, the whole of me was made of sand. Of course it was true that I was composed of particles, and I thought my delirium had found a metaphor for that. But the grains that floated through my inner vision were neither sand nor atoms. A member, dark and vague, was reaching for them. I struggled to awaken; I didn't want to distinguish its shape, and still less did I want to learn what it meant to do with the grains—for as the member sucked them into itself, engulfing them in a way that I refused to perceive, I saw that the grains were worlds and stars.

I woke shivering. My body felt uncontrollable and unfamiliar. I let it shake itself to rest—not that I had a choice, but I was concentrating on the problem of why I'd woken head raised, like a watchdog. What had I heard?

Perhaps only wind and sea: both seemed louder, more intense. My thoughts became entangled in their rhythm. I felt there had been another sound. The bushes threshed, sounding parched with sand. Had I heard Neal returning? I stumbled into his room. It was empty.

As I stood by his open window, straining my ears, I thought I heard his voice, blurred by the dull tumult of waves. I peered out. Beyond the low heads of the bushes, the glow of the beach shuddered towards me. I had to close my eyes, for I couldn't tell whether the restless scrawny shapes were crowding my eyeballs or the beach; it felt, somehow, like both. When I looked again, I seemed to see Neal.

Or was it Neal? The unsteady stifled glow aggravated the distortions of my vision. Was the object just a new piece of debris? I found its shape bewildering; my mind kept apprehending it as a symbol printed on the whitish expanse. The luminosity made it seem to shift, tentatively and jerkily, as though it was learning to pose. The light, or my eyes, surrounded it with dancing.

Had my sense of perspective left me? I was misjudging size, either of the beach or of the figure. Yes, it was a figure, however large it seemed. It was moving its arms like a limp puppet. And it was half-buried in the sand.

I staggered outside, shouting to Neal, and then I recoiled. The sky must be thick with a storm-cloud; it felt suffocatingly massive, solid as rock, and close enough to crush me. I forced myself towards the bushes, though my head was pounding, squeezed into a lump of pain.

Almost at once I heard plodding on the dunes. My blood half deafened me; the footsteps sounded vague and immense. I peered along the dim path. At the edge of my vision the beach flickered repetitively. Immense darkness hovered over me. Unnervingly close to me, swollen by the glow, a head rose into view. For a moment my tension seemed likely to crack my skull. Then Neal spoke. His words were incomprehensible amid the wind, but it was his voice.

As we trudged back towards the lights the threat of a storm seemed to withdraw, and I blamed it on my tension. "Of course I'm all right," he muttered irritably. "I fell and that made me shout, that's all." Once we were inside I saw the evidence of his fall; his trousers were covered with sand up to the knees.

IV

Next day he hardly spoke to me. He went down early to the beach, and stayed there. I didn't know if he was obsessed or displaying pique. Perhaps he couldn't bear to be near me; invalids can find each other unbearable.

Often I glimpsed him, wandering beyond the dunes. He walked as though in an elaborate maze and scrutinised the beach. Was he searching for the key to the notebook? Was he looking for pollution? By the time he found it, I thought sourly, it would have infected him.

I felt too enervated to intervene. As I watched, Neal appeared to vanish intermittently; if I looked away, I couldn't locate him again for minutes. The beach blazed like bone, and was never still. I couldn't blame the aberrations of my vision solely on heat and haze.

When Neal returned, late that afternoon, I asked him to phone for a doctor. He looked taken aback, but eventually said "There's a box by the station, isn't there?"

"One of the neighbours would let you phone."

"No, I'll walk down. They're probably all wondering why you've let some long-haired freak squat in your house, as it is."

He went out, rubbing his forehead gingerly. He often did that now. That, and his preoccupation with the demented notebook, were additional reasons why I wanted a doctor: I felt Neal needed examining too.

By the time he returned, it was dusk. On the horizon, embers dulled in the sea. The glow of the beach was already stirring; it seemed to have intensified during the last few days. I told myself I had grown hypersensitive.

"Dr Lewis. He's coming tomorrow." Neal hesitated, then went on "I think I'll just have a stroll on the beach. Want to come?"

"Good God no. I'm ill, can't you see?"

"I know that." His impatience was barely controlled. "A stroll might do you good. There isn't any sunlight now."

"I'll stay in until I've seen the doctor."

He looked disposed to argue, but his restlessness overcame him. As he left, his bearing seemed to curse me. Was his illness making him intolerant of mine, or did he feel that I'd rebuffed a gesture of reconciliation?

I felt too ill to watch him from the window. When I looked I could seldom distinguish him or make out which movements were his. He appeared to be walking slowly, poking at the beach with my stick. I wondered if he'd found quicksand. Again his path made me think of a maze.

I dozed, far longer than I'd intended. The doctor loomed over me. Peering into my eyes, he reached down. I began to struggle, as best I could: I'd glimpsed the depths of his eye-sockets, empty and dry as interstellar space. I didn't need his treatment, I would be fine if he left me alone, just let me go. But he had reached deep into me. As though I was a bladder that had burst, I felt myself flood into him; I felt vast emptiness absorb my substance and my self. Dimly I understood that it was nothing like emptiness—that my mind refused to perceive what it was, so alien and frightful was its teeming.

It was dawn. The muffled light teemed. The beach glowed fitfully. I gasped: someone was down on the beach, so huddled that he looked shapeless. He rose, levering himself up with my stick, and began to pace haphazardly. I knew at once that he'd spent the night on the beach.

After that I stayed awake. I couldn't imagine the state of his mind, and I was a little afraid of being asleep when he returned. But when, hours later, he came in to raid the kitchen for a piece of cheese, he seemed hardly to see me. He was muttering repetitively under his breath. His eyes looked dazzled by the beach, sunk in his obsession.

"When did the doctor say he was coming?"

"Later," he mumbled, and hurried down to the beach.

I hoped he would stay there until the doctor came. Occasionally I glimpsed him at his intricate pacing. Ripples of heat deformed him; his blurred flesh looked unstable. Whenever I glanced at the beach it leapt forward, dauntingly vivid. Cracks of light appeared in the sea. Clumps of grass seemed to rise twitching, as though the dunes were craning to watch Neal. Five minutes' vigil at the window was as much as I could bear.

The afternoon consumed time. It felt lethargic and enervating as four in the morning. There was no sign of the doctor. I kept gazing from the front door. Nothing moved on the crescent except wind-borne hints of the beach.

Eventually I tried to phone. Though I could feel the heat of the pavement through the soles of my shoes, the day seemed bearable; only threats of pain plucked at my skull. But nobody was at home. The bungalows stood smugly in the evening light. When I attempted to walk to the phone box, the noose closed on my skull at once.

In my hall I halted startled, for Neal had thrown open the living-room door as I entered the house. He looked flushed and angry. "Where were you?" he demanded.

"I'm not a hospital case yet, you know. I was trying to phone the doctor."

Unfathomably, he looked relieved. "I'll go down now and call him."

While he was away I watched the beach sink into twilight. At the moment, this seemed to be the only time of day I could endure watching—the time at which shapes become obscure, most capable of metamorphosis. Perhaps this made the antics of the shore acceptable, more apparently natural. Now the beach resembled clouds in front of the moon; it drifted slowly and variously. If I gazed for long it looked nervous with lightning. The immense bulk of the night edged up from the horizon.

I didn't hear Neal return; I must have been fascinated by the view. I turned to find him watching me. Again he looked relieved—because I was still here? "He's coming soon," he said.

"Tonight, do you mean?"

"Yes, tonight. Why not?"

I didn't know many doctors who would come out at night to treat what was, however unpleasant for me, a relatively minor illness. Perhaps attitudes were different here in the country. Neal was heading for the back door, for the beach. "Do you think you could wait until he comes?" I said, groping for an excuse to detain him. "Just in case I feel worse."

"Yes, you're right." His gaze was opaque. "I'd better stay with you."

We waited. The dark mass closed over beach and bungalows. The nocturnal glow fluttered at the edge of my vision. When I glanced at the beach, the dim shapes were hectic. I seemed to be paying for my earlier fascination, for now the walls of the room looked active with faint patterns.

Where was the doctor? Neal seemed impatient too. The only sounds were the repetitive ticking of his footsteps and the irregular chant of the sea. He kept staring at me as if he wanted to speak; occasionally his mouth twitched. He resembled a child both eager to confess and afraid to do so. Though he made me uneasy I tried to look encouraging, interested in whatever he might have to say. His pacing took him closer and closer to the beach door. Yes, I nodded, tell me, talk to me.

His eyes narrowed. Behind his eyelids he was pondering. Abruptly he sat opposite me. A kind of smile, tweaked awry, plucked at his lips. "I've got another story for you," he said.

"Really?" I sounded as intrigued as I could.

He picked up the notebook. "I worked it out from this."

So we'd returned to his obsession. As he twitched pages over, his feet shifted constantly. His lips moved as though whispering the text. I heard the vast mumbling of the sea.

"Suppose this," he said all at once. "I only said suppose, mind you. This guy was living all alone in Strand. It must have affected his mind, you said that yourself—having to watch the beach every night. But just suppose it didn't send him mad? Suppose it affected his mind so that he saw things more clearly?"

I hid my impatience. "What things?"

"The beach." His tone reminded me of something—a particular kind of simplicity I couldn't quite place. "Of course we're only supposing. But from things you've read, don't you feel there are places that are closer to another sort of reality, another plane or dimension or whatever?"

"You mean the beach at Strand was like that?" I suggested, to encourage him.

"That's right. Did you feel it too?"

His eagerness startled me. "I felt ill, that's all. I still do."

"Sure. Yes, of course. I mean, we were only supposing. But look at what he says." He seemed glad to retreat into the notebook. "It started at Lewis where the old stones were, then it moved on up the coast to Strand. Doesn't that prove that what he was talking about is unlike anything we know?"

His mouth hung open, awaiting my agreement; it looked empty, robbed of sense. I glanced away, distracted by the fluttering glow beyond him. "I don't know what you mean."

"That's because you haven't read this properly." His impatience had turned harsh. "Look here," he demanded, poking his fingers at a group of words as if they were a Bible's oracle.

WHEN THE PATTERNS READY IT CAN COME BACK.

"So what is that supposed to mean?"

"I'll tell you what I think it means—what he meant." His low voice seemed to stumble among the rhythms of the beach. "You see how he keeps mentioning patterns. Suppose this other reality was once all there was? Then ours came into being and occupied some of its space. We didn't destroy it—it can't be destroyed. Maybe it withdrew a little, to bide its time. But it left a kind of imprint of itself, a kind of coded image of itself in our reality. And yet that image is itself in embryo, growing. You see, he says it's alive but it's only the image being put together. Things become part of its image, and that's how it grows. I'm sure that's what he meant."

I felt mentally exhausted and dismayed by all this. How much in need of a doctor was he? I couldn't help sounding a little derisive. "I don't see how you could have put all that together from that book."

"Who says I did?"

His vehemence was shocking. I had to break the tension, for the glare in his eyes looked as unnatural and nervous as the glow of the beach. I went to gaze from the front window, but there was no sign of the doctor. "Don't worry," Neal said. "He's coming."

I stood staring out at the lightless road until he said fretfully "Don't you want to hear the rest?"

He waited until I sat down. His tension was oppressive as the hovering sky. He gazed at me for what seemed minutes; the noose dug into my skull. At last he said "Does this beach feel like anywhere else to you?"

"It feels like a beach."

He shrugged that aside. "You see, he worked out that whatever came from the old stones kept moving toward the inhabited areas. That's how it added to itself. That's why it moved on from Lewis and then Strand."

"All nonsense, of course. Ravings."

"No. It isn't." There was no mistaking the fury that lurked, barely restrained, beneath his low voice. That fury seemed loose in the roaring night, in the wind and violent sea and looming sky. The beach trembled wakefully. "The next place it would move to would be here," he muttered. "It has to be."

"If you accepted the idea in the first place."

A hint of a grimace twitched his cheek; my comment might have been an annoying fly—certainly as trivial. "You can read the pattern out there if you try," he mumbled. "It takes all day. You begin to get a sense of what might be there. It's alive, though nothing like life as we recognise it."

I could only say whatever came into my head, to detain him until the doctor arrived. "Then how do you?"

He avoided the question, but only to betray the depths of his obsession. "Would an insect recognise us as a kind of life?"

Suddenly I realised that he intoned "the beach" as a priest might name his god. We must get away from the beach. Never mind the doctor now. "Look, Neal, I think we'd better—"

He interrupted me, eyes glaring spasmodically. "It's strongest at night. I think it soaks up energy during the day. Remember, he said that the quicksands only come out at night. They move, you know—they make you follow the pattern. And the sea is different at night. Things come out of it. They're like symbols and yet they're alive. I think the sea creates them. They help make the pattern live."

Appalled, I could only return to the front window and search for the lights of the doctor's car—for any lights at all. "Yes, yes," Neal said, sounding less impatient than soothing. "He's coming." But as he spoke I glimpsed, reflected in the window, his secret triumphant grin.

Eventually I managed to say to his reflection "You didn't call a doctor, did you?"

"No." A smile made his lips tremble like quicksand. "But he's coming."

My stomach had begun to churn slowly; so had my head, and the room. Now I was afraid to stand with my back to Neal, but when I turned I was more afraid to ask the question. "Who?"

For a moment I thought he disdained to answer; he turned his back on me and gazed towards the beach—but I can't write any longer as if I have doubts, as if I don't know the end. The beach was his answer, its awesome transformation was, even if I wasn't sure what I was seeing. Was the beach swollen, puffed up as if by the irregular gasping of the sea? Was it swarming with indistinct shapes, parasites that scuttled dancing over it, sank into it, floated writhing to its surface? Did it quiver along the whole of its length like luminous gelatin? I tried to believe that all this was an effect of the brooding dark—but the dark had closed down so thickly that there might have been no light in the world outside except the fitful glow. He craned his head back over his shoulder. The gleam in his eyes looked very like the glimmering outside. A web of saliva stretched between his bared teeth. He grinned with a frightful generosity; he'd decided to answer my question more directly. His lips moved as they had when he was reading. At last I heard what I'd tried not to suspect. He was making the sound that I'd tried not to hear in the shells.

Was it meant to be an invocation, or the name I'd asked for? I knew only that the sound, so liquid and inhuman that I could almost think it was shapeless, nauseated me, so much so that I couldn't separate it from the huge loose voices of wind and sea. It seemed to fill the room. The pounding of my skull tried to imitate its rhythm, which I found impossible to grasp, unbearable. I began to sidle along the wall towards the front door.

His body turned jerkily, as if dangling from his neck. His head laughed, if a sound like struggles in mud is laughter. "You're not going to try to get away?" he cried. "It was getting hold of you before I came, he was. You haven't a chance now, not since we brought him into the house," and he picked up a shell.

As he levelled the mouth of the shell at me my dizziness flooded my skull, hurling me forward. The walls seemed to glare and shake and break out in swarms; I thought that a dark bulk loomed at the window, filling it. Neal's mouth was working, but the nauseating sound might have been roaring deep in a cavern, or a shell. It sounded distant and huge, but coming closer and growing more definite—the voice of something vast and liquid that was gradually taking shape. Perhaps that was because I was listening, but I had no choice.

All at once Neal's free hand clamped his forehead. It looked like a pincer desperate to tear something out of his skull. "It's growing," he cried, somewhere between sobbing and ecstasy. As he spoke, the liquid chant seemed to abate not at all. Before I knew what he meant to do, he'd wrenched open the back door and was gone. In a nightmarish way, his nervous elaborate movements resembled dancing.

As the door crashed open, the roar of the night rushed in. Its leap in volume sounded eager, voracious. I stood paralysed, listening, and couldn't tell how like his chant it sounded. I heard his footsteps, soft and loose, running unevenly over the dunes. Minutes later I thought I heard a faint cry, which sounded immediately engulfed.

I slumped against a chair. I felt relieved, drained, uncaring. The sounds had returned to the beach, where they ought to be; the room looked stable now. Then I grew disgusted with myself. Suppose Neal was injured, or caught in quicksand? I'd allowed his hysteria to gain a temporary hold on my sick perceptions, I told myself—was I going to use that as an excuse not to try to save him?

At last I forced myself outside. All the bungalows were dark. The beach was glimmering, but not violently. I could see nothing wrong with the sky. Only my dizziness, and the throbbing of my head, threatened to distort my perceptions.

I made myself edge between the bushes, which hissed like snakes, mouths full of sand. The tangle of footprints made me stumble frequently. Sand rattled the spikes of marram grass. At the edge of the dunes, the path felt ready to slide me down to the beach.

The beach was crowded. I had to squint at many of the vague pieces of debris. My eyes grew used to the dimness, but I could see no sign of Neal. Then I peered closer. Was that a pair of sandals, half buried? Before my giddiness could hurl me to the beach, I slithered down.

Yes, they were Neal's, and a path of bare footprints led away towards the crowd of debris. I poked gingerly at the sandals, and wished I had my stick to test for quicksand—but the sand in which they were partially engulfed was quite solid. Why had he tried to bury them?

I followed his prints, my eyes still adjusting. I refused to imitate his path, for it looped back on itself in intricate patterns which made me dizzy and wouldn't fade from my mind. His paces were irregular, a cripple's dance. He must be a puppet of his nerves, I thought. I was a little afraid to confront him, but I felt a duty to try.

His twistings led me among the debris. Low obscure shapes surrounded me: a jagged stump bristling with metal tendrils that groped in the air as I came near; half a car so rusty and misshapen that it looked like a child's fuzzy sketch; the hood of a pram within which glimmered a bald lump of sand. I was glad to emerge from that maze, for the dim objects seemed to shift; I'd even thought the bald lump was opening a crumbling mouth.

But on the open beach there were other distractions. The ripples and patterns of sand were clearer, and appeared to vibrate restlessly. I kept glancing toward the sea, not because its chant was troubling me—though, with its insistent loose rhythm, it was—but because I had a persistent impression that the waves were slowing, sluggish as treacle.

I stumbled, and had to turn back to see what had tripped me. The glow of the beach showed me Neal's shirt, the little of it that was left unburied. There was no mistaking it; I recognised its pattern. The glow made the nylon seem luminous, lit from within.

His prints danced back among the debris. Even then, God help me, I wondered if he was playing a sick joke—if he was waiting somewhere to leap out, to scare me into admitting I'd been impressed. I trudged angrily into the midst of the debris, and wished at once that I hadn't. All the objects were luminous, without shadows.

There was no question now: the glow of the beach was increasing. It made Neal's tracks look larger: their outlines shifted as I squinted at them. I stumbled hastily toward the deserted stretch of beach, and brushed against the half-engulfed car.

That was the moment at which the nightmare became real. I might have told myself that rust had eaten away the car until it was thin as a shell, but I was past deluding myself. All at once I knew that nothing on this beach was as it seemed, for as my hand collided with the car roof, which should have been painfully solid, I felt the roof crumble—and the entire structure flopped on the sand, from which it was at once indistinguishable.

I fled towards the open beach. But there was no relief, for the entire beach was glowing luridly, like mud struggling to suffocate a moon. Among the debris I glimpsed the rest of Neal's clothes, half absorbed by the beach. As I staggered into the open, I saw his tracks ahead—saw how they appeared to grow, to alter until they became unrecognisable, and then to peter out at a large dark shapeless patch on the sand.

I glared about, terrified. I couldn't see the bungalows. After minutes I succeeded in glimpsing the path, the mess of footprints cluttering the dune. I began to pace toward it, very slowly and quietly, so as not to be noticed by the beach and the looming sky.

But the dunes were receding. I think I began to scream then, scream almost in a whisper, for the faster I hurried, the further the dunes withdrew. The nightmare had overtaken perspective. Now I was running wildly, though I felt I was standing still. I'd run only a few steps when I had to recoil from sand that seized my feet so eagerly I almost heard it smack its lips. Minutes ago there had been no quicksand, for I could see my earlier prints embedded in that patch. I stood trapped, shivering uncontrollably, as the glow intensified and the lightless sky seemed to descend—and I felt the beach change.

Simultaneously I experienced something which, in a sense, was worse: I felt myself change. My dizziness whirled out of me. I felt light-headed but stable. At last I realised that I had never had sunstroke. Perhaps it had been my inner conflict—being forced to stay yet at the same time not daring to venture onto the beach, because of what my subconscious knew would happen.

And now it was happening. The beach had won. Perhaps Neal had given it the strength. Though I dared not look, I knew that the sea had stopped. Stranded objects, elaborate symbols composed of something like flesh, writhed on its paralysed margin. The clamour which surrounded me, chanting and gurgling, was not that of the sea: it was far too articulate, however repetitive. It was underfoot too—the voice of the beach, a whisper pronounced by so many sources that it was deafening.

I felt ridges of sand squirm beneath me. They were firm enough to bear my weight, but they felt nothing like sand. They were forcing me to shift my balance. In a moment I would have to dance, to imitate the jerking shapes that had ceased to pretend they were only debris, to join in the ritual of the objects that swarmed up from the congealed sea. Everything glistened in the quivering glow. I thought my flesh had begun to glow too.

Then, with a lurch of vertigo worse than any I'd experienced, I found myself momentarily detached from the nightmare. I seemed to be observing myself, a figure tiny and trivial as an insect, making a timid hysterical attempt to join in the dance of the teeming beach. The moment was brief, yet felt like eternity. Then I was back in my clumsy flesh, struggling to prance on the beach.

At once I was cold with terror. I shook like a victim of electricity, for I knew what viewpoint I'd shared. It was still watching me, indifferent as outer space—and it filled the sky. If I looked up I would see its eyes, or eye, if it had anything that I would recognise as such. My neck shivered as I held my head down. But I would have to look up in a moment, for I could feel the face, or whatever was up there, leaning closer—reaching down for me.

If I hadn't broken through my suffocating panic I would have been crushed to nothing. But my teeth tore my lip, and allowed me to scream. Released, I ran desperately, heedless of quicksand. The dunes crept back from me, the squirming beach glowed, the light flickered in the rhythm of the chanting. I was spared being engulfed—but when at last I reached the dunes, or was allowed to reach them, the dark massive presence still hovered overhead.

I clambered scrabbling up the path. My sobbing gasps filled my mouth with sand. My wild flight was from nothing that I'd seen. I was fleeing the knowledge, deep-rooted and undeniable, that what I perceived blotting out the sky was nothing but an acceptable metaphor. Appalling though the presence was, it was only my mind's version of what was there—a way of letting me glimpse it without going mad at once.

V

I have not seen Neal since—at least, not in a form that anyone else would recognise.

Next day, after a night during which I drank all the liquor I could find to douse my appalled thoughts and insights, I discovered that I couldn't leave. I pretended to myself that I was going to the beach to search for Neal. But the movements began at once; the patterns stirred. As I gazed, dully entranced, I felt something grow less dormant in my head, as though my skull had turned into a shell.

Perhaps I stood engrossed by the beach for hours. Movement distracted me: the skimming of a windblown patch of sand. As I glanced at it I saw that it resembled a giant mask, its features ragged and crumbling. Though its eyes and mouth couldn't keep their shape, it kept trying to resemble Neal's face. As it slithered whispering toward me I fled toward the path, moaning.

That night he came into the bungalow. I hadn't dared go to bed; I dozed in a chair, and frequently woke trembling. Was I awake when I saw his huge face squirming and transforming as it crawled out of the wall? Certainly I could hear his words, though his voice was the inhuman chorus I'd experienced on the beach. Worse, when I opened my eyes to glimpse what might have been only a shadow, not a large unstable form fading back into the substance of the wall, for a few seconds I could still hear that voice.

Each night, once the face had sunk back into the wall as into quicksand, the voice remained longer—and each night, struggling to break loose from the prison of my chair, I understood more of its revelations. I tried to believe all this was my imagination, and so, in a sense, it was. The glimpses of Neal were nothing more than acceptable metaphors for what Neal had become, and what I was becoming. My mind refused to perceive the truth more directly, yet I was possessed by a temptation, vertiginous and sickening, to learn what that truth might be.

For a while I struggled. I couldn't leave, but perhaps I could write. When I found that however bitterly I fought I could think of nothing but the beach, I wrote this. I hoped that writing about it might release me, but of course the more one thinks of the beach, the stronger its hold becomes.

Now I spend most of my time on the beach. It has taken me months to write this. Sometimes I see people staring at me from the bungalows. Do they wonder what I'm doing? They will find out when their time comes—everyone will. Neal must have satisfied it for a while; for the moment it is slower. But that means little. Its time is not like ours.

Each day the pattern is clearer. My pacing helps. Once you have glimpsed the pattern you must go back to read it, over and over. I can feel it growing in my mind. The sense of expectancy is overwhelming. Of course that sense was never mine. It was the hunger of the beach.

My time is near. The large moist prints that surround mine are more pronounced—the prints of what I am becoming. Its substance is everywhere, stealthy and insidious. Today, as I looked at the bungalows, I saw them change; they grew like fossils of themselves. They looked like dreams of the beach, and that is what they will become.

The voice is always with me now. Sometimes the congealing haze seems to mouth at me. At twilight the dunes edge forward to guard the beach. When the beach is dimmest I see other figures pacing out the pattern. Only those whom the beach has touched would see them; their outlines are unstable—some look more like coral than flesh. The quicksands make us trace the pattern, and he stoops from the depths beyond the sky to watch. The sea feeds me.

Often now I have what may be a dream. I glimpse what Neal has become, and how that is merely a fragment of the imprint which it will use to return to our world. Each time I come closer to recalling the insight when I wake. As my mind changes, it tries to prepare me for the end. Soon I shall be what Neal is. I tremble uncontrollably, I feel deathly sick, my mind struggles desperately not to know. Yet in a way I am resigned. After all, even if I managed to flee the beach, I could never escape the growth. I have understood enough to know that it would absorb me in time, when it becomes the world.

Fantasy Tales *Vol. 5, No. 10, Summer 1982. Cover art by David Lloyd*

JUST BEHIND YOU

Ramsey Campbell

I'VE HARDLY SLAMMED the car door when Mr Holt trots out of the school. "Sorry we're late, head," I tell him.

"Don't send yourself to my office, Paul. It was solid of you to show up." He elevates his bristling eyebrows, which tug his mottled round face blank. "I'd have laid odds on you if I were a betting man."

"You don't mean no one else has come."

"None of your colleagues. You're their representative. Don't worry, I'll make sure it goes on your record somehow."

I want to keep this job, whatever memories the school revives, but now it looks as if I'm attending his son's party to ingratiate myself rather than simply assuming it was expected; the invitations were official enough. I'm emitting a diffident sound when Mr Holt clasps his pudgy hands behind his back. "And let me guess, this is your son," he says, lowering his face at Tom as if his joviality is weighing it down. "What's the young man's name?"

I'm afraid Tom may resent being patronised, but he struggles to contain a grin as he says "Tom."

"Tom Francis, hey? Good strong name. You could go to bat for England with a name like that. The birthday boy's called Jack. I expect you're eager to meet him."

Tom hugs the wrapped computer game as if he's coveting it all over again, and I give him a frown that's both a warning and a reminder that his mother promised we'd buy him one for Christmas. "I don't mind," he says.

"Not done to show too much enthusiasm these days, is it, Paul? Cut along there, Tom, and the older men will catch you up."

As Tom marches alongside the elongated two-storey red brick building as if he's determined to leave more of his loathed chubbiness behind, Mr Holt says "I think we can say it's a success. A couple of the parents are already talking about hiring the school for their parties. Do let me know if you have any wheezes for swelling the funds."

I'm distracted by the notion that a boy is pacing Tom inside the ground-floor classrooms. It's his reflection, of course, and now I can't even see it in the empty sunlit rooms. "It was tried once before," I'm confused enough to remark. "Hiring the place out."

"Before my time," the headmaster says so sharply he might be impressing it on someone who doesn't know. "There was a tragedy, I gather. Was it while you were a pupil here?"

Although I'm sure he doesn't mean to sound accusing, he makes me feel accused. I might almost not have left the school and grown up, and the prospect ahead doesn't help – the schoolyard occupied by people I've never seen before. The adults and most of the boys have taken plastic cups from a trestle table next to one laden with unwrapped presents. "I'm afraid I was," I say, which immediately strikes me as an absurd turn of phrase.

"Can we start now, dad?" the fattest boy shouts. "Who else are we supposed to be waiting for?"

"I think you've just got one new friend, Jack."

I hope it's only being told it that makes him scowl at Tom. "Who are you? Did you have to come?"

"I'm sure he wanted to," Mr Holt says, though I think he may have missed the point of the question, unless he's pretending. "This is Paul Francis and his son Tom, everyone. Paul is proving to be the loyallest of my staff."

Some of the adults stand their cups on the table to applaud while others raise a polite cheer. "Is that my present?" Jack Holt is asking Tom. "What have you got me?"

"I hope you like it," Tom says and yields it up. "I would."

Jack tears off the wrapping and drops it on the concrete. A woman who has been dispensing drinks utters an affectionate tut as she swoops to retrieve it and consign it to the nearest bin. "Thank you, dear," Mr Holt says, presumably identifying her as his wife. "Even if it's your birthday, Jack – "

"I'll see if it's any good later," Jack tells Tom, and as Tom's face owns up to hoping he can have a turn, adds "When I get home."

"Do pour Paul some bubbly, dear. Not precisely champers, Paul, but I expect you can't tell on your salary."

As a driver I should ask for lemonade, but I don't think I'll be able to bear much more of the afternoon without a stronger drink or several. As Mrs Holt giggles at the foam that swells out of my cup, her husband claps his hands. "Well, boys, I think it's time for games."

"I want to eat first." With a slyness I'm surely not alone in noticing Jack says "You wouldn't like all the food mother made to go stale."

I take rather too large a gulp from my cup. His behaviour reminds me of Jasper, and I don't care to remember just now, especially while Tom is on the premises. I look around for distraction, and fancy that I glimpsed someone ducking out of sight behind the schoolyard wall closest to the building. I can do without such notions, and so I watch Mrs Holt uncover the third table. The flourish with which she whips off its paper shroud to reveal plates of sandwiches and sausage rolls and a cake armed with eleven candles falters, however, and a corner of the paper scrapes the concrete. "Dear me," she comments. "Don't say this was you, Jack."

"It wasn't me," Jack protests before he even looks.

Someone has taken a bite out of a sandwich from each platter and sampled the sausage rolls as well, though the cake has survived the raid. Jack stares at Tom as if he wants to blame him, but must realise Tom had no opportunity. "Who's been messing with my food?" he demands at a pitch that hurts my ears.

"Now, Jack, don't spoil your party," his mother says. "Someone must have sneaked in when we all went to welcome your guests."

"I don't want it any more. I don't like the look of it."

"We'll just put the food that's been nibbled out for the birds, shall we? Then it won't be wasted, and I'm certain the rest will be fine."

I do my best to share her conviction for Tom's sake, although the bite marks in the food she lays on top of the wall closest to the sports field look unpleasantly discoloured. Jack seems determined to maintain his aversion until the other boys start loading their paper plates, and then he elbows Tom aside and grabs handfuls to heap his own plate. I tell myself that Tom will have to survive worse in his life as I promise mentally to make up to him for the afternoon. If I'd come alone I wouldn't be suffering quite so much.

I let Mrs Holt refill my cup as an aid to conversing with the adult guests. I've already spoken to a magistrate and a local councillor and an accountant and a journalist. Their talk is so small it's close to infinitesimal, except when it's pointedly personal. Once they've established that this is my first job at a secondary school, and how many years I attended night classes to upgrade my qualifications, and that my wife doesn't teach since she was attacked by a pupil, except I'd call her nursery work teaching, they seem to want me and Tom to feel accepted. "He certainly knows how to enjoy himself," says the magistrate, and the councillor declares "He's a credit to his parents." The accountant contributes "He's a generous chap," and it's only when the journalist responds "Makes everybody welcome even if he doesn't know them" that I realise they're discussing not my son but Jack. The relentlessly sparkling wine helps me also understand they're blind to anything here that they don't want to see. I refrain from saying so for Tom's sake and quite possibly my job's. I do my best not to be unbearably aware of Tom's attempts to stay polite while Jack boasts how superior his private school is to this one. When Jack asks Tom if his parents can't afford to send him to a better school than he's admitted to attending, my retort feels capable of heading off Tom's. It's Mrs Holt who interrupts, however. "If everyone has had sufficient, let's bring on the cake."

If she meant to cater for the adults, Jack has seen off their portions, either gobbling them or mauling them on his plate. He dumps it on the pillaged table as his mother elevates the cake and his father touches a lighter to the candles. Once all the pale flames are standing up to the July sun, Mr Holt sets about "Happy birthday to you" as if it's one of the hymns we no longer sing in school. Everybody joins in, with varying degrees of conviction; one boy is so out of tune that he might be poking fun at the song. At least it isn't Tom; his mouth is wide open, whereas the voice sounds muffled, almost hidden. The song ends more or less in unison before I can locate the mocking singer, and Jack plods to blow out the candles. As he takes a loud moist breath they flutter and expire. "Sorry," says his father and relights them.

Jack performs another inhalation as a prelude to lurching at the cake so furiously that for an instant I think his movement has blown out the candles. "Who's doing that?" he shouts.

He glares behind him at the schoolyard wall and then at his young guests. His gaze lingers on Tom, who responds "Looks like someone doesn't want you to have a birthday."

Jack's stare hardens further. "Well, they'd better play their tricks on someone else or my dad'll make them wish they had."

"I'm sure it's just these candles," Mrs Holt says with a reproachful blink at her husband and holds out the cake for him to apply the lighter. "Have another try, Jack. Big puff."

The boy looks enraged by her choice of words. He ducks to the candles the moment they're lit and extinguishes them, spraying the cake with saliva. I won't pretend I'm disappointed that the adults aren't offered a slice. I can tell that Tom accepts one out of politeness, because he dabs the icing surreptitiously with a paper napkin. Mrs Holt watches so closely to see all the cake is consumed that it's clear she would take anything less as an insult to her or her son. "That's the idea. Build up your vim," she says and blinks across the yard. "Those birds must have been quick. I didn't see them come or go, did you?"

Mr Holt hardly bothers to shake his head at the deserted field. "All right, boys, no arguments this time. Let's work off some of that energy."

I suspect that's a euphemism for reducing Jack's weight, unless Mr Holt and his wife are determined to be unaware of it. I'm wondering what I may have let Tom in for when Mr Holt says "Who's for a race around the field?"

"I don't mind," says Tom.

"Go on then. We'll watch," Jack says, and the rest of the boys laugh.

"How about a tug of war?" the magistrate suggests as if she's commuting a sentence.

"I don't think that would be fair, would it?" the councillor says. "There'd be too many on one side."

Jack's entourage all stare at Tom until the accountant says "How do you come up with that? Twelve altogether, that was twice six when I went to school."

"I mustn't have counted the last chap. I hope it won't lose me your vote," the councillor says to me and perhaps more facetiously to Tom, and blames her drink with a comical grimace.

"I don't care. It's supposed to be my party for me. It's like she said, if we have games it isn't fair unless I win," Jack complains, and I can't avoid remembering any longer. Far too much about him reminds me of Jasper.

I didn't want to go to Jasper's party either. I only accepted the invitation because he made me feel I was the nearest to a friend he had at his new school. I mustn't have been alone in taking pity on him, because all his guests turned out to be our classmates; there was nobody from his old school. His mother had remarried, and his stepfather had insisted on moving him to a state school, where he could mix with ordinary boys like us. I expected him to behave himself in front of his family, but whenever he saw the opportunity he acted even worse than usual, accusing the timidest boy of taking more than his share of the party food, and well-nigh wailing when someone else was offered whichever slices of the cake Jasper had decided were his, and arguing with his parents over who'd won the various games they organised unless he was the winner, and refusing to accept that he hadn't caught us moving whenever he swung around while we were trying to creep up on him unnoticed. Now I remember we played that game among ourselves when the adults went to search for him. As if I've communicated my thoughts Tom says "How about hide and seek?"

I could almost imagine that someone has whispered the suggestion in his ear. He looks less than certain of his inspiration even before Jack mimics him. "How about it?"

"Give it a try," Mrs Holt urges. "It'll be fun. I'm sure Mr Francis must have played it when he was your age. I know I did."

Why did she single me out? It brings memories closer and a grumble from Jack. As his allies echo him, his father intervenes. "Come on, chaps, give your new friend a chance. He's made an effort on your behalf."

I wonder whether Mr Holt has any sense of how much. Perhaps Jack takes the comment as an insult; he seems still more resentful. I can't help hoping he's about to say something to Tom that will provide us with an excuse to leave. Despite his scowl he says only "You've got to be It, then."

"You see, you did know how to play," his mother informs him.

This aggravates his scowl, but it stays trained on Tom. "Go over by the wall," he orders, "and count to a hundred so we can hear you. Like this. One. And. Two. And. Three, and don't dare look."

Tom stands where he's directed – overlooking the sports field – and rests his closed eyes on his folded arms on top of the bare wall. As soon as Tom begins to count, Jack waddles unexpectedly fast and with a stealth I suspect is only too typical of him out of the yard, beckoning his cronies to follow. There must be a breeze across the field; Tom's hair is standing up, and he seems restless, though I can't feel the wind or see evidence of it elsewhere. I'm distracted by Mr Holt's shout. "Boys, don't go – "

Either it's too late or it fails to reach them, unless they're pretending not to hear. All of them vanish into the school. Mrs Holt puts a finger to her lips and nods at Tom, who's counting in a loud yet muffled voice that sounds as if somebody is muttering in unison with him – it must be rebounding from the wall. I take Mrs Holt not to want the game to be spoiled. "They won't come to any harm in there, will they?" she murmurs.

Jasper didn't, I'm forced to recall: he was on the roof until he fell off. Mr Holt tilts his head as though his raised eyebrow has altered the balance. "I'm sure they know not to get into any mischief."

Tom shouts a triumphant hundred as he straightens up. He seems glad to retreat from the wall. Without glancing at anyone, even at me, he runs out of the yard. Either he overheard the Holts or his ears are sharper than mine, since he heads directly for the school. Someone peers out to watch his approach and dodges back in. I don't hear the door then, nor as Tom disappears into the school. It's as if the building has joined in the general stealth.

I remember the silence that met all the shouts of Jasper's name. For years I would wonder why he was so determined not to be found: because he didn't want to be It, or on the basis that we couldn't play any games without him? In that case he was wrong about us. As the calls shrank into and around the school, we played at creeping up on one another while he wasn't there to ruin it for us. It was my turn to catch the others out when I heard his mother cry "Jasper" in the distance – nothing else, not so much as a thud. The desperation in her voice made me turn to see what my friends made of it. Could I really have expected to find Jasper at my back, grinning at the trick he'd worked on us and on his parents, or was that only a dream that troubled my sleep for weeks?

He must have resolved not to be discovered even by his parents; perhaps he didn't want them to know he'd been on the roof. I assume he tried to scramble out of sight. We didn't abandon our game until we heard the ambulance, and by the time we reached the front of the school, Jasper was covered up on a stretcher and his parents were doing their best to suppress their emotions until they were behind closed doors. As the ambulance pulled away it emitted a wail that I didn't immediately realise belonged to Jasper's mother. The headmaster had emerged from his office, where no doubt he'd hoped to be only nominally in charge of events, and put us to work at clearing away the debris of the party and storing Jasper's presents in his office; we never knew what became of them. Then he sent us home without quite accusing us of anything, and on Monday told the school how it had lost a valued pupil and warned everyone against playing dangerous games. I couldn't help taking that as at least a hint of an accusation. If we hadn't carried on with our game, might we have spotted Jasper on the roof or caught him as he fell?

It seems unlikely, and I don't want to brood about it now. I attempt to occupy my mind by helping Mrs Holt clear up. This time she doesn't leave any food on the wall for whatever stole away with it, but drops the remains in the bin. From thanking me she graduates to saying "You're so kind" and "He's a treasure," none of which helps me stay alert. It's the magistrate who enquires "What do we think they're up to?"

"Who?"

She answers Mr Holt's tone with an equally sharp glance before saying "Shouldn't some of them have tried to get back to base by now?"

At once I'm sure that Jack has organised his friends in some way against Tom. I'm trying to decide if I should investigate when Mr Holt says "They should be in the fresh air where it's healthier. Come with me, Paul, and we'll flush them out."

"Shall we tag along?" says the accountant.

"Two members of staff should be adequate, thank you," Mr Holt tells her and trots to catch me up. We're halfway along the flagstoned path to the back entrance when he says "You go this way and I'll deal with the front, then nobody can say they didn't know the game was over."

As he rounds the corner of the building at a stately pace I make for the entrance through which all the boys vanished. I grasp the metal doorknob and experience a twinge of guilt: suppose we call a halt to the game just as Tom is about to win? He should certainly be able to outrun Jack. This isn't the thought that seems to let the unexpected chill of the doorknob spread up my arm and shiver through me. I'm imagining Tom as he finds someone who's been hiding – someone who turns to show him a face my son should never see.

It's absurd, of course. Just the sunlight should render it ridiculous. If any of the boys deserves such an encounter it's Jack, not my son. I can't help opening my mouth to say as much, since nobody will hear, but then I'm shocked by what I was about to do, however ineffectual it would be. Jack's just a boy, for heaven's sake – a product of his upbringing, like Jasper. He's had no more chance to mature than Jasper ever will have, whereas I've had decades and should behave like it. Indeed, it's mostly because I'm too old to believe in such things that I murmur "Leave Tom alone and the rest of them as well. If you want to creep up on anyone, I'm here." I twist the knob with the last of my shiver and let myself into the school.

The empty corridor stretches past the cloakroom and the assembly hall to the first set of fire doors, pairs of which interrupt it all the way to the front of the building. My thoughts must have affected me more than I realised; I feel as though it's my first day at school, whether as a pupil or a teacher hardly matters. I have a notion that the sunlight propped across the corridor from every window won't be able to hold the place quiet for much longer. Of course it won't if the boys break cover. I scoff at my nerves and start along the corridor.

Am I supposed to be making a noise or waiting until Mr Holt lets himself be heard? For more reasons than I need articulate I'm happy to be unobtrusive, if that's what I am. Nobody is hiding in a corner of the cloakroom. I must have glimpsed a coat hanging down to the floor, except that there aren't any coats – a shadow, then, even if I can't locate it now. I ease open the doors of the assembly hall, where the ranks of folding chairs resemble an uproar held in check. The place is at least as silent as the opposite of the weekday clamour. As the doors fall shut they send a draught to the fire doors, which quiver as though someone beyond them is growing impatient. Their panes exhibit a deserted stretch of corridor, and elbowing them aside shows me that nobody is crouching out of sight. The gymnasium is unoccupied except for an aberrant reverberation of my footsteps, a noise too light to have been made by even the smallest of the boys; it's more like the first rumble of thunder or a muted drum-roll. The feeble rattle of the parallel bars doesn't really sound like a puppet about to perform, let alone bones. Another set of fire doors brings me alongside the art room. Once I'm past I wonder what I saw in there: one of the paintings displayed on the wall must have made especially free with its subject – I wouldn't have called the dark blotchy peeling piebald mass a face apart from its grin, and that was too wide. As I hurry past classrooms with a glance into each, that wretched image seems to have lodged in my head; I keep being left with a sense of having just failed to register yet another version of the portrait that was pressed against the window of the door at the instant I looked away. The recurrences are progressively more detailed and proportionately less appealing. Of course only my nerves are producing them, though I've no reason to be nervous or to look back. I shoulder the next pair of doors wide and peer into the science room. Apparently someone thought it would be amusing to prop up a biology aid so that it seems to be watching through the window onto the corridor. It's draped with a stained yellowish cloth that's so tattered I can distinguish parts of the skull beneath, plastic that must be discoloured with age. While I'm not sure of all this because of the dazzle of sunlight, I've no wish to be surer. I hasten past and hear movement behind me. It has to be one if not more of the boys from Jack's party, but before I can turn I see a figure beyond the last set of fire doors. It's the headmaster.

The sight is more reassuring than I would have expected until he pushes the doors open. The boy with him is my son, who looks as if he would rather be anywhere else. I'm about to speak Tom's name as some kind of comfort when I hear the doors of the assembly hall crash open and what could well be the sound of almost a dozen boys charging gleefully out of the school. "I take it you were unable to deal with them," says Mr Holt.

"They were all hiding together," Tom protests.

Since Mr Holt appears to find this less than pertinent, I feel bound to say "They must have been well hidden, Tom. I couldn't find them either."

"I'm afraid Master Francis rather exceeded himself."

"I was only playing." Perhaps out of resentment at being called that, Tom adds "I thought I was supposed to play."

Mr Holt doesn't care for the addition. With all the neutrality I'm able to muster I ask "What did Tom do?"

"I discovered him in my passage."

Tom bites his lip, and I'm wondering how sternly I'm expected to rebuke him when I gather that he's fighting to restrain a burst of mirth. At once Mr Holt's choice of words strikes me as almost unbearably hilarious, and I wish I hadn't met Tom's eyes. My nerves and the release of tension are to blame. I shouldn't risk speaking, but I have to. "He wouldn't have known it was out of bounds," I blurt, which sounds at least as bad and disintegrates into a splutter.

Tom can't contain a snort as the headmaster stares at us. "I don't believe I've ever been accused of lacking a sense of humour, but I fail to see what's so amusing."

That's worse still. Tom's face works in search of control until I say "Go on, Tom. You should be with the others" more sharply than he deserves. "Sorry, head. Just a misunderstanding," I offer Mr Holt's back as I follow them both, and then I falter. "Where's – "

There's no draped skull at the window of the science room. I grab the clammy doorknob and jerk the door open and dart into the room. "Someone was in here," I insist.

"Well, nobody is now. If you knew they were, why didn't you deal with them as I asked?"

"I didn't see them. They've moved something, that's how I know."

"Do show me what and where."

"I can't," I say, having glared around the room. Perhaps the item is in one of the cupboards, but I'm even less sure than I was at the time what I saw. All this aggravates my nervousness, which is increasingly on Tom's behalf. I don't like the idea of his being involved in whatever is happening. I'll deal with it on Monday if there's anything to deal with, but just now I'm more concerned to deliver him safely home. "Would you be very unhappy if we cut our visit short?"

"I'm ready," says Tom.

I was asking Mr Holt, who makes it clear I should have been. "I was about to propose some non-competitive games," he says.

I don't know if that's meant to tempt Tom or as a sly rebuke. "To tell you the truth" – which to some extent I am – "I'm not feeling very well."

Mr Holt gazes at Tom, and I'm more afraid than makes any sense that he'll invite him to stay even if I leave. "I'll need to take him with me," I say too fast, too loud.

"Very well, I'll convey your apologies. A pity, though. Jack was just making friends."

A hint of ominousness suggests that my decision may affect my record. I'm trailing after the headmaster, though I've no idea what I could say to regain his approval, when he says "We'll see you on Monday, I trust. Go out the front. After all, you're staff."

It feels more like being directed to a tradesman's entrance. Tom shoves one fire door with his fist and holds it open for me. It thuds shut behind us like a lid, then stirs with a semblance of life. Perhaps Mr Holt has sent a draught along the corridor. "Let's get out of his passage," I say, but the joke is stale. I unlatch the door opposite his office and step into the sunlight, and don't release my grip on the door until I hear it lock.

My Fiat is the smallest of the cars parked outside. I watch the door of the school in the driving mirror until Tom has fastened his seat belt, and then I accelerate with a gnash of gravel. We're nearly at the gates when Tom says "Hadn't I better go back?"

I halt the car just short of the dual carriageway that leads home. I'm hesitating mostly because of the traffic. "Not unless you want to," I tell him.

"I don't much."

"Then we're agreed," I say and send the car into a gap in the traffic.

A grassy strip planted with trees divides the road, two lanes on each side. The carriageway curves back and forth for three miles to our home. Tom doesn't wait for me to pick up speed before he speaks again. "Wouldn't it help if I did?"

I'm distracted by the sight of a Volkswagen several hundred yards back in the outer lane. It's surely too small to contain so many children; it looks positively dangerous, especially at that speed. "Help what?"

"You to stay friends with the headmaster."

This may sound naïve, but it's wise enough, and makes me doubly uncomfortable. As the Volkswagen overtakes me I observe that it contains fewer boys than I imagined. "I don't need to use you to do that, Tom. I shouldn't have used you at all."

"I don't mind if it helps now mother hasn't got such a good job."

The next car – an Allegro – to race along the outer lane has just one boy inside. He's in the back, but not strapped in, if he's even seated. As he leans forward between the young couple in front I have the disconcerting impression that he's watching me. I don't know how I can, since I'm unable to distinguish a single detail within the dark blotch of his face. I force my attention away from the mirror and strive to concentrate on the road ahead. Until I brake I'm too close to a bus. "Look, Tom," I hear myself say, "I know you mean well, but just now you're not helping, all right? I've got enough on my mind. Too much."

With scant warning the bus halts at a stop. The Allegro flashes its lights to encourage me to pull out. Its young passenger is unquestionably watching me; he has leaned further forward between the seats, though his face still hasn't emerged into the light. The trouble is that the man and woman in front of him are middle-aged or older. It isn't the same car. This confuses me so badly that as I make to steer around the bus I stall the engine. The Allegro hurtles past with a blare of its horn, and I have a clear view of the occupants. Unless the boy has crouched out of view, the adults are the only people in the car.

The starter motor screams as I twist the key an unnecessary second time. I'm tailing the bus at more than a safe distance while cars pass us when Tom says "Are you sure you're all right to drive, dad? We could park somewhere and come back for it later."

"I'll be fine if you just shut up." I would be more ashamed of my curtness if I weren't so aware of a Mini that's creeping up behind us in the inner lane. The old man who's driving it is on his own, or is he? No, a silhouette about Tom's size but considerably thinner and with holes in it has reared up behind him. It leans over his shoulder, and I'm afraid of what may happen if he notices it, unless I'm the only person who can see it. I tramp on the accelerator to send the Fiat past the bus, only just outdistancing an impatient Jaguar. "I mean," I say to try and recapture Tom's companionship, "let's save talking till we're home."

He deserves more of an apology, but I'm too preoccupied by realising that it wasn't such a good idea to overtake the bus. The only person on board who's visible to me is the driver. At least I can see that he's alone in the cabin, but who may be behind him out of sight? Suppose he's distracted while he's driving? A woman at a bus stop extends a hand as if she's attempting to warn me, and to my relief, the bus coasts to a halt. The Mini wavers into view around it and trundles after my car. I put on as much speed as I dare and risk a glance in the mirror to see whether there was anything I needed to leave behind. The old man is on his own. Tom and I aren't, however.

My entire body stiffens to maintain my grip on the wheel and control of the steering. I struggle not to look over my shoulder or in the mirror, and tell myself that the glimpse resembled a damaged old photograph, yellowed and blotchy and tattered, hardly identifiable as a face. It's still in the mirror at the edge of my determinedly lowered vision, and I wonder what it may do to regain my attention – and then I have a worse thought. If Tom sees it, will it transfer its revenge to him? Was this its intention ever since it saw us? "Watch the road," I snarl.

At first Tom isn't sure I mean him. "What?" he says without much enthusiasm.

"Do it for me. Tell me if I get too close to anything."

"I thought you didn't want me to talk."

"I do now. Grown-ups can change their minds, you know. This is your first driving lesson. Never get too close."

I hardly know what I'm saying, but it doesn't matter so long as he's kept unaware of our passenger. I tread on the accelerator and come up fast behind a second bus. I can't avoid noticing that the object in the mirror has begun to grin so widely that the remnants of its lips are tearing, exposing too many teeth. The car is within yards of the bus when Tom says nervously "Too close?"

"Much too. Don't wait so long next time or you won't like what happens."

My tone is even more unreasonable than that, but I can't think what else to do. I brake and swerve around the bus, which involves glancing in the mirror. I'm barely able to grasp that the Fiat is slower than the oncoming traffic, because the intruder has leaned forward to show me the withered blackened lumps it has for eyes. I fight to steady my grip on the wheel as my shivering leg presses the accelerator to the floor. "Keep it up," I urge and retreat into the inner lane ahead of the bus. "I'm talking to you, Tom."

I will him not to wonder who else I could have been addressing. "Too close," he cries soon enough. I scarcely know whether I'm driving like this to hold his attention or out of utter panic. "Too close," I make him shout several times, and at last "Slow down, dad. Here's our road."

What may I be taking home? I'm tempted to drive past the junction and abandon the car, but I've no idea what that would achieve beyond leaving Tom even warier of me. I brake and grapple with the wheel, swinging far too widely into the side road, almost mounting the opposite kerb. Perhaps the lumps too small for eyes are spiders, because they appear to be inching out of the sockets above the collapsed shrivelled nose and protruding grin. I try to tell myself it's a childish trick as the car speeds between the ranks of mutually supportive red-brick semis to our house, the farther half of the sixth pair on the right. As I swing the car into the driveway, barely missing one concrete gatepost, Tom protests "You don't park like this, dad. You always back in."

"Don't tell me how to drive," I blurt and feel shamefully irrational.

As soon as we halt alongside Wendy's Honda he springs his belt and runs to the house, losing momentum when his mother opens the front door. She's wiping her hands on a cloth multicoloured with ink from drawing work cards for the nursery. "You're early," she says. "Wasn't it much of a party?"

"I wish I hadn't gone," Tom declares and runs past her into the house.

"Oh dear," says Wendy, which is directed at least partly at me, but I'm busy. Reversing into the driveway would have entailed looking in the mirror or turning in my seat, and now I do both. I have to release my seat belt and crane over the handbrake to convince myself that the back seat and the floor behind me are empty. "Done your worst, have you?" I mutter as I drag myself out of the car.

This isn't meant for Wendy to hear, but she does. "What are you saying about Tom?" she says with a frown and a pout that seem to reduce her already small and suddenly less pretty face.

"Not him. It was – " Of course I can't continue, except with a frustrated sigh. "I was talking to myself."

The sigh has let her smell my breath. "Have you been drinking? How much have you drunk?"

"Not a great deal under the circumstances."

"Which are those?" Before I can answer, however incompletely, she says "You know I don't like you drinking and driving, especially with Tom in the car."

"I wasn't planning to drive so soon."

"Was it really that awful? Should I have come to support you?"

"Maybe." It occurs to me that her presence might have kept the unwelcome passenger out of my car, but I don't want her to think I'm blaming her. "I wasn't going to make an issue of it," I say. "You didn't seem very eager."

"I'm not completely terrified of school, you know."

Despite the sunlight and the solidity of our house, I abruptly wonder if my tormentor is listening. "Me neither," I say louder than I should.

"I hope not, otherwise we'll never survive. Come inside, Paul. No need for anyone to hear our troubles."

"All I was trying to say was I've already made one person feel they had to tag along with me that shouldn't have."

"I expect one of you will get around to telling me about it eventually." Wendy gazes harder at me without relinquishing her frown. "Taking him with you didn't put him at risk, did it? But driving like that did. He's the best thing we've made together, the only one that really counts. Don't endanger him again or I'll have to think what needs to be done to protect him."

"What's that, a threat? Believe me, you've no idea what you're talking about." The sense that I'm not rid of Jasper is letting my nerves take control of my speech. "Look, I'm sorry. You're right, we shouldn't be discussing this now. Leave it till we've both calmed down," I suggest and dodge past her into the hall.

I need to work out what to say to Tom. I hurry upstairs and take refuge in Wendy's and my room. As I stare at the double bed while Tom and Wendy murmur in the kitchen, I have the notion that my fate is somehow in the balance. Now there's silence, which tells me nothing. No, there's a faint noise – the slow stealthy creak of a stair, and then of a higher one. An intruder is doing its best not to be heard.

I sit on the bed and face the dressing-table mirror. It frames the door, which I didn't quite shut. I'll confront whatever has to be confronted now that I'm on my own. I'll keep it away from my family however I have to. The creaks come to an end, and I wonder if they were faint only because so little was climbing the stairs. How much am I about to see? After a pause during which my breath seems to solidify into a painful lump in my chest, the door in the mirror begins to edge inwards. I manage to watch it advance several inches before I twist around, crumpling the summer quilt. "Get away from us," I say with a loathing that's designed to overcome my panic. "Won't you be happy till you've destroyed us, you putrid little – "

The door opens all the way, revealing Tom. His mouth strives not to waver as he flees into his room. I stumble after him as far as the landing and see Wendy gazing up from the hall. "He wanted to say he was sorry if he put you off your driving," she says in a low flat voice. "I don't know why. I wouldn't have." Before I can speak she shuts herself in the front room, and I seem to hear a muffled snigger that involves the clacking of rotten teeth. Perhaps it's fading into the distance. Perhaps Jasper has gone, but I'm afraid far more has gone than him.

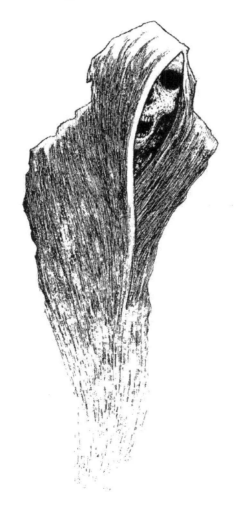

COMING TO AMAZON IN MAY 2021 . . .

It's "ALIENS" vs VICTORIANS vs ZOMBIES! in

DEVIL'S ACRE

EPISODE 1: THE GREAT STINK

ADRIAN BALDWIN

VIVA THE SUBTERRANEAN RESISTANCE LEAGUE!

IT'S THE 1840s AND THE SUBTERRANEANS HAVE HAD IT WITH HUMANS POLLUTING THE PLANET!

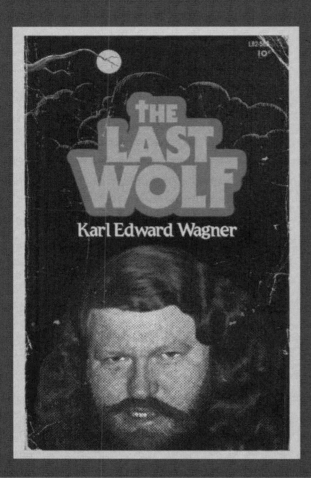

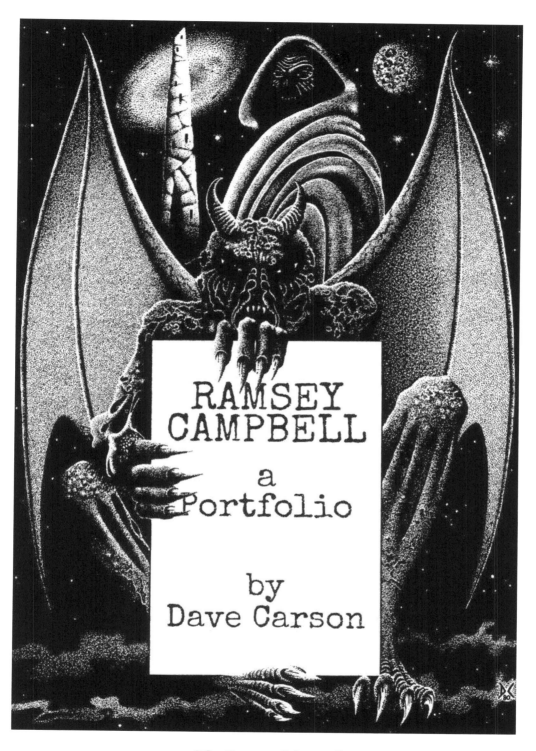

'The Stages of the God'

'The Hands'

'The Tomb-Herd'

144

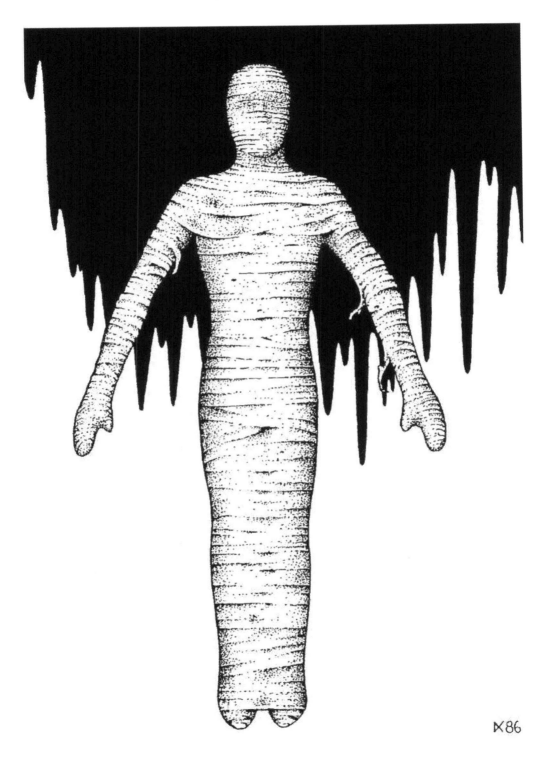

'A New Life'

'Asylum'

'Book shop'

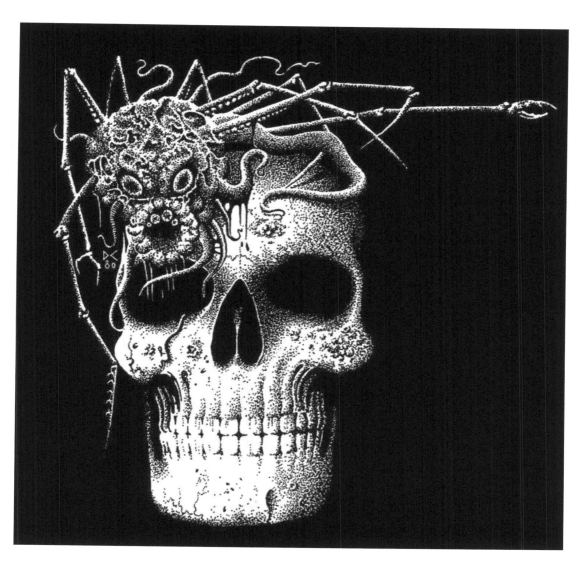

'Skull Demon'

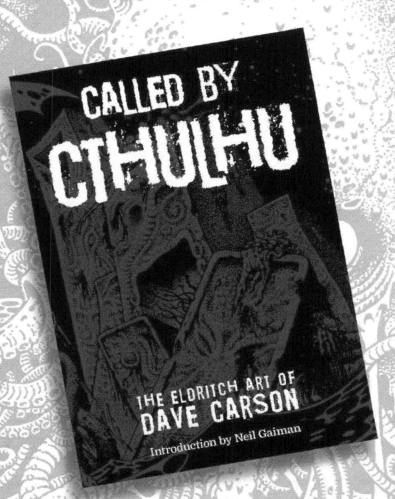

NEWMAN ON CAMPBELL

Kim Newman

*From 2008, the UK's leading critic, **Kim Newman**, presents us with his Introduction for the PS Publishing edition of the Ramsey Campbell novel* Thieving Fear.

Front cover of Thieving Fear *(PS Publishing)*

CONGRATULATIONS. YOU'VE BOUGHT – *and are about to read* – a novel by Ramsey Campbell. You are clearly a person of taste. You are unafraid – though, once you get into the book, that's almost certainly going to change.

Before you plunge into *Thieving Fear*, I'm obliged to detain you a few moments. Of course, those who prefer 'Afterwords' to 'Forewords' are joining us now – probably in something of a state after the emotional and intellectual wringer of Ramsey's uniquely pertinent approach to horror fiction. He's a writer who has no truck with euphemisms like 'dark suspense' or 'occult mystery'. In an era where 'horror' is again something of a dirty word, Ramsey Campbell proudly writes it – indeed, he has the habit of smearing it on padded walls in his own blood, insisting Ancient Mariner-style that you pay attention.

I first encountered Ramsey Campbell's work in the mid-1970s, when I bought the Star paperback of his second collection, *Demons By Daylight*. In my early teens, I had what was then the usual introduction to horror: late-night TV screenings of Universal and Hammer films spurred an interest in the books they were adapted from; once the key texts – Stoker, Shelley, Stevenson, Wells, Wilde, Doyle, even H. Rider Haggard – were devoured, the 'horror' section in W.H. Smith's beckoned, and mostly consisted of Dennis Wheatley's pompous Black Magic novels, with the odd 120-page New English Library proto-nasty (*Orgy of Bubastis*, *Night of the Vampire*, *Dracula and the Virgins of the Undead*) thrown in.

Stephen King was a high school teacher, James Herbert was dreaming up ad slogans, Anne Rice was a poet's wife and Dean Koontz wrote new-wave science fiction. The revolutionary name in literary horror in 1973 was H.P. Lovecraft, dead for decades but paperbacked by Grafton with wonderful covers and finally a mass-market success – which prompted lookalike releases of authors associated with HPL (Clark Ashton Smith, Frank Belknap Long, Robert E. Howard) or hailed by Lovecraft in his influential 'Supernatural Horror in Fiction' essay (Arthur Machen). Ramsey Campbell came across Lovecraft a few years earlier, and was similarly besotted with the work: his first collection, *The Inhabitant of the Lake*, written (and published) at an age which made me (and a lot of others) envy and admire the achievement, consists of Lovecraft/Cthulhu Mythos pastiches which already strain the limited form, reaching beyond HPL's horrors to touch on Campbell's own. *Demons By Daylight* was already the mature Ramsey Campbell – shorn of the apparatus of Lovecraft, and rooted in a sense of place and social context that was all Ramsey's own.

Stephen King writes that Americans think Ramsey sounds like the Beatles – well, maybe John Lennon in his darkest moments (Lennon's experimental/horror fiction gets a tiny reference in *Thieving Fear*), or those chilling throwaway lines ('all the lonely people, where do they all belong?' 'I'd rather see you dead, little girl') between the yeh-yeh-yeh gear. Certainly, Campbell *owns* Liverpool as a setting the way Lovecraft owns New England or King owns Maine. Clive Barker is from the 'pool too – but note how rarely he sets any of his work there, out of professional courtesy. In this book, we have an array of Northern settings – even some forays to London: all written from deep experience, with an M.R. Jamesian sense of the haunted aspects of landscape, though Ramsey is as strong on urban or suburban seediness as desolate shorelines.

Thieving Fear is thematically a follow-up to Ramsey's novel *Obsession*, and is an essay in what we might call the 'four friends' sub-genre. *Four Friends* is the title of an interesting Arthur Penn film from 1981 (scripted by Steve Tesich), following high school comrades on their subsequent, entwined paths – always linked by intense shared experience that hobbles, shapes and inspires the courses of their lives. Other examples of this little-noted form in various media include the TV miniseries *Our Friends in the North*, Robert Silverberg's *The Book of Skulls*, my own novel *The Quorum* (Ramsey was first – but not the last – to notice how much it owes to *Obsession*), the Stan Lee-Jack Kirby run of *The Fantastic Four* (seriously), Alexandre Dumas' *Vingt Ans Aprés* (what ever happened to the Four Musketeers?), the unloved movie sequel *More American Graffiti*, Peter Straub's *Ghost Story* (in which there are *five* friends, though the film drops one), *The Deer Hunter*, and – which is where we came in – the album and documentary *Let It Be*.

Here, the four friends are related and more intensely bound up with each other, even as they are isolated in their shrouds of nightmare. There's magic involved, but it doesn't take the supernatural to make life almost unlivable in Campbell's domain – he is a master at depicting (with only the slightest satirical exaggeration) the way trends in modern business and cultural life erode every possible human value and make the world that bit worse *every single day* (thank you, FrugoCo), but also at showing how *other people* can scrape your nerves – a parade of jolly unsympathetic phone-in callers, co-workers who all seem in on a joke you're the butt of, conversations which always turn around to bite no matter what you say – and seal you into a bubble of despair. Even well-intentioned folks can be devastating, and close friends can do more harm than strangers.

So, read the new Ramsey Campbell. Enter his world of horror. You'll probably find that you've been living there all along. . .

RAMSEY CAMPBELL

a Portfolio
by Jim Pitts

'Above the World'

Fantasy Tales, *Vol. 7, No. 14, Summer 1985*

'The Sneering'

'Mackintosh Willy'

'The Song at the Hub of the Garden'

'The Pit of Wings'

The B.F.S. Bulletin, *Vol. 9, No. 1, May/June 1981*

Jim Pitts Prints

Each print is on high quality A4 paper, approved and signed by the artist before being sealed for protection inside a plastic envelope.

Colour prints are £7.00 each incl p&p

Black & white prints £5.00 each incl p&p

Any orders for 5 or more prints qualify for a 20% discount.

To order please email paralleluniversepublications@gmx.co.uk, listing which prints you would like. You will then be emailed a Paypal invoice.

Jim Pitts is an award-winning artist (two-times winner of the prestigious British Fantasy Award, plus Science Fiction's Ken McIntyre Award), whose work has appeared in numerous magazines and books, both professional and small press.

Check our website: paralleluniversepublications.blogspot.com/

COMPETITION! WIN A SIGNED AND INSCRIBED COPY OF *RAMSEY CAMPBELL'S LIMERICKS OF THE ALARMING AND PHANTASMAL!*

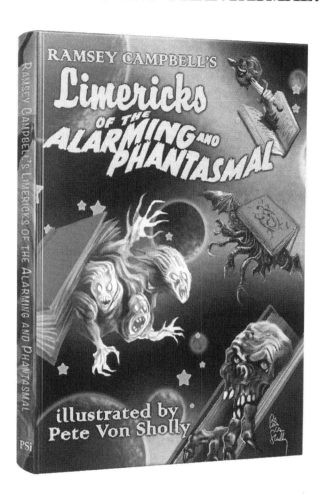

To enter this competition, exclusive to readers of Phantasmagoria, simply(!) identify the original novel, story or film which forms the basis and inspiration for each of the following limericks by Ramsey Campbell himself!

The winner will be selected at random (based on correct entries, of course) on August 1st 2021 and will receive a copy of Ramsey Campbell's Limericks of the Alarming and Phantasmal (illustrated by Pete Von Sholly), signed by the author and inscribed with a limerick based on their name!

All entries must be sent via email to tkboss@hotmail.com no later than 15th July 2021. Good luck!

A SELECTION OF RAMSEY CAMPBELL'S
LIMERICKS OF THE ALARMING AND PHANTASMAL

Though you're missing the Lady Ligeia,
You may think that you'll nevermore see her.
But your previous wife
Is possessive of life,
And your subsequent wives will all be her.

You may think you were nothing but thumbs
And wish for a potion that numbs,
For they'll see that you're mental
About articles dental
When Berenice shows off her gums.

It really won't do to be vague
Or mistake your condition for ague,
For you'll shortly be dead,
Since the chap masked in red
Has delivered the gift of the plague.

There's many a rogue and a sot'll
Rue meeting old Justice Harbottle.
But the end of his life
Is the start of the strife
That will cause him to wobble his wattle.

You may find that he prompts little mirth,
The chap who flops out of the berth.
His cadaverous hug'll
Turn into a struggle
That's more than your voyage is worth.

You may find that you're fit to be tied
When at last you track down Mr Hyde.
Then you may want to heckle
The good Dr Jekyll
For hiding Hyde in his inside.

There once was a fellow named Gray
Who was fond of a life that was gay.
But his need was emphatic
To keep in the attic
A picture that let him make hay.

It's no use to protest even louder
When you find what you took for a powder.
While it sat on the shelf
It transmuted itself
Into something that turns folk to chowder.

You may think that it must be sublime
To be able to travel through time.
But you'll find it's a pox
If you meet the Morlocks,
Which is all I can do for a rhyme.

You'll be shivering more than a leetle
If you meet the prodigious Beetle.
There's no room in a rug
For that magical bug,
Which may make you revert to the foetal.

Never think that the fellow's a boor
To tell you to stay off the moor,
For a nocturnal hound
May be drawn to your sound
And bring a bad end to your tour.

You may find your decision was rash
If you sleep in the room by the ash,
For a witch in the bole
May peek out of a hole
And send spiders to settle your hash.

It's a thing like a pig, not a mouse,
That's at large in the borderland house.
Though the swine is infernal,
Views of the eternal
Will give you less reason to grouse.

If you seek entertainment that's wacky,
The fellow to hear is Carnacki.
His guests he regales
With mysterious tales,
Although sometimes the payoffs are tacky.

Arthur Jermyn was glad to expire
Once he learned of his lineage dire.
The Darwinian truth
Showed his stock was uncouth
And he turned himself into a pyre.

Take care you don't do yourself ill
When you go for a view from a hill.
For the folk who provide
The odd contents inside
The glasses are in for the kill.

It may prove to be hard to explain
That what the hand dropped was a brain.
And if you should face
Those consumers of space,
They'll give your brain worse than a pain.

You must voyage on more than a boat
Before you can see what you wrote.
There's temporal travel
You'll have to unravel,
For the future produces your note.

Beware of the creature called Carker,
For he's eager to make your life starker.
Once he fastens his jaws
He just mindlessly gnaws,
Till you're gone without even a marker.

You might want to have written your will
When you stay in the house that's called Hill.
Once you've chosen your room
You may find it's your tomb
So that you'll be a ghost who's there still.

Let us hope that you'll come to no harm
While you're sojourning at Poroth Farm.
If your hosts fail to blink
It will tip you the wink
That they'll give you good cause for alarm.

Don't ever imagine that hicks
Constructed those shapes made of sticks.
For they're based on old lore
That it's rash to ignore
Or the life you've got left will be nix.

They're a force that you'll struggle to stem,
Those ladies whose names are A--- M---.
And they'll grow more dramatic –
Near anagrammatic –
Till you've killed every last one of them.

If you booked at the premium rate
No wonder you're scratching your pate.
With the personal service
You'll be worse than nervous
When you stay in room 1408.

And a quartet of films:

The Egyptian explorer cries "Lumme!
Do you medicos think I'm a dummy?
I'm confined in a cell
For the stories I tell
About muttering words near a mummy."

Could the method of naming be wrong
That makes us refer to King Kong?
That gigantic ape
May well make us gape,
Yet too teeny to spot is its dong.

Though it looks like a helping of Jell-O,
Its antics may well make you bellow.
A meteorite
Is the source of the fright –
It's the lair of this inchoate fellow.

Your teenager's head's in a whirl,
And the demon inside makes her hurl.
To contend with the beast
You must send for a priest,
And his stole he will have to unfurl.

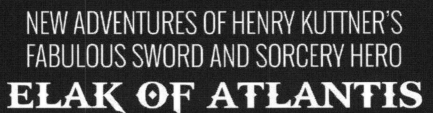

'The Urge'

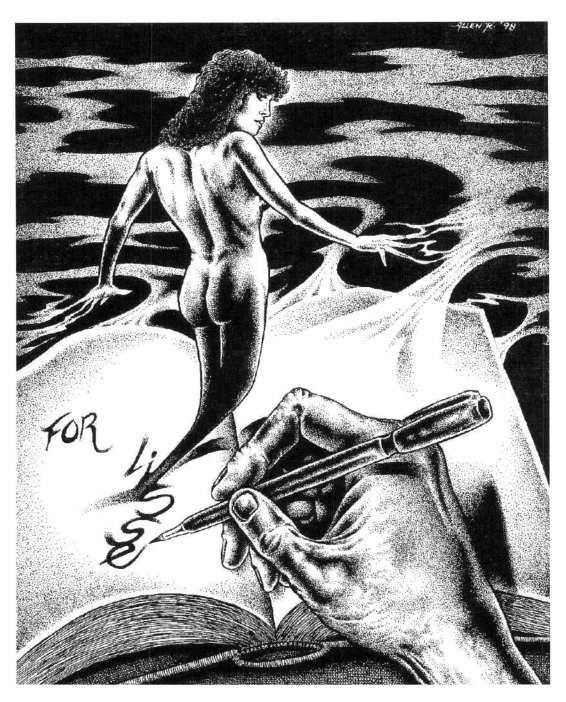

'Kill Me Hideously'

'The Void'

'Macintosh Willy'

Slow

Slow

Slow

Slow

Medusa

Medusa

HAPPY (BELATED) 60th BIRTHDAY! ON THE OCCASION OF RAMSEY CAMPBELL'S 75th BIRTHDAY

Feature prepared by David Mathew

Ramsey Campbell. Photograph by Peter Coleborn

This piece was originally prepared in 2005, in time for Ramsey Campbell's 60th birthday in January of 2006. Unfortunately, it was not published at that time, and appears here for the very first time. Not all of the contributors are still with us, and perhaps – while celebrating Ramsey's 75th birthday – we might also remember absent friends.

—**David Mathew**

Ramsey Campbell: Tributes to the 60th Birthday Boy

I'm sure everyone involved in celebrating Ramsey's 60th will talk about what a cunning, marvellous writer he is. That's a given, but the vegetable I'd like to drop in this pot of Ramsey soup is a memory of his kindness and generosity. We met right after I had published my first novel, The Land of Laughs, *with about as much fanfare as a flea circus receives when it comes to town. When someone told me I was meeting RC at a convention in Birmingham, I gulped because he was one of my great heroes and what the hell could I say to him that wouldn't sound either dumb or fawning? But there was no reason to worry because when we were introduced, he clapped me on the shoulder in his way and went on to tell me how much he had liked my novel and on and on until I almost started purring like a cat. Me first novelist, he Ramsey Campbell. Over the years, I have heard tales like this again and again about this man. What a pleasure it has been to know a person who is as fine an artist as he is a human being. Happy Birthday, Ramsey. A big hug to you from Vienna, with schlag on top.*

—Jonathan Carroll

Although our paths had already crossed at one or two conventions, I only properly met Ramsey in the flesh (a word that assumes suitably macabre undertones when used in any conjunction at all with Mr Campbell) in the mid- to late-eighties.

I had travelled to Liverpool to interview him for Jessie Horsting's Midnight Graffiti *magazine having arranged to meet him at the local cinema where he and Jenny, his ever-delightful wife and all-important First Reader, had been given full access to a mid-morning screening of* The Dead Poets Society *prior to its general release. The objective was that Ramsey could prepare a finger-on-the-pulse review of the movie for his weekly spot on Mersey Radio.*

I arrived around thirty or maybe forty minutes before the end of the film and a cleaner showed me into the darkened auditorium where, able to see three heads around fifteen or twenty rows in front of me (think here of Mystery Science Theater 3000*), I took a seat on the back row and attempted to make sense of the story unravelling on the Big Screen. It didn't take long. And it took even less time for me to succumb to the old lump in the throat (I never watched the full film – haven't been able to face it after such a baptism of fire).*

Thus it was that as Ramsey and Jenny wandered jauntily up the aisle with the Manager, discussing the finer points of camera technique, direction and acting skills, they encountered a bleary-eyed Yorkshireman replete with notebook, recorder and enough stringy saliva to house a squadron of alien spiders hell-bent on world domination. But ever the gentleman, Ramsey did not falter. We bade thanks and farewell to the Manager and made our way to lunch amidst mumbled small talk from yours truly.

That was what happened first.

After lunch – salads, burgers etc, as I recall, all accompanied by the soft whir of my recorder – I was invited back to the Campbells' home to finish off the interview, see some of Ramsey's book collection and have a cup of tea before heading homewards. Back in the car, Ramsey donned a pair of black leather gloves which he then displayed, fingers waggling threateningly, while moaning, Ygor-like (or perhaps Marty Feldman would be closer to the truth...), 'Ah, the hands. . . they have the black gloves on them. . .' Once on the way, Ramsey delighted in pointing out places of local interest – otherwise known as spots where some unfortunates had met their untimely ends – while Jenny (presumably having heard it all before) watched the road ahead.

Campbell Towers (it does not bear that name, though it should) is a cross between the Psycho house and the Addams Family's mansion, all gables, architraves and turrets, squatting feral-like in a sedate suburb of Wallasey. It stretches up to three floors, many of which are now home to books, magazines, videos, DVDs and CDs. They were not quite in such number back then, but they are now. The Campbells still live there, by themselves now – their son and daughter (Matty and Tamsin) having fled the nest for their own adventures – but with occasional mutterings and murmurings, creakings and knockings to keep things interesting. (I can vouch for these, incidentally, having only recently spent the night at their place following one of our occasional reading appearances. Certainly, it would appear that whenever the Campbells walk there, they do not do so alone.)

And that was it.

We've become friends, the four of us (including my wife, Nicky), over the intervening years. Indeed, I'm fortunate enough to have been entrusted by Ramsey with the task of ensuring his work continues to find at least some kind of a home – albeit a modest one – here in the UK. To date, we've published three novels (The Darkest Part of the Woods; The Overnight and, most recently, Secret Stories), a story-collection (Told by the Dead) and Ramsey Campbell, Probably, a collection of his non-fiction essays which went on to win the British Fantasy Award, the Bram Stoker Award and the International Horror Guild Award. With so many novels behind him and so many hundreds of stories, not to mention essays, reviews and articles, it's fair to say that Ramsey is as prolific as – if not more prolific than – he has ever been. That the high quality of his output has been steadfastly maintained is truly remarkable.

And here we are now, at sixty years. A landmark, or so they would have us believe. Well, as we all know... you're either here or you're not here: the rest is just numbers. And he certainly doesn't look sixty. Though he used to.

—Peter Crowther

Talent doesn't much give a damn where it builds its nest. Some of the most ethically indefensible shits I've ever been forced to acknowledge are so jampacked with breathtaking ability that one is forced to conclude that gawd (or whoever's in charge) has a truly warped sense of equilibrium.

Such, happily for all of us, is not true of Ramsey Campbell. The 'shite' part, not the talent part.

Ramsey Campbell is one of those people who, if you're lucky enough in a normal lifetime to meet, is a dear man with a sweet manner and a good heart. Though his writing is obstinately without blemish, engaging, often enough brilliant to want to club the old man out of frustration and naked envy, he is in person as noble and as decent and as charming as the fiction.

As one who is known for holding grudges for decades, I am also grudgingly acknowledged (even by sluggards) as one who does not truckle, either out of friendship or fear. So when I say that calling Ramsey a friend, and a very fine man, even the horned and hamhanded must recognize it as devil's due of a high order.

Happy birthday, Ramsey. Champagne to our real friends. . . real pain to our sham friends. Toss one down for me, mate.

—Harlan Ellison

I'd like to say Thank You as well as Happy Birthday, Ramsey. You may not realise it, but you gave me my first-ever printed quote. You said "Christopher Fowler is writing the kind of horror stories I didn't think anyone wrote anymore." In true

Campbell style, you'd given me a slightly sardonic, back-handed compliment by implying it was better to keep moving on and breaking new ground. I took your advice, and therefore owe you more than I've ever told you. So thank you, for making me afraid of rain and dolls and broken windows, of shadowed corners and deserted backstreets and terraced houses, for defining all the things that made me most uneasy. You were the master of urban unease back then – you're still the master now.

—Christopher Fowler

Every genre needs a figurehead, whether it's a father-figure or a matriarch; someone who links everyone, seems to have a handle on just about every aspect of the field, is as rooted in the past as they're interested in the future, and that everybody looks to whenever things get serious. What I find strange is that 60 seems awfully young for someone who's been the natural great High Kahunga of British horror for as long as I can remember.

My first, albeit indirect encounter with Ramsey was through his debut story 'The Church in the High Street', published in August Derleth's Dark Mind, Dark Heart anthology. He was sixteen when it was published and I must have been about twelve or thirteen when I got to read it. Out of all the stories in that landmark collection, it's the one that's stayed most vividly in my mind. I had an outsider's connection to the genre then, but Ramsey was already right there at its heart.

It's remarkable that someone with such a psychologically harrowing upbringing (documented in his non-fiction pieces as well as being the engine for so much of his fiction) should have grown not only to be our professional rock, but also our Number One Party Animal. If I had to pick out a single memory, it would be of a Saturday night in Liverpool and a convention at the Adelphi. A bunch of us had followed Ramsey's lead to Chinatown and at the end of the evening, as we were leaving the restaurant, the owner was waving away the guarantee cards we offered to back up our personal cheques.

And as he waved them away, he was grinning happily. "Any friend of Ramsey Campbell's is okay by us," he called after us as we spilled out into the street.

Happy Birthday, Ramsey.

—Stephen Gallagher

I probably have an idiosyncratic take on Ramsey's work. His most powerful images for me are those of blighted, dirty, dank neighborhoods that should have long ago been plowed under but that still support a population filthy and leprous in body and soul. This isn't to say they are bad people, simply frightened ones – scurrying scurrying – and grateful for the little rooms that give them the illusion of safety from the human monsters that roam when the moon is high. Days are always overcast here and the rains are as grimy and cold as sewer water. There are never sirens to be heard because these are the forgotten people, where even the meannest coppers fear to tread, and there are only two kinds of music – the wails of human misery and ancient Victrolas playing the music of the dead.

—Ed Gorman

Happy Birthday, Ramsey. Stop being so talented and brilliant and give the rest of us a chance. You should be wearing slippers, taking up lawn bowling and starting to flick through SAGA brochures, instead of which you insist on continuing to be one of the most exciting, original and exhilarating writers in British horror writing. It's not fair. Act your bloody age.

    Lots of love,
    Muriel

—Muriel Gray

The Seven Faces of Ramsey Campbell

Let me explain what I don't mean by the above title. I'm not suggesting that Ramsey Campbell is a shoggoth who can make simulacra of a human visage appear at various sites on his apparently human form. Nor that he is a psychopath capable of assuming a number of radically different personalities. Nor that he is a revenant whose spectral features appear in every flapping newspaper or broken window in the district.

Rather, what I mean to say is that Campbell is the kind of writer who is equally at home in all three types of horror story – and more. Not only is his prose instantly recognisable and consistently disturbing, but he has also brought his distinctive vision and style to bear on practically every type of dark fiction.

Let's begin with the Campbell of The Nameless *and 'The Brood': the master of urban supernatural horror. In the 1970s, Campbell produced an astonishing series of novels and short stories that identified the weird in the modern city: in its claustrophobic environment, its fragmented culture, its neurotic people. Building on ideas developed by Fritz Leiber and Robert Bloch, Campbell went further than either of them in showing how urbanisation had created new shapes and habitats for the unknown.*

Then there's the Campbell of Needing Ghosts *and 'The Second Staircase': the dissonant modernist of horror fiction, echoing both literary and cinematic techniques in his use of imagery to suggest fractured and distorted identity. Like Beckett, Campbell finds something both horrific and benign in the ability of human consciousness to paper over the cracks, to read meaning into the jagged nonsense of the built environment.*

From that, it's not far to the Campbell of The Face That Must Die *and* Silent Children: *a master of the grim psychological thriller. His use of paranoid thoughts and 'real-time' narrative recalls such classic noir writers as Bardin and Woolrich, while his readiness to explore the darkest recesses of the human libido place him alongside Ellroy and Raymond on the shelf marked 'For adults only. P.S. We mean it.'*

Perhaps Campbell has another desk at which he has written 'Old Clothes', 'Out of the Woods' and The Influence: *old-style supernatural tales that echo the ironic, reticent approach of M.R. James. Campbell brings to the 'traditional' weird story the same conviction and attention to detail that characterise his 'modernist' stories. And as with the best of James, the apparent cosiness of the framework is thoroughly shaken up by the time the story ends.*

According to über-critic S.T. Joshi, the Jamesian ghost story operates within the boundaries of a familiar moral universe. A bolder Campbell has used the combined influence of Lovecraft and Blackwood to explore how the unknown might corrode the fabric of reality. His novels Midnight Sun and The Darkest Part of the Woods are bitter metaphysical fables, suggesting that our consensus reality is the tip of a very cold, very dark iceberg towards which our world is blithely sailing.

Another Campbell has ably completed three of Robert E. Howard's tales of Solomon Kane: heroic adventures tainted by the corrupt breath of the macabre. He has gone on to write his own cycle of weird fantasies, including 'The Pit of Wings' – a story whose core image, I suspect, was inspired by a bad experience with Kentucky Fried Chicken. It's worth noting how well Campbell's approach to narrative resonates with Howard's: the close adherence to a single viewpoint, the distortion of subjective time around a horrific incident. Not to mention the appropriateness of Margaret Brundage illustrations to some of Campbell's tales.

The seventh face of Ramsey Campbell is the one that no human witness has described.

—**Joel Lane**

Ramsey is a true original. But he talks funny. The first time I met him, we had trouble understanding one another. His accent and my Southern accent collided like trucks. But we got around it. He is an original and one of the all time greats.

But he does talk funny.

—**Joe R. Lansdale**

While it was H.P. Lovecraft who, for better or worse, led me to devote myself to horror literature, it was Ramsey Campbell who revealed to me that it was still possible to follow one's deepest and most idiosyncratic impulses for self expression without abandoning the genre. More than anything else in my life, I wanted to write horror stories. I could not conceive of writing to any other purpose than to convey my personal nightmares as well as those which I viewed as dominating human life in general. Toward this end, horror fiction seemed to hold the greatest potential. However, this potential had been exploited, at least in my estimation, only in rare instances. Those who had most conspicuously excelled in this literary form in the past were also those who risked alienating its audience by doing what only 'real' writers were allowed to do: create works that seemed entirely strange to the reading public. I wrote 'seemed' because nothing produced by the human imagination can ever be entirely strange to others—it can only have gone unrecognized until someone like Poe or Lovecraft or Campbell comes along. With the death of Lovecraft, I thought that horror literature had made its last leap into strange territory. It seemed to me that the best I could hope for would be to imitate him. Campbell's own career started down that road before it took an amazing turn and showed that the greatest potential of the horror genre did not die with Lovecraft. I do not find it impossible to imagine contemporary horror fiction without Ramsey Campbell. But I do find it impossible to conceive of it as being of any particular interest or worth without him.

—**Thomas Ligotti**

I first met Ramsey Campbell in December 1991. At the time I was Co-President of the Bangor English and Dramatic Society; I was in my second year at university, in North Wales. I'd invited him to give a reading.

As it turned out, I would see many of the core characteristics that make up the man on that one evening. First, the Chinese dinner: our Ramsey writes passionately, as we all know, but he dines passionately, drinks passionately and entertains passionately as well. Having worried about what he would be like to meet, I enjoyed this dinner immensely. He's great company.

Then there was work to be done. Ramsey read ('Apples' was one story but I regret that I can't recall the second), and afterwards I chaired the Q and A. I had warned Ramsey (I thought it only fair) that there would be a certain person in the audience who would be gunning for him in the interview section, she having taken a gross dislike to his story 'The Other Woman'. What impressed me most, not least because – to be frank – we'd had a few glasses by that point, was his steadfast and, again, passionate defence, not only of that story but of the horror genre in general. Clearly a planned defence, granted; but it left me in no doubt that here was an author who could discuss his field as comprehensively and with as much authority as he could participate in it.

At the author's insistence, we took the moonlit short cut back to my place at the end of the evening, this necessitating a walk through the cemetery in Hirael. I can think of no better commendation of Ramsey Campbell than this: he did everything that night, and on the many subsequent times we've met up, to the limit. Even tripping over the border of a grave. . . but that's another story.

—David Mathew

When I was young I sent Ramsey a story. It was terrible and I cringe to think of it. A real window-licker. But at the time I suppose I thought it was great and off it went, and a little while later I got a reply. Ramsey Campbell had taken the time to read my story, give a short critique and encourage me in my endeavours. I've still got the letter. It was a lovely thing to get. I met him a long time later at a convention in Birmingham. He signed my books and introduced me to Dave Mathew and, graciously, had no recollection of my story. Happy Birthday, Ramsey!

—Paul Meloy

As a predictably unbearable teenager, there was a short time – a very short time – when I was a bit embarrassed about my predilection for horror. I could just about finesse SF, but horror was just so. . . naff. At best, I told myself, it was a guilty pleasure. Then I found Ramsey Campbell. I have him to thank for knocking all that nonsense out of me, because there was just no way I could pretend that I didn't think his books were superb. When I pushed them at friends, there was nothing 'ironic' about it. "Read this," I'd say simply. "It's fucking brilliant." I still do. Thank you, Ramsey, for showing what can be done, and thank you for the books, and many many happy returns.

—China Mieville

Ramsey cares more about the traditions and integrity of this wonderful genre of ours than anyone else I know. Not only that, but he is not backward in coming forward (as we say up north) when he feels that the genre has been maligned or misrepresented in some way. To illustrate my point, allow me to share this memory with you:

Several years ago, a major bookstore in Manchester, which shall remain nameless, arranged a Horror Night as one of a series of literary events to launch their new, swish Events Suite (or whatever they had elected to call it – my memory is hazy on such details). It was a filthy winter's night in late January or early February. Rain was lashing down, the wind was howling, fog was wreathing the motorways, making driving conditions treacherous, and public transport was all to cock. Despite this, thanks to the gallant efforts of British Rail (ahem), I somehow managed to traverse the Pennines and arrive at my destination more or less on time. Other guests were not quite so lucky. If I remember correctly (and I probably don't; I've done so many of these events over the years that they tend to blur into one joyous melange after a while) one guest (it may have been Simon Clark, but then again...) had arrived wind-swept and ruddy-cheeked, whilst another (Steve Gallagher?) had rung to say he had been forced back by elemental forces beyond his control and would not, sadly, be joining us.

That left only Ramsey to account for, who was driving over from Liverpool with his wife, Jenny. While we waited for Ramsey and any other late arrivals to appear, we hardy few who had braved the elements milled around, sipping wine, nibbling canapés and making polite conversation. Now, upon my arrival in the store, I have to say that among the many posters and displays advertising other such literary evenings, I had not noticed a single one informing the public of this particular event. I remember feeling surprised and a little disappointed at the lack of publicity, but had resigned myself, as I often do, to the literary world's tendency to nudge horror fiction to the back of the queue, or even dismiss it altogether.

Not so Ramsey. When he finally arrived, having endured a hellish journey in abysmal conditions, he erupted into the Events Suite like an avenging angel, bringing some of that evening's storm with him. Regardless of the prevailing atmosphere of polite conviviality, he angrily requested the presence of the store manager and, when that unhappy, cowering individual appeared, loudly demanded to be told why there was not a single poster, a single display, a single flyer even, advertising that evening's event. Some people looked shocked, even affronted, at his outburst, but I remember thinking how justified his fury was and how delighted I was that he was giving voice to the silent indignation in my own mind. I also remember feeling ashamed that I had said nothing, that I had been quite prepared to stand by and silently accept that once again the horror field and its practitioners, by the non-action of being ignored, had been treated shabbily, shown little or no respect, by those who ought to be glorying in its diversity, emphasising its literary merits, celebrating its noble traditions.

And so, ladies and gentlemen, I give you Horror's Champion, Mr Ramsey Campbell, a man who I am proud to know and who I continue to be proud to call a friend...

Happy Birthday, Ramsey.

—**Mark Morris**

Ramsey Campbell is the best horror writer in Britain today. Actually, that's underrating him – he's the best horror writer of his, and several other, generations. He's also among the best critics of the genre, an erudite advocate of a form often lazily dismissed by dolts and a tireless champion of personal freedoms in a country that sometimes seems compelled to throw them away.

By the time they were sixty, Edgar Allan Poe and H.P. Lovecraft were too busy being dead to do their best work. Ramsey Campbell, by contrast, still has a lot of writing to do.

There should be a Campbell statue put up in every underpass in Liverpool, equipped with a tape-recorder whispering his creepiest stories in the author's own voice.

Happy birthday, Ramsey.

—**Kim Newman**

Go Ramsey! It's your birthday! Seventeen years after discovering your work and I've never looked back. You've been a huge influence on me and have shown me how rich and diverse a genre horror can really be.

—**Jonathan Oliver**

My young man memories – a heated debate on the merits of Losey's film, Secret Ceremony, the awesome fear of M.R. James, Beatles psychedelic joys and the quality of the fishcake and chips we were eating as we walked home one chilly November night in Liverpool (1968).

Happy birthday, Ramsey!

—**Alan David Price**

Ramsey Campbell has been doing small, nice things on my behalf for almost two decades now. He provided my then-publishers with a terrific quote to put on the cover of my debut novel. He wrote the introduction to my first stand-alone novella. I'm not the only person he does stuff like this for by a very, very lengthy chalk, always happy as he is to lend his weight to the task of promoting some fledgling talent or getting some new project off the ground.

And then you meet him. You're expecting some acidic, near-reptilian figure, thin as a wisp and dressed entirely in black, who'll gaze at you unnervingly with darkly-hooded eyes and greet you in a voice like the death-rattle of a beetle. Instead of which, Ramsey turns out to be cheery, often downright jolly, spouting gobbets of demented humour like rounds from some surreal mortar, the life-and-soul of the convention.

Which raises a perennial question in this genre of ours. Why's it always the nicest guys who write the nastiest stories?

—**Tony Richards**

Ramsey and I go back to the Seventies when I had just started my literary agency and he had completed his first novel. The introduction came from Stephen King. In those days they dubbed me The Queen of Horror, with Ramsey, King and Straub on my client list.

We all worked hard but had a huge amount of fun; I still remember how much *we drank. Our lunches in Bianchi's in Soho lasted all afternoon. Ramsey, with his hippie hair and slow, adorably Merseyside chuckle, seemed far removed from the nightmare landscapes he evoked. Reading his manuscripts late at night, the hair on my neck would steadily rise. One scene he wrote stayed with me for years, try as I might to expunge it. Now I have finally shaken it off but Ramsey will remember which one it was.*

Good luck, mate, on your sixtieth birthday. I look forward to being scared to death for at least another thirty years.

—Carol Smith

When I first started reading and writing horror, Ramsey Campbell was a massive inspiration. I'd never read anything like him before - or since, actually – and I can still remember discovering his trademark chill. Fifteen years later, he's still the master – our finest living exponent of the eerie, and the all-time king of unease. Happy birthday, Ramsey!

—Michael Marshall Smith

My profound love to my dear old friend, Ramsey.

—Peter Straub

I'd been aware of Ramsey Campbell as a short story writer since at least the early 1970s, and liked his work, but it was The Nameless, *which I read in 1981, not long after I'd moved from Texas to live in England, that really made an impact. I was so impressed that, most unusually, I read it again, almost immediately, trying to figure out why it was so good, and how he'd done it. In those days (I admit I still incline towards this view) I felt supernatural horror was most effective at short story or novella length – this in spite of the fact (or maybe, who knows, because of it) that I'd just written my own first horror novel.* The Nameless *immediately went onto a little shelf of what I considered to be the rare, brilliant exceptions of completely successful, full-length novels of this kind, along with Bram Stoker's* Dracula, *Shirley Jackson's* The Haunting of Hill House, *and Jonathan Carroll's* The Land of Laughs.

And then, in 1983, he did it again, and even better, with Incarnate.

And has gone on doing it – while never abandoning short stories – ever since, and will continue, let us hope, for at least another forty years.

—Lisa Tuttle

*For more about **Dr. David Mathew**, including his latest titles, please visit his Amazon page.*

MEETING RAMSEY CAMPBELL

Frank Duffy

Frank Duffy

Frank Duffy *reflects with great fondness about the times over his life when he met Ramsey Campbell in person.*

I WAS ONLY eighteen years of age when I first met Ramsey Campbell at a book signing launch in Liverpool at the end of the 1980s. I remember it was a Saturday afternoon, match day for many of the football mad people in the city. For me, it was my monthly pilgrimage to Chapter One Bookshop at the corner of London Road, a stone's throw from the Empire Theatre. It was the type of bookshop which no longer exists, crammed to the ceiling with genre books by Michael Moorcock, Ursula K. Le Guin, Ray Bradbury, and Fritz Leiber, and seemingly endless copies of magazines such as *Cinefastique*, *Fangoria*, and *The Twilight Zone*. It's display windows were just as mesmerising, replica spaceship models from famous American TV shows, and first edition copies of books I was never able to afford.

The second I walked through the door, I hadn't realised how nervous I was. I'd been reading Ramsey Campbell since I was eleven years old, after picking up a copy of *Demons By Daylight* from an outdoor market in Prestatyn, North Wales, in the summer of 1982. The book had a transformative effect on my reading life, although at such a young age it would have been difficult articulating what had appealed to me.

I waited in line, but was unable to catch a glimpse of the author, but sensed his presence lurking somewhere ahead of me, the scratching of his pen originating from between racks of pulp horror paperbacks. I suddenly had the urge to leave the shop, to escape. I'd come with my friend, Tony, one of those unflappable, relaxed personalities who rarely seem out of sorts no matter what the occasion or situation, and it was they who managed to persuade me to stay.

As the line took me along on its unpredictable currents, I finally laid eyes on Ramsey Campbell. He was impossibly cheery-faced for a literary icon. Surely, he should have exuded the po-faced seriousness I'd presumed was the default position most famous authors exhibited. But here he was, laughing, and chatting away with undeniable ebullience, while signing copies of his latest novel, *Ancient Images*. This only made me more nervous, his affability throwing me off guard. There was now a chance I wouldn't scurry away book in hand after a cursory, polite introduction. In fact, I was eager to enquire about his 1988 collection *Dark Feasts*, whose ambiguity and narrative complexities had made me realise how little I sometimes understood. Was I now brave enough to voice my questions?

When that moment arrived, my knees were shaking badly. It wasn't that Ramsey Campbell was an author whose work I admired, it was that he was *the* author. They say never meet your heroes, but in this case I guess the expectations were reversed.

The first thing I remember was shaking hands with him, a courtesy few adults extended me, let alone my literary idol. I showed him the books I'd brought for signing, the aforementioned *Dark Feasts*, as well as *Cold Print*, *The Doll Who Ate His Mother*, and *The Hungry Moon*. He asked me what I thought of them, and, excited that I was speaking to him, I gushed poetically, most of which was most likely unintelligible.

As he was signing my copies, I asked about 'Seeing the World', the penultimate story in *Dark Feasts*. Ramsey responded with enthusiasm, asking for my take on the story, before explaining what I had so obviously missed. Buoyed by my success, I was about to ask another question, before realising the queue was getting much longer.

I thanked Ramsey, and as I was about to leave, he asked me to wait, while speaking to the bookshop owner. I heard him ask for a chair, and although I hoped, in my heart I never for one moment believed it was meant for me. Once the chair was deposited at the table at which he was signing books, he invited me to sit, to continue our conversation. It's one thing to meet your boyhood hero, it's another for the experience to become something altogether unexpected, and in the best way conceivable.

I can't recall most of what we talked about, but I suspect a lot of the questions I asked him might have bordered on the absurd. And yet, I never felt I was an annoyance to Ramsey, who did everything to put me at ease. This must have taken some doing, considering my age and excitability. The only detail which still eludes me is leaving the bookshop, and what I might have said as I departed. There was every chance I floated home rather than take the train back, high on the fumes of the unexpected.

That was 1989. My next encounter with Ramsey Campbell, although not face-to-face, was equally memorable.

In the mid-'90s, I was living in Greater Manchester, in a small dingy flat that almost defied description due to the god-awfulness of its interior. My neighbours were of the nocturnal variety, some of whom I suspect were low-level street dealers. It was without a doubt the worst period of my life, which had stagnated to the point of cliché. And one day, probably not all that surprising considering my environment, somebody stole the majority of the hardbacks from my book collection, including copies of *The Parasite* and *Incarnate*. I was heartbroken by the theft, since it had taken me so long to save up for those books, and more significantly, because my Ramsey Campbell editions were the pride of my collection.

Two weeks later, my mother visited me bearing a large parcel. To my amazement, I discovered it contained several Ramsey Campbell hardbacks, including *The Parasite* and *Incarnate*. Also included was a handwritten letter from Ramsey to my mother. On reading its contents, I'm not ashamed to say I burst into tears. I still have that letter somewhere, and can remember the majority of what was written. I laughed when Ramsey signed off with a flourish, putting a curse on anyone else who might dare to come near my recently depleted book collection. The letter was headed, bearing Ramsey's face engulfed in monstrous inky black tentacles.

Wanting to replace the books stolen from my collection, it turned out my mother had contacted Ramsey through BBC Radio Merseyside, where he often reviewed the latest film releases. This being pre-Internet days, she was seeking advice about the best place to start. Ramsey asked for her address, and promised to contact her once he had more information. Several days later a package arrived, and to my mother's astonishment, Ramsey had sent her the same books from his own collection. All of this despite never having met her, and most likely, having no memory of meeting me either. I wrote to Ramsey thanking him, sending him a couple of bottles of wine, which admittedly my mother selected, knowing my knowledge of oenology was about as proficient as my knowledge of string theory.

Shoot forward twelve years to Christmas 2006, by which stage I was living and working abroad in Poland. At the time I was back in the UK visiting my mother. We were drinking wine and watching a documentary on BBC4 about the evolution of the horror genre. To be perfectly honest, I'm not entirely convinced my mother was as enthusiastic about the documentary as I was, not until Ramsey Campbell suddenly appeared on screen, at which she point perked up. Naturally, our conversation turned to the previous occasions which I'd briefly entered Ramsey's orbit. A couple of glasses of wine later, and I was dishing out superlatives about Ramsey's *importance in the genre*, waxing lyrical about the generosity he'd shown me years earlier. I guess my mother must have been impressed that at thirty-five years of age, I was still as passionate about his work as I'd ever been, so much so, she set into motion a plan I almost dismissed as a practical joke.

I was woken the very next morning by my mother, a cordless phone clutched in one hand, a piece of paper in the other (on which was written a phone number), grinning away at me, which automatically set alarm bells ringing. She proceeded to tell me that I had an interesting day ahead of me, urging me to get out of bed sooner rather than later, saying she'd *just gotten off the phone with Ramsey Campbell*, that he was waiting for me to call him back. Unsurprisingly, I dismissed the story as a practical joke, in fact quite a peculiar one. For although my mother has a cracking sense of humour, she's never been the type to pull someone's leg. Perhaps my abundance of praise for Ramsey the previous evening had awakened in her a devilish sense of mischief.

She pursued me around the house, insisting I was making a mistake if I didn't ring *him*. She was so unlike my mother that eventually curiosity got the better of me. I dialled the number, firing scornful glances across the living room, while waiting for *somone* to pick up. If I'd been expecting anyone to answer, it certainly wasn't Ramsey Campbell.

Someone did pick up. I instantly recognised the voice despite the intervening seventeen years since we'd last spoken. All at once I was calling him Mr Campbell, reverting to a school boy persona in the breadth of single dizzying second. And exactly like the first time we met, he told me to call him Ramsey. I can't really remember much of what we talked about, because all of that was snuffed out in a second when he invited me over to his house for the annual Campbell Christmas party. I said yes before my brain had had time to digest the difficulty of the logistics. I didn't drive a car, and Ramsey lived across the Mersey in Wallasey, over thirty-five miles away.

"That's okay, love, I'll drive you," my mum said.

I was plagued with nerves the entire way there, wondering what on earth I was going say to him, Ramsey Campbell, the greatest living horror author of his generation. The first time I'd spoken to him I'd only been eighteen years old, my worry smothered by excitement. Now in my mid-thirties, I felt stranded in a sea of anxiety.

When I turned up at his front door, armed with bottles of wine (it seems wine plays a significant theme within this article), Ramsey appeared. I heard no music or heady conversations emanating from within. Grinning ruefully, Ramsey informed me that I was indeed the first guest. I might have blushed at my eagerness to attend, but Ramsey was having none of it, ushering me inside to meet Jenny, his wife. If my nerves were palpable, neither Ramsey or Jenny ever let on. Instead they set about making me as comfortable as possible, no doubt aware my barely concealed awe was akin to being the first person on Mars, incredulous it had transpired in the first place.

Soon the other guests started to arrive, a collection of family and friends who poured into the house with infectious, noisy good will. More wine was dispensed, and I soon settled into the *spirit* of things. There was such a variety of people, some of whom came from the exotic world of theatre and TV, including Samantha Giles, who at the time was famous for playing Bernice Blackstock in ITV's *Emmerdale*. My Lord, if only my mother had been present!

Ramsey kept checking to see if I was acclimatising, often introducing me to people as a published author. I confess I was riddled with impostor syndrome when

I heard the words, sometimes imagining I was required to provide credible evidence. Maybe that was evident on my face, for Ramsey invited Samantha Giles and myself to the front living room, telling us he wanted us to bear witness while he tested out the new speakers on his television.

Now, knowing Ramsey's encyclopedic knowledge of films, and that one of his favourites was Max Ophüls's *Letter from an Unknown Woman*, it entered into my head that Samantha and I were about to be treated to perhaps something of similar weight and sophistication. What could it be, I wondered? Perhaps Luis Buñuel's *Viridiana*, or no, how about Ken Russell's *The Devils*, or . . . a list of arthouse classics paraded before my eyes as I took a comfy armchair, settled back and waited for a cinematic revelation . . .

Final Destination 3! The one with the rollercoaster. The one with Mary Elizabeth Winstead. The one whose onscreen sound effects proved the perfect litmus test for Ramsey's speakers. *Final Destination 3*, the one with the nail gun and the cherry picker. *Final Destination 3*, the last film on earth I expected Ramsey Campbell would choose. Of course, in hindsight, when testing out the audio qualities of a pair of new speakers, it makes perfect sense: the screaming, the machinery, the explosions. And yet at the time, and by choosing this film, I realised I also related to Ramsey on a more personal level now. Sure, he was a true cinephile, but he was also, and still is, one of the most approachable people I've ever met.

At around 11pm, my mother returned to pick me up, which prompted Ramsey to run out of the house and across the street in order to coax her inside. I was quite merry when my mother joined the party, although I had strategically stayed alert throughout not wanting to forget the evening. My mother later told me how happy it made her to see me in the company of my hero, relaxed and not at all out of my depth as I had felt I might be. However, she says she became completely lost when Ramsey launched into an impromptu scene from a film (Jack Arnold's *The Incredible Shrinking Man*), especially when he started staggering around the kitchen miming someone of minuscule stature weighted down by a giant hypodermic syringe.

That was the last time I met Ramsey face-to-face. Of course, the Internet and social media have meant that people like myself have managed to stay in touch with Ramsey regularly (for many years I frequented the message board on his official website), or at least with the kind of frequency denied us in the past. If I were speaking about some other author of similar accomplishment, I might suppose this to be the antithesis of what they'd want, or choose, but with Ramsey, I have the feeling he still very much enjoys the camaraderie and normalcy of speaking with people of a similar mentality.

I'm forty-nine now, happily married, and I still live in Poland. My mother talks about Ramsey every time I see her, as does my friend Tony who accompanied me to Chapter One all those years before. Most people who know me know the name Ramsey Campbell, even if they've never read any of his books. I'll be forever thankful for the kindness he showed me, not once, but three times.

For Patricia Duffy who made two of these stories happen

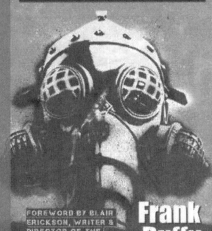

CAMPBELLIAN FICTION

Alison Littlewood, Michael Marshall Smith, Dean M. Drinkel and Frank Duffy provide us with some haunting tales written in the vein of Ramsey Campbell.

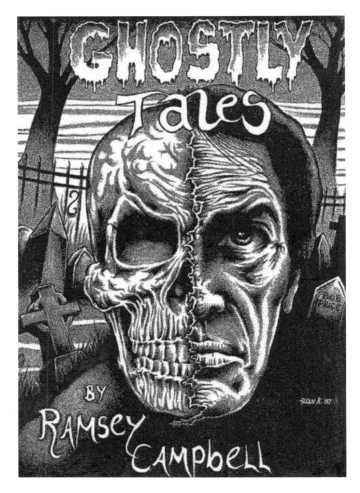

Artwork by Allen Koszowski from Crypt of Cthulhu *#50*

THE ENTERTAINMENT ARRIVES

Alison Littlewood

THE PROFESSOR DROVE slowly down the rain-lashed promenade, passing sign after dispirited sign that marked the boarding houses still clinging to whatever sorry living this place could afford. Westingsea in early May, and the angry sky flung handfuls of rain at its houses and pavements and the battered old black Wolseley he drove, drowning out any other sound. He could see the sea, black and heaving to his right, shifting in as surly a fashion as it always did, but only the rain was listening to any murmur it made. He knew without looking that the belligerent clouds, fierce as he'd ever seen them, were indifferent to whatever lay beneath. Of humanity there was no sign, unless it was the mean slivers of light trying to escape the windows of the blank-faced, three storey properties along the front.

None of it mattered to the Professor. In fact, it was probably better this way; there was no one to see him arrive and no one to see him leave. He required no witnesses, no applause; there would be enough of that later. He knew where he was going and he knew what he would find when he got there, since it was always the same. The jaded, the worn out and the mad: that was who he had come for. Momentarily, he closed his eyes. *After the strife*, he thought, *after the rain, the entertainment*. He could almost smell their clothes, redolent of over-boiled potatoes and their own unloved skin. He could almost feel the texture of it on his hands, and his fingers, resting on the steering wheel, twitched – though sometimes it seemed to him that the car responded to his thoughts, or someone else's, rather than his touch.

He suddenly wanted to look over his shoulder at the things on the old and clawed back seat, but he didn't need to look. He could feel them, as if their eyes were fixed on his shoulder blades, boring into him. Punch had woken, then. He must be nearly there; he saw the spark of irritation from a neon sign to his left, *HO EL*, it said, the T too spent to play its part any longer, and he spun the wheel, or it spun under his hands; he wasn't sure which. The even movement of wheels on road gave way to the jolt and judder of potholes and the car drew to a halt facing a crumbling brick wall, drenched and rain-darkened. He stared at it. He still didn't want to turn around, though he never eluded what he did; it was his – what? Duty? That seemed too mild a word, for duty could be shirked. It's who he *was*. He was the entertainment, and he was here to entertain, and entertain he would. *After the rain . . .*

But for now the rain showed no sign of ceasing. It hammered on the roof and spat at the windows, and he switched off the engine and thus the wipers, and the deluge blurred the world entirely. He realised he hadn't even looked for the name of the hotel, but he had no need to do so; it had called him here and he had answered, just as he always did, even when the day wasn't special, as this one was.

He pushed open the car door, his right sleeve soaked through at once, but that didn't give him pause. Rain seemed to follow him even in the height of summer, and at least this smelled right: of ozone and tarmac and, peculiarly, of dust. He stepped out, retrieving the heavy duffel bag from the back seat before heading for the hotel entrance. He heard the cackle of the neon sign and turned to see that the 'O' had also given up the ghost. A matching spurt of electricity ran down his spine, and he savoured it; he hadn't felt anything like it for a long time. It was a special night indeed. The shadow of an echo of a smile tried and failed to touch his lips, and he reflected that such a thing hadn't happened for a long time either.

The glass doors slid aside at his approach – unusual for the establishments he frequented – and the rain was suddenly cut off and other sounds, human sounds, returned. From an opening to one side came the clink of glasses. Somewhere someone was vacuuming, which made him frown, and he stared down at the dust-free carpet. His shoes were as wet as if he'd emerged from the sea and he shifted them, watching the moisture darken the floor with something like satisfaction. Then a voice, a cheery voice, said: "Can I help you, sir?"

A young woman with sleek hair pulled back against her head was seated behind a reception desk, smiling at him with reddened lips. The desk was grey, as was her uniform, and the wall behind her, and indeed that too-clean carpet. It looked anonymous; the hotels he frequented were often shabby and dirty, but they were never anonymous. The Professor frowned in answer, but he felt a sudden jolt of – what? Hunger? Eagerness? – from within his bag, and the contents shifted as if they were settling, or perhaps its opposite. He walked towards the girl and simply said, "Snell?"

His voice was dry and cracked. In truth he was unused to using it; his real voice, anyway. Sometimes he used his clown voice, or his jolly comedian voice, but not today. Generally, until it was time, he didn't need to; he certainly didn't like to.

"Welcome, Mr Snell. One night, is it?" She wrinkled her nose as if she could smell something unpleasant, then covered her expression by parting those red-painted lips once more. It wasn't quite a smile.

"No." He leaned in closer until he could sense her wanting to recoil, *needing* to recoil, and he stared at her and he did not blink. "The manager. Snell. Booked the entertainment. Snell."

Her forehead folded into wrinkles. "Our manager – Miss Smith – she's not on tonight, I'm afraid sir, but I don't—"

"Snell."

His voice was implacable, and she knew it was implacable, he could see it in the way her eyes struggled to focus when she raised them to meet his. "Of course. I'll get someone for you, sir. I'll only be a moment."

She was as good as her word, trotting into the room from whence he'd heard the sound of glasses and returning a few seconds later with a gangling lad in dark, ill-fitting trousers and a waistcoat with grey panels down the front. He looked puzzled, was muttering something to her, but he fell silent when he stood in front of the Professor, who stared at the pock-marks in his skin until he was forced to look away.

"I'm sorry," the lad began, but suddenly another voice rang out behind him, so bright and full of excitement and somehow *pure* that they all turned to look.

"Punch!" the voice cried. It belonged to a small boy of maybe six or seven, his hair curling and golden, and he grinned and pointed at the Professor's bag.

The Professor looked, though as soon as he saw the shadow of a hand reaching across the carpet towards the child he knew what he would see. The crimson sugarloaf hat with its jolly green tassel had escaped the fastening and was poking from the top of the bag, along with the beaked nose, the hooked chin, the single avaricious eye, staring and endlessly blue.

"Mr Punch!" the boy said again, his voice disturbing the very air, which seemed to reconfigure itself around them. "Is there a show? Is Judy in there? Can we go, Mummy, can we?"

The child looked up at the slender woman with the fond gaze who was holding his hand, and she smiled back at him. "We'll see."

"We will," the Professor said, but it was like being in the car, that odd feeling that he wasn't always the one steering, the one forming his lips into words. It was better when he had the swazzle in his mouth. Everything he said felt right then, even though the sound emerged as a series of shrieks and rasps and vibrations, words that no one else could understand. He realised he didn't know if Judy was in the bag, as the boy had asked. Sometimes it was the earlier one, the older one: Joan. Sometimes it was the newer one, the one he never quite knew where she came from: Old Ruthless.

The waistcoated lad who'd only managed to say *I'm sorry* drew a sigh. "I suppose we could – in a corner of the bar, if it's just a booth."

The Professor answered him with a look.

"Just the one show, is it? Just one? Because we're kind of busy."

"And dinner."

The boy looked puzzled. "I'm afraid service just finished. Chef might be able to plate something up for you, before he goes."

The Professor scowled. "I'll be fed."

He nodded in relief. "Our manager – she left no information about paying you—"

"I'll be paid." The Professor started to walk across that grey, too smooth carpet, leaving the youth to follow in his wake. A special night, and nothing was ready: he did not suppose his theatre would be set up waiting for him, as it usually was, nor his watery soup turning tepid upon the table. It was lucky he always carried his booth; and his puppets – his special puppets – were always at hand, as they should be, or he wouldn't deserve the name Professor, or Punchman, or, as some were wont to call the entertainment, Beach Uncle. And without such a name, what would he be? He supposed, once, he had borne some other moniker, but if he had, he could no longer remember it.

The space opened around him, larger than he had expected; perhaps the night was special after all. The walls were painted a slightly paler grey, too bright, but it was flaking in the corners and the edges of the sofas were scuffed. The bar was grey too, and the high ceiling, lost to the dim lighting, was a deeper shade. He saw at once where he would set up his booth. There was a little nook off to one side, too small to be of use for anything else, where he knew the floors would not have been swept and the dim corners would have been abandoned to the spiders or whatever else cared to take up residence there. Yes: that was the way to do it.

He did not look at the faces of the occupants of the room, not yet. It wasn't time. But his gaze went towards the wall of windows, which were dark, reflecting back the interior of the bar and the deeper shadow where he stood. He nodded with satisfaction. The rain, finally, had stopped.

In the long pause, in the silence and the darkness, the Professor waited. He was on his knees, his back bent; the bag was at his feet with Mr Punch still supine, half in and half out of the opening. Above the Professor's head was the little waiting stage and beyond that was the bar, entirely stilled, its patrons gathered in to a row of chairs hastily brought forward by the lad who'd said *I'm sorry.*

Outside the booth nobody spoke, but he could picture their faces, all turned expectantly to the little rectangular opening draped in fabric that had once been brightly striped in red and white. Without looking, the Professor slipped the swazzle from his pocket and into his mouth, tasting the old, cold bone, and he held it in position with his tongue. He could still sense the excitement creeping from the bag and towards his hands. It was *the* night. Early in May on the seafront, and not just any day in May: it was the 9th, the evening that was recognised throughout the land as Mr Punch's birthday.

In answer to that thought a faint wheezing, a little like a laugh, emerged into the quiet. He was not sure if it came from his own breath passing through the swazzle or the bag on the floor or from the air around him. It didn't matter. Soon they would begin and everything else would end. It was almost time. He reached down, his fingers seeking out Mr Punch's hat, passing over the soft nap of its fabric and finding the opening into which he would slip his fingers. He couldn't see it but he pictured the soft brown substance; its touch felt like skin against his hand as he pulled it home.

He closed his eyes. *That's the way to do it.*

He pictured the little boy's face. *Is Judy in there?* He knew, despite his excitement, the child would not be watching. He was too new, too fresh for any of this. The show wasn't meant for the likes of him. He knew who would make up his little audience: ladies in voluminous chintzy skirts, their face powder clogging the wrinkles beneath; old men, tired from years of stale marriages and disappointing jobs, disillusioned and spent; the worn out, the mad and the lost. That's who would be waiting for him, who was always waiting for him.

In the next moment, he had poked Mr Punch's head up over the stage and an odd sort of sigh rose from the audience. With his other hand he stretched down and rummaged in the bag, finding another soft, leathery opening. As Mr Punch began to shout for his wife, he slipped it on. It wasn't Judy, he felt that at once. It was the original: it was Joan, though he knew the people watching wouldn't know the difference. Sure enough he heard a call of "Judy, Judy!" as he used her little hands to grab her baby from within the bag's innards and sent her up to join her irascible husband.

He spoke through the swazzle, every word and gesture coming as if from somewhere miles distant, the show drifting over him as if he wasn't the one in control at all, and yet it was the same as always; a sense of being in the very right place at the very right moment, though he felt discomfited at that, and an image of that hotel sign rose before him, flashing its maimed sign as a woman's voice said: *Mr Snell. Mr Snell . . .*

As he thought of it, Mr Punch dropped the baby, Joan screamed, and the couple set to, her beating him with her hands, he fighting back with his stick until the sound the swazzle made rose to a scream. Joan fell, though within reach, as she always did; he pulled her into the dark with the tip of his shoe. He knew that she was waiting; she was only ever waiting. And then he realised that no one had yet laughed.

He listened, hearing only silence on the other side of the booth, and felt the stillness creeping from that side of the grimy fabric and into the dark, and the little twist of discomfiture inside him grew a little. But of course all was still; nothing was happening, and he grasped in the bag for the policeman and sent him up to make his arrest until Mr Punch beat him too and flung him into the void.

At last there came a titter, too high and too clear, but there was no time to think of it. The words were forming, the next puppet fitting itself slick and snug onto his hand.

"It's dinnertime." The words were clear, even swazzle-distorted as they were, but as he said them the Professor thought *No, it's not, I haven't had my dinner*, and he knew something was wrong even as Joey the Clown entered stage right and waved his string of sausages at the onlookers. Punch descended once more into the dark and nestled in close. He didn't speak in words, not exactly, but the Professor heard him anyway: *Hungry.*

I know. I know you are.

It's my birthday. I want cake.

The Professor swallowed, carefully, around his swazzle. Punchmen had been known to die that way, choking on the thing that made them what they were: when their time was up. He felt suddenly very tired. His time would never be up, he knew that. The characters were all there, in his bag, waiting: Scaramouche and the skeleton; the hangman; the ghost; the lawyer; Jim Crow; the blind man. The crocodile, who would soon go up and wrestle the clown for his sausages. All had made their appearance in his show so many times, appearing in the very right place at the very right time. Old words ran through his mind:

With the girls he's a rogue and a rover
He lives, while he can, upon clover
When he dies – only then it's all over
And there Punch's comedy ends.

As if in answer, laughter finally came from the other side of the curtain, as the sausages and then the clown went to join Mr Punch's wife in the nothingness beyond the booth. It wasn't the right kind of laughter though, he knew that, *felt* that, and he found himself wondering if tonight was the night and an odd kind of hope rose within him. Tonight, the devil might come, the one character from the show who never did; the devil might come and take them all.

That's the way to do it, he thought but didn't say, because it wasn't yet time: he always knew when it was time. First Punch went back to dispose of the crocodile and then the doctor tried to treat him only for Punch to beat him with his slapstick – "Take that!" said the swazzle – and he too was thrown into space, emptied and wrinkled without the enlivening force of the Professor's hand, nothing but an empty skin.

Another delve into the bag and a jolt of that same electricity he'd felt earlier crackled through him. Jack Ketch, the Hangman, was soft yet cold against his hand. Suddenly, he knew he had to look. He didn't know why but he felt almost sick with the need to do it, and he used Ketch's arm to draw the awning back, just a slit.

The breath seized in his throat. The golden haired boy he'd seen earlier was there after all, sitting in the front row, his smiling mother on one side and a man who must be his father on the other, all of them smiling, not used up, not worn out, not *ready*. It wasn't right. None of it was right, and he realised he'd known it when the steering wheel had turned in his hands and he'd felt the greed rising from the back seat where Mr Punch lay, watching with his blank blue eyes and hungering, always hungering, but especially today.

I want cake.

The Professor closed his eyes. He knew suddenly it was not the right time; it wasn't the right time and it wasn't the right place. It never had been. Snell was waiting, he knew that too. Mr Snell had called him and booked him, the entertainment to follow the strife, to follow the rain, but Mr Snell wasn't here.

The Professor opened his eyes and saw Punch's blue orbs staring back.

"I don't know how to do it," he said, except it came out in a series of wheezing growls, the words lost, because this was what he did: a duty that could not be shirked. Mr Punch whipped his head back up onto the stage and Jack Ketch chased him with his noose, Punch pointing at it, condemned but not ready to go quietly, not yet. "I don't know how to do it." The words, this time, were clear.

Here, the Professor knew, was where the hangman would put his own head in the noose to show Punch how to do it, only to be kicked off the stage and hung himself. That's what was supposed to happen. It wasn't what happened in his show, however, because Joan was back, taking Ketch's place, holding the noose herself and looking about, shading her painted eyes with one hand.

"I need a volunteer," she said, every word crystal-sharp despite the swazzle, the old bone that was cold in the Professor's mouth. He recalled that it was sometimes called a *strega*. The word meant "witch". He had never known why, not properly, and yet somehow he had always understood and had felt strangely proud of the fact, because it showed that he belonged: he was the Professor, the Punchman, the Beach Uncle.

He realised the boy was staring directly at the slit in the curtain, looking straight at him. He nudged it back into place even as the child pushed himself to his feet.

"A volunteer!" Joan shrieked, waving her little hands in excitement, jangling the noose, beckoning him on, and the Professor heard footsteps approaching, too soft and light.

For a moment there was silence. Then Joan made prompting noises, little wheezy nudging sounds, and she waved the noose, and he heard:

"I don't like it," spoken softly and with a little breathy laugh at the end, and the same footsteps retreated, and Joan shrieked more loudly than she had ever shrieked, so loudly that it hurt the Professor's ears.

Then came another voice, a louder, smoother voice, which said "Don't worry, it's fine, I'll show you," and louder, more tappy footsteps approached, and the Professor knew without looking that the child's mother was coming forwards; that she was going to show him the way to do it.

Joan showed her the noose. She slipped it over the woman's head. And then there was a pause because Mr Punch wanted a souvenir; he always wanted a souvenir. He bobbed down and reached his camera from the bag – an old, heavy, Polaroid camera, and he bobbed up and had her pose, trying this angle and that before there was a loud bang and a flash drowned the world in light, just for an instant, and the woman's son caught his breath.

The camera whirred and spat its picture onto the floor. The Professor could just see it, below the old tangled fringe that ran around the bottom of the booth. Faintly, like a ghost, the woman's grin was appearing in the photograph: only that, her lips parted in the strained semblance of a smile, revealing teeth a little less white than the paper.

Then Mr Punch stepped forward and hit her with his slapstick. There was another bang, this time so loud that everyone would be forced to close their eyes, just for a moment, just as long as it took, and the woman was hung, her body limp and falling, emptied of enlivening force; nothing but an empty skin.

"I don't know how to do it," said Mr Punch.

"I need a volunteer," said Joan.

A rough shout came from the other side of the booth, of mingled surprise and awe, followed by loud clapping, albeit from a single pair of hands. The Professor peeked out to see the woman's husband looking impressed, grinning and clapping. They always grinned and clapped. And he realised that the child and his father were the only ones watching the show. There were no worn-out old ladies, no tired and ancient men. The boy wasn't grinning and clapping, however. He was peering to left and right of the booth at the blank grey walls and the grey floor, no doubt wondering when his mother was going to appear again, laughing at his surprise and perhaps, too, his fright.

But his mother didn't appear. Instead his father was coming forward, his smooth-soled shoes making hardly any sound on the carpet. Joan placed the noose over his head. There came a *bang – flash – whirr*, and a photograph drifted to the floor, the ghost of another fixed smile already beginning to form.

"Dad," the boy said from his place in the front row. "I don't like it."

"Come on, son!" his dad replied, his voice full of humour. "It's all jolly good fun!"

The words didn't sound right, even to the Professor who didn't know the man, who should never even have seen him, and yet Joan tightened the noose about his neck and held him steady for Mr Punch, who grasped his slapstick in both little hands and spun, and the man slid to the floor, as empty and used up as his wife.

This time there was no laughter; there was no applause. There was only a pensive little boy looking up at the stage, waiting for his mum and dad to come back.

"I need a volunteer!" said Joan.

The boy shook his head. The Professor peeked once more through the curtain and thought he saw, in the dim light, the glisten of a tear on his cheek. *Don't*, he thought, *don't you do it, that's not the way*, and something in the child sagged and he pushed himself to his feet, as weary as any old lady in chintzy skirts, as any man waiting to use up his retirement, and he stepped forward.

The Professor felt his hands carry out the motions as Joan slipped the noose over the boy's golden head. He felt it as she tightened the rope. He heard the bang and the whirr but he didn't see the flash because his eyes were already pressed tightly closed. He realised he hadn't felt much at all in a very long time. He wasn't certain he ever wished to again. There was only the darkness behind his eyes and then Mr Punch said, "That's the way to do it!" and it was so full of excitement, so full of triumph, and the Professor opened his eyes to see another little square of white, a photograph of a child's clean smile. He knew the boy hadn't been smiling, that he would never smile again, but Mr Punch's camera had caught it anyway, just as it always did.

He lowered his hands, feeling the strain in his elbows and shoulders, feeling suddenly very old. He caught only disjointed words as he started to thrust the puppets, without looking at them, back into their bag. Soon he would be on the road again. He would be driving somewhere else, anywhere, and he knew that it would be raining, and that the rain would smell inexplicably of dust.

Dinnertime, said Joey the Clown.

Birthday, said Joan.

Cake, said Mr Punch, and his voice was the most contented of all: *Cake*.

The Professor slipped his hands under the booth's fringe and felt for the puppets that had fallen. He grabbed Joey and the crocodile and the doctor, feeling the old, cold skin, and then he grabbed the new ones, those who had fallen. He paused when he felt their touch on his hands.

The skin was still warm, and it was supple, and smooth, and soft. He drew them towards him and picked them up, holding them to his chest, then stroking them against his cheek. He *felt* them and their warmth went into him. It awakened parts of him he had rather hadn't awoken because it was wonderful, conditioned by their love, seasoned by their life. They weren't used up and they weren't jaded. They weren't mad or spent or lost. They were fresh and new and something inside him stirred in response.

Cake, Punch murmured again, and the hard unyielding surface of his face pressed up close to the Professor's. *Cake*.

The Professor pressed his eyes closed, though he could see everything anyway. There were beaches outside, not just rain-tossed promenades. There were hotels limned in sunlight. There were roads he had not yet taken. All he had to do was see where the Wolseley wished to go, and grip the wheel, and force it to go somewhere else.

The entertainment would arrive, and he did not suppose they would welcome him in. He had a sudden image of Mr Snell, thin and bent and grey, twitching the dingy curtains of a faded boarding house and waiting, fruitlessly waiting. The Professor decided he did not care. He had tasted cake, the only kind he wanted, but he had not had his dinner; and he found he was very, very hungry indeed.

One day, he supposed the devil might come and take them all. Until then, he would find them: the golden little boys and girls who did not laugh and did not clap. He would find every one of them. He whispered under his breath as he emerged from the booth into the empty and quiet bar. He began to dismantle the stage, his whisper sounding different as he slipped the swazzle into his pocket, speaking in his own voice at last the words that were always waiting there for him: *That's the way to do it*.

This story – a sequel to Ramsey Campbell's own tale 'The Entertainment' – was first published in Darker Companions, *edited by Scott David Aniolowski and Joseph S. Pulver, Sr. PS Publishing, 2017.*

Alison Littlewood's latest novel is *Mistletoe,* a winter ghost story. Her other books include *A Cold Season, Path of Needles, The Unquiet House, The Hidden People* and *The Crow Garden.* Alison's short stories have been picked for a number of year's best anthologies and she has won the Shirley Jackson Award for Short Fiction. Alison lives in Yorkshire, England, in a house of creaking doors and crooked walls. Visit her at www.alisonlittlewood.co.uk.

BEFORE YOU BLOW OUT THE CANDLE

Books One and Two

"Revamped third edition - with two bonus creepy Christmas stories"

Preparing for a Nightmare...

BEFORE YOU BLOW OUT THE CANDLE
Book One

Edited by Marc Damian Lawler

Edited by Marc Damian Lawler

Now available from Amazon

Voted Best New Horror Collection by the Undead Book Club of Britain!

DIFFERENT NOW

Michael Marshall Smith

SHE WAS OUT of the door before Chris had time to grasp what was going on. What had started as a run of the mill argument had suddenly escalated out of control, bored misery giving way to alarm. Then the flat seemed very empty, and she was gone.

Until moments before it had just been the usual depressing bickering, the holding up of past hurts for inspection, and he'd been wondering how much longer he was going to defend his corner. There had been a time when he'd been prepared to stay up all night, had felt bound to hang on in there until the swapping of grievances could be steered towards a new compromise. A time when he could not have contemplated sleeping next to her unless they did so as friends.

But *so many nights*. For a few months or weeks things would be alright, and then the familiar slow spiral towards confrontation would start. She would shout, and he would mutter: both completely in the right, and both utterly in the wrong. These days he didn't have the energy to argue until dawn when he knew any truce was only temporary; or the stomach to put up with melodrama when what they needed was discussion. When the point of diminishing returns had clearly been reached he usually went to bed, to be joined an hour later by Jo, vicious and sniffling. The next day would be very unpleasant, the day after less so. Sooner or later both would apologise so they could start living their lie for a little longer, go on inhabiting the same fragile world.

Chris grabbed his keys and ran for the door. He tripped over the pile of newspapers left in the middle of the floor by leave-it-where-it-drops Jo, and almost fell, but his beat of irritation was perfunctory. This was very bad. He'd looked at her and for the first time seen that he didn't know her any more, as if he was in the room with an utter stranger. Suddenly it hadn't been just another row, a chance for both to be flamboyantly hurt: the cord which had always somehow remained between them had lain there, exposed, waiting for the axe.

Fumbling to lock the door Chris dropped his keys and swore. He didn't like the note of slight hysteria in his voice. It wasn't like him. However loud the shouting, he always stayed distant enough to watch, even when he was centre stage. Stuffing the keys in his jeans he leapt down the steps to the hall four at a time.

The outside door was open, swaying slightly from the strong wind outside. Rain spattered the familiar black plastic bags habitually left in the hall by the tenants of the downstairs flat, who he suspected were also responsible for the grey camper van which had sat outside on four flat tires since before he'd moved in.

He shouted at their door with all his strength, throat rasping: "Oh what a surprise: someone's left some fucking rubbish in the hall!"

Frightened by his fury he bolted out of the door and ran to the end of the short path, wildly looking up and down the street. All he could see was waving branches and wet moonlit patches. He'd hoped that she would grind to a halt just outside the house, but clearly she'd got further. Swearing desperately he trotted back and pulled the door shut before heading out onto the pavement.

She couldn't have had much more than two minutes' start on him, which made it very likely that she'd gone right. Though it was theoretically possible she could have covered the two hundred yards or so to the end of the road on the left side, it seemed unlikely.

Chris jogged to the nearer corner and stood at the insignificant cross-roads, straining his ears for the sound of footsteps. All he heard was the sound of distant traffic on the Seven Sisters Road: the featureless cramped streets of terraced houses facing him were silent apart from the sound of rain on swaying leaves. He called her name and heard nothing more than the thin sound of his own voice. Head down and shoulders hunched against the wind-whipped rain, he trotted out of Cornwall Road, across the small junction and into the road that began the most direct route to the station.

After a couple of minutes he stopped, panting slightly. There was still no sign of Jo, and there were now a couple of choices as to which way she might have gone. Assuming she would have been walking towards the station to head for home, she should have taken the left fork – but she had only walked the route a couple of times, and always with him. Chances were that she wouldn't have had any clear idea of the way, and the alternative road was actually slightly wider than the one which led to the station. Chris had a sneaking suspicion that faced with the choice she might have assumed that was the best way to go. Not that there was any real way of telling: he didn't know if she had headed for the station at all.

Shivering, simultaneously wishing he'd thought to bring a coat and realising that going back for one would lose him any chance of catching up, Chris headed for the wider road, walking quickly.

It was impossible to see very far down the road, as it curved quite sharply round to the left, presenting a blank face of wall broken by occasional squares of light. From his level all Chris could see was patches of ceiling and snatches of curtain. It seemed very easy to believe there was no-one on any of the rooms, that they were empty and always had been. In one ground floor room a black and white television flickered by itself, somehow making the sight even less hospitable than the windows that were dark and reflective black. Disturbed, Chris turned his attention back to the pavement. Somewhere, a long way off, a car horn sounded.

Suddenly he saw a movement some way ahead, and hurried forwards. It was difficult to see very clearly in the steadily falling rain, and hard to see what might be there against the pocks and puddles in the pavement. A shape moved out from behind a car, but it was only a small dog, white and shivering. Wiping rain from his face Chris trotted up to the next junction.

The streets all looked the same. All bent slightly, all had pavements torn apart through years of patching, and all looked orange and shiny black with water, the patterns of light changing as branches of grey leaves slashed in front of the streetlights. There was still no sign of Jo, no sign of anyone. Chris picked a road at random and headed down it.

He was far from sure what would happen when he found her. Nothing like this had ever happened before. If she'd headed for home, which would involve a tube to a mainline station and then an hour on a train, that was bad. If she'd not even been thinking as clearly as that, but had just set off, that was even worse, given her paranoia about walking any streets late at night. Either way it seemed possible that things might finally have broken down, and he realised suddenly that he didn't want them to. However bad things might be between them, she was the only person who really knew him. And more than that, he loved her.

Another turning, another road. Chris felt increasingly desperate, felt an already bad situation getting away from him, and he was now far from sure where he was. Not having a car meant that he didn't know the area very well, his movements restricted to walking to the station and the nearest shops. He thought that the station was probably still over to the left, but when he started to choose left turns the roads bent and doglegged, bringing him back or taking him in the wrong direction, through rows and rows of three storey brick punctuated by sheets of dark glass.

Finally he stopped and rested, hands on his knees and chest aching.

After a few moments the pain felt at once less urgent but more deep-seated, a feeling he remembered from horrific cross-country runs at school. Then, too, the rain had sheeted down, as if settled in for ever. Chris raised his head, squinting into the lines of water.

Someone was standing at the top of the street.

Chris straightened, and took a pace forward. About fifty yards away, motionless and grey behind the rain stood a woman of Jo's size and shape. It had to be Jo. Feeling a lurch of compassion, Chris walked quickly towards her, and then started to trot.

As he neared her he slowed to a walk. She was facing away from him, shoulders slumped, heedless of the rain which coursed down her soaking hair and clothes. She made no movement as he approached and Chris felt tears welling up: Jo hated the rain, and there are always things about someone which, however trivial, make them more them than anyone else.

He stood at her side for a moment, and then gently touched her shoulder. For a moment there was no response, and then she looked up slowly, timidly.

It wasn't Jo.

Chris took a step backwards, confused. The woman continued to look at him as rain ran down her face, not staring, just including him in her gaze.

"I'm sorry, I thought . . ." Chris stopped, unable to finish the obvious sentence, transfixed by her face. It wasn't Jo, but it so nearly was. The face was so similar, so *equal* to Jo's face, and yet something was different. He took a few more steps backwards, shrugging to show his harmlessness, and started to turn away.

As he did so the woman turned too, and he caught a glimpse of her face in three-quarter view. The woman began slowly to step through the puddles, heading up a road he'd already tried. Chris stared after her, and knew what it was about her face.

It was the face of someone he didn't know. The face of someone you catch sight of across a room, the face of a stranger you don't understand yet, a face before you've seen it thousands of times, loved and kissed every inch of it, seen its every smile and frown. It was the face that Jo would always have had had he not plucked up his courage on a night four years ago, and walked across the room to timidly make her acquaintance.

Had he not met her and loved her, had she not become his world, she would always have had that face. The woman's face was Jo's in a world where they'd never met.

Chris started up the road after her, just as she turned the corner. Anxious to keep sight of her, he slipped on a patch of lurid moss glistening blackly on the pavement. Narrowly avoiding a sprawling fall he awkwardly maintained his balance, twisting his knee. Slowing to a fast lurch he painfully rounded the corner in time to see the flap of a coat disappearing from sight. He rubbed his knee for a moment and then set off in pursuit.

He hadn't tried this particular road, and didn't recognise it or the turning. Wiping water from his face he trotted into the sheets of rain, feeling the silence behind the hissing patter of drops. He slipped again navigating the turn at speed but kept his balance. At the end he stopped, chest heaving again. She had disappeared.

There was no obvious way she could have gone. The other three roads all stretched straight for many yards before curving, and it should have been possible to see her whichever way she'd taken. Chris glanced about wildly, peering into the rain. Then he noticed something. The road opposite was Cornwall Road.

Bewildered, he took a few steps forward, into the middle of the road. He turned and looked the way he'd come. The road was unfamiliar, curving a wholly different way to the road he walked down to the station. The road that cut across was different too: it was narrower and had more trees. The whole junction was different, and yet . . .

He walked slowly into Cornwall Road. There, about ten yards up on the left, was the familiar white gateway, the entrance to Number 7, and light fell weakly down from the upper window. Proceeding forwards like a nervous gunfighter, casting frequent glances behind, Chris tried to marry the two views in his mind. But they wouldn't gel, couldn't.

Cornwall Road now joined with different roads, and the grey camper van was gone.

He pushed open the dark green gate and stepped up to the door. Through misted glass he saw that the hallway was clear. He turned and looked at the entryphone. The label by the topmost buzzer said "Price", which was not his name. He wondered briefly where Jo was now, but already the name seemed unfamiliar, ordinary, like that of someone he'd met once at a party, some years ago. His key did not turn the lock, was made for a different door.

Chris took a last look at the house and then turned and faced the rain, pausing for a moment before stepping out into it. He had no idea where he lived, who he loved, where he should go.

Things were different now.

Michael Marshall Smith is a novelist and screenwriter. Under this name he has published nearly a hundred short stories and five novels, and is the only author to have won the British Fantasy Award for Best Short Fiction four times. 2020 saw a *Best Of Michael Marshall Smith* collection. Writing as **Michael Marshall** he has written seven internationally-bestselling conspiracy thrillers, and now additionally writing as **Michael Rutger**, in 2018 he published the adventure thriller *The Anomaly*. A sequel, *The Possession*, was published in 2019.

He is Creative Consultant to the Blank Corporation, Neil Gaiman's production company in Los Angeles. He lives in Santa Cruz, California, with his wife, son, and cats. Find out more about him at: www.michaelmarshallsmith.com.

THEY DREAMT OF ALBERT TOO

Dean M. Drinkel

Author's note: *This is a story written in homage to Ramsey Campbell and his* Scared Stiff: Tales of Sex and Death *collection. I will admit it's a little tongue in cheek and probably a bit transgressive with some Bret Easton Ellis, Dante, Umberto Eco and John Polidori thrown in for good measure. Oh, and it's semi-based on a true story. So you're getting quite a bang for your buck I think. I hope you enjoy it! And thank you Ramsey!*

—**Dean M. Drinkel**

Towson State University, Maryland, United States of America, 1988

I

"NO-ONE WANTS TO be fooled." I flipped the coin over—it wasn't the face of God that stared back at me but some woman ascending/descending a throne. Not what I was expecting. I didn't know her. I wasn't an animal. I dropped the coin, kicked it under a chair—at the party I met Tom. Tom seemed super-cool. He drank beer out of plastic cups like in the movies. He told me he was big in the music scene; there was this band out of Seattle who was going to be massive (even if they were headbangers). He said he'd lend me a bootlegged mixtape he'd got from mail-order. In fact, he told me, there was such an important scene going on right now that if I had nothing better to do we could ride the Greyhound across country and check it out. That way I'd get out alive, he surmised. I didn't hear any mirth—so I said I'd think about it . . . I hadn't seen my schedule yet. Tom scratched his neck and his arms and his chest. He said if this party was a blow-out we'd go to his place (he lived off-campus) and play some records. His favourite band was Throwing Muses or somesuch. Tom spoke a mile-a-minute about music, art, sports, history. When I eventually got a word in he heard my accent and asked me where I was from. I said Liverpool. He said cool. His eyebrows arched. He took a gulp from his red plastic cup and asked if I loved the Beatles. After a pause and after I saw the way he was staring at me I said sure, didn't everybody? Tom slapped me on the back (hard) and let his hand linger on my spine (awkward) then finished his beer and asked if I wanted one. I was gagging for booze. I'd only been in the country a couple of hours and couldn't sleep on the plane and wasn't sure whether it was before or after or whatever the hell the time was. I knew it'd be better to suffer from a hangover rather than jet-lag. Above the DJ's thumping music I shouted yes, I'd murder for a beer. I watched the not-too-pretty girl stick a video in a Betamax player and a film started (it was *Love At First Bite*) but they played it on slow-speed. Tom noticed I was watching so grabbed my hand, pulled me into the kitchen. A book fell out of my pocket. He scooped it up. You like this shit? I nodded. Oh, I thought you'd like something esoteric or even French poetry, know what I mean? Not really. I snatched back Clive Barker's *Books of Blood*, stuffed it back in my jeans. I'm not like the others I said. The others? Yeah, I swirled my beer, you know: poncing around with *On The Road* or *Naked Lunch* or some pretentious shit. Tom wasn't sure if I was serious so burst out laughing. Finish your drink, he suggested, this scene isn't happening. I'll take you somewhere safer. Okay, I said, I slurped my cup. He offered me his hand. I took it. Tom said don't worry, we won't fool around, unless you want to—but I'm not your sweetheart, he stressed. I didn't reply. He dragged me off. Of the guy and the girl screwing against the refrigerator, he never said a word, though he'd never taken his eyes from them the whole time they were there. I'd seen her and she'd seen me and it turned me on. The blood that poured from his neck: a sign of the times.

II

Outside, Tom walked towards the parking lot. It was in darkness. Wings flapped above. Maybe a nest nearby. I wondered what birds made that racket though because it was damn loud. I followed Tom. He seemed confused. Are you okay, I asked. He bent over. His face was red. Blotchy. Was he going to have a heart attack? I told him to take deep breaths—which he did. When he could speak he told me not to worry as now and again this kind of thing happened. His soul sometimes felt so electric. He said if he didn't know better a witch had put a curse on him. I laughed but I could see he was being serious. A lot of witches in Towson? I wondered. He shrugged and said maybe not, but Baltimore? That was different. A lot of dark shit when down there, he added. He must have been high because his eyes were really sparkling. I didn't know why a witch would want to curse him. He shrugged again, said they had their reasons 'cause they were sneaky bitches. He ran a hand over his dirty blonde buzz-cut and pulled off his t-shirt. His chest, his stomach, his arms were covered with what looked like tattoos but the more I stared I realised they were bite marks. Tom smirked. I'm hard-bodied aren't I? And tan. He pointed into the darkness of the lot. You want me to jerk you off now or later? My throat went dry. My heart beat a little faster. Is that on the cards? I asked. He replied that if that was what I wanted, he was okay with it. All English were queer weren't they? I said I wasn't sure that was actually true, anyway I . . . he grabbed my hand and stuck it between his legs, told me to squeeze, so I did. I think I did that just to put a stop to whatever game he was playing but it was obvious he was enjoying it. Tom stared into my eyes—they were a cobalt blue but dead-looking—pushed me away. He said I was cute but I didn't have to worry, he wasn't in the mood. I said I wasn't worried. He said the night was young. I was getting a bit hard myself just like him. He said cool. I said cool too. He waved then stared past me. I looked up as I heard those wings flapping but then there was a truck with some people in it. They'd been at the party. They called Tom's name. He said everyone was going into Baltimore to a séance. Did I want to go? I said sure. Great, he said. What about the witches? He said tonight was their night off. I said cool, he was probably right. He nodded and said yes, he probably was. I went with him to the truck. REM was playing on the radio (some dirge about the end of the world). There wasn't room inside so I climbed in the back. I like the wind on my face. Everybody seemed happy to see Tom, nobody paid me any attention so when we pulled away I almost fell out. I tried not to take it personally. I wasn't alone. There was an oriental-looking girl sitting near me. She wore a long fur coat, not much else. Hello again, she said. She was the girl screwing the guy against the fridge. I held out my hand. She laughed. We've already met—just not in this life. It started to rain, a shower. The drops were deep red. Tom was right, witches existed.

III

What do you think you are doing here? She asked. There was something else but the wind drowned the words. She rolled something between her fingers. Silver. Familiar. She saw me watching (it was hypnotic), made it disappear. She asked me again, what do you think you're doing here? Was she having an existential crisis or perhaps it was too early in American sojourn to come over all Wittengestein so I assumed she meant what was I doing in the back of the truck? I said we were going to the same place. She said, oh, where was that? I said Baltimore. She looked past me. The flapping again. Was it above us? Behind us? Seemed everywhere at once. What had I been drinking? She came closer. Her eyes were green. Her fur coat had opened. She was naked. On her right breast there was a mark. Some skin hung lose. The injury was raw. Fresh. She didn't do anything to close her coat. She smiled. Her teeth were red, something caught between them. I knew I was stoned because she reminded me of that shark from *Jaws*. The girl licked her lips and moved again, got in between my legs. She knelt, fiddled with the button and zip on my jeans. Her coat flapped in the breeze. I started getting hard, of course I did—she was stunning. Her skin, porcelain. She had my jeans and pants down before I was fully up. She grabbed my cock, opened her mouth but stopped. A car behind us honked their horn. She pulled her furs around her, crawled away. I sat there not moving until she said I'd better put my dick away, so I hitched up my clothes. I hadn't gone down. Severely disappointed. She mumbled something about me being dead cute. The car sped past, disappearing into the darkness of the roads. The moment was awkward so I started yattering, telling her stuff about me—I was an exchange student and was going to be around for a while. Her eyes narrowed, said I should be careful, nothing was promised. The truck slowed. A stop-light. It'd turned red. A car on the other side of the road. The one that had been following us. Its lights were out, the engine off and the windows blackened but I knew somebody was sitting inside. She asked me my name, I told her. I asked her hers. She said, Apple. Apple? Yes, Apple. Apple then stood up. I warned her to be careful. She made a noise, said I should watch out for Tom, he couldn't be trusted. I asked why. Apple said he wasn't kind and was the devil. I told her that was over-dramatic. She swirled her finger in the air. I asked what was she doing. She said protection. I said mine? She said, oh no, not yours. I didn't understand but as the truck drove away (the light had gone green), she fell forward. I went to grab her but caught thin air. She'd vanished. As had the blacked out car. There was only the truck and the open road. From the cab I heard laughter. They were smoking. We carried on for ten, fifteen minutes then we were in the city. We found a place to park. You okay? Tom asked as he got out of the cab, helped me down. Did you know there was a girl back here? I asked. Girl? He sounded jealous. I said yeap, Apple. He stepped forward but paused as if something was stopping him. He was enraged. That fucking bitch! He spat.

IV

Tom was raring up, ready to scrap but then his body suddenly expunged the anger. One moment it was powering him, the next it had vanished. Tom turned on his heels, flounced away. I went after him, asked what I'd done wrong. He didn't answer at first but eventually stopped and with his back to me he called me an asshole. I wasn't getting it. He spat on the floor again. With his foot he ground it into the tarmac. He then, very delicately in my opinion, drew his foot up, down, along to the side, up, down, to the other side—was that a pentagram? He asked me whether I was jerking his chain. I said, how could I know anything, I'd only just met him. He said right, right, yeah, okay, okay. He smiled. He came real close up to me. I'll tell you but you're not going to like this. I shrugged, go for it. Apple was my queen, *my* queen. And she died. Six days ago. There's a séance for her in there. He motioned to the club. But you know what? I shrugged again. No. They're not the crowd for you . . . for us . . . should we get the ferry? I was trying to process what he'd said. How could she be dead? I saw her at the party and in the truck. Tom scratched his chin, she was at the party? I nodded. That's interesting, he said. He slapped me on the ass. Let's get the ferry, there's somebody I want you to meet. He walked away. I stayed where I was so he came back, grabbed my hand, pulled me along the street. What about your friends? I asked. Friends? They're no friends of mine. Never met them before. He dragged me down some of the back streets of Baltimore. I wasn't sure I wanted to go anywhere with this guy, I knew I thought he was cool, super-cool but perhaps what Apple had said was true because it did seem he had a screw loose or two but then again, maybe it was me that was losing it because how could I have had a conversation with a dead girl. I wasn't making it up. We got to the port. There weren't many people around. Tom told me to wait outside the office. He went inside then came out after ten minutes or so. He held two tickets in his hand, playfully waved them in my face. I only got singles, he said, because of the time. We can stay over at the Point. Point? Yeah, he nodded really enthusiastically, we're going to Fells Point. He looked at his watch then hugged me. We've got five minutes. I let him pull me along. There was the ferry. We were the only passengers. We punched our tickets, he helped me on board. It was cold but Tom wanted to sit on top. I didn't see any staff but somebody must have untied the ropes, we drifted out onto the water. Christ, I spluttered, I wish we had some drink. Tom stared at me, liquor? Oh I've got something better than liquor. I stared up at the night (could I hear flapping above the noise of the engine and the water?) then he nudged me in the stomach. When I looked his mouth was open. Something on the edge of his tongue. Shall we? He asked. Sod it. Yeah, why not. We moved into one another, kissed. The tab or whatever it was ended up in my mouth and then moments later, fireworks exploded. What was I doing here?

V

I must have passed out. We'd passed through to the other side. Fells Point. Fireworks were exploding all around me. Such vibrant colours. And sounds. Bangs and whizzes and pops and screams. Yeah, the screams were the loudest. This is heaven isn't it? Tom slurred. I stumbled off the ferry but he caught me before I fell ass over tit. The world was nothing more than a blur, Tom in particular—except for his face, that always was in focus even if the rest of him wasn't. He led me from the jetty. It was still night. Was I unconscious? I asked. He nodded. How long? He shrugged, said not to worry because we were both experiencing the same thing. Strong stuff, I mumbled, he said yes. Magical almost. He laughed. From the jetty we made our way up a path towards an area where there were some buildings, shops, that kind of thing. I wasn't able to concentrate, felt so light-headed that if it wasn't for Tom holding me I would have floated away on the wind now blowing. It wasn't all roses though, I had a pain in my neck. Literally. I prodded it. It felt wet. A bit spongy. Tom knocked my hand away. I asked him what had happened, he said something about me tumbling. He laughed again and his laugh was contagious so I started laughing too. I asked him if there was anybody about and he said not anymore, which was odd but I had to sit down so he carried me to a bench. Are you going to throw up? He asked. I don't think so. Nonetheless he forced my head between my legs. I didn't think that was going to make much difference. I was hot and sweaty but bloody freezing. When I spoke I could see mist. I said to Tom I could do with some water and he said when we got where we were going there would be plenty to drink. He asked me if I could stand and I said I wasn't sure. Tom wrapped his arms around me, pulled me into him. He was mumbling to himself. It sounded like he was saying sorry, sorry, sorry over and over again. He asked me if I could walk, I said I wasn't sure because my legs were jelly and he said his were too and that not to worry as it'd all be over soon and soon I could sleep. I said great. I could hear something . . . no, someone . . . people. People were coming from over the hill. There was light too and suddenly I was warm. We were surrounded. All these people carrying burning torches. They were naked. There was a girl and a guy and they stood in front of me and held out their hands. I turned to Tom and he smiled and nodded and said I should go with them. I said was he coming and he said not this time. I let the girl and guy lift me to my feet. Somebody removed my clothes. Somebody else stroked the wound to my neck and said that it had begun. Begun? What had begun? The blood ceremony, someone whispered. I was naked but so was everybody else so what was the point of being ashamed? There was chanting and singing and we danced from the bench through the trees to a building, it was small and wooden. There were people waiting for us. And then somebody, somebody I thought I recognised, though they looked different touched my forehead and I fell backwards. Tom wasn't there to catch me.

VI

They'd forced me onto my knees—wood dug into my flesh. I was aflame. I was a bit more compos mentis though my breathing was heavy. The building was a large chamber. A church. Rose petals covered the floor. As my eyes focused I realised they weren't petals but slabs of skin. I tried to lift my head but somebody pushed me down. In reverence. But I'd managed to see that the walls of the church were lined with naked people. Their energy was expectant. Rampant. Before me was a throne and perched on the throne like a crow, was an old woman. She wasn't just old, ancient. She looked oriental. She was naked too but covered in furs. She issued a command—I was lifted and carried, dropped unceremoniously by her feet. She reached down and caressed my face. Is this the ending you thought you'd see? She asked. I could put you in a cage if that was what you wanted? I could have slit your throat and pirouetted in your red tears. I went to answer but when I opened my mouth, a waterfall of blood cascaded out. The pain hit me—they'd taken my tongue. You don't even know where you end and I start, she chuckled. She dipped a finger into my scarlet self and prodded the wound on her breast. The others started swaying. They started to fuck. Men and women. Women and men. Men and men. Women and women. The Queen, Empress, whatever the hell she was, opened her legs. Maggots fell from her rotting corpse. I did dream of you once, she whispered, but you were stolen from me. We were connected by a ruby coloured umbilical then he came and—she motioned as if her fingers were scissors and fell silent. Somebody kissed me, no several people were kissing me. I was grabbed between the legs and my body began to pull/push. This will be the way of things, the old woman cackled. The chamber was suffocated by the stench of sex. It was offensive. I mounted the man, I mounted the woman. I was close . . . I was close . . . my hips moved as I too was mounted. Then this Empress stood, placed something in my mouth. A silver coin. You are mine and I want you all to myself, she screamed and the world around me shimmered and evaporated. Are you okay? The girl asked. I took a breath. I was leaning up against the fridge. I was at a party. Her legs were wrapped around me. Are you okay? She asked again. I said I wasn't sure. She kissed me. Her hand down the front of my jeans. She could tell that I wasn't really into it. Don't you want me? She asked. She didn't wait for me to answer. She stepped backwards, wiped her mouth with the back of her hand. There was blood. Did you bite me? I asked, touching my neck. Only because you offered yourself, she said. Somebody was watching us. He was kind of cute. He offered a half-eaten apple to me. He pulled a maggot from it. I smiled. He beckoned me to him. As the girl spun around the kitchen, I joined him by the window. You ever feel you've lost your crown? He asked. I know what you mean, I replied, watching the drunken girl dance. I liked this guy. I was going to be him, he was that cool. I've dreamt of you many times, we whispered. I took his hand and when nobody was looking, and under a black crescent moon we plummeted from the room . . .

Ambitious, **Dean M. Drinkel** is a published author, editor, award winning script-writer and film director and was Associate Editor of *FEAR* magazine. In 2018 he established the horror press Demain Publishing. In 2020 he joined the board of film and TV production company Mystic & Mainstream. More about him can be found at: www.deanmdrinkel.com.

THE DEPTHS OF BELIEF

Frank Duffy

FOR A MOMENT Theo forgot he was no longer a pupil but a teacher, and flicked his cigarette over the hedgerow as Lambeth stalked into view.

"I'll have you lot out on the rugby pitch first thing tomorrow morning," the chemistry teacher yelled at a group of second years.

Theo heard someone shout *fuck off* in response, which made Antonia giggle. Ahead of them, pupils shambled along the narrow countryside pavements, irate teachers volleying commands at them. The annual sponsored walk was despised by everyone.

"Tell me those aren't ours," Antonia said.

He turned to see a couple sprinting away, the sun glaring down on them as they passed a sign for *Black Temple Caves*.

Antonia cupped her face.

"Hard to say."

"We should go after them."

"They won't thank you for it."

"I know."

"So why bother?"

"Lambeth will go ballistic, and they're just kids."

Antonia gave him a quick kiss.

"That was risky," he said, grinning.

"You're such a strategist."

"I'm not."

"You are, and you know it. Showing me you're a soft touch. Appealing to my caring sensitive side."

"You don't have one," Theo grinned.

They followed the pupils to the top of a grassy hill overlooking acres of cabbage fields. In the flitting shadows below, the pupils were momentarily visible, laughter drifting away as they darted into some trees.

"They're heading to the caves."

"Little bastards. They probably think we won't bother."

They trotted down the hill, scuffing up dirt, coming across a fence lying toppled in the grass, wooden posts jutting from the earth.

"This way," Theo said.

He glanced back over his shoulder, the hill looking much further away. Spiky bushes filled the gloom, rocks appearing from the undergrowth like tumorous infestations. The ground became a muddy slope, trees bent crookedly, roots exposed. Antonia put a finger to her lips, listening. Voices. Only they weren't so audible for Theo to make out where they were heading.

"Why the caves?" Antonia asked.

"Maybe they want some alone time."

She grinned at him.

"Good idea."

Theo saw how dark it was in the spaces between the trees, continuing down the slope, grabbing branches to stop from falling. Antonia slid past with far more agility.

"Steady there, Mr Williams."

They followed a mud-spattered avenue, daylight scarcely piercing the murkiness. The path narrowed, trees replaced by solid rock. Theo threw up his arms, an explorer proving his doubters wrong.

"Here we are."

The cave entrance was as fathomless as a black hole. Antonia craned her neck inside.

"They can't have gone in."

A decade spent teaching geography to year four students told Theo they were naïve to assume the opposite. There was a noise from within the cave, someone clambering over rocks.

"It's time we called Lambeth."

"I thought you said they were just kids?"

"I'm not breaking my neck for them.

"I was right. You are a strategist."

Theo pulled out his iPhone.

"About what?

"Making me think you weren't going to grass them up."

"That's a bit harsh."

He waited for a dialling tone, but instead got only the blank nothingness of a phone without a signal.

"Out of range."

Antonia tried hers.

"Same here."

"Shit."

"We don't have a choice."

"Lead on."

"In your dreams."

Theo shone his phone backlight into the cave, very little emerging except for a curvature of rock dripping with moisture. Antonia was close behind him, her breath amplified.

"Can't make out a thing," he said.

Antonia answered, but sounded much further away.

"Say that again."

Her voice receded.

"Wait."

He aimed his phone, but was met by blackness. Somewhere deep within the rockface he could hear her, so faint he couldn't tell whether it was anything more than his imagination. He walked a couple of paces before coming up against dripping limestone walls which sloped away into even blacker depths. He held the phone up to his face, his breath a misty white vapour floating out into the echoing subterranean darkness.

"Antonia?"

Someone moved to his right, or at least he thought they had, except any attempt to shine the backlight was swallowed by unfathomable blackness.

"Can't see a thing," he shouted.

There was a glimmer from up ahead, the backlight illuminating a crevice just about wide enough for his body. Who knew where it might lead, but he couldn't stay here, his phone battery wouldn't last much longer.

The crevice was much narrower than it had first appeared, Theo manipulating his limbs in ways he never thought possible. For a terrifying moment, he thought he was going to get stuck, before managing to slide his arms and hands free, wriggling out onto the other side.

He landed on his knees, cold moist air passing over his face like clammy hands searching for definition. Up ahead light flickered off the walls, a passage zigzagging towards it with unmistaken human precision. A way out?

He bent low, following the passage, and after a minute or so, was standing in an enclosed space about thirty metres across. The light came from dozens of candles on a large limestone rock protruding from the ground. He stared, as if he could renounce its existence with the power of disbelief, ironic considering what it was.

In the chilly subterranean darkness someone had built an altar. A threadbare sacrament cloth covered its jagged surface, with a small wooden communion dish at one end. Encumbered with such human meaning, and yet removed from its normal environment, it was an anomaly. It had no right being here.

There was an old childhood story about the caves, about exiled Catholics conducting illegal masses to escape the Elizabethan purges of the late sixteenth century. Up until now hadn't believed it.

The ground swayed with the flickering candle light, a rhythmical blackness undulating across the chamber. This time he was mistaken, not realising until almost too late that he was looking at a carpet comprised of human limbs. Lying prostate before the altar were many human forms. One of them sensed he was there, and turned their face towards the backlight, eye sockets fleetingly illuminated. Theo spun about, his throat constricting, and ran back into the passage, panting breathlessly.

The ceiling was lower than he remembered, and he had to crouch as he manoeuvered along the passage. Soon he was crawling, pushing against the immovable rockface, dust scratching at his eyeballs. It was a different passage, he was going in the wrong direction. It was too late to turn back, even if he'd wanted to.

There was a sudden violent vibration in his hand as the backlight vanished faster than the stammering of his heart. Ordinarily, he might have considered his options, but something else crystalized his terror into a single overriding imperative. Survival. One trouser leg rose up his shin, exposing his ankle, fingers enclosing about it, pressing into the flesh.

Theo pulled away, screaming so loudly he thought it would bring the passage crashing down on him. But not even this could stop him from moving forward, knowing without hesitation what would happen if he did.

He was starting to imagine he was going to die down here, when the passage ended. Sunlight poured into his upturned face. He was on his feet within seconds, dodging rocks, intuiting their presence.

"Theo."

Antonia.

He almost stopped running, turning his head, except his legs refused to be slowed. Perhaps she was outside, calling him to safety. The world beyond the cave entrance resembled a diorama, tempting in its authenticity, achingly close.

"Don't leave me."

This time he saw her on the opposite side of the cave, emerging from a hole in the ground. Forcing her body out, the muscles in her face contorted with the effort. Her blackened face, eyes rimmed with dirt, fixed on him. He knew her well enough to know she was willing him to her rescue.

She squirmed out of the hole and was almost on her feet, when something writhed out after her.

"Wait."

He didn't look at what happened next, not even when she called his name one last time, before falling silent.

Theo hurtled out into the daylight with the necessity of a sprinter, knowing in his heart that Antonia's description of him had been accurate. He was indeed a strategist.

Frank Duffy is the author of five short story collections, *The Signal Block and Other Tales* (Sideshow Press), *Unknown Causes* (Gallows Press), *Hungry Celluloid* (Dark Minds press), *Distant Frequencies* (Demain Publishing), and *Night Voices* (joint author collection with Paul Edwards – Demain Publishing). He's also the author of three novellas collected together in a single volume, *Mountains of Smoke* (Gallows Press), as well as a chapbook, *Photographs Showing Terrible Things* (Sideshow Press). In 2021, his debut novel, *The Resurrection Children* will be published by Demain Publishing. Laird Barron once described his fiction as: "Frank Duffy approaches the dark night of human existence from oblique angles and with a craftmanship akin to Thomas Ligotti and the late, great Joel Lane." Originally from the UK, Frank now lives in Poland with his wife Angelika, where he runs a small video production company.

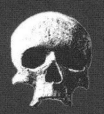

DEMAIN PUBLISHING

HORROR
FROM DEMAIN

A SHORT SHARP SHOCK! BOOK

#1

SCI-FI & FANTASY
FROM DEMAIN

WEIRD, WONDERFUL, OTHER WORLDS.

#1

A MYRIAD OF BOOKS

MURDER MYSTERY
FROM DEMAIN

MURDER! MYSTERY! MAYHEM!

#1

POETRY
FROM DEMAIN

BEATS, BALLADS & BLANK VERSE

#1

ALL AVAILAIBLE

on
amazon

DemainPublishing.com

Artwork by Dave Carson

*Fronted by none other than **Stephen King**, the* Phantasmagoria *team reviews a variety of **Ramsey Campbell**'s many titles over his career so far, while the UK's leading film critic, **Kim Newman**, also takes a look at the Spanish film adaptations of the author's work.*

LITERATURE

THE DOLL WHO ATE HIS MOTHER

Stephen King

From 1978, the King of Horror reviews Ramsey Campbell's first novel.

GOOD HORROR NOVELS are not a dime a dozen, but I have noticed that there never seems any serious shortage of good ones – and by that I mean that you seem to be able to count on a chiller of some stature every year or two, and a vintage year may produce as many as three amid the usual paperback-original dreck and the rather too-large number of embarrassing hardcover publications. But, maybe paradoxically, good horror *writers* are quite rare.

Consider the one-book horror writers if you will; their numbers are legion. Robert Marasco and his *Burnt Offerings*, Blatty's *The Exorcist*, even Bram Stoker's *Dracula*. Of course Stoker wrote other horror novels, but have you met anyone who was carrying a copy of *The Lair of the White Worm* under his arm lately? Similarly there are writers such as Henry James who dipped into the field of supernatural horror only once and then left it forever.

This is the reason why I was so pleased with Ramsey Campbell's first novel, *The Doll Who Ate His Mother*. Campbell is a young (thirty-ish) writer who has worked with consistent artistry and painstaking honesty in the horror field since publishing his first book, *The Inhabitant of the Lake*, with small but highly-respected Arkham House some years ago. I think his short story, 'The Companion' (originally published in an original anthology *Frights*), the best post-war story of supernatural horror I have ever read. He is literate in a field that has attracted too many comic-book intellects, cool in a field that tends towards panting melodrama by virtue of its subject-matter, fluid in a field where many of the best practitioners often fall prey to cant and stupid "rules" of fantasy composition.

But not all good short story writers in this field are able to make the jump to the novel. Poe did it once with *The Narrative of A. Gordon Pym*, and Lovecraft failed ambitiously several times (more because of his own ponderous writing style than any fault in conception, I think). I'm happy to say that Ramsey Campbell has made the jump almost effortlessly, with no attenuation of imagination or weakening of effect. Writing novels is a lot like long-distance running, and you can almost feel some would-be-novelists getting tired; they begin to breathe a little hard by page one hundred, to pant by page two hundred, and limp over the finish line with little to recommend them beyond the bare fact that they have finished. Campbell runs well – especially in a genre where the hills tend to be steeper than in some others.

The story begins with Clare Frayn's brother Rob losing an arm and his life in a car accident. The arm is important because it is made off with . . . and eaten, we are led to suppose, by a shadowy young man named Chris Kelley. Clare meets Edmund Hall, a crime reporter who believes that the man who caused Rob's death was the grown-up version of a boy he knew in school on Mulgrave Street in Liverpool, a boy fascinated with death . . . and with the eating of the dead.

Clare, Edmund Hall and George Pugh, a cinema owner whose elderly mother has also been victimised by Kelley, join together in a strange and reluctant three-way partnership to track Kelley down. And so they do, at least in a fashion. The climax of the hunt takes place in the rotting cellar of a slum building marked for demolition, and it is one of the most effective sequences in modern horror fiction (in modern fiction *period*, for that matter). In its surreal evocation of ancient evil, in the glimpse it gives us of "absolute power", it is a voice from the 1970s finding its own viable and believable version of Lovecraft's horrid and indescribable Elder Ones.

The characters are well-drawn – Clare with her stumpy legs and dreams of grace, Edmund with his baleful dreams of glory and self-aggrandisement, George Pugh holding onto the last of his cinemas and admonishing two teenage girls who walk out before the playing of the national anthem has finished – but perhaps the central character here is Liverpool itself, with its orange sodium lights, its slums and docks, its cinemas converted into HALF A MILE OF FURNITURE. Campbell's best short stories have lived and breathed Liverpool in what seems to be equal amounts of attraction and repulsion, and that sense of place is here as well, often as textured as Raymond Chandler's LA or Larry McMurtry's Texas. *Children were playing ball against the church*, Campbell writes. *Christ held up his arms for a catch.* It is a small line, understated and almost thrown away. But this sort of thing, indicative of a good eye and ear, accumulates.

The Doll Who Ate His Mother is perhaps not one of the great horror novels, but it is a very good one. Campbell has fine control of his potentially tabloid-style material, even playing off it occasionally (a particularly dull and almost viciously-insensitive teacher sits in the faculty room with a paper headlining HE CUT UP YOUNG VIRGINS AND LAUGHED near at hand – the blackly hilarious sub-title being *His Potency Came from Not Having Orgasms*), and he carries us down inexorably past levels of abnormal psychology into something that is much, much worse.

This is a novel of many various pleasures, and not the least of them for the reader is the fact that it may serve as an introduction to a young writer who bids fair to join the company of the greats. Britain has supplied more than its share of good supernatural writers over the years, and it may well be that Ramsey Campbell is presently the best of them. *The Doll Who Ate His Mother* is a fine piece of work.

Editions of *The Doll Who Ate His Mother* are available to purchase from Amazon and other outlets.

THE ONE SAFE PLACE

Kim Newman

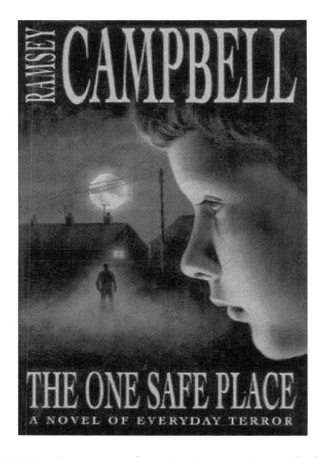

NO OTHER HORROR writer currently active is engaging with the real world quite as rigorously as Ramsey Campbell. *The One Safe Place* can be compared with *The Face That Must Die* and *The Count of Eleven* in that it contains no overt supernatural activity, concentrating instead on a mix of suspense, reportage and satire. However, it does adopt the structure of earlier Campbell novels (*The Hungry Moon*, *The Influence*, *The Long Lost*) in that it presents us with a vividly-characterised 'normal' family who are progressively tormented and pulled apart by contact with malevolent circumstance. Though as complex as the protagonists of earlier Campbell novels, the Travis Family of *The One Safe Place* are used to force us to conclusions which are as much political and social as they are psychological and individual.

Much horror, especially American horror, is essentially solipsist, turning inward to chronicle the extraordinary oppressions felt by people who have always believed they deserve better. Campbell, who can match anyone when writing from inside the viewpoint of individuals deep in the country of the demented, is always concerned with larger issues. It is as much to his credit as it is to the discredit of the world that, in much of his work, the larger forces that torment the individual owe as much to Kafka's vision of the state and society as an instrument of torture as it does to Lovecraft's extra-dimensional, inhuman monsters.

Often, Campbell writes best from anger. No one can present more believably infuriating jobsworths than he does, epitomised by the toadishly eager police constable who helps with the seizure of the heroine's video collection (Susanne Travis is an American academic who teaches a course about violence in Manchester) or the self-serving headmaster who rules that the murder of young Marshall Travis's father is no excuse for his vandalising of a newsagent's sign that seems to impugn his mother. Of course, these people are seen through the viewpoint of the understandably distressed Susanne and are therefore stereotypes, but Campbell's brilliance is to make them as convincing as they are horrifying. And these are walk-on players not merely grotesque furniture, but integral to the author's vision of the society that empowers them to make Susanne's life hard.

Early in the novel, Susanne takes part in a *Kilroy*-style tabloid TV debate on real-world and media violence which allows Campbell to deploy his underappreciated gift for satiric observation but also foreshadows the meat of the novel's bleak substance. Like too few practitioners in the business of horror, Campbell has been paying attention to the headlines and the general drift of ill-informed argument about the interface between what he does for a living and the symptoms of the societal disease he writes about here. Without ever stooping to explicit references to the Jamie Bulger case, Campbell dissects that particular media frenzy, contrasting the world of Marshall Travis with that of his dark equivalent Darren Fancy.

Marshall is growing up surrounded by action movies, Sharon Stone posters and Stephen King novels but has got from his academic mother and bookseller father a complex and questioning attitude to the media. Darren, the son of an extended family of violent criminals, is actually less interested in violence on screen than Marshall, because he has enough personal experience of it and has no equipment to deal with fiction or representation of any kind. Subtly, Campbell shows that Marshall – who is terrorised personally by Darren's Dad, whose father is murdered by Darren's uncles, and who is drugged and abducted by Darren himself – is traumatised not by Schwarzenegger films or even the video nasties his mother has to watch, but by the eruptions into his life of the irrational as represented not only by the Fancy Family but by the British justice system, the media and a stifling school. By contrast, Darren puts into action his revenge fantasies because he has no other idea of what a fantasy actually is.

Often, the criminal classes are as literally demonised in horror as they are in the gutter press. Stephen King frequently presents trailer trash evil in terms of middle-class paranoia (cf: *Christine*), with the subtly reactionary effect of absolving America of responsibility for a monstrousness that grows out of poverty. The Fancy Family are classically grotesque, allowing Campbell almost to parody a soap opera vision of sordidness, but Darren is presented as a monster we cannot but understand. He is part of a cycle of resentment, emotional and physical deprivation and casual violence that goes back well beyond his bed-ridden child-molester grandfather. They are awful people, admittedly, but no more so than the policeman or the headmaster. In the end, Campbell indicts not merely the disadvantaged – actually, the Fancys are rich from crime and choose to live in squalor – but the collapsing infrastructure of a society that allows them to exist.

Though not steeped in party politics – there's a one-scene bunch of communist die-hards who seem as intolerant as anyone, and Campbell dares to present a meddling but not unsympathetic Tory neighbour character – *The One Safe Place* can only be read as an analysis of a world that has been shaped by the Reagan-Thatcher 1980s and has been exacerbated by the Murdoch-Maxwell coarsening of the culture. In the end, with a variety of meanings, this is a novel about poor people: deprived and pitiable, meagre and suffering. The title is, of course ironic, as we see all safeties as illusional: governments, the police, schools, families, homes – all are oppressive or violated. Finally, we are taken into Marshall's head, which is not so much safe as fortified.

The depressing and horrifying central strand of *The One Safe Place* follows Marshall's changing perceptions of violence. A sufferer from bullying in America and the victim of a series of calamities in Britain, he is depicted as a strong, intelligent, open and compassionate kid. Under the influence of the LSD with which Darren has spiked his Coke, he becomes amazingly suggestible and even develops a heroic attachment to the kid who has duped him into playing Russian roulette. But at the end, in a coda as chilling as the insight into psychopathic minds Campbell manages in *The Face That Must Die* and *The Count of Eleven*, Marshall too is warped, not merely by his experience of violence but by the messages he has been given from authority figures, and seems set on the course to grow up into a monstrous vigilante.

Editions of *The One Safe Place* are available to purchase from Amazon and other outlets.

THE GRIN OF THE DARK

Joe X. Young

YOU HAVE AT your disposal a body of published work going back over half a century; you have a wealth of knowledge of times long since passed in the history of entertainment, times when there were legendary performers of the Music Hall stage as well as that new kid on the block . . . 'The Moving Picture Show'. During those early days there were the masters of movie manipulation such as George Méliès who created such astonishing visuals with the newest of media that audiences were taken way out of what we would nowadays refer to as their 'comfort zones' and plunged into intense experiences that they were ill prepared for. *The Grin of the Dark* harnesses that history for a similar experience.

For those expecting a straightforward horror journey I would say to turn back now, as this is certainly not one, instead it is a meandering sojourn into the life of Simon Lester, a reviewer who fell on hard times only to be offered an opportunity to get his life on track. The 'big bad' of this story is difficult to get into as there's far more going on here than it would appear, and I got the overall impression that the disjointed nature of the first person narrative was created with the intention of screwing with the reader. Had this been in third person we would have been in our own familiar spectator role, but seeing everything unfold through Simon's eyes and only gathering his perspectives puts us every bit in the dark as he is throughout the mundane occurrences of a regular existence tinged with peripheral weirdness provided by the flogged-to-death trope of 'evil clowns'.

The reason I read *The Grin of the Dark* was definitely not because of the evil clowns aspect, as I was for a brief time a circus clown back in the days before Stephen King ruined things for us once and for all. This is not to say that he was solely responsible, coulrophobia (fear of clowns) has long since been a thing with people and in recent years has exploded to the point where I am tired of seeing clowns being represented as things of evil, so much so that I generally avoid any 'killer clown' fiction, but this offering from Ramsey Campbell had me intrigued as it touched upon several things I had a fondness for as a youth. I'm part of the generation which saw the last knockings of the variety show, when the likes of Billy Dainty, Roy Castle, Comedy Acrobats and a wealth of other unusual acts would take to the stage on shows such as *The Good Old Days*, *The Wheeltappers and Shunters Social Club* and, of course, *Sunday Night at the London Palladium* to show us the kind of entertainment which has nowadays been relegated to little more than an historical footnote. *The Grin in the Dark* harks back to such acts, to the time when Roscoe 'Fatty' Arbuckle was king of the silent funnies.

It is not the author's first dip of the toe into archaic entertainment waters as anyone who has read *Ancient Images* which treads in Universal Monsters territories can contest to, but *The Grin in the Dark* is very different. The 'Fatty Arbuckle' of this story is Thackeray Lane aka 'Tubby Thackeray', a British silent movie comedian whose screen presence was more unnerving than comedic and whose works were mostly forgotten and would be destined to stay that way if not for the determination of Simon Lester who is attempting to write the definitive work on Thackeray.

The Grin of the Dark *artwork by Joe X. Young*

We know from the get-go that Simon has his work cut out for him, and I could absolutely relate to the difficulties involved in gathering information on niche subjects, especially as this book was written back in the days when internet modems were attached by wires and made annoying chirruping noises for ten minutes before connecting. Limitations to info gathering are not all that get in his way – his relationship with a single mother is in need of attention and she hopes he will straighten his life out as both she and her son adore Simon but her parents disapprove of him and to make matters worse actually own the flat he lives in. He does however have a golden opportunity to come good in the shape of a ten grand advance on a book with the possibility for a series if things go well, which will potentially put him in the good graces of his future in-laws.

It isn't long before things take a turn for the weird, with a hideously freaky clown watching him from the shadows and a mysterious internet troll who is definitely realistically portrayed as even to this day there are forums where such people get to have their unrestricted opinions. I can't discuss much of the ins and outs of the plot beyond that as there really isn't that much of one; the deeper Simon delves into the background of Thackeray the more difficulties he finds in a story which is written in such a way that very little is clear. There are twists which may seem important but turn out to be nothing, whilst seemingly insignificant things early on double back and expose themselves toward the end. With this, a pace slower than wading through knee-high porridge in flippers, and deliberately misspelled language, it is often a trial to read, but those who stick with it will either cry 'foul' or shout 'genius'. One thing is for certain; you'll probably read a hundred other books and still not find another one like this.

Can I recommend it? That is something of a double-edged sword as there is so much of the story which really isn't a story at all but more of a backdrop of a life which is so incredibly dull that I regretted choosing it to read, but the seamless blending of the factual old-time acts with the Thackeray legend strengthens the story considerably. If you like fast pacing and lots of viscera this is perhaps not going to delight, but for those of you who like a meticulous slow-burner there is much here to please you.

Editions of *The Grin of the Dark* are available to purchase from Amazon and other outlets.

RAMSEY CAMPBELL'S
LIMERICKS OF THE ALARMING AND PHANTASMAL

Trevor Kennedy

THERE'S A FINE line between comedy and horror. Both are essentially the theatre of the absurd and both are very tricky to do well also. So, it is therefore an even more daunting task to attempt to combine the two mediums with glowing results, as more often than not one or the other (or both) suffers.

However, when it does work the end result can be something very special indeed. Examples of this that come to my mind straight away are the films *An American Werewolf in London*, directed by John Landis, and Sam Raimi's *Evil Dead II*. There are more, of course, but they are rare. *Ramsey's Campbell's*

Limericks of the Alarming and Phantasmal is one of this elite group.

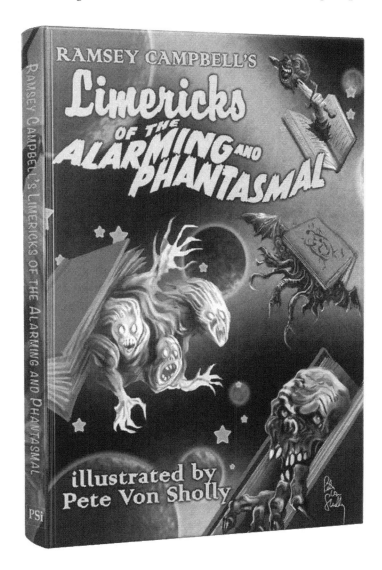

One of the world's foremost and prolific authors of horror presents us with a collection of brief verses based upon classic horror literature, a wonderful, fun-filled book aimed at children. Practically all of the historical genre greats are delightfully and macabrely referenced within – Stoker, Shelley, Dickens, Lovecraft, Wells, Le Fanu, Poe, James, Conan Doyle, Wheatley, Bradbury, Bloch, Amis, King and even Campbell himself. Jeez, even Jack the Ripper and my old mate, the charismatic, cannibalistic anti-hero (I don't care what anyone says, he's an anti-hero and NOT a villain, to me!) Hannibal Lecter are in there too! The gloriously vivid colour illustrations by Pete Von Sholly are just the icing on the cake.

As a self-confessed comedy snob, it really can take a lot to get me to guffaw (I like my comedy served dark and outrageous – think of a weird three-way hybrid of Rik Mayall, Kenny Everett and Alan Partridge topped with lashings of *Little Britain*, *Father Ted* and *The League of Gentlemen*), but I did indeed laugh out loud at some of the off-the-wall eccentricities contained inside this book.

It's like a brief history of horror literature for kids, but in verse form, with a huge nudge and a wink to the readers too – we're in on the jokes with Campbell, we're a part of it, and that feels pretty cool. The child readers themselves will love it as well, of course!

I strongly urge you to buy a copy of this book, enjoy it for yourself for a day or so, and then pass it onto a kid for them to relish too.

Great fun!

Ramsey Campbell's Limericks of the Alarming and Phantasmal is published by PS Publishing and is available to purchase from their website, Amazon and other outlets.

For more information please go to: www.pspublishing.co.uk

THE INHABITANT OF THE LAKE
& OTHER UNWELCOME TENANTS

Con Connolly

HAVING BEEN A long-time aficionado of Ramsey Campbell's psychological and "horror in the mundane" style of fiction, full of suggestion and restrained unease, I was intrigued as to what his take on the otherworldly horror and tentacular terror of H.P. Lovecraft would read like.

As with almost all of Campbell's work, of course, this book surprised me. For starters, it was written when the author was a mere stripling of 18 and contains some of his first published stories by Arkham House. Campbell freely admits in his original Introduction (1964) that these stories are pastiches of Lovecraft's Cthulhu mythos and adds in an afterword written in 2010 that he wrote them "as a way of trying to pay back the pleasure his (HPL's) work had given (him)" and for "the pleasure of convincing (him)self that they were almost as good as the originals". On the advice of friends, he forwarded his stories to the (generally!) acknowledged custodian of Lovecraft's work, the renowned August Derleth who obviously agreed they were good, as he published the stories reprinted here.

Derleth also suggested that Campbell adapt his stories to an English milieu, rather than the traditional "Lovecraft Country" setting of homages to HPL, which led to the creation of the fictional landscape of the Severn Valley, where Campbell has set these tales and more of his oeuvre since.

In addition to the stories themselves, the aforementioned Introduction and Afterword, the inclusion of earlier drafts (annotated by Derleth) of some of the stories and, best of all, correspondence from August Derleth, make this an enlightening and fascinating read for anyone with an interest in the Mythos. Derleth's advice in the art of writing Lovecraftian fiction is both instructive and amusing (the word "shit" and other "vulgarities" belong in Henry Miller's *Tropic of*

Cancer but not in a weird tale – who knew?!), as is Campbell's own gloss on the stories in his Afterword.

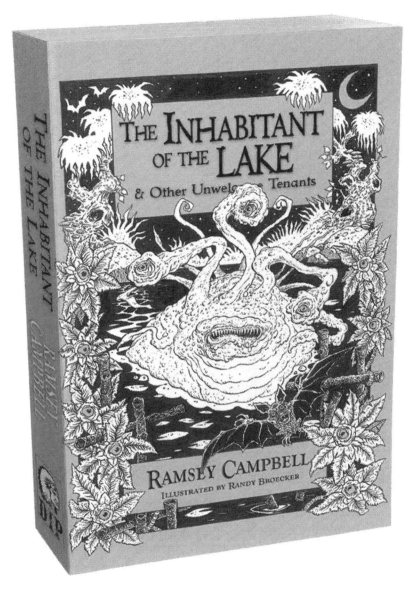

In the same Afterword, Campbell explores Lovecraft's dismissal as a "pulp" writer, criticized even by other writers who are fans, such as Stephen King and Charles L. Grant, as an "adolescent phase", (as Campbell puts it), who possesses a "rococo style and very little else" (quoted from Grant). While Campbell refutes this, stating that he enjoys and appreciates Lovecraft's work more now than he did then, he does point out that many imitators who concentrate too much on HPL's ornate prose fall down badly, creating parody rather than pastiche.

I unconsciously alluded to such parodies at the start of this review, as for many not overly familiar with his work, Lovecraft is all hideously indescribable monsters and unspeakable threats from other worlds and dimensions and little else. Writing, as he did, within the editorial requirements of the pulp magazines he practically despised, Lovecraft included these elements but is remembered when many of his more successful contemporaries have been forgotten. There is a cold and scary rationalism and pessimism about the best of HPL's work, a feeling of wrongness that builds as each story progresses: Unlike M.R. James (another influence on Campbell), Lovecraft firmly links science to horror, his hypothesis being that each of us is alone and cosmically insignificant in an indifferent universe – if a creator God does exist, He is the blind idiot, Azathoth, dreaming an insane cosmos into existence.

While Campbell has evolved his own very distinct and unmistakable style and voice since those early days, I think his appreciation of HPL remains undimmed because both writers share that feeling of wrongness in their work, that uncertainty as to whether the wrongness is internal, external or the influence of one upon the other.

As with most HPL devotees, Campbell gleefully adds to the Mythos and his invented occult grimoire 'The Revelations of Gla'aki' features in more than one story here, leading unwary readers towards horrible fates. The tome and the abominable Gla'aki himself take centre stage in the title story, a tale of possession told in a classically Lovecraftian semi-epistilatory narrative.

Other stand-outs include 'The Plain of Sound' and 'The Render of the Veil', both taking up Lovecraft's fascination with non-Euclidian physics and his theme that the world as we experience it is a construct of our minds and that experiencing the full multi-dimensionality of it will bring madness and torment. This is also touched upon in 'The Insects from Shaggai', a tale of unpleasant mind-controlling, dimension-travelling insectoids who serve an even more unpleasant master.

'The Mine on Yuggoth' and 'The Moon-Lens' share protagonists who are hideously transformed following fleeting encounters with the Old Ones as Campbell interprets them, while 'The Will of Stanley Brooke' and 'The Return of the Witch' are more evocative of 'Herbert West – Reanimator'. 'The Room in the Castle' deals with Things best left locked away and sinister histories, as does 'The Horror from the Bridge' involving a cursed family history and sinister amphibians on the rampage in Clotton, Campbell's translocation of Innsmouth.

All the stories here are great fun to read and it should be remembered that while Lovecraft references and homages are commonplace now, Campbell was a pioneer in this field back in 1964. These stories show the signs of a writer still learning his craft (some of the attempts at rustic and local dialect are unintentionally hilarious, as is a telegram interrupted horribly in mid-composition [". . . IA! YOG-SOTHOTH! CTHULHU FHTAGN!!"] contained in 'The Tomb Herd' and subsequently edited out when that story was published as 'The Church in High Street') but are all the more fascinating for that and a credit to the man for including warty first drafts and his typical wry self-deflationary commentary.

Ramsey Campbell has revisited what has since become known as "The Brichester Mythos" in the novella *The Last Revelation of Gla'aki* (2013) and the trilogy *The Searching Dead* (2016), *Born to the Dark* (2017) and *The Way of the Worm* (2018).

Special mention also goes to the wonderful and unsettling cover and illustrations by Randy Broecker.

Note: *One of the high points of 2019 for this reviewer was to shake hands with the great man himself at WorldCon in Dublin.*

The Inhabitant of the Lake & Other Unwelcome Tenants is published by Drugstore Indian Press (PS Publishing) and is available to purchase from their website, Amazon and other outlets.

For more information please go to: www.pspublishing.co.uk

THIRTEEN DAYS BY SUNSET BEACH

Louise McVeigh

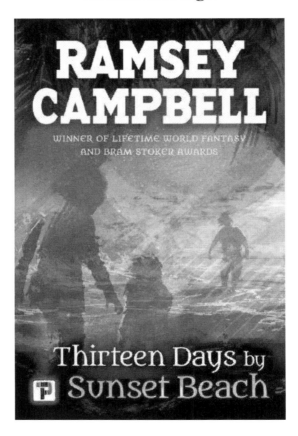

OVER THE YEARS, my family and I have enjoyed holidays abroad, including America twice. Before my husband and I get any older we had booked another holiday to the USA with my son and daughter, for July, 2020, a trip I had, as usual, planned out with great excitement. But then came the Covid pandemic and with the greatest of disappointment the holiday had to be cancelled (and rebooked twice – we still haven't been!).

It was during the period of lockdown, one day when I was feeling a little bored, that I began reading *Thirteen Days by Sunset Beach* by Ramsey Campbell and I can honestly say that I could hardly put the book down.

From the very beginning I felt as if I was going on holiday with Mr and Mrs Thornton and their family to the Greek island of Vasilema (one of my own past holidays was also to a Greek island which made the story even more interesting). The detailing of travelling through the airport, being on the coach, the boat etc is amazing, along with the description of their arrival at the hotel, meeting up with other members of their family, the staff at the hotel, and their planning of day trips.

Strange things then begin to be noticed by the family, such as the lack of mirrors, the oversized beach umbrellas, the cloudy skies etc.

One of the family's tours takes them to a resort deserted during the day and a strange cave where 'things' happen. Some of the islanders soon begin to follow them too. But will the Thorntons and their family find out what exactly is happening on the island and will they eventually be able to make it out in one piece?

I enjoyed reading this novel so much that I have began reading it again. The mix of that holiday feeling with the subtle, creeping horror is just great.

Thirteen Days by Sunset Beach is published by Flame Tree Publishing and is available to purchase from their website, Amazon and other outlets.

For more information please go to: www.flametreepublishing.com

JUST BEHIND YOU

Carl R. Jennings

WHEN I WAS a child, my family and I went to the Grand Canyon National Park in the state of Arizona for a vacation. It was a lovely day: my father, mother, and multiple siblings rode down into the canyon on donkeys; toured the khaki, russet, and red landscape; we interacted with some of the Native American reenactors, and they performed in shows which I'm sure someone today would happily be offended on their behalf. After a long day, my family and I camped at the bottom of the canyon for the night.

Except, one of my brothers and I didn't go to sleep. We were young and as intelligent as the rock that surrounded us. We went exploring on our own, eventually finding a ghost town. It was a thrillingly terrifying place to be in, right up until the point my brother and I accidentally locked ourselves in a jail cell. Old that metal may have been, lacking in structural integrity it was not.

We tried cutting ourselves out with a variety of things around us, which of course didn't work. We even fashioned a grappling hook from our shoe strings and my brother's glasses in an attempt to reach the jail cell keys on a hook across the room. This succeeded, but ultimately ended up in failure when the heavily rusted key broke off in the lock. Eventually a search party found us the next day. The door to the jail cell had to be cut off with the same motorized saw that rescue services typically use for extracting people from wrecked vehicles.

That was quite the harrowing story, wasn't it? Was it not compelling and succinct? Well, no, it wasn't really, but that's okay because it was a complete fabrication. I've never been to Arizona and I'm an only child. Also, I stole many of the elements from a *Brady Bunch* two-part episode.

I made up this story to demonstrate that the craft of writing short stories requires a certain type of skill. I would wager there have been many students throughout the years who thought their English class assignment of writing a short story was going to be a breeze. In actuality, with such a flippant mindset, it's like trying to cut through a series of iron bars with a wedge shaped rock. Doing the craft of short story well requires quite a different set of skills from novel writing, the primary among them is wielding brevity like a highly paid cosmetic surgeon wields a scalpel.

Not everyone who is mad enough to choose to put words together in a compelling order as a profession can achieve the skill of the short story. I've heard of a few who won't even try.

Ramsey Campbell is one who tried his hand at short stories and ended up becoming quite renowned for it. That's what you'll find in the collection *Just Behind You*: eighteen short stories which demonstrate Ramsey Campbell is nowhere near the level of having to rip-off *Brady Bunch* episodes to create an amazing, yet brief, narrative. I've picked out three that I'm confident will whet your appetite for more.

'The Place of Revelation'

I like the way this story plays out. The protagonist, Colin, is a young boy with a set of parents who are at one time overbearing and neglectful. Neglectful in the sense that they clearly have no respect for him as a developing person. His aunt is kind enough, but, again, not seeing him for *him*.

Not his uncle, however – he does see Colin for the special person he is. He, like his uncle, has the the ability to see and interact with more than what everyone else can. It's not something Colin is thrilled about. While he may be a part of a chosen few, what is beyond the mundane world is fantastical, it's wondrous, it's . . . deadly. Colin can navigate this world that lies over ours like cling wrap with the occasional kink, but only if he learns from his uncle's stories.

Although the night of this story is different: Colin's uncle wants *him* to tell the stories, in a sort of passing of the torch. Which is more apt of a phrase than it at first sight appears.

'One Copy Only'

This one is a book-lover's dream. The protagonist is certainly a book lover. She's a judge, but she is at the point in her career and her life which shows how continually disappointing the application of the law is. Life has become grey and dreary, and the only escape she has is books. Except, recently, books, or, rather, those who write them, have begun to disappoint her as well. She is in an age of cynicism, an age in which the villainous are presented as victims. She yearns for the solid heroism of high fantasy.

Fortunately for her, a second hand magazine purchase leads her to a particular used bookstore. Within its dingy walls and sagging roof, she finds her Elysium between the pages of a certain book. However, this book comes with a weight that has nothing to do with how it feels in her hands; a weight heavy enough to start warping her life around it as soon as she sees it.

'Breaking Up'

This is one of Campbell's horror stories where mobile phones feature. I've read many who lament having a mobile phone as an anathema to horror; that one is in constant communication with the artificial human hive mind. Campbell seems to have taken this on as a personal challenge, and has made strong headway into pushing back against this presumption.

The title is a pun. Not only is the sound from protagonist Kerry's phone seemingly increasingly unreliable throughout the story, but she is also having an issue with an old flame.

I'm sure there are many among us who have had the misfortune of dating someone who won't accept when the relationship is over. Kerry is plagued by an older man she once dated. She was somewhat uneasy about the whole relationship to begin with, but she became too unnerved by the large age gap between them. However, he has not stopped trying to restart the relationship, continuing to call her on her mobile and begging her to take him back.

This comes to a head one winter's day, when the weather is all snow and wind and ice, and Kerry has to walk home. Her former boyfriend calls her time and again along this walk. He, along with the situation, slides downhill on black ice from there.

Just Behind You is published by Drugstore Indian Press (PS Publishing) and is available to purchase from their website, Amazon and other outlets.

For more information please go to: www.pspublishing.co.uk

TOLD BY THE DEAD

Jessica Stevens

RAMSEY CAMPBELL IS described as one of Britain's most respected living horror writers, and after reading his collection *Told by the Dead*, one can certainly understand his importance in the community. This collection of chilling stories was first published by PS Publishing in 2003, then made available in trade paperback by Drugstore Indian Press, an imprint of PS Publishing Ltd. Ramsey Campbell has received many awards for his work including the Grand Master Award of the World Horror Convention, the Lifetime Achievement Award of the Horror Writers Association, and the Living Legend Award of the International Horror Guild.

The author has a powerful way of reaching into one's innermost thoughts, and dissecting them until he has crafted unsettling portraits within his own characters. *Told by the Dead* showcases his ability to harness the ordinary, then as if a magician, twist these settings into instruments of fright.

The collection opens with 'Return Journey'. Our reader finds themselves on an old train pulling out of a station littered with wartime paraphernalia. Campbell sets the scene with three children engaged in a dark game of pretend, along with a restless woman in search of nostalgia. Memories of the blackout are awakened upon entering a darkened tunnel. Footsteps of the past are retraced, as Hilda unearths her anxieties, ones that spiral downward toward forgotten shelters. She can still see the childhood masks pressed against the very membrane of darkness.

Another story that articulates Campbell's inventive ability is 'Agatha's Ghost'. The reader is presented with a woman held prisoner by an unpredictable intruder. Objects within her home play hide and seek, while cutlery arranges itself in religious ridicule. Agatha seeks support in the phone-in show presented by Barbara Day, a host who deals in the unusual. Campbell is a master of suspense as the reader eagerly devours each sentence in order to discover the truth.

'Little Ones' is a glimpse into two teachers' lives. Gill, a young woman, and Mrs Lavelle, the oldest instructor in their school. During Gill's bus ride she often views a hunched figure beyond the heavy curtains of the Lavelle's front window. There are others as well, muted shadows tucked behind a netted cloth. Events take an interesting turn when Gill confides in the older woman, and is allowed into her home. What takes place next is proof that anything is conceivable within our own private worlds.

Ramsey Campbell touches upon themes worthy of *The Twilight Zone*. 'The Entertainment' is a dark cautionary tale that begins with a man caught in a downpour seeking asylum for the night. He stumbles upon a location he stayed in once with his parents fifty years ago. There in the window of a three-story house is a notice, and a signboard that reads "Hotel". Campbell's talent really shines within his brilliant description, as the reader is submerged into a world both familiar and distinctive all at once. Tom Shone, the story's protagonist, is enlisted as the entertainment for the night in exchange for room and board. Uncertainty is instilled when the reader is introduced to a variety of unsettling explanations, as well as characters. 'The Entertainment' is one of those stories that remains with you, despite the passage of time.

'All For Sale' is another story that delves into mankind's most primal fears. Three friends embark on a trip to the Mediterranean. The reader is introduced to Barry, and a girl named Janet that he first encounters on a plane. They meet again along the seafront at one of the various clubs. He escorts her back to her place, only to find she has forgotten her key. They return back to the seafront, but soon he finds himself abandoned once she is safely inside. The next morning Barry ventures into the market hoping he will find her, but the deeper he travels into this foreign world of awnings and stalls, the more he realizes that danger doesn't always play by the same rules. Campbell is an absolute master when it comes to suspense, along with chilling conclusions. 'All For Sale' is nothing short of an intense page turner.

'The Worst Fog of the Year' begins with pure poetic flair, a gift Campbell holds in spades. The reader can feel the thick fog encircling them as Gaunt moves toward a house and the scene of two women inside, one brandishing a pistol. Gaunt is heard whispering commentaries in the background, while the women wait for a presence that has long since been dead. This tale unravels like a dark opera, one that promises an unsettling end.

Ramsey Campbell is truly a credit to his profession. Wonderfully illustrated by Randy Broecker's front cover and Richard Lamb's interior work, *Told by the Dead* is a marvellous collection, one that houses a unique voice that will certainly inspire for generations to come.

Told by the Dead is published by Drugstore Indian Press (PS Publishing) and is available to purchase from their website, Amazon and other outlets.

For more information please go to: www.pspublishing.co.uk

THE COMPANION & OTHER PHANTASMAGORICAL STORIES

Helen Scott

WAY BACK IN the 1990s when I was a librarian, I got my first taste of Ramsey Campbell when I read *The Hungry Moon*. Since then I've dipped in and out of his novels, always coming away thinking that I need to read more of his work. In recent years that has been the case. Most recently I reviewed his novel, *The Wise Friend*, and the collection *By the Light of My Skull*.

Ramsey writes with such a keen eye, he picks up on people's little nuances and translates them to the page. This makes his reader feel like they are being told a tale by a friend. His ability to transport you into each story makes you think about it long after you've finished reading. That is the mark of a craftsman – to embed his tale in your head is truly a talent.

This collection, *The Companion & Other Phantasmagorical Stories*, is a huge tome of tales that does not disappoint. Celebrating sixty years of publishing short stories, these have been selected by Ramsey himself. There is a lovely Introduction from Ramsey to get the juices going and then it's straight into the content.

The story 'Bradmoor' is the first one I read (included as part of the Introduction and written by the author when he was very young). It reads like a Hammer Horror or BBC Christmas special. There is an antiquity feel to this story, like it happened long ago in another time and place. Frank sends a message to his friend, a psychic investigator. The message simply says, "Come at once. I am in a horrible trap." His friend leaves immediately for Frank's home, Bradmoor. When he gets there Frank informs him that he has sold his soul to a man named de Ville. Frank holds out little hope of making it through the night. Walpurgis night is upon them and Frank is sure that de Ville will come to collect his soul.

'The Render of the Veils' starts out as an unassuming story about Kevin who after missing his last bus home is contemplating staying put until morning rather than walk home in the heavy downpour. He decides however to brave the weather and begins walking. After a few minutes, he pulls over a taxi and the driver agrees to take him home even though he was just clocking off. As Kevin is talking to the driver another man approaches and asks if he can share the cab. Kevin agrees. Rather than talk to his cab mate, Kevin starts to read a book about witchcraft but this just starts a conversation with the cab mate, Fisher, who is an occultist. By the time they reach Fisher's home they've had a very intriguing conversation about the Necronomicon and seeing without using your eyes. As Fisher gets out of the cab, Kevin impulsively decides to accompany Fisher and find out more about this "seeing things as they really are" and goes inside despite being warned of the danger.

This story is a real highlight of the collection and showcases Ramsey's interest in Lovecraft and his amazing knowledge of the occult. It's all done in such an understated way as to be believable.

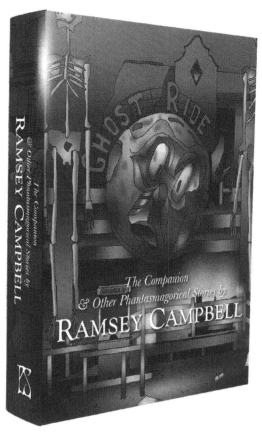

In 'The End of a Summer's Day', two newly-weds, Maria and Tony, are part of a tourist group looking at caves. Maria is unnerved by the experience when she thinks she sees faces in the walls of one of the caves. Tony reassures her and tells her everything is fine. As part of the tour, the guide turns off his torch, to demonstrate just how dark and foreboding the cave really is. Maria reaches for Tony's hand but when the torch goes back on she finds she is holding the hand of a blind man. Tony is nowhere to be seen and no one has any memory of the man Maria describes. The other tourists keep telling her that the blind man is her husband and he is the man she's been with all along.

In the Introduction to the book, Ramsey says that this story was influenced by his whirlwind romance with fellow librarian Rosemary Prince. Knowing this, the reader can see how that heady flush of romance has been used to play on the also heady rush of fear you get when circumstances pivot for the worst.

This book is peppered with tales told from a child's point of view. 'The Guy' is about Bonfire Night and friends Denis and Joe. Joe is the new boy in town and has moved from a bad neighbourhood to a better one. Denis's mum doesn't approve of their friendship but what do mums know?

'The Chimney' is a story that I've read in a previous anthology but enjoyed re-reading. We all remember being scared of a cupboard, a room, or in this case, a chimney, in our childhood home. That irrational fear of hearing a noise and your imagination going into overdrive. This is what happens one evening when a boy is putting together a jigsaw puzzle. But just as he begins to forget about the incident something else happens. . .

Two other stories, 'The Fit' and 'The Man in the Underpass' are also worth mentioning.

Ramsey is a master at telling things from a child's perspective. He's very good at playing on that fear of the unknown that we all remember from childhood and exacerbating it by using dramatic irony. I particularly enjoy this aspect of his writing. His stories in this collection, along with *The Wise Friend* and another short, 'The Moons', all make me nostalgic for my childhood and the way even the slightest scare would manifest itself into a saga.

The selection that Ramsey has chosen is a reflection of his diversity and ability to appeal to all. It is complemented by James Hannah's amazing cover and artwork within. There is something for everyone in this beautiful book.

The Companion & Other Phantasmagorical Stories is published by PS Publishing and is available to purchase from their website, Amazon and other outlets.

For more information please go to: www.pspublishing.co.uk

THE INFLUENCE

David R. Purcell

THE INFLUENCE IS the story of a family haunted by the death of an elderly matriarch, 'Queenie'. The story begins with Queenie's untimely passing. Not long after the funeral, strange happenings begin to occur around the old house that Queenie bequeathed to her niece Alison, Alison's husband Derek and their young daughter Rowan. In time, the family begin to worry that Rowan's mysterious new friend, Vicky, has a part to play in Rowan's increasingly odd and worrying behaviour.

Right from the start, Campbell wastes no time in drawing the reader into the story with vivid and atmospheric descriptions, making you feel the cold, smell the damp and hear every creak of the house. Here, we are immediately introduced to Queenie. Larger than life, cantankerous and permanently abusive, she embodies the archetype of the domineering matriarch, so wretched, yet morbidly rich of character, even though she dies at the end of chapter one, it is a testament to Campbell's genius that her lingering presence is felt throughout the rest of the book.

Alison is our protagonist, although over the course of the book's thirty-six chapters we do at times experience the story through other characters' points of view. She is sympathetic, compassionate and caring and this is shown through her interactions with her patients (she works in a children's care facility) and her family.

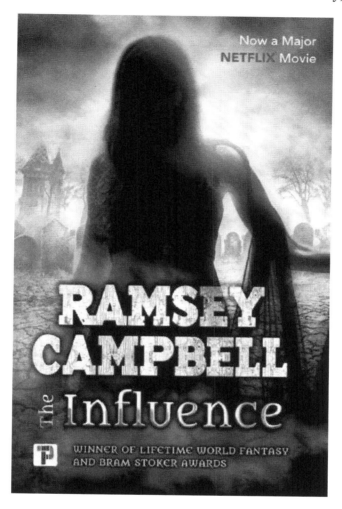

Derek is a supportive husband and a loving father to Rowan, who herself is thoughtful, brave and smart beyond her years. Each character is nuanced and unique with a healthy balance of qualities, both positive and negative. Family is one of the main themes of the story and it is the love of the family that carries them through the story's darker moments, and, boy, like any horror tale worth its mettle, there are a lot.

Campbell pulls no punches when it comes to the darker elements, but never crosses the line into the obscene or gratuitous. His real mastery, however, is in building tension and using subtlety. At several points, the reader's fear is heightened not by what is seen or witnessed by the character, but rather by what is imagined by them. I refer to one particular scene where Alison is locked in the pitch-black room with Queenie's body. The body is, of course, lifeless, but inside Alison's mind, she can imagine the corpse upended and scuttling around the room behind her. I don't frighten easily, but whilst reading that particular scene, I'm glad my room light was on, and not just the glare from my iPad!

My final observation: The pacing was skilfully laid out. Quite often with the horror genre does the storyteller overcook their narrative, pouring their best into key scenes and letting the rest feel flat, and that is where Campbell's true talent lies. He tells a consistent story with thrilling peaks and gentle lulls without ever making the reader feel bored.

Overall, I was hooked from the beginning. A compelling and exciting story about life and death, people's needs and desires and, most importantly; family. 4.5/5.

The Influence is published by Flame Tree Publishing and is available to purchase from their website, Amazon and other outlets.

For more information please go to: www.flametreepublishing.com

RAMSEY CAMPBELL, PROBABLY

Abdul-Qaadir Taariq Bakari-Muhammad

RAMSEY CAMPBELL, PROBABLY, edited by critic S.T. Joshi, is a collection of essays, or perhaps to take it a step further, conversations, by one of Britain's most prolific writers of horrific fiction, Mr Ramsey Campbell. In the United States he may not have the notoriety of Stephen King, Wes Craven, George A. Romero or John Carpenter, but nevertheless, he is considered one of the most respected living writers of British literature. In this book, the reader is treated immediately to an introduction by Douglas E. Winter, in the form of an appreciation of Campbell's work that he recalls reading nearly thirty years prior in a collection of short stories titled *Demons By Daylight*, this being one of his most fondest memories in comparison to work done by well known movie moguls. I can understand that completely. It doesn't matter the fame of the producer or director of a piece of work, but rather how the work resonates with its viewers. The good ones always manage to stay with you over the years. Due to space limitations, for my review of this collection I'll concentrate mainly on nine of the sections contained within.

The first two sections are titled 'Fiedler on the Roof' and 'The Crime of Horror'. It is here where Campbell discusses how Leslie Fiedler is one of the lamest and inaccurate critics of horror that he has ever read. He highlights his disgust based on a speech of Fiedler's published in the June 1984 issue of *Fantasy Review*.

On the other hand, Campbell speaks highly of some writers and the works they have produced. People such as Edgar Allan Poe, Arthur Machen, H.P. Lovecraft and my own favorite, Ray Bradbury. Yet, he also goes on in detail about how some of the best crime and horror fiction blends so naturally well together. Campbell finds of particular interest a Penguin omnibus which contains the first three novels of John Franklin Bardin, *Black Flowers* by Steve Mosby and *The Art of Murder* by José Carlos Somoza .

In 'Dig Us No Grave' the focus is on his bread and butter the supernatural. The first author he mentions is M.R. James and he doubts there will ever again be a writer of the ghost story of the calibre of James. Campbell also talks about how nostalgia should not take away the effect aimed at by the ghost story. He feels as though the supernatural experience should convey a message of intensity. This concern is raised in reference to Susan Hill's novel *The Woman in Black*. Hill suggests that the ghost story is best suited in the past whereas Campbell vehemently disagrees.

With 'A Horror Writer's Lexicon' the reader is treated to some comedy from Mr Campbell. He talks about the catchphrases, terminologies, and questions that horror writers will encounter. I found here familiar questions like 'Do you write under your own name?' and 'Have you had anything published?' These never stop being asked and I have been writing for ten years now. Perhaps they will never stop. New readers and the unfamiliar will always pop up.

'Horror Fiction and the Mainstream' sees Campbell addressing his encounters with the public and how people like to compare his personality with the stories he has written. People don't seem to realize that what they are reading are works of fictitious lives and settings. Still, I can attest to this having some relevance. As Campbell states, in a way he is the stories that he writes. In other words, as a writer there are always some elements of us inside the work that we produce on paper.

Even if it's within the 5-7-5 rule of a haiku. Before this section concludes, Campbell states his admiration for classic horror stories written by authors outside of the genre and that he writes his tales simply for the love of the art.

In 'Unconvincing Horror' Campbell turns up the heat again. This time he cites the adaptation of works done by Robert Louis Stevenson and W.W. Jacobs that was turned into a play called *Nightmares* and performed at the Chester Gateway Theatre, and which was a big disappointment and a shame to the original content, but at the same time honest in its description of using subject matter from authors already associated with horror. Perhaps the lesson, or play rather, should have been never to assume anything. I think I would have been pissed too and demanded a refund to go along with it.

On to the next two sections of my focus, 'To the Next Generation' and 'On Horror and Fantasy Film'. I found this part to be like an introductory session before you begin the 'Master Class' portion on horror writing and the genre. It asks the question of why do we as horror writers write such tales. Campbell elaborates that the writer will also throughout their career question one's authenticity. It is in fact, as he says, a natural position the writer will always come back to. This is so true as I have heard many other creatives that are long time veterans in their fields of choice who still have their doubts if they are the real deal, irregardless of the amount of awards or money that fill their living rooms or bank accounts. With that said, as he goes on to explain, never should a writer give up on their passion of putting ink to paper. Once more M.R. James is mentioned, in particular as a go-to source to learn the technique of ghost story writing. The same is also said of Lovecraft in the area of the supernatural.

Furthermore, Campbell advises all writers to read outside of their genre until they have found their own voice. When doing so he also advises several things. For one, he is against using clichés as he proclaims they are a strong indicator of lazy writing. If you must write about traditional horror figures, such as King Kong for example, that monster should always be re-imagined minus the woman being a damsel in distress or the object of his affection. Remember he also says that the monsters we write about could very well be the one in the mirror and not one wearing a mask of any sorts. Like I've read from Stephen King, Campbell reminds the writer to write each day to improve their craft.

The last section I'm focusing on, 'Horror Films and Society', deals with a very serious matter. It focuses on the abduction and brutal murder of James Patrick Bulger, a two-year-old boy from Kirby, Merseyside, England on February 12th, 1993, by two ten-year-old boys. At the time, Campbell took issue with people and more than likely this would have included the media, unless the media is different in the UK as opposed to the United States, that tried to sway public opinion in the negative sense against the field of horror. In this case the vehicle used was the horror film *Child's Play 3* (1991). During the investigation of the case, the film was linked to one of Bulger's murderers, Jon Venables, who was said to have acted out a scene from the movie during the crime, but it was later determined from a psychiatric evaluation that he disliked horror films. Campbell adds his take on the matter; to defend not the film per se, but the absurdity that horror invokes people to lose their sanity, especially in this case of James Bulger. He points out that critics or hate-mongers of this form of art were so quick to condemn the film and not the murderers that they used evidence against it that did not even occur in the film itself, but in a scene from a previous sequel in the franchise. This is not surprising for someone who already has an established bias and this kind of negligence of the facts happens all the time. As you read this, in my home country of the United States gun shootings and the murders that they often produce do not really separate us from our Wild Wild West heritage. Instead of it being isolated to a particular area as it once was, it is now all over the country, as I'm sure it has been reported throughout the BBC and British media. This I am sad to say is the preferred method of choice that many Americans use for a myriad of reasons. One of the main reasons is our perverted usage of the right to bear arms. In any event, when this happens often video games and violence in films get blamed for our lack of gun control. No one looks with seriousness at the triad of political parties, corporate entities, and the fact that this is America's culture. I agree with Campbell. Art should not be blamed for heinous crimes. Violence exists from an established culture, not from Jason Voorhees.

Other sections of this fascinatingly interesting collection of non-fiction again combine the humorous with the more serious, all told in Campbell's intellectual and unique voice, including his takes on topics as broad and diverse as pornography (specifically bottom spanking), more on censorship (and moral crusader Mary Whitehouse), real life apparent ghostly encounters, fake vampire hunters, trash movies, his fellow writers and colleagues, further on the literary side of our genre, and more. Overall, a great insight into the mind of one of the most respected British authors today.

Ramsey Campbell, Probably is published by PS Publishing and is available to purchase from their website, Amazon and other outlets.

For more information please go to: www.pspublishing.co.uk

You Never Know Who Might Be in Your House

Marc Damian Lawler

For Ramsey

AS SOON AS their feet touch the top stair—they have to fly.
They have no fear of falling—that is nothing compared to what is coming after them.
The little devils in the bedroom get to keep the bling . . . and if the robbers can run fast enough, they get to keep their heads—literally.
You never know who might be staying in your house; and when you might be required to buy a bottle of deep-clean carpet cleaner.

THE RETROSPECTIVE &
OTHER PHANTASMAGORICAL STORIES VOLUME II

Barnaby Page

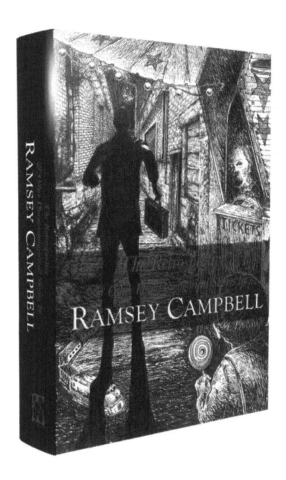

THE SENSE OF disquiet is relentless in Ramsey Campbell's new collection; whether a schoolboy nagged by something glimpsed in a derelict house, an elderly woman fearful of a particular Christmas decoration, or (in the black comedy 'A Street Was Chosen') the denizens of an entire road driven wild by a sadistic psychology experiment, none of Campbell's characters is ever given much in the way of peace, and nor is the reader. These are, almost without exception, stories where the mundane only barely conceals the uncanny.

Still, the first thing that jumps out from the 33 stories here *is* the mundanity of reality, and in fact the monstrous often isn't overt until the closing words of a story confirm that it was there all along. Many are set in anonymous and depressing British towns (Campbell seems to have a rather jaundiced view of contemporary

Britain), and on the rare occasions that they do stray to more exotic locations (Greece, Turkey) it is to follow holiday-makers. Many deal in the same themes: urban decay (sometimes literally) and the underclass, for example, although the awfulness is not confined to the mean streets – forests and trees provide their share, too. Many of the stories have child protagonists (their vulnerability sometimes magnified by being away from home) whose difficulty in rationalising fears accentuates the pervasive sense of being stranded in a world that is not quite *doing anything bad to you*, at least not yet, but is certainly considering it. Many feature much older people, dementia and mental illness, to similar effect.

These are not new stories; although there is disappointingly no publication history in the volume, they date back to at least 1989 ('Meeting the Author'), and several were collected in the anthologies *Just Behind You* (2009), *Told By the Dead* (2003) and *Ghosts and Grisly Things* (1998). That may disappoint some, but it does mean that *The Retrospective & Other Phantasmagorical Stories* (which follows on from 2019's similar collection *The Companion & Other Phantasmagorical Stories* from the same publisher) will make a substantial introduction to Campbell's shorter fiction for those who don't know it, as well as a handsome addition to the library for completist collectors; attractively designed and very nicely typeset, it includes suggestive illustrations by Glenn Chadbourne for most of the stories, as well as a chatty introduction by Campbell.

Anyone other than Number One Fans would be best advised to dip in and out rather than read it cover to cover; the family resemblances among the tales can be quite strong, and just occasionally two rather similar ones are placed together. Close attention is called for, too, for these are not skimmable stories; often heavy on description and light on dialogue, they can almost conceal vital clues. But of course that – as well as the sheer inventiveness with which Campbell repeatedly remixes familar real-life situations and horror tropes into grippingly fresh tales – is what makes them so absorbing, even immersive.

There isn't a dud among them, but several stand out. The title story, 'The Retrospective', takes us on an almost-literal trip down Memory Lane with a weird museum serving as a metaphor for the past (or perhaps more than a metaphor). 'The Rounds' is powerful in its implications of a character trapped in circular time, with a terrorism backdrop and hints of mental illness only heightening the nightmarish quality. Unusually among these stories, it may need to be read more than once.

That is not the case with 'At Lorn Hall', which makes a fantastically atmospheric conclusion to the collection; here, the idea of giving so much important dialogue to the (supposedly) recorded audio-tour accompanying a solo visitor around a deserted country house is one of the volume's master strokes, adding a novel element to a much-used horror setting. It also allows Campbell to indulge in his fondness for lines with sinisterly double meanings, seen elsewhere in 'Holding the Light' – where we are always just ahead of the characters in terms of comprehension and fear – as well as in the children's dialogue of 'The Moons' ("we're in his cage", "it's taking us") and in the misheard railway-station announcements of 'Passing Through Peacehaven' (or are they misheard?).

'At Lorn Hall' also contains one of the few implausibilities in the book (our hero would surely have figured out that there's something unusual about the audio tour much earlier; another occurs in 'The Alternative', where it is very unlikely anyone could have traced the money the protagonist gives to strangers). But these are so rare as to barely interfere with enjoyment, and occasional other apparent incongruities (like the reference to a "traveller's cheque" in 'Where They Lived') are attributable to a story's age.

Further highlights include 'With the Angels', one of several featuring children and their adult relatives, but the protagonist here is an older woman, and *her* long-dead grandmother is a real presence in the story; the central character is haunted by a now-distant childhood as much as by any things which may, or may not, dwell in the family home. 'The Dead Must Die' is a striking take on the fervent extremes of Christianity, drawing us into a mind where blood transfusions have become confused with vampirism. 'Digging Deep' is an original development of the buried-alive premise, and although it's not quite credible (the unfortunate internee figures out his predicament too quickly and abruptly), a hilarious twist is followed by a truly horrifying one.

Brief but thematically rich, 'No Strings' is one of the most thought-provoking stories in the volume, with a sympathetic main character facing disturbingly but not-quite-definably Other homeless people. 'The Place of Revelation', meanwhile, is an intriguing ghost story where a kind of animism suggests that haunting need not be an entirely negative thing. This last is compared by Campbell to the work of Arthur Machen, and there are odd moments throughout where one gets a pleasant whiff of other writers: several of the urban stories slightly recall Stephen King's 'Crouch End', for example, while the sinister bingo game in 'The Callers' is reminiscent of Shirley Jackson's 'The Lottery'.

Inevitably a few stories are about writers and writing (for example 'The Wrong Game', where the source of an author's good fortune comes back to trouble him, and 'The Word', where the misanthropic editor of a tiny fanzine does not welcome an apparent Second Coming – it is impossible to tell whether it is his sanity that is deteriorating, or the world's). Others have fun with specific aspects of modernity: the trivia quiz show is viciously lampooned in 'Getting it Wrong', for example, and the Frugo business empire (including the Frugoplex cinema chain and the wonderfully named Frugolé tapas bar) appears in several tales. The liberal middle class come in for ribbing several times, notably in 'Feeling Remains' with its amusingly well-observed do-gooder mum (woke when it suits her) and in 'The Moons', funny until it becomes very unfunny on a path in the woods, with the painfully-named kids Claude and Ludwig (presumably parental homages to Debussy and Beethoven).

But although there is plenty of social observation and not a little humour in *The Retrospective*, these never dominate. It is firmly a collection of ghost stories, or perhaps more accurately probably/possibly-ghost stories, for in many cases some ambiguity remains. Campbell is more or less conventional in his approach to them, not trying to push too many boundaries but instead giving us new angles on familiar scares, and doing it with language that is sometimes magnificently evocative (*tiles as white as a blizzard, frantic bushes, indifferent as outer space, trees . . . reaching for the larger dark*).

Perhaps two or three times in the entire collection an over-fanciful description brings the reader up short, trying to figure out what it means. But for the rest of *The

Retrospective's 550-plus pages, you will be transported to Campbell-world, one so easy to believe yourself in because it's so very like ours; it's just that the darkness is that little bit more insistent.

The Retrospective & Other Phantasmagorical Stories Volume II is published by PS Publishing and is available to purchase from their website, Amazon and other outlets.

For more information please go to: www.pspublishing.co.uk

THE WISE FRIEND

Gabrielle (G.C.H.) Reilly

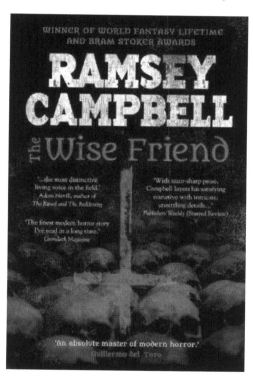

LOOK WHO'S COMING to dinner . . .

Smouldering straight out of the fiery furnace that is the fevered machinations of veteran British horror talent Ramsey Campbell, we find ourselves attentively coerced in these dark days by the mysterious *The Wise Friend*, Campbell's latest offering to his beloved horror fiction community. As with many (if not all) of Campbell's works we are confronted with a multi-faceted, subtle and mysterious tale that lingers on in the mind, well after the experience of descension down the rabbit hole has abated.

Meet Patrick, single father of one teenager, Roy. Like much of Campbell's other psychological etchings, here we see real, perfected characters. Campbell exposes the tensions familiar to many of us within our own families – even royal ones! The pathos of getting older, the gulf that exists between generations and the inability of youth to fully permeate the wisdom of elders.

Another theme explored is the alchemy of creating art. This mused on mysticism close to art is nearly as timeless as antiquity itself. Take, for instance, the questions we have around da Vinci or how little we know about the exceptionally unprolific genius of Vermeer. It is said blues guitarist Robert Johnson sold his soul at midnight by crossroads, way down in old Mississippi, in bargaining for god-like musical skill in a modern Faustian pact. They say artistic genius is a gift. If so, then to whom should we leave the thank you note?

Years before, the family Torrington experienced the death, possible suicide, of Patrick's Aunt Thelma when he (Patrick) was a teenager. She was a well respected individual within the somewhat cliquey world of artistic circles. Decades after her death, teen Roy is drawn to her works. Father tries to bond in this shared interest and they attend a gallery where they meet enigmatic stranger Bella Noel. Seemingly possessing the same interests, Bella bewitchingly proceeds with the allurement of Roy into accompanying her to various occult locations cited in the late artist's journal. This puppy-love obsessional relationship starts gaining prominence as Roy embarks on his own coming of age. As well as that comes contemporary growing up, including the commonplace interest in illicit materials – that by which far too many have lost themselves within. Bella and Roy are a distorted mirror version of Patrick's failing marriage to Julia, Roy's mother. Notions of what is the role of modern masculinity, or that of fatherhood, and not being a husband any more, are suggested within this increasing fractious father/son dynamic. Images of redundancy in natural species come to mind like that of arachnids or the praying mantis. The familial tension with its crumbling relationships, unsettling themes and the mapped out descent through the dark jaunty Campbellian mirror are analogous to those in Ari Aster's *Hereditary* – a similarly creepy slow-burn of a different medium.

As well as being a foreboding journey, Campbell deftly reminds us that nature can be cruel and black, beyond us and ancient. To be respected. This is a book steeped in mature and skilful writing. A patchwork quilt of influences, from Lovercraft's 'The Colour Out of Space', the madness of Lady Macbeth, as well as old folk tales, gnosticism, the unquiet dead and the ambiguity of memory. Ignorance of youth and ego, and the unyielding foghorn of the past, a modern cautionary warning to the curious.

For fans and newcomers alike this is a sublime and refined work. So close to reality, you will start seeing oddities in the corner of your eye (and not just within the woods . . .). This is no Clive Barker, however *The Wise Friend* is indeed incredibly well researched and laboured over lovingly – akin somewhat to Giles in *Buffy*. Ramsey Campbell demonstrates exquisitely how to linger an uncanny yarn, expertly drawing out the mystery with finesse, just like the combined beauty and horror of a spider quietly spinning her silk. As Hamlet once said: "There are more things in Heaven and Earth, Horatio, than are dreamt of in your philosophy."

The Wise Friend is published by Flame Tree Publishing and is available to purchase from their website, Amazon and other outlets.

For more information please go to: www.flametreepublishing.com

THE SEARCHING DEAD

David Brilliance

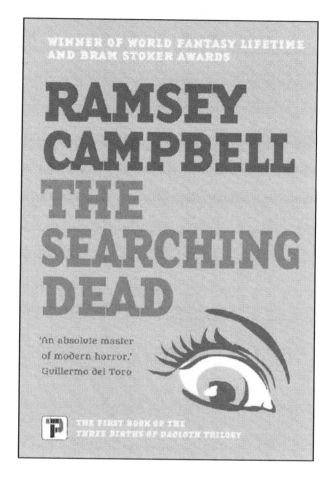

MY EXPERIENCE OF Ramsey Campbell is mainly confined to DVD extras, where Mr Campbell pops up occasionally to 'wax lyrical' (what does that actually *mean*??) on films such as the 1957 masterpiece *Night of the Demon* or somesuch. Coming to this novel fresh, I had no pre-conceived ideas about Campbell's writing but the fact he was apparently a fan of the stories of M.R. James was a very good start. In fact, the James influence seems to suffuse a good portion of this book, with specific references to gargoyles and old churches that evoke memories of the creepy old English settings James employed in his tales. There's even a nice in-joke at one point, with the central schoolboy character Dominic Sheldrake seeming to see the face of a dead man imprinted on a settee cushion (which brings to mind the end of James's "'Oh, Whistle, and I'll Come to You, My Lad'" in which the narrator describes an "intensely horrible face" imprinted on a floating bed sheet).

The book gets underway with a brief interview with Campbell, in which the first paragraph cheerfully blows ninety percent of the plot! Fortunately, I didn't bother to read any of this Q&A piece until *after* I'd read the story itself. The story is prefaced by an introduction by the, now grown-up, character of Dominic, in which he laments on a life "littered with mistakes" (yes, I know the feeling, Mr Sheldrake!) and then it's onto the story proper.

Set in the 1950s, we are introduced to schoolboy Sheldrake and his bestie Jim Bailey, who are just bidding goodbye and keeping their upper lips stiff as they say a temporary farewell to the third member of their little gang, female Bobby, who is heading to the delights of an all girls school while Dom and Jim are starting at a deeply religious school which has a dislike of "pansies" as well as US horror comics of the like that caused a great stir back then. The horrors of school life are evocatively conveyed by Campbell, with descriptive passages of the smell of boys, and chalk dust that seems common to every such hell hole in the land (school days in the 1970s were bad enough; the 1950s must have been unendurable!), as well as the teachers and all their accompanying quirks. The boys' Form Master, the creepy but affable Mr Noble, plays a large part in the novel, and is recognised by Dominic as the sinister figure he'd seen shuffling about in a cemetery which his house is next to, and his bedroom overlooks – there's more sinister shuffling about in that cemetery later, as Dominic encounters Noble and his young pram-bound daughter, Tina, followed by Noble's acerbic and suspicious missus Bernadette. These three immediately come across as wrong 'uns, and we know that Dominic must be in for some creepy shit involving them later . . .

Without giving too much away, it seems Mr Noble has an ability to "bring back the dead". We first get an inkling of this when another character who plays an important role, Mrs Norris, chats amiably to Dominic's parents about her dead husband, who won't stay dead it seems and is apparently keeping her company! Is Mrs Norris off her rocker, or is something more sinister going on? Clue: it's the latter. A school trip to France, to check out some of the battlefields from the War, confirms this, as Dom and Jim follow Noble from the dormitory one night, to see him doing something rather strange in a field . . .

As well as all the atmospherics and sense of sinister foreboding, there's also some nice humour – though I'm not sure if it's meant to be humorous, or am I just sick? – involving Noble Snr, who fought in the War and comes to the school to give an assembly hall speech to the boys about his experiences during wartime, mainly involving rats, lice and his losing a toe due to "trench foot"! The characters of the "Tremendous Three" (Dominic, Jim and Bobby) are fun too, and could have spun off into their own Enid Blyton-type series.

This review, by necessity, has to be brief, but summing up, I enjoyed this book. Campbell writes descriptively but breezily, never becoming boring or turgid and with a good grasp on interesting and, in some cases, likeable characters who we don't mind spending some literary time with. An interesting book – the only gripe I can reasonably make is with the rather unengaging (to me, anyway) title. That's rather a minor point though, so I can comfortably give this one a ten out of ten.

The Searching Dead is published by Flame Tree Publishing and is available to purchase from their website, Amazon and other outlets.

For more information please go to: www.flametreepublishing.com

FILM

Kim Newman

Poster for Los sin nombre *(1999)*

LOS SIN NOMBRE (1999, English: *The Nameless*)

Directed by: Jaume Balagueró.

Written by: Jaume Balagueró and Ramsey Campbell (story).

Starring: Emma Vilarasau, Karra Elejalde, Tristán Ulloa, Toni Sevilla, Brendan Price, Jordi Dauder and more.

AN EXERCISE IN creepy atmospherics, Jaume Balaguero's film transfers Ramsey Campbell's novel from its British setting to Spain and reins in the supernatural aspects. It opens with the discovery of the corpse of a crippled little girl and the trauma of the parents who have to identify the body of their kidnapped daughter, then picks up five years later as the traumatised mother (Emma Vilarasau) receives a telephone call which purports to be from the supposedly dead girl. She retains ex-cop Elejalde to investigate the possibility that another child was murdered in her daughter's place and that the girl (Jessica Del Pozo) has been raised by a mysterious cult, the Nameless.

The story owes a little to *Don't Look Now* (1974), with the mother drawn into a trap by her blind love for a child who may have become a monster, but the film's strength is in its unsettling details: the faces of the sinister extras who lurk around the heroine, ranted exposition about the cult without a name, explorations of the old dark house where the cultists live, sinister nuns and nurses, jarring little bits of David Fincher-style dementia, a sacred statue weeping blood, mutilation rites executed with a stanley knife, a domed roof covered with snapshots of missing children. However, the last reel is a little hasty, with some major characters incidentally killed and a touch too much grinning on the part of one revealed villain before a have-it-both-ways punchline.

EL SEGUNDO NOMBRE (2002, English: *Second Name*)

Directed by: Paco Plaza.

Written by: Ramsey Campbell (novel), Fernando Marías (screenplay) and Paco Plaza (screenplay).

Starring: Erica Prior, Trae Houlihan, Denis Rafter, Craig Stevenson, John O'Toole, Frank O'Sullivan and more.

IT OUGHT TO be a source of national shame that there are no British films adapted from the works of Ramsey Campbell – and it's just rubbing it in that three of his novels have been filmed in Spain. Directed by Paco Plaza, who co-wrote with Fernando Marias, this is a slightly too solemn version of Campbell's paranoid, but also satirical *The Pact of the Fathers*. The filmmakers made a decision that probably accounts for the movie not getting any kind of release in Britain – though shot in Barcelona, it uses Campbell's character names and casts a lot of ex-pats who have to be dubbed into Spanish, resulting in a film that seems to take place nowhere.

Entomologist Daniella (Erica Prior) is upset when her father (Craig Hill) commits suicide on her birthday and her alzheimer's-suffering mother (Teresa Gimpera) suddenly stirs and seems to react to her – only to call her by the wrong name ('Jospehine'). Meanwhile, scarred ex-convict Toby Harris (Craig Stevenson) is mixed up in things, and Erica starts to investigate . . . learning from a mad priest (John O'Toole) about a sinister sect of Abrahamites who practice child sacrifice, and that her own (complicated) family history is wound up with them. She turns out to be the third person we thought she might be, which shows that the film at least knows we'll try to second-guess the plot – but the basic *Rosemary's Baby*-type paranoid conspiracy cult premise means that it's not so much a matter of which characters will turn out to be implicated in it all as when the heroine will catch on and whether it'll be too late for her to do anything about it. Spoiler – it is: and the film goes for a downer finish which seems more cruel than earned.

Poster for El segundo nombre *(2002)*

It has some nice touches – like casting Spanish horror veterans Hill and Gimpera in small significant roles – and Plaza manages to catch some of Campbell's distinctively queasy family relationships . . . including a finish in which the villains stand around numbed by the terrible things they've done rather than exulting in them, and the weirdly affecting relationship that grows between the heroine and the mangled man who has cause to believe he's her real father.

LA INFLUENCIA (2019, English: *The Influence*)

Directed by: Denis Rovira van Boekholt.

Written by: Michel Gaztambide (screenplay by), Daniel Rissech (screenplay by), Denis Rovira van Boekholt (screenplay by) and Ramsey Campbell (based on the novel by).

Starring: Manuela Vellés, Maggie Civantos, Alain Hernández, Claudia Placer, Emma Suárez, Daniela Rubio and more.

IT'S STILL A mystery to me why Ramsey Campbell – the Terence Davies of horror – is unfilmed in his native land, but has had a run of adaptations made in Spain. Like *The Nameless* and *The Pact of the Fathers*, this transposes a Liverpool-set story to Spain – losing a great deal of the local colour and nuance of the original, but replacing it with a different kind of gloomy mood. Fine as these films are, I'd still like to see them made on their home turf with Campbell's excruciating character interplay as well as his general creepiness. It's also an issue, perhaps, that in the adaptation a slow-building supernatural plot becomes less opaque – the penny drops almost immediately that bedridden witchy Victoria (Emma Suárez) has set things up so that she can possess her granddaughter Nora (Claudia Placer) while avenging herself on her two daughters, Alicia (Manuela Vellés) and Sara (Maggie Civantos), whom she blames for the (fairly accidental) death of her beloved husband (Ramón Esquinas) in a childhood 'gotcha' incident. We get flashbacks to establish how nightmarish the girls' childhood was – their cousin is still traumatised (and missing a fingertip) – and the backstory is doled out piecemeal, but mostly we follow Alicia, a nurse who has come home to help her sister care for their comatose mother (this is an entry in the *Patrick/Medusa Touch* psychic-bastard-in-a-coma sub-genre), and Nora, who has a hard time at a new school and starts hanging around with creepy waif Luna (Daniela Rubio), who Victoria has possessed as a half-measure.

It's actually an interesting wrinkle on the possess-a-kid-to-become-immortal premise (another sub-genre, cf: *The Mephisto Waltz, Nothing But the Night*) that Victoria has already transferred herself successfully into a younger host body but wants one that's of her bloodline so she can will her worldly goods to her but mostly to inflict horrible pain on her own children. It offers regular sacrifices, as the evil one racks up a body count – with the possessed children as catspaw – and glimpses of the demonic entity Victoria serves, who might not be best pleased with the pettiness of her witchery. The setting is a standard creepy old house with dodgy wiring and the look is typical intimate Spanish horror, privileging the drawn, haggard, glamorous women and making the few men who stray into the ménage – Alicia's electrician husband Mikel (Alain Hernández), mostly – feebs who take a lot of abuse.

One odd plot lapse – much is made of the machines keeping Victoria alive, with several desperate attempts to disconnect them, but a key incident involves a power cut that somehow doesn't affect the gadgets. Scripted by Michel Gaztambide, Daniel Rissech and Denis Rovira van Boekholt.

Poster for La influencia *(2019)*

Ramsey Campbell's 'The Guide' artwork by Pete Von Sholly

SOME TITLES
CURRENTLY AVAILABLE
ON AMAZON

FROM THE
TIME WARRIORS
SERIES

BY OWEN QUINN

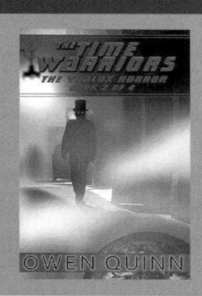

Space is no longer
the final frontier

ACKNOWLEDGEMENTS

'Ramsey Campbell' front cover artwork copyright © Pete Von Sholly.

All book cover, competition and advertisement images used within *Phantasmagoria Special Edition Series #4: Ramsey Campbell* copyright © the relevant publishers/artists/authors etc.

'Ramsey' artwork copyright © Les Edwards.

Opening Ramsey Campbell photograph copyright © Peter Coleborn.

Page 2: Cover illustration for the Ramsey Campbell novel *Midnight Sun*, 2019 (Drugstore Indian Press/PS Publishing Ltd.). Artwork copyright © Randy Broecker.

Pages 5, 8, 12, 21, 33, 40, 65, 91, 105, 139, 152, 166, 187, 217, 221 and 250: All 'spot' illustrations copyright © Randy Broecker 2021.

Page 6: 'Introduction: Ramsey @ 75' copyright © Stephen Jones 2021.

Page 6: Photograph copyright © Mandy Slater 2018.

Page 8: Photograph copyright © Mandy Slater 2018.

Page 9: Artwork copyright © Allen Koszowski. From the book *Made in Goatswood: New Tales of Horror in the Severn Valley: A Celebration of Ramsey Campbell* (Call of Cthulhu fiction, published by Chaosium Inc.).

Page 10: 'Ramsey Campbell: Selected Biography' copyright © Stephen Jones 2021.

Page 14: 'For Ramsey' and accompanying photographs copyright © Trevor Kennedy and Allison Weir 2021.

Page 17: 'Rising Generation' artwork copyright © Stephen Jones 1975. Originally published in *World of Horror* No.4, January 1975. Reprinted by permission of the artist.

Page 18: Page : 'Introduction: Rising Generation' copyright © Stephen Jones 2021.

Page 18: 'Rising Generation' copyright © Ramsey Campbell.

Page 22: 'Ramsey Campbell Interview: Master Storyteller, Literary Giant' copyright © John Gilbert and Ramsey Campbell 2021.

Page 22: Photograph copyright © Peter Coleborn.

Page 25: Photograph copyright © Peter Coleborn.

Page 26: Photograph copyright © Gerry Adair 1993.

Page 29: Photograph copyright © Mandy Slater 2012.

Page 31: Photograph copyright © Peter Coleborn.

Page 33: Photograph copyright © Jo Fletcher 1980.

Pages 35, 36, 38 and 39: Artworks/images copyright © Pat Kearney/*Goudy* magazine/the Estate of Eddie Jones/Ramsey Campbell. Originally published in *Goudy* magazine, issue 2, 1961. Reprinted by permission.

Page 36: 'The Inhabitant of Liverpool' copyright © Pat Kearney 2021.

Page 42: 'The Uneasy Worlds of Ramsey Campbell' and accompanying cover artwork copyright © *Shadow: Fantasy Literature Review*/David A. Sutton/the Estate of Eddy C. Bertin. Originally published in *Shadow: Fantasy Literature Review*, #16, March 1972. Reprinted by permission. Cover artwork by Alan Hunter.

Page 54: 'Eddy C. Bertin (1944–2018)' copyright © David A. Sutton 2021.

Page 56: 'From "The Franklyn Paragraphs" to Daoloth: Ramsey Campbell and Lovecraft Over Fifty Years' copyright © S. T. Joshi 2021.

Page 61: Image source: Google Images.

Page 66 to 73: All artworks copyright © Les Edwards.

Page 76: 'My Favourite Ramsey Campbell Story . . .' copyright © 2021 the individual contributors.

Page 76: Illustration from the chapbook, *Two Obscure Tales* (Necronomicon Press). Artwork copyright © Allen Koszowski 1993.

Page 88: *The Last Revelation of Gla'aki* by Ramsey Campbell (PS Publishing Ltd.), cover spread artwork copyright © Pete Von Sholly 2013.

Page 90: 'The Inhabitant With Visions from Demons!' copyright © Randy Broecker 2021.

Page 92: Cover illustration for the Ramsey Campbell collection *The Inhabitant of the Lake & Other Unwelcome Tenants* (PS Publishing Ltd.). Artwork copyright © Randy Broecker 2011.

Page 93: Illustration for the Ramsey Campbell story 'The Room in the Castle' from *The Inhabitant of the Lake & Other Unwelcome Tenants* (PS Publishing Ltd.). Artwork copyright © Randy Broecker 2011.

DAVE JEFFERY'S CaTHEDRAL

OUT NOW

Paperback & Kindle

"An exciting and enthralling new world in horror fiction, from an author who only seems to be growing in confidence and talent with each installment."

– Thomas Joyce

"There is a melancholy and desperation that is painful and beautiful to experience and this work will stay with you for a long time."

– Breathtaking Literature

amazon

The end is hear ...

DEMAIN PUBLISHING

Page 94: Illustration for the Ramsey Campbell story 'The Horror from the Bridge' from *The Inhabitant of the Lake & Other Unwelcome Tenants* (PS Publishing Ltd.). Artwork copyright © Randy Broecker 2011.

Page 95: Illustration for the Ramsey Campbell story 'The Return of the Witch' from *The Inhabitant of the Lake & Other Unwelcome Tenants* (PS Publishing Ltd.). Artwork copyright © Randy Broecker 2011.

Page 96: Illustration for the Ramsey Campbell story 'The Moon-Lens' from *The Inhabitant of the Lake & Other Unwelcome Tenants* (PS Publishing Ltd.). Artwork copyright © Randy Broecker 2011.

Page 97: Illustration for the Ramsey Campbell story 'The Stone on the Island' from *Visions from Brichester* (PS Publishing Ltd.). Artwork copyright © Randy Broecker 2015.

Page 98: Illustration for the Ramsey Campbell story 'Before the Storm' from *Visions from Brichester* (PS Publishing Ltd.). Artwork copyright © Randy Broecker 2015.

Page 99: Illustration for the Ramsey Campbell story 'Cold Print' from *Visions from Brichester* (PS Publishing Ltd.). Artwork copyright © Randy Broecker 2015.

Page 100: Illustration for the Ramsey Campbell story 'The Other Names' from *Visions from Brichester* (PS Publishing Ltd.). Artwork copyright © Randy Broecker 2015.

Page 101: Illustration for the Ramsey Campbell story 'The Last Revelation of Gla'aki' from *Visions from Brichester* (PS Publishing Ltd.). Artwork copyright © Randy Broecker 2015.

Page 102: Illustration for the Ramsey Campbell story 'Made in Goatswood'. Artwork copyright © Randy Broecker 2021.

Page 104: 'Ramsey's Favourites' copyright © Ramsey Campbell 2021.

Page 104: Photograph copyright © Peter Coleborn.

Page 106: 'The Voice of the Beach' copyright © Ramsey Campbell.

Page 126: *Fantasy Tales* Vol. 5, No. 10, Summer 1982. Cover art by David Lloyd. Copyright © Stephen Jones/*Fantasy Tales*.

Page 128: 'Just Behind You' copyright © Ramsey Campbell.

Page 142: Illustration for the Ramsey Campbell story 'The Stages of the God', FantasyCon VI programme booklet. Artwork copyright © Dave Carson 1980.

Page 143: Illustration for the Ramsey Campbell story 'The Hands'. Artwork copyright © Dave Carson.

Page 144: Illustration for the Ramsey Campbell story 'The Tomb-Herd' from the *Haunters of the Dark* portfolio. Artwork copyright © Dave Carson.

Page 145: Illustration for the Ramsey Campbell story 'A New Life' from *BFS Winter Chills* 1. Artwork copyright © Dave Carson 1986.

Page 146: 'Asylum' artwork copyright © Dave Carson 1980.

Page 147: 'Book shop' artwork copyright © Dave Carson 1978.

Page 148: 'Skull Demon' artwork copyright © Dave Carson.

Page 150: 'Newman on Campbell' copyright © Kim Newman 2008.

Page 154: Illustration for the Ramsey Campbell story 'Above the World', *Northern Chills*, edited by Graeme Hurry (Kimota Publishing). Artwork copyright © Jim Pitts 1994.

Page 155: Front cover of *Fantasy Tales*, Vol. 7, No. 14. Artwork copyright © Jim Pitts 1985.

Page 156: Illustration for the Ramsey Campbell story 'The Sneering', *Fantasy Tales*, Vol. 7, No. 14. Artwork copyright © Jim Pitts 1985.

Page 157: Illustration for the Ramsey Campbell story 'Mackintosh Willy', *Northern Chills*, edited by Graeme Hurry (Kimota Publishing). Artwork copyright © Jim Pitts 1994.

Page 158: Illustration for the Ramsey Campbell story 'The Song at the Hub of the Garden', *Savage Heroes*, edited by Eric Pendragon. Artwork copyright © Jim Pitts 1977.

Page 159: Illustration for the Ramsey Campbell story 'The Pit of Wings', *Fantasy Tales*, Vol. 13, No. 7. Artwork copyright © Jim Pitts 1991.

Page 160: Front cover of *The B.F.S. Bulletin*, Vol. 9, No. 1. Artwork copyright © Jim Pitts 1991.

Page 163 to 166: Limericks copyright © Ramsey Campbell.

Page 168: 'The Urge' from the Ramsey Campbell chapbook, *Two Obscure Tales* (Necronomicon Press). Artwork copyright © Allen Koszowski 1993.

Page 169: Illustration for the Ramsey Campbell story 'Kill Me Hideously' which first appeared in *Weird Tales*. Artwork copyright © Allen Koszowski.

Page 170: 'The Void' from the Ramsey Campbell chapbook, *Two Obscure Tales* (Necronomicon Press). Artwork copyright © Allen Koszowski 1993.

Page 171: Illustration for the Ramsey Campbell story 'Macintosh Willy'. Artwork copyright © Allen Koszowski.

Page 172 to 175: Illustrations for the Ramsey Campbell chapbook, *Slow* (Footsteps Press). Artworks copyright © Allen Koszowski 1985.

Page 176 to 177: Illustrations for the Ramsey Campbell chapbook, *Medusa* (Footsteps Press). Artworks copyright © Allen Koszowski 1987.

Page 178: 'Happy (Belated) 60th Birthday! On the Occasion of Ramsey Campbell's 75th Birthday' copyright © David Mathew and the individual contributors.

Page 178: Photograph copyright © Peter Coleborn.

Page 188: 'Meeting Ramsey Campbell' and accompanying photograph copyright © Frank Duffy 2021.

Page 194: Artwork from *Crypt of Cthulhu* #50, copyright © Allen Koszowski.

Page 196: 'The Entertainment Arrives' copyright © Alison Littlewood.

Page 206: 'Different Now' copyright © Michael Marshall Smith.

Page 212: 'They Dreamt of Albert Too' copyright © Dean M. Drinkel 2021.

Page 218: 'The Depths of Belief' copyright © Frank Duffy.

Page 224: Artwork copyright © Dave Carson.

Page 224: 'The Doll Who Ate His Mother' copyright © Stephen King 1978. Originally published in *Whispers* #11–12, October 1978. Reprinted by permission of the author.

Page 227 to 263: Reviews copyright © Kim Newman, Joe X. Young (plus accompanying *A Grin in the Dark* artwork), Trevor Kennedy, Con Connolly, Louise McVeigh, Carl R. Jennings, Jessica Stevens, Helen Scott, David R. Purcell, Abdul-Qaadir Taariq Bakari-Muhammad (accompanying poem copyright © Marc Damian Lawler 2021), Barnaby Page, Gabrielle (G.C.H.) Reilly and David Brilliance 2021.

Page 258: Picture copyright © Filmax/P.C. Joan Ginard.

Page 260: Picture copyright © Castelao Producciones/Filmax International/Just Films/Vía Digital.

Page 262: Picture copyright © La Ferme! Productions/Mogambo (producer)/Nadie es Perfecto/Recording Movies, S.L./The Influence Movie, A.I.E.

Page 263: Ramsey Campbell's 'The Guide' artwork copyright © Pete Von Sholly.

Phantasmagoria

HORROR, FANTASY & SCI-FI

ISSUE #18

Featuring Interviews with Mike Chinn, Peter Crowther, Nancy Kilpatrick and Andrew Smith, plus Features, Fiction, Reviews and Artwork!

COMING to **AMAZON** in MAY 2021

Printed in Great Britain
by Amazon